The Forbitten

The Full Moon

J.L. Miller

authorHOUSE®

AuthorHouse™
1663 Liberty Drive
Bloomington, IN 47403
www.authorhouse.com
Phone: 1-800-839-8640

First published by AuthorHouse   5/12/2010

ISBN: 978-1-4520-2080-8 (e)
ISBN: 978-1-4520-2079-2 (sc)
ISBN: 978-1-4520-2078-5 (hc)

Library of Congress Control Number: 2010906561

Printed in the United States of America
Bloomington, Indiana

This book is printed on acid-free paper.

For my wonderful children
Austin, Cody, Emma and Madison
Love Mom

1 NEW BEGINNINGS

BEEP, BEEP, BEEP......

"Err," I groaned as I turned over and hit the loud alarm clock that was blaring out the steady beeps that were getting louder the longer as I let it ring. I struck it with such force I knocked it off my night stand and it clattered to the dark wood floor. Thoughts ran through my mind as I laid there motionless on my bed. The thought of pulling the covers over my head and going back to sleep was just so tempting, but that wasn't going to happen, and the nightmare that I was trying to avoid was staring me straight in the face.

Another fabulous day, I thought. My life as I knew it was over, and I know me being a teenager you would say that all teenagers say's that at one time or another. But it's the truth in my case because today was the day that my mother was taking me across the country to a place that I am not sure you could even find in a map. My mother just got married to someone she barely knew, and I was not overly excited. She had only met Ben 6 months ago. My mom worked as a hair-dresser in a small shop down the road from our house, and Ben just happen to walk into her shop needing a haircut.

Yeah, I know, give me a break. He was so taken by my mother and, I'm sure, the assets that he thought she had to offer, I thought with some hostility. All right, let me give him some credit: he is a nice guy and he truly seems to care about Mom. Well in any case, he asked her out, and they have been inseparable ever since. Like magnets, they seem to pull to each other. Truly I wouldn't think they wouldn't act so...*so gooey.* After all, they are adults. Shouldn't they show some restraint, especially in public or around me in public?

So now that brings us to the present, where my mom has shattered my whole life and I can't even groan about it. It's been a long time since my mom has been truly happy about anything and I don't want to ruin it, even though it feels like she has turned into a tornado and trashed my life.

"Abigail," I heard my mother yell up the stairs, "It's time to get up!"

"Err,"I groaned again. I kicked my blue fluffy comforter off and sat up. "I can't believe she is doing this to me," I grumbled quietly. I have lived in this house since I was born. I had my first birthday here. The tree house that I played in when I was small is still in the back yard. All my friends, what few I had of them were here. Everything I knew was in this small town. I had already said goodbye to the few friends I had here. I wasn't really popular, I tried to keep under the radar of most of the students that lived here, and I was sure that I wouldn't be missed. The friends I had begged me to keep in touch, and I agreed, knowing that this was the only way I was going to keep my sanity. I had all of their emails, of course, and their phone numbers.

As I looked around the room full of brown boxes that I had finished packing last night, I fought the tears that were threatening to be exposed. Everything I owned was pack into boxes that filled the room, with a few exceptions like my bedding and the clothes. I had barely managed to convince my mom to leave my personal stuff unpacked; she was ready to go and wanted everything that wasn't bolted or screwed to the walls ready for the movers. The clothes that I would wear on my nightmarish travel to Klamath Falls were the only thing that my mom had left out. Everything that had to do with clothing was packed. *My mother is taking me across country to a place I hadn't even heard of, and I just know I am going to hate it.*

As I walked quietly towards the bathroom trying to avoid the squeaky floor board that had never been fixed in the hall, I heard my mom calling up the stairs.

"Abigail," my mother said, "Did you get the rest of your stuff packed?"

"Yes, mom," I answered. "I did it last night before I went to bed". I had known that the movers were coming today to pack up what was left of my life.

"Great," she said, with a hopeful tone in her voice, like the fact that she had just ruined my life didn't even register with her. "I just know you'll like Klamath Falls."

I didn't want to hurt her feelings so I just said, "Yes, mom. It will all be great." I tried to keep the grimace off my face and the sadness out of my tone that were going to expose my true feelings, but my mom was so happy that I knew she wouldn't even catch it. She must have been in denial, thinking I was going to enjoy being ripped out of the place that was my comfort zone. *God, I hate the sound of that place, Klamath Falls. It sounds like a place that has been in the news a dozen times for some catastrophe or another.*

Ben, which was the name of my mother's new husband, had left right after the honeymoon to get everything settled. With my mother's help he had managed to get me enrolled in the local high school in the middle of my sophomore year. This would be the last day that I would spend in the house that held all my memories.

A small lump appeared in my throat, threatening to choke me. My dad left when I was three and my mother never speaks of him. I have no idea why he left or if I would ever see him again. Except for me, there was no actual physical proof he existed; no pictures, no clothes, no memories. My mother had pretended to be a pyro on the day he left and burnt all evidence of their time together, or at least that's what she told me. I mentioned it once and my mother just looked for a way to change the subject. I wasn't sure if it was the fact that he had left her that she hated, or if there was more to the story that my mom was not comfortable talking about, but whatever happened stayed locked in the vault that was my mother and so I just let it go. I didn't want to upset her.

As I walked though the house, running my fingers against the wall, I thought through all the memories. My stomach felt uneasy and it was hard to breathe. There was nothing on the walls. My mother had packed all the pictures that were hanging on the walls. You couldn't even tell that there were any pictures ever hung there except for the darker shade on the wall where the picture once hung. With everything almost gone in the house, you couldn't even tell that we had ever lived here.

I couldn't help but feel this move was a very bad thing. My stomach twisted when I thought of it, like one of those things that people know is a truly a bad thing, but they don't say anything to prevent their friends from getting angry at them for offering their opinion. My mom was set on leaving today and it was all happening so fast I couldn't catch my breath. It was like she had taken a break from parenting, or taken a break from her senses, and my guess was both. It seemed like she couldn't spend too much time away from her new hubby, like it was causing her pain to be separated from him. Ben was a nice guy, don't get me wrong, and he was nice-looking. I was sort of grateful for that, with his dark black hair and dark eyes, and his pale white skin. The fact that he was in good shape helped too. I guess one word about his physique was that it was perfect. Everything in the man's face was perfect: he had a straight nose and perfect eyes that were spaced just the right distance from each other. The only think that wasn't perfect was his pale skin, probably from the lack of sun in Klamath Falls. I almost let out a hysterical laugh on that one. My mom had told me the weather climate there was quite a bit different and that we would have to make a shopping trip to get new clothes to accommodate for a new winter wardrobe. I had let a curse slip at that one. I groaned in despair when she told me it rained quite a bit, and then quickly regained my composure, not wanting to hurt her feeling.

I slowly headed into the bathroom, dragging my feet the whole way, not in a hurry to get ready. I shut the door with a small thud and stared in the mirror. There was not too much special about me; I have soft white skin that tends to burn quite easily if I stay out too long in the sun. I have blue eyes with just a hint of green that shows in the light. I have light brown hair that hangs straight to the middle of my back, my frame was quite little, and of course I was very short, only standing a whopping 5 ft 3 inches. Right now I have dark purples circles under my eyes, I am sure it is from the lack of sleep that I haven't gotten from the day my mom had told me we were moving. When I was younger, I always hoped I would manage to be at least 5 foot 8 inches, which is what the normal supermodels are, but as I grew older my hopes were dashed; and now, only standing at 5 foot 3 inches…let's face it, I would be no supermodel .

Besides, I thought with a chuckle, *you have to starve yourself to be a model*, and of course I liked food way too much to give that up. *I will leave all the starving and finger jamming down the throat to the real supermodels.* I am sure that if I stood looking in the mirror long enough, I could start pointing out lots of flaws, beside my most obvious feature that I am short. I guess my self-esteem is lacking, but really, what teenager is ever happy with their appearance? The rich girls that went to my school who had enough money to fix their flaws don't count as regular teenagers. I was a very quiet girl, never got into trouble; I preferred to be left alone, and I am sure my mother was very relieved over that one. You could say that I was more adult than my youth-stricken mother. My mother had tried various new things. She was always up for a new adventure. Although she never thought to bring me along for the ride, I was always grateful for that. This time, though, I couldn't fathom what changed her mind enough to want to marry Ben.

I was trying to settle my emotions so the sick feeling in my stomach would eventually pass. I took once last fleeting look in the mirror, ran my finger through my disheveled hair, and turned to the shower. I was one of those people who always felt better after I have a shower, so naturally every day I took one and sometimes two. There wasn't a whole lot that my mother hadn't packed – or should I say, tried to pack, because I found myself repacking most of the stuff she had jammed in the boxes – so finding shampoo and conditioner was going to be a test.

"God, I don't even want to know where my toothbrush is," I whispered under my breath. I turned the shower on as hot as it would go without burning my skin off. I carefully got in the shower, letting the water hit my back and run to my toes, and then I stuck my head under. I think I was subconsciously trying to drown my thoughts away. It didn't help. As I washed my hair my mind raced. What would the new city be like? Would I get along with any of the kids my age? I wondered what kind of house my mother was to subjecting me to.

I heard my mom call again, "ABIGAIL!" I shut off the water and grabbed a towel. Thank god my mom thought to leave one out for me. I opened the door just a crack as I wrapped the towel around myself.

"I'll be ready in a few minutes!" I yelled down stairs. It never took me very long to get ready. I wasn't into makeup or high fashion, I lived my life fairly plain and I guess you could say I was a little odd, which my mom truly hated. She thought every girl should wear makeup and be into the latest trends. I jumped into my jeans, grabbed my t-shirt and put that on quickly, although I wasn't sure why I was in a hurry. *Slow it down, Abby*, I thought to myself. It wasn't me who was so excited about the move, and my mom could wait a few extra minutes for me to collect myself. The huge gold framed mirror that hung over the sink had completely fogged over. I grabbed my towel and wiped the mirror off. *Yep, my face looks just as depressed as last time I saw it*, I thought, and I tried to smile. As of late, I practiced smiling a lot so I could look convincing, but I still looked really pathetic when I tried.

I ran a brush thought my wet hair quickly, getting any snags that were there, and not even bothering to blow dry it. *What's the point, I thought. Who was I trying to impress? If it rained as much as mom had said in Klamath Falls, my hair would probably get drenched. No point in doing anything about it.* Then I looked at the bag my mom had left on the counter. *Aaw, she was thinking about me. She left me my toothbrush.* Once I got done brushing my teeth and my mouth tasted of mint, I packed up the rest of my toiletries and opened the door and headed down the oak staircase. I sighed, as I knew it would be for the last time.

"Are you ready?" My mother asked with a hopeful glance. It took everything in me to keep from screaming, so I paused, and when I thought it was safe to answer without screaming I replied with one single word.

"Yes," I said as we headed out the door. "Mom?" I asked as we step out the front door.

"Yes, Abby," she said and stopped to look me full in the face. It was hard to look her straight in the eyes. I could see it, the look in her eyes: It was like Ben was the sun, was my mom's whole world, and I was some small planet that got to live in her orbit.

"Aren't you going to miss Florida at all?"

She paused and then started to speak. "Abby, I will miss it here, but this is our past. Our future is with Ben. You are young, Abigail; you'll see that this will work out just fine."

I like how she used the word "our." *Doesn't she mean her future, I* thought, as she continued to talk.

"Please see this as an adventure; you never know. You actually might like where we are moving to. Please give it a chance."

"All right, mom," I said, trying to smile. I took one quick glance back at the little white house with the blue shutters that had had meant so much to my mother and I, and then sighed and got in the cab. I shut the door to the past and headed into the future. *Here's to new beginnings,* I thought.

I can't say that I was overly chatty on the plane, but under the circumstances I was doing quite well. My mom was so excited that she talked most of the way and I listened; her mouth was like a speed boat and the motor was running at top speed. Ben, my mom's new husband, was used to the finer things in life so that why I wasn't so shocked when I saw that we had gotten first class tickets. I guess the flight could have been worse; I could have been stuck in back of the plane where they herded most passengers like cattle, with no leg room, close enough for someone to breathe on me. The thought actually made me about *gag*.

There was a tall leggy female flight attendant with blonde hair pulled up in a tight bun who constantly asked me if there was anything she could get me. I thought about saying, *Wake me up from this nightmare, that's what you can get me...or maybe a plane ticket home*. I held my tongue and just answered, "No, thank you."

After my mom's mouth got tired and she had been quiet for a while, she reached over and said, "How are you doing, Abby?" She actually sounded a little concerned for the first time in six months. She actually sounded like my mother again and not some infatuated teenager.

"Fine, mom," I said as nicely as I could.

"You know, you are really going to like Klamath Falls. There are lots of kids your age there," she said, trying to convince me. I could see the look in her face; my mother could never hide her emotions. She's a small woman with dyed blonde hair, petite like me. I think it made her feel better to know none of her grey hair was ever detectable. She also got her nails done every two weeks, whether she needed it or not. *I think it's part of her religion,* I chuckled to myself.

During all the years that we lived in Florida I don't think my mom dated once, so you could see why I was a little hesitant that my mother could fall in love and get married in only six months. Don't get me wrong, Ben seemed to be a nice guy, but didn't the nice guys always turn out to be the scary ones, with body parts buried in the back yard? I didn't even notice that we were coming in for a landing until the passenger seat belt sign came on.

"Better put on your seat belt," my mother said. I finally looked out the windows, but all I could see was fog.

Great, just great, I thought. *I can't even see the prison that my mother is subjecting me to for the next two or three years.* I gave up and shut the window visor. Since it was so foggy anyway that you couldn't see anything, what was the point trying to look out the window? As the plane descended my heart beat raced faster. The plane came down with a jolt and then quickly came to a stop... I was not looking forward to this.

We departed the airplane and headed into the terminal, and there was Ben, of course. He was waiting to greet us, or should I say, ready to greet my mother.

"Rebecca," he said to my mom. Ben grabbed my mother up in his arms with one swoop and kissed her passionately.

Kill me, no strike me dead, I thought to myself. This was crossing the line. Public affections were not part of the deal she made when she dragged me to this forbidding place. They didn't seem to be aware of anyone in their small bubble. It was just my mom and Ben. I couldn't believe my mother was putting on a show. People began to stare.

"Newlyweds," I stated to an older couple who must have been in their 80's, with withered faces and white hair. They had to pick up their faces off the floor, and I was surprised their dentures didn't fall out. It looked like the man was going to have a heart attack. Only when the older women hit him in the gut, and he let out a groan, did he close his mouth. I guess I had to giggle at that one, it was actually funny.

Ben set my mother down with a laugh. "How was your trip?" he asked.

"Wonderful," she said with a glowing look on her face. My mom had such a glow to her face, she could have lit up a complete town for a year, like a personal town power plant with all that energy and excitement.

I wasn't even sure if he had even noticed me, but then he looked back at me and asked, "What about you, Abigail?"

"You can call me Abby," I said, "And it was fine, thanks." After that long flight, I really wasn't up to playing nice and having small talk. Of course this was the man who single-handedly destroyed my life with one giant swoop.

Whatever makes my mother happy, I thought and then let out a sigh. My mom was so happy in Ben's arms that she completely forgot about me behind them. Which was okay, I liked being invisible. Better to be invisible than have to pretend to be happy.

"Wait till you see the house, you're going to love it," Ben said with so much enthusiasm, it was going to make me puke.

"I can't wait," my mother said. "You're going to like it, Abigail." Mom sounded like she was giving a pep talk. I didn't realize how long the drive was; *thank god I brought some technology to this godforsaken place,* I thought, putting my headphones on and turning on mp3 player. I stared out the window of Ben's SUV and tried to go back to a time when my thoughts had been happy. My life was not very exciting but it had to be better then what waited for me in Klamath Falls, I was sure of that.

As we drove through the city I felt like I was in a "Leave It to Beaver" rerun. Everything looked so old, even the people looked like they were from a really bad flashback to the '40's, though I could only guess the '40's since I was not actually living at that time. They didn't look very friendly; the lady at the general store, a short plump lady with gray hair and an apron, was out sweeping the front walk. The look she gave me when we drove past looked like she was shooting daggers right at me. As we drove though the city and started heading out into the country, I was a little curious.

"So you don't live in the city, Ben? I asked with confusion on my face.

"No," he said with a smirk on his face. "We live just outside of town, about 3 miles."

From what my mom had told me, Ben and his family were all from Klamath Falls, and they were all in the wine-making business. That was confusing, because I thought you needed sunshine for that. As we started to slow I saw all the vines with grapes, for the wine I guessed. Then we turned off the main road and through some iron gates and started up the long drive.

"What are the iron gates and fencing for?" I asked Ben as we continued up the lane. He hesitated before he answered, I wasn't even sure he was going to answer.

"It's to keep out animals and unwanted visitors," he answered, closing that subject. Then I saw it, the huge house on the hill: the Manor, my mom had called it when she tried to describe it. I never thought it would be like this. My first impression was that it wasn't even a house, it was a castle, like Dracula castle. My mouth hit the floor. The house was made of old kinds of white and brown stones with a huge over-hang over the front doors. My guess is they had made it so they could get out of the car without getting wet, since it rained all the time here. The drive was paved until we got to the house. There was a huge fountain in front of the massive front doors, and the drive turned into bricks that wrapped around the huge fountain.

Ben must have sensed something, because he said, "Yes, it is quite large, but you'll get used to it. It's your home now too, Abigail."

It will never be my home, I thought with grimace on my face. As we walked to the door of the house, the house seemed to get bigger as we got closer. I looked up and there were even gargoyles on the top of the roof on the edge. As we reached the massively large doors, they began to open.

"Welcome home, sir," said an older looking gentleman, with grey hair and deep wrinkles across his face that never seemed to change from that one expression when he talked.

"This is Albert, our butler," Ben said.

"Welcome Mrs. Moore," he said to my mother and then he turned to me and said, "Welcome, miss."

Somehow, I didn't feel at peace by the way he greeted us.

"Albert will help you get settled, Abigail. Please take Abigail up to her room, Albert," Ben said with a smile. Then he did something I didn't expect. He turned and looked at my mother and then picked her up to carry her over the threshold, making it look like she was light as a feather.

She laughed, "What are you doing?" she giggled.

"It's customary to carry the bride over the thresh-hold," he said with a gigantic smile on his face. She was still laughing as I watched them head into the house.

"Right this way, miss," Albert said. I grabbed what few bags that Albert hadn't managed to grasp. "Just a few rules," he continued, as he showed me to my room. "Please don't walk the halls at night and keep out of rooms that aren't yours. If you make a mess, please clean it up, and also, do not go out at night," he said with a stern look on his face. I was not use to having rules; my mother had always trusted me enough to know that I would always do the right thing. This did not sit well with me but I kept my composure and refrained from saying some snide remark. As we trotted up the steps to the second floor, Albert keeping a constant pace, I noticed my surroundings.

I gasped. *This isn't a house,* I thought, *it's a museum.* It had tall ceilings with one huge chandelier that hung above the steps in entry way it had, portraits of people I could only guess were once important people in Ben's family. The pictures looked so old. There were what looked like priceless vases around every corner, and a huge tapestry hung at the top of stairs, which I could only guess had his family crest on it. It was black and red with a silver shield in the middle of it. A sword ran right through the shield. It was quite impressive. We made our way down the long hallway and finally Albert stopped.

"Your room, miss" Albert said with the strange still look on his face. He turned to open two massive doors to show me the room.

I started to say, *you can just call me Abby,* when he turned and said, "Good night, miss," and then shut the two big oaks doors. I was finally alone; I set my stuff on the floor, and took a look around the room.

The tall ceilings seemed to run throughout the house. There was a large oak bed in the middle of the room with a canopy over it, a massive wood dresser in the corner with a large mirror over it, and also across from the bed there was a desk with a computer. My mom must have suggested it. There was no way Ben would come up with it on his own. I was glad that my mom had left me alone to unpack; that way I could go to pieces alone.

Well, I thought to myself, *I am sure these clothes aren't going to put themselves away.* I grabbed the largest suitcase and set it on the bed. I unzipped it and started to pull clothes out. Then I realized I hadn't even looked for the closet. I looked around room and finally saw it. I opened the door, but it wasn't just a closet; it was a whole huge bathroom with a gigantic closet. I wasn't really into the clothes thing, so this was much more than I needed, but it would be nice to have my own bathroom. I guess I couldn't complain about that. I started hanging my clothes in the oversized closet. *I think my clothes could take up 1/4 of this, what I am going to do with all rest of the space*, I thought to myself.

After I got everything put away, I thought it might be a good idea to take a quick glance my new home. *God, how weird is that, to think about calling this creepy Dracula castle my new home.* I opened the door, which let out a high pitch creak. *Shh*, I thought, *I don't want them to think I am snooping*, which I was. *Who cares*, I thought. If my mom was going to move me halfway across country and make me live in a place that looked like Dracula himself could live in the castle, I was going to get a peek. Since I knew tomorrow would be my dreaded first day of school, I was thinking I shouldn't snoop too much; after all, I did need some sleep. That is, if I was able to sleep in this manor which looked like a giant tomb.

As I walked down the hall and looked at all the antiques, I gasped. *Oh no*, I thought. I wasn't the most coordinated person in the world; god forbid I knock something over in this house. It would take me more than a century to pay for it. As I went down the stairs to the main floor, I heard laughter coming from the room off to the right. I peeked my head through the door. It was my mom and Ben, laughing and joking like they were teenagers with their first crush. As I looked through the doors at my juvenile mother, the door creaked. *Oh crap, doesn't anyone grease these doors around here?* I thought.

"Oh, Abigail," my mom said, looking a little embarrassed, her face going red. She straightened out of the embrace she and Ben were in. Thank god! No teenager wants to see their parents getting frisky, it's just so gross.

"Sorry," she said. "I didn't see you there."

That was the point, I thought to myself.

"Did you get everything put away okay?"

"Yep, sure did," I said, trying to put smile on my face, I knew this marriage was a bad idea, and moving across country, even worse, but for the sake of my mother I would grin and bear it.

"Well, you must be famished," my mother said with concern on her face.

"Where are my manners?" Ben said. "We should get ready for dinner. I'll have the cook prepare something."

"Don't bother Ben," I said, trying to keep the hostility out of my voice. "I'm not real hungry." *I wasn't in the mood to try to keep food down,* I thought to myself. "I think I'll just head off to bed."

"Sleep tight," my mom said.

"Good night, Abby. I am sure this place will grow on you," Ben said, with a hopeful glance.

"I'm sure it won't," I thought quietly to myself. I tried to smile as I turned and walked out the door heading to the massive staircase. I entered the room that was now mine and headed into the huge bathroom where the closet was. I picked out a simple white t-shirt and a pair of black loose fitted shorts. I guess you could say that I wasn't your normal frilly girl. I hated pj's so most nights I would just sleep in a t-shirt and shorts; not trendy but damn comfortable. I finished getting undressed and brushed my teeth and washed my face. For some reason, I always felt better my little routine of washing and brushing. As I looked in the mirror I whispered under my breath, "So plain."

Well there wasn't anything to do about my face, as if it would help anyways, I thought. Then my stomach fluttered with the thought of my first day of school. My old school was large enough that I could fly under the radar, and no one really bothered me. But this school was so small, I was guessing everyone was informed on my arrival and there would be plenty of stares and, I was sure, lots of gossip. That thought just seemed to make things worse. I wasn't sure how I was going to make through the first day. My social skills were next to nothing and I wasn't pretty or funny, and I was sure all the kids had their own opinions on what I was going to look like and act like. *Well, I can't do anything about it tonight, so I might as well not dwell on it.*

2 The Fall

MY ALARM WENT OFF AND I groaned, rolled over, and shut it off, thinking it was too early to get up. Then I realized, no it's not too early, the sun just never shines in Klamath Falls. I stumbled out of the bed and headed to the bathroom, almost tripping over myself. I was in a hurry, thinking I didn't want to be late for my first day. I hopped in the shower, scrubbed down as fast as I could, not even waiting for the water to warm up. I jumped out, grabbed the towel, and almost fell in the closet. *I am going to have to work on my balance or I am not sure that I will make through the day.* I grabbed a blue long-sleeved shirt with a low v in the front and a pair of faded blue jeans. I put them on as fast as I could without injuring myself. I brushed my hair, trying to get all the snarls out, and then I grabbed the blow dyer from one of the cabinets. Ben must have had the butler stock it. I didn't wait till my hair was completely dry; I was in a hurry, still rushing. I guess I should be glad that I didn't yank all my hair out in the rush. I brushed my teeth, grabbed my socks and shoes, and headed out the bedroom door. I ran down the steps, surely making all the noise I could manage.

As I reached the first floor, Ben and my mom were there waiting for me, smiling. "Abby, do you want some breakfast?" my mom asked.

"No, I'm really not hungry," I replied. She didn't push, which was a little different. Usually she made sure I ate breakfast, being that it was the 'most important meal of the day' as she constantly reminded me.

"You look wonderful," my mom said.

"Are you ready for your first day," Ben asked with a curious look on his face.

"As ready as I'll ever be," I said with the attempt of a smile on my face.

"Well," Ben said with a big smile on his face, "Your mother and I thought, since we didn't really do anything for your birthday, and you don't want to be dependent on us, we would give your an belated birthday present." I had just turned 16 right after the wedding, so it kind of got pushed on the back burner. As he opened the gigantic front doors I saw it, it was like a dream. It was black with huge tires which I sure that I was going to get pretty bruised getting in and out of it.

"You got me a Jeep," I said with a shocked voice.

"Well, it was Ben's idea," my mom said.

"I just thought it would be nice to have something to get you around since we live out in the country," Ben said with a pleased look on his face.

"Have a good day," mom said as she gave me a hug and then Ben dropped the keys in my hand.

"Thanks," I said as I headed out the door. *Maybe this move won't be so bad*, I thought as I got into the huge Jeep.

"Drive carefully, Abby," my mom called out in her worried voice. I knew it wouldn't worry her for long because she got distracted easily.

"Don't worry, mom. I will," I said, trying to soothe her. As I sat behind the wheel, I actually smiled. *My very own Jeep*, I thought to myself as I started the Jeep. It started with a great roar.

"This baby has a lot of power," I said out loud. I put the car into gear and started -to move, the vibration of the jeep shaking my frame. I wasn't really sure where I was going, but I knew my way into town, and I was pretty sure the school wasn't going to be that hard to find.

As I came into the city I realized that my first impression was probably right. The city was very small and the people still looked like they should be on one of those old TV show reruns, the ones where everyone was nice to the neighbors and took over cookies and cake to someone's house daily. As I pulled into what I figured would be the school, I realized that schools always looked the same, no matter where you are. They're just an institution, where kids can be off the streets until 3:00 rolls around and their parents can take their turn to babysit.

The school wasn't that big. Klamath Union School had a total of 970 students – my old school was 4 times bigger – and all brick. I was sure that the parking lot was probably bigger than the whole school. I found the first parking spot I could and pulled in and shut off the engine, trying not to draw attention to myself. The parking lot looked like fresh gravel had just been laid; I could still smell the tar under the gravel. I chose this parking spot because it was close to the exit of the school so I could get out in a hurry if I needed to. I got out of the Jeep and headed towards the front door. I could feel the stares on my back, burning me like their eyes were lasers. Or like an overweight person looks at a cupcake. I was starting the school in the middle of my sophomore year. I was sure that all of these kids had been together since day one so I wasn't sure how I would be received. I knew that I would be a curiosity to them, and I would probably get quite a few stares, but hopefully by day two they would all get over it and I could endure my punishment in Klamath Falls being on everyone's back burner.

I entered the school. As I walked in, I noticed a trophy case right there, and two massive staircase on each side of me. Then I noticed the office sign over a door to the right. I walked into the office and saw a brown-headed, chubby women kneeling on the floor. She wore a button-down shirt with flowers on it and a pair of brown pants. At that part, I wondered if she actually worked that hard to mismatch herself or if it was a god-given talent.

Stop right there, Abby, I thought to myself. *Where are your manners?*

"Gosh darn it," the woman said, sounding frustrated. I cleared my throat so she would know that she had an audience.

"Oh!" She said, looking embarrassed as she looked up at me, her face flushing. "Can I help you?" She asked with a smile, and got up off the floor. "I am sorry, dear. I lost my earring and I was trying to find it..."

"That's okay; my name is Abby Watson."

"Oh yes," she said. "You moved out to Ben Moore's place."

I just nodded.

"Yes, dear," she grabbed a stack of papers from the edge of her very messy desk. "Here is your schedule, and the teachers will give you the books you need." She explained very clearly the directions to my first class as she handed me the schedule and locker number and combination.

I walked down the hall, taking in the little touch of perfume, bubble gum and sweat that lingered in the air. I was aware that the kids were staring; one girl almost lost her books when she was paying more attention to me than them. *God, don't let me trip,* I thought to myself as I headed to my first class. I kept my eyes down at my feet to avoid any eye contact with the other students.

It wasn't hard to find my first class; the school had only three floors and of course the older students were on the top floor. Composition happened to be the first door as I came up the steps. I looked at the door before I walked in. The name on the door said, "Mr. Murphy."

I sighed and walk through the door preparing to face the firing squad. I tried to sneak in without saying anything but Mr. Murphy seemed to be very perceptive, though that should be hard in a school where not much ever changed.

"Excuse me, miss," he said with a startled expression. "Are you sure you belong in this class?"

"Yes, my name is Abby Watson, and we just moved here."

"Oh, that right," he said as some kind of recollection came back to him. "Go ahead and find an empty seat." I looked at the semi-empty class room, with kids still piling in through the door. I headed for the last seat in the back, trying to melt into the background. Just then a group of guys strolled in, laughing and drawing quite a bit of attention to themselves. There were five of them, and they were all very tall; they each had to be over six feet and muscular with short dark hair and deep black eyes. They were all wearing black shirts and blue jeans. They were very loud with their deep rich voices. They looked dangerous, the kind of guys you would take home to make your parents freak out.

"All right everyone, take your seats." The bell rang as the teacher began to talk.

Just then another boy walked into class. He was very much like the other five with the black shirt and jeans. His hair was lighter brown though, and instead of his eyes being a dark black like the other boys, they were blue, ice blue, and he seemed somewhat younger.

He was *gorgeous*. My heart raced as I gawked at him. There was something about him, something so familiar. I dropped my head very quickly as I realized I was staring. *Good one, Abby,* I thought to myself, *the only thing that would have been worse is if I started drooling.* Disgusted with myself, I kept my eyes low, still watching him.

"Nice of you to join us, Mr. Wilkins," Mr. Murphy said with a grimace. The boy started to head over to sit with the other five. Just then his head jerked and he looked at me, and then he looked away very quickly. I gathered from the look on his face that, for that split second, something had disturbed him.

Through the rest of the class, I tried not to stare at the gorgeous boy. I felt like the group of strange boys were all looking at me. *I am a new student; maybe I am just being paranoid;* I thought to myself. Class was boring and the teacher's voice was a dull monotone. I felt my head bob a few times, and just when I thought I was going to fall asleep and my head would crash on the table, the bell rang, making me jump. *Thank god,* I thought to myself. The girl who had sat in front of me turned around.

"Hi," she said in a sweet voice with a perky personality. "My name is Julie." She said, showing every one of her perfectly straight white teeth in an eye-crinkling smile.

"Hi," I replied, a shocked look on my face. "I'm Abby," I introduced myself. Julie had straight brown hair that came to her shoulders and glasses. She was petite like me, and had a bubbly personality that could put anyone into a good mood. She seemed nice enough.

"Well, what's your next class," she asked.

"Math," I said, with a frown on my face.

"Oh, you got Mr. Stewart; he's a real peach," she said with sarcasm in her voice. "Well, I can show you the way."

"Thanks," I said, with a grateful look on my face. And I was grateful; nothing says "new student" like getting lost on the first day. As we walked out of class, I noticed the group of boys standing right outside the classroom, leaning against lockers with their arms folded, not looking as if they were in any hurry to get to their next class. They were still joking and laughing, except the one with the ice blue eyes. He was looking at me as though he could see right into my soul. He wasn't joining in conversation with the other boys, and there was no amusement on his face. My heart started to race, and I blushed as I walked by and headed to class.

"Who was that," I whispered to Julie. She giggled; she must have seen him looking at us too.

"Oh, that was Ethan Wilkins," she said with a smile on her face. "Don't get too close, she whispered. "He's very different. Actually, all the boys he hangs with are weird," she added.

I wanted her to clarify that comment, but I didn't want to be rude. Since it was a small town, I was sure that I would learn all the gossip sooner or later. As the school day dragged on and on, it seemed that I was constantly running into Ethan. He never said anything; he just looked at me with those beautiful eyes and a look on his face that ranged from confusion, to worry, to intrigue.

The final bell rang. *Thank god, the day is over.* I headed back to my Jeep, and I managed to stay off the radar of most of the students. Only Julie seemed to be brave enough to talk to me, a fact for which I was truly grateful. From what I learned about the school, everyone pretty much stayed in the social circle everyone else expected them to be in. You had the geeks, the ones who would play chess or join the glee club. You had the cheerleaders, with their short skirts and blonde hair, always worried about their weight, and the jocks who played all the sports. When you tried to carry on a conversation with them, it was like they had got tackled one too many times and were showing signs of brain damage. Then of course there were the bad boys like Caleb's crew who were hot, mysterious, and dangerous all wrapped into one. I secretly wondered where I would fit in and what group would accept me into their fold. I hurried out to the Jeep as fast as I could without tripping. As I started to get ready to jump into my Jeep I noticed him. Ethan. Staring at me in the parking lot. He was standing by a group motorcycles. *God this is getting a little old,* I said, so low that I didn't think anyone heard me. Just then his head turned away and he started talking to the other five boys who were in our first period class. A chill ran through my body. I shrugged and jumped into my jeep, trying to act as if I hadn't even noticed.

If this was going to continue tomorrow, I was going to have to say something, I thought to myself. I started to head out of town and back towards Ben's house. I couldn't even call it home; It wasn't my home. It was a prison that my mother was subjecting me to. My home was in Florida, with the ocean and the sun and, yes, even the alligators. As I pulled up to the house, I decided that that a walk might calm my nerves a little. I wasn't ready to go in and have to put on my happy face. I left my keys in the jeep, jumped out, and shut the door quietly. I hoped that no one had noticed me drive up and shut the door, and I headed out the forest behind the big mansion. I looked up at the mansion as

I passed, and I could have sworn I could see someone on the second floor staring at me. I looked away very quickly. Then I looked back to see if I was mistaken. There was no one there, but the curtains waved ever so slightly.

As I headed into the forest I noticed a small rock path, which I was happy about. I didn't really want to get lost and my sense of directions was never very good. I guess that evened things out because it coincided with my crappy balance. I knew it was going to get dark soon, and the words of wisdom the creepy butler had given me were ringing in my head. So I knew I couldn't stay out too long. I must have gone at least a mile on the path. It was so dark in the forest with the trees like a canopy letting very little light through. It was then that I came upon an opening in the woods. As I came through the openings in the trees, I noticed the ground was rocky now, and as I walked forward I realized the ground dropped off and away. I slowly walked up to the edge. It was a big cliff with water flowing down below. I kicked one of the rocks that were near my feet. It rolled off the edge; it seemed to fall forever before it finally splashed into the river below.

I looked over the edge and a shiver ran down my spine. I took a step backwards not wanting to lose my balance and fall over the edge. That would have been quite possible for me. I was depressed, but not suicidal, so falling off a cliff didn't appeal to me. It was so beautiful, like one of the pictures you see hanging at a museum, though I could see why they didn't want anyone out at night. God forbid I fall over this cliff the first full day I was here. With my balance issues, this probably wasn't the best place for me.

I probably should head back, I thought. A cold breeze blew, and I was suddenly in a hurry to get back. It was then that I heard a twig snap. It made me jump. I looked around to see if anyone was there, but I could only see the tree tops sway with the wind.

"Hello? Is anyone there?" I said. I heard nothing. Then, I felt really stupid for letting my imagination get out of control. *There's no one out there*, I said to myself. *This is private property and there was a ten foot wall around the property.*

Out of the corner of my eyes, I saw something whirl past. It was so fast! I turned to see what it was, but as I turned, I lost my balance. I felt the thud as I hit my head on the side of the cliff and the last thing I remembered was falling over the edge.

The first thing I noticed as I opened my eyes was how dark things were, and how very cold. Then I realized I was lying on the forest floor about 10 feet from the edge of the cliff. The last thing I was aware of was losing my balance and falling over the cliff. *How can that be? I had to be at least 10 feet back!* My head started to spin and hurt, which was proof that my memory wasn't faulty. My wrists were aching like they had been in a tourniquet too long and it ached as the blood flow slowly returned to my fingers. Just then, I heard my name being yelled.

"ABIGAIL!" I heard from a distance.

"Mom," I whispered,

Then I heard another voice, a man's voice. "Abigail! Abigail Watson, where are you!"

I tried to yell but it didn't seem like the words could come out of my mouth. I was chattering so bad from the cold that it felt like there was a jackhammer in my mouth. Just then I saw my mom running towards me.

"Abigail! Are you all right?"

I could see the worry in her eyes and terror in her voice. "Yes mom," I managed to get out through my chattering teeth. "I just slipped." I shook my head trying to remember what had happened. "I slipped and fell, but I don't know what happened after that," I told her with a confused look on my face.

I felt myself being lifted off the ground. "Let's get her home," Ben said to my mom. He carried me easily back to the house. When we got to the house it seemed like I couldn't keep my eyes opened. They kept trying to close.

"Maybe we should take her to the hospital, or at least call a doctor," my mother said with a tremor in her voice.

"I don't think that will be necessary," Ben said, trying to calm my mother down. "We'll keep an eye on her tonight. If we see any sign of a concussion we will take her to the hospital."

"But she hit her head, Ben! We should take her in. What if she has internal bleeding or something?" It was just like my mom to overact.

Ben always had a calming effect on her, and it didn't take him long to work his magic on her. "Rebecca. Please calm down," he said, while sweeping her disheveled blonde hair out of her face. "Abigail will be fine."

"Mom," I said with a shaky voice that almost came out in a whisper. "I'm fine; I could use a warm shower and some sleep."

"Are you okay to walk," Ben asked.

"Yeah, I am fine; just a little tired."

He set me down, I wavered for just a moment and Ben caught me. "Abby, are you sure you can walk?" Ben asked with a concerned look on his face.

"I really am fine, gravity's just not my thing."

"I am starting to get that impression," he said with a nervous look. I started up the stairs

"Maybe you should stay home from school tomorrow," my mom said, but it was more a question than an order.

"No, mom. It's only my second day. These people probably already think I am weird. I don't want to give them something else to talk about." I started up the stairs holding the massive would rail, just so I wouldn't fall. I finally reached my room and shut the massive doors, still trying to get a grip on what had happened. I was walking; I heard something in the trees. I knew I saw something, but what? *What did I see? And how did I survive the fall?* I knew that it didn't make any sense. As I got into the shower and the water started hitting my back, I could see I was shaking; *I must be going into shock,* I thought to myself. As I took inventory to make sure that I was in one piece, I noticed that my wrist had strange purplish bruises. They almost looked like they were finger marks, but they were too big to belong to anyone I knew. I couldn't see any more damage, but I knew that I fell. *Why don't I have more scrapes, or how am I alive at all? I should be dead at the bottom of the cliff.* Nothing made sense.

I could have probably stayed in the shower all night, but I knew soon the hot water would run out. I shut off the water and grabbed the towel that hung to the right of the shower. As I wrapped the towel around me, I noticed that the mirror had fogged over. I grabbed a washcloth out of the drawers that Ben must have had stocked for me. *Great, just great,* I let out a whisper. *Now I have the creepy butler in my private bathroom.* I wiped the mirror off and then stared at the plain person in the mirror; I notice that a small but prominent bump was forming over my left eye. So that proved that I had fallen and bumped my head.

Fabulous, I thought. *As if I wasn't a big enough freak to begin with. Now I'm going to have a big goose-egg on my head.* I grabbed my t-shirt and shorts, and got dressed for bed.

I headed back into the bedroom and realized that my window was opened. With a shiver I ran over and shut the big window. I had to shove pretty hard to get it closed, but finally it shut with a thud. I could have sworn that this window was shut when I walked in, but I probably couldn't tell what I saw. The small concussion probably took care of anything I had thought I had seen.

Well, I'm sure my mother is going to be checking on me at least a dozen times tonight, so I better get some sleep. Just then, I noticed a glass of water and two aspirin sitting on a nightstand by the bed. I knew I loved my mom. It's nice that were so in sync that she would know that I needed aspirin. I grabbed the glass of water and took the pills as I hopped into bed. I couldn't keep my eyes open any longer; I fell fast into a deep sleep.

3 Nightmare

I WALKED THOUGH THE DARK massive forest, stumbling on the rocks below my feet. A cold breeze blew, ruffling the trees above. I could feel that I was being watched, and it sent a cold chill though my body. I could hear branches and twigs snapping in the deep, dark forest. There only seemed to be a small amount of light from the moon set high behind the trees. I could see the cold breath coming out of my mouth. Another chill ran through me. There was a thin fog that seemed to linger on the forest floor, untouched by the air that blew all around.

I searched into the trees, seeing nothing. It was so dark. I started to run, tripping and stumbling on the twigs below my feet. I couldn't run far enough or fast enough. I tried to scream, but I couldn't find my voice. It was like something was keeping me from screaming. Then, all of a sudden, I froze. In front of me in the darkness, I could see a set of eyes. Not just any eyes but light, ice blue eyes, looking at me. It knocked the breath right out of me and made my heart stop. Then it was over.

I jolted upright with a scream. My heart was still pounding, and sweat was rolling down my face. It took me a moment to realize that it was just a nightmare. I wasn't sure what the nightmare was about, though the vivid details I ran over and over in my head. The only thing I was sure of was the eyes, the eyes that seemed to be so familiar, but I couldn't place them. I fell back into my pillow, grateful it was just a dream. I took a breath to slow my heart, and after it returned to its regular beat, I turned my head to the left to look at the clock that was on the night stand. 6:30.

I signed. Time to get ready for school, although after that nightmare I was not sure school was what I needed. I slowly climbed out of bed and sluggishly made it to the bathroom. I hopped in the shower, washed up, grabbed my towel and wiped the mirror that was always foggy after the shower. I brushed my teeth meticulously. It was like I was on autopilot. Then I really looked in the mirror. The small bump that I had from last night's misadventure had grown three times bigger, and it was more of a dark purple, almost black now. Then I looked at my wrist and there was 5 long lines that looked like giant hands had gripped them. I thought back to last night, trying to remember how I had got the bruises on my wrist or the bump on my head, but I could think of nothing to explain the marks or the bump.

What happened last night? I tried to remember, and the more I thought, the more my head felt like it was going to rip off my shoulders and roll onto the floor. *I'm a freak*, I thought to myself. *I can't go to school looking like this.* I hurried and grabbed a long black shirt and a pair of blue jeans. Hopefully the shirt would keep people from noticing the bruises on my wrists. I grabbed a band-aid that was in the medicine cabinet hanging on the wall above the light switch. It was nice that I had my own personal first aid kit. No doubt I would need it. I had no clue what I was going to do about the huge lump protruding from my forehead but I was sure the band-aid would help a little. I decided leaving my hair down would cover some of it. Thank god my bangs had grown out somewhat from last time I cut them. *What am I going to tell people*, I thought to myself. *It was bad enough that people stared yesterday, but the thought of having them stare at me today almost sent me into convulsions.*

"What am I going to tell everyone at school?" I whispered under my breath. As I walked out of the bathroom I heard a small knock at my door. The knock wasn't loud but it seemed to echo off the high ceiling. Before I could say, "Come in," the door cracked open.

"Can I come in?" my mom whispered.

"Sure, mom."

"How are you feeling, honey?" she asked, a concerned look on her face.

"I'm fine, just a little bruised up," I said to reassure her.

"You gave me quite a scare, Abigail." She almost sounded mad as the words came out. I knew that she wasn't mad; it was just that I had frightened her. I was usually more responsible than to wander off in a strange place. The look on her face made me feel even worse.

"Sorry mom, I just went for a walk. I'm really not sure what happened."

"Well I am glad you're all right," she said. "I know this has been a hard move for you, but please try, honey. If you just give it a chance, I know you'll really like it here." For some reason she kept repeating her statement, probably trying to convince herself that if she kept saying it, it would make it true. I almost laughed at that thought. To be happy here was not remotely a possibility.

"Mom," I said, with compassion in my voice, "I am happy if you are happy. I will adjust."

"Abby," she started, "I don't just want you to adjust, I want you to be happy, too." She still had a concerned look on her face, and I wished that I could make her feel better, but trying to lie was not an option. I was a terrible liar, and eventually I would feel guilty enough that I would give in and tell the truth. I decided the truth would be better this time.

"Mom, it's a lot to take in. I am trying, just please give me some time."

"Okay, Abby, I won't push." I could see that she was really making an effort not to pry so I guess I should give her some brownie points.

"Really, Mom, I am fine," I said with a smile.

"Do you want to stay home today?" Again she said it with the concerned look all over her face. The thought of staying locked up in Dracula's castle for an entire day was worse than me plunging to death over the cliff.

"No, it's only my second day, and I don't want to get behind," I quickly said. I really didn't think I was going to get behind at school, but at least it was better than here.

"Okay," she said with a resigned looked on her face. "Well, why you don't come downstairs and get breakfast.

"All right, Mom. I will be down in a few minutes."

"Okay, Abby, I will leave you alone to finish getting ready." As she shut the door behind her I felt relieved. I finished getting my socks and shoes on and then took a look out the window and sighed. Another gloomy day. I thought the clouds were so thick it barely let light through. Rain was a given. I hurried downstairs, trying not to trip down the massive wood stair case, and I made it to the dining room. It wasn't hard to find, because it was off the entryway. As I walked into the dining room I noticed it fit with the rest of the house. It was full of antiques. There was a long table that stretched across the room with twenty chairs, nine on each side and one at each end. *I swear I walked back in time,* I thought. Over the massive table covered in a beautiful white lace table cloth was an elegant crystal chandelier.

I've died and gone to hell, I thought. *The table looks too beautiful to even eat at. God forbid I spill something and give the butler something to pop a vein over.* The thought of the butler actual having any reaction at all almost made me smile. I walked in and noticed my mom and Ben were nowhere in sight. Just then, the creepy butler came through the door behind me. He was so quiet that it made me jump when he said, "Mr. and Mrs. Moore have already had their breakfast and have left for the day."

"Oh," I said with a frown on my face. *I didn't think it took me that long to finished getting ready but I must've just missed them,* I thought.

Just then, I noticed that he was caring a tray full of food, he looked like one of the fancy waiters from the city.

"Here is your breakfast, Miss," he said with the same expressionless look on his face. It looked like his face was permanently etched that way. Then he quickly set the food down on the table. I looked at all the food: pancakes, eggs, toast, sausages, bacon, milk, and juice.

I started to protest. "I really don't need all this, cereal would be just fine."

His face didn't change and he didn't respond to my protest. He just turned and started heading out the door that he come through. "Good day, miss," he said as he walked out the door.

"What a friendly, creepy guy," I said to myself. "There is just something about that guy that gives me the chills." The food did look good and I was extremely hungry. I hadn't had much of an appetite since we moved here, and the food smelled and looked surprisingly good. I sat down and started to eat. Everything was delicious. I started to drink the juice and it was gone in under a minute. *Gosh, I didn't realize that I was that thirsty.* Silently I wondered what my mom and Ben were going to do today. I knew it had only been two days since we moved here, but it didn't seem that I had gotten to see my mother in that time.

"It's the honeymoon stage," I said to myself. "It will get better in the next couple of months," I tried to reassure myself. Just then I noticed the clock. "OH, CRAP!" I said out loud; 7:45. I only had 10 minutes to get to school and 5 minutes to get to class. I started to pick up the dishes to take them to the kitchen, but I heard the butler outside the door.

"Just leave the dishes, miss," he said in a monotone voice. I didn't have the time or the energy to argue with the creepy butler. I ran out of the dining room to the great room, grabbed my keys from where my mom must have put them after they brought me back to the house last night. Then I turned to looked around for my bag and remembered that I had left in out in my jeep. I was very grateful that I hadn't been assigned any homework on my first day. I was sure that was going to change. I headed out to my jeep without giving Albert the creepy butler a glance. I opened the door to my jeep and jumped in and turned the keys.

The jeep rumbled to life with a great roar. *I will never get tired of this truck,* I thought to myself, *it's the best gift I have ever been given.* I loved it, and all the freedom that came with it. I decided not to turn the radio up, which I normally did. I usually had it blasting crazy 80's rock songs; Bon Jovi was my favorite. I would play the same 80's songs over and over, singing along with them as long as no one was around, I wasn't the best singer in the world and didn't want to kill anyone with my singing. I know I wasn't born in the 80's, which my mother continues to remind me. There's just something about those songs that makes me feel good. Most of the ones I actually liked were rock ballads; something about the undying love in them.

My head was still reeling from the bump I had suffered from last night, so turning on the radio was not an option. As I rolled into town and made to the school, I thought I had just minutes to spare. When I pulled into the school parking lot, I noticed it was awfully crowded for me being so late. I glanced down at the clock on the dash and realized it was only 7:30.

"Oh, no," I grumbled. Ben's clocks must have been running ahead. Nothing scared me more than being the center of everyone's attention. I sat in the Jeep and thought for a moment. I didn't really want to get out, knowing that everyone was curious about the strange new girl. I decided to stay in the Jeep.

I gave in and turn on my radio, which I knew was going to give me more of a headache. It was much better than the prospect of getting out and being stared at, knowing that they probably already were. I took a chance to glance out, to see if anyone had noticed me pulling into the parking spot. It seemed I hadn't interrupted anyone's activities.

Just then, I noticed a large group of guys, all very big. I realized this was the group from my first hour class. They didn't seem to notice me, which was good in my book; they were all very large and very intimidating. Today they were wearing matching leather jackets and faded blue jeans. How strange that they were riding motorcycles in a place that saw more rain than sun. Just then, I saw *him*; those light ice blue eyes were watching me.

It was a knee jerk reaction; I looked down, dropping my head so that my hair covered my face. There was something about his face. He was different than the other boys. I couldn't figure it out. I knew he was gorgeous, with that light brown hair and his eyes and his body, built like a rock star. He was just so mesmerizing. I felt a chill run down my body and my heartbeat sped erratically. I took a breath to try and relax myself.

I don't really know how long I sat there, frozen, but I was conscious of when the parking lot started to empty. I took a deep breath, turned off the engine and stepped out of my Jeep. I was hoping that today wasn't going to be too much of a nightmare; maybe I could stay somewhat invisible so I didn't have to explain the big bump on my head. I walked into class and realized even before I sat down that it wasn't going to be as easy as I hoped. Julie was sitting there with a concerned look on her face. Before she could ask, I mumbled, "I fell in the woods."

She seemed to sense that I didn't really want to talk about it so she let it drop. I could see that she was trying to fight the smile that was slowly building on her face, but she didn't ask me anything more about it. I could see that Julie and I were going to get along just fine, she didn't press so I didn't talk. About 30 seconds before the bell rang to get class started, the six massive boys walked through the door.

"Caleb, Isaac, Jeremiah, Cain, Samuel and last but not least, Ethan," Mr. Murphy announced as they walked through the door. "It's nice to see you in class, but maybe you shouldn't wait till the last minute," he said, with a stern look on his face. "Take your seats," he ordered in a low gruff voice.

They didn't say anything. They just had wide grins on their face, almost like they were laughing at him. As they sat down I couldn't help but stare. They almost looked like they could be in college, they were quite a bit bigger than the other boys sitting around them. They were so big I wasn't sure how the desk didn't crumble into pieces the minute that they sat down. I had never seen anyone as big as these boys. I could feel my jaw drop, and closed it fast with a loud pop where my bottom teeth hit my upper teeth. I was sure that my jaw was going to hurt later. I hoped that no one saw my response to the massive boys, but Julie must have, because I could hear her giggle.

As I watched them I realized that most of the other kids in class didn't notice them. Actually, you could say they pretty much ignored them. I noticed the one with the ice blue eyes and the light brown hair had turned his head my way. He looked at me with some interest, and I was embarrassed so I dropped my head, letting the hair fall around my face. That seemed my normal reaction now anytime he looked at me. I heard Julie giggle again. I knew that Mr. Murphy had started the class, but I was so engrossed in my thoughts about the blue-eyed boy that to tell you the truth I had no Idea what he was talking about.

Time seemed to go by in a flash. The bell rang and startled me. I started to gather up my books and to get up. I was the last one out the door with Julie right in front of me. As I walked out the door, I noticed the 6 boys standing around the lockers on the outside of the door, but they weren't laughing and joking this time. They were all looking at Julie and me as we passed through the door. I wasn't paying much attention to my walk, which was highly dangerous. I tripped over my feet, but before I could fall, Julie caught my arm.

"Thanks," I said, "for saving me from the embarrassment of picking myself off the floor."

"No problem," she said with a laugh. As I looked out of the corner of my eyes I could see the blue eyes and the smirk that came with it, I grimaced and then began walking to math. Mr. Stewart was starting to talk about formulas, but it seemed like I couldn't concentrate. After math class was over, I made it though the hours in a daze.

Finally it was lunchtime. I really didn't feel like eating. Julie was hoping that I would sit with her and her friends, who I had sat with yesterday. I knew she was dying to find out what I did to my head. In my embarrassment over the whole situation, I wasn't in the mood to talk to anyone about it. I told her I was just going to get a soda and head out and listen to music in my Jeep. I paid for my soda and slowly made my way outside. As I was walking to my jeep, I noticed the group of five guys sitting at the back of the cafeteria, laughing and joking. Except for one. Caleb, who was the biggest of course, was staring at me with those deep black eyes. I tried to ignore him as I headed out the doors.

When I opened the cafeteria door and notice it was raining. I groaned. I thought about making a run for it, but chances were that I would trip and get muddy as well as wet. I stood under the cafeteria overhang, thinking about my options. I had a strange feeling that I was not alone. I turned around, and there, leaning against the wall to the cafeteria, was the beautiful brown-haired, blue-eyed boy. It seemed like forever that he stood there and looked at me with those beautiful blue eyes. His face was unreadable, not even a smirk.

He shrugged off the wall and took three long steps and stopped at my feet. I could feel my jaw start to drop, but I stopped myself.

He said in a deep angelic voice, "Hello. My name is Ethan Wilkins. You must be Abigail Watson."

It was like he sent an electric shock thought my body; I couldn't say anything. It was like my airway shut down, like my brain had shut down. I just nodded, trying to remember to breath. He was taller than I thought from only seeing him from a distance, and he was more beautiful than I could think possible. Before I could get my brain to work so I could talk, he smiled, and my breathing became erratic. He smiled like he could my heart speed up. Just then he turned and walked past me, and the smell that came through the breeze as he walked past was a strong woodsy, musky scent. A warm chill ran though me, like there was fire running though my veins.

Without another word he walked from underneath the protection of the cafeteria overhang into the rain, which was starting to come down harder. It drizzled down his hair, just making him that much more appealing.

So mysterious, I thought, as he walked towards his bike and got on. It took him one quick kick start and the monstrous bike roared to life, and I watched him ride away. The first thoughts that came to my mind was, *I'm such in idiot.* I couldn't understand why I didn't open my mouth and talked to that beautiful boy.

There were a lot of other things that ran through my mind. One was, *why did he introduce himself only to walk away?* Also, school wasn't over for the day. *Why did he leave, and what's with the bike, in the rain?* So many questions and no answers. *This should keep me up tonight; I haven't had a good night sleep since we moved to this horrible place.* Just then the bell rang, and I ran to class. I didn't want to be late. I met up with Julie, who was walking up the hall.

"Julie," I said, with a shaky voice.

"Yes, Abby?" she asked.

"Can I ask you a question?"

"Sure, Abby."

"What do you know about Ethan Wilkins?" I asked.

She giggled again. "You're interested in him," she said, and it wasn't even a question, more like a statement.

"Well, I said, ignoring her, "He introduced himself at lunch and then he took off on his bike. He just seems a little strange."

"Ethan and his friends," she lumped them together, "are very different," she said with a composed look, and she wasn't giggling now. "They pretty much stay to themselves, they don't really notice anyone. They do whatever they want, come and go as they please. I'm really even shocked he would say anything to you; usually they go on with their day not paying attention to anyone."

"Oh," I said, with more questions burning in my head.

"What did he say?" Julie asked.

"He just told me his name and asked me mine, and then he left. It was all very strange," I said.

"Well, that's Ethan for you," she said, almost spitting out the words. I got the impressions from the way Julie said his name that she had gotten a bad taste about Ethan and his friends.

"Julie, can I ask you another question?"

"Sure, Abby. Go ahead."

"Well, "I started, "what's with the rest of the kids in school? They don't like them much either, do they?"

She stopped walking; she looked as if she was being very careful about how she was going to answer. "Not really, Abby. Most of the kids see them as troublemakers and try to steer clear of them."

"Oh," I said.

"You have to remember, Abby," she continued, "most of our families have lived here for a very long time, and things that happened in the past affect the future."

I wasn't sure what she meant by that, but I was starting to run late for my next class so I just said thanks and headed off to Home Economics, or Home Ec. I groaned internally. One thing I hadn't been able to demonstrate yet was my lack of skill at cooking. I couldn't cook, not one bit, but I could burn just about anything. At my last school, after almost burning down the classroom, I had managed to weasel out of the class. Here at Klamath Union High School this class was required, whether I burned down the school or not. I was starting to get to know most of the kids in my classes now, a couple of them were in quite a few of my classes, so I guess you could say that it didn't feel like I was in front of the firing squad anymore.

As the small frail teacher began to speak in her little voice, I noticed her glasses were as thick as coke bottles. Her hair looked like it was done in the 50's in the beehive look, and I was guessing it had just as much hair spray in it as what little hair she had. Mrs. Teasly was her name, and I figured that named fit her pretty well, since I was stuck in a sitcom. Thankfully she didn't get all the speeches for safety done today so that let me off actually having to cook anything, or should I say burn anything. The bell rang and I was off to another boring class. The school was very small and even with the small population of kids, it seemed like we were in an ant farm and everyone was walking over each other.

I had gym next, which I think I hated just as much as Home Ec. There was a girl named Sarah there. Sarah was a tall quiet girl with long blonde hair and a pale face. She seemed to get along with everyone, although she tried to stay beneath the radar as much as I tried to. The first terror in gym that the teacher had lined up for us was running around the gym for 10 minutes. I was certain that if I didn't get Ethan of my mind and concentrate on my feet, I was sure to trip and break something. Or worse, I'd trip and fall on someone and then they would break something…but those eyes and that smell and the way he walked…just then, down I went. Thank god I didn't end up tripping Sarah, who was running beside me. If there was any question about the bump on my head, I am sure those questions were answered now. I was surprised that no one had come out and asked me what had happened. I was sure that there must have been questions but either they were too afraid to ask or they just liked talking behind my back. My guess was that they just like talking about the new girl behind her back.

As soon as the last bell rang I was off to the locker room. Without my concentration, it seemed like I was the last one out of the locker room. It took me forever to get undressed and redressed. What a weird day, I thought. I headed to my locker and grabbed my bag. Just then 5 large boys walked behind me, laughing. I tried to ignore them, but then abruptly the laughter stopped. I thought they had already walked by. I grabbed my bag and turned around and stopped dead in my tracks. All five boys were around me with dark eyes staring.

"You must be Abigail Watson…" The biggest boy said in a gruff voice with a half-cocked smile. The other boys started to laugh in harmony. I was in shock. These boys towered over my 5 ft 3 inch frame.

"Cat got your tongue?" Again it was only the biggest boy who said anything. I tried to speak, but nothing would come out of my mouth.

Just then Mr. Murphy came out of his class room "Do we have a problem, Caleb?" he asked with stern voice.

"No, sir, Mr. Murphy. Just introducing ourselves to the new student," Caleb said with a wicked grin on his face. Again the boys let out a laugh.

"Well, school's over for today so why don't you guys head out?"

"Yes, sir!" Caleb said, spitting the words out. He turned his head toward me with the wicked smile. "I guess we'll be seeing you around," he said with a laugh. My stomach did a flip; it took everything in me to keep my knees from collapsing from underneath me. He gave me one quick wink and headed out the door with the other four boys following.

"Are you all right, Ms. Watson," Mr. Murphy asked with a concerned look on his face.

"Yes," I said as soon as I could find my voice. *What strange day I was having,* I thought to myself.

"Will you be okay to walk out to your car?"

"Yes." Again with the single-word answer.

He still looked a little worried but he just smiled and said, "Have a nice night, Ms. Watson." He turned and walked out the door, and I managed to gather myself together to head out to my jeep. I took a quick glance out the door, just to make sure the boys weren't out in the parking lot waiting for me. I let out sigh when I heard the motorcycles revving in the distant. I headed out to my jeep, thanking god that the day was finally over. Then a thought occurred to me, which hadn't come to my attention until I got into the comfort of my jeep. *Why wasn't Ethan with his friends?* Anytime I had ever seen Ethan, all of them were together. I started my jeep, looked over my shoulder, and then proceeded to pull out. I turned on my radio and flipped it to a couple of stations. Most of the stuff they played was country, not my favorite. I finally managed to find a station that played some of my music, or at least close to it, but trying to drown out my thoughts through the loud music didn't seem to be working. I knew I was going to have to think through today's events. Putting it off was probably just going to make things worse.

When I pulled the drive, I was relieved to see Ben's SUV in the driveway, which meant my mom would be home. I put the jeep into park, grabbed my bag as I opened the door and then jumped down. I was just about to open the front door when my favorite creepy butler graciously opened the door first.

"Thanks," I muttered.

The only greeting he gave me was, "Welcome home, Miss."

I grumbled as I walked through the door and set my bag on a chair that was sitting to the right. I could hear voices coming from the living room. Before I walked through the door I cleared my throat to give advance warning that I was coming, just so I didn't happen to walk in on my mom and Ben.

"Welcome home," my mom gasped. Just then a chill ran down me, and not a good chill. It was a "welcome to living in hell" chill I can't believe she called this my home.

"Thanks, mom," I managed to get out of my mouth without trying to seem nasty.

"How's your head feeling?" She asked.

"Fine."

"It doesn't hurt?" She asked. I knew my mom was concerned but I really didn't want to get into last night's misadventures.

"No, mom, really, I'm fine," I tried to convince her. She didn't look convinced.

Just then, Ben managed to get a word in. "Abby," he said in a low voice. "You must be very careful when you are walking the grounds or in the forest. There are many dangers. One of them you found last night. There are many canyons, and you could fall quite easy. Also we have a lot of large predators that roam this area; bears, coyotes, and wolves. Please don't go out in the woods by yourself and especially don't go at night. You are very lucky that your mom and I were the ones to find last night. You almost gave your mom a heart attack and I know that she doesn't want anything to happen to you. It would kill her."

"I'm sorry," I said. I know I had said that a dozen times since yesterday, but I think they needed to hear it again, and I guess I was going to keep on saying it until they forgot about the accident. My mom still looked emotional, and she pulled me into a bear hug.

"It's all right, Abigail, my mother started to say. I cut her off.

"Mom, I'm fine. Let's talk about something else. How was your day?" I asked, trying to lead her away from the subject of me.

"Oh," she said, "It was wonderful. Ben took me over most of the property. He showed me how they make their wine, and the acres and acres of grapes. It was all very interesting." I couldn't see my mom getting excited about wine, and the way they make wine, but my guess was that my mom was eager to make Ben happy, so it probably didn't bother her that she spent the whole day on a subject that clearly didn't interest her.

"That's great, mom, I'm glad you had fun."

"If you'll excuse me," Ben said, "I will see when dinner will be ready." With that he headed out the door. My mom turned to me,

"Abby," she said. "How was your second day?"

"Great," I lied. She didn't seem to buy my one-word answer.

"Abby," she repeated, now with a stern look on her face.

"Really, mom, the day passed without anything special happening."

"Did you make any friends?"

More questions? I thought. "Yes, there's a girl named Julie that is pretty nice, also a girl named Sarah who is in my gym class. Mom," I said, "I am pretty tired and I have a lot of homework. If you don't mind, I will just grab a sandwich and some milk and head upstairs to do my homework."

"That's fine, Honey. We have all weekend to catch up." She gave me a kiss on the cheek as I headed to the kitchen to grab a sandwich. I walked in and there was a pale lady behind one of the counters. She was dressed in all white, and quite pudgy. She had short red curly hair.

"Can I help you?" She asked in a shrill voice. *She's just like the butler,* I thought, and sighed.

"I was just going to grab a sandwich and head off to bed. "

She almost looked offended. "No one is allowed to cook in this kitchen but me!" Her voice was almost hostile. She didn't say another word, just got the bread and peanut butter out of the cupboard and started making my sandwich. When she was done she grabbed a tray and placed the sandwich on the tray, and then grabbed a glass and headed over to the fridge. She got out the milk and poured it in the glass. She set that on the tray and then snatched an apple out of the basket on one of the tables.

"Anything else?" She asked in the same snippy tone.

"No, thank you," I managed to mumble out.

"Dinner is at 6 pm sharp. I only cook one dinner, so if you want to eat, be in the dining area at six." Then she stared at me.

"I understand."

"Just leave your tray outside your bedroom door and Albert will be around to pick it up when you are done."

I turned to walk out the door and then I heard her say, "Welcome to Klamath Falls. I am sure we will get along, as long as you stay out of my kitchen. And you can call me Mrs. MacAfee."

I walked out of the kitchen and headed up to my room, feeling worse than I had at school. I shut my doors and set the tray down, not in the mood to eat anymore. I set my bag on the desk and opened it to grab the little homework I had. I guessed they were trying not to overwhelm me during the first week, but as I sat down homework was the one thing that really wasn't on my mind. I replayed all the day's events in my head: the unusual way Ethan had talked to introduced himself; him just leaving in the middle of the school day; the way that Julie had talked about him and his friends. Although I didn't think she was that far off about them. They were very intimidating. But not Ethan, there was just something about him, like the way he held himself, the way he talked, and those eyes with no hint of evil in them. I was starting to obsess a little too much over him.

I slammed my book shut and sighed. Just then I heard a knock on my door. I knew that knock. I knew it was my mother, although in this house, or should I say museum / castle, the knocks seemed to echo and fill the huge room.

She opened the door and asked, "Can I come in?"

"Sure," I said.

"I know that we haven't had a lot of time to talk since we moved here, and I really want to know how you are doing," she said with a guilty expression on her face. I knew she was worried, due to the fact that the worry lines seemed to be forever on her forehead.

"Mom," I said, with a cool, calm expression, "I really am fine. School seems to be just like home, just a lot smaller. I have made a few friends."

"Have you met any boys you like?"

"No, not really," I lied, but I answered too quickly.

She let out a laugh, but secretly I knew she was relieved. "Did you get your homework done?" She asked.

"Just started," I said, "But the cook was nice enough to make me a sandwich so I could eat and work up here." The look on my face must have not been convincing because she didn't look convinced.

"So you met the cook, Katherine."

"Oh, is that her name?" I replied back.

"Yes, she's a nice lady," my mother said. I didn't want to make my mom feel bad by telling her the truth about the cook and the creepy butler, so I just nodded in agreement. "Well, I should let you get back to work. Try not to stay up too late," my mother said as she headed out the door.

"Don't worry, mom, I am so tired I will probably pass out as soon as my homework is done."

"Night, Honey," she said.

"Night, mom." As she shut the massive wood doors with a silent thud, I stared back at my homework. It only took me 45 minutes to my home work done. After I had finished, I took a look at the sandwich that the witch of a cook made for me, and decided I was a little hungry. I finished the sandwich, and chugged down the glass of milk. I hadn't realized how thirsty I was. I set the glass back on the tray and hurried to put it outside the door. I didn't want to catch the wrath of the crazy cook. I shut the door and headed over to my desk where I had left my MP3 player I grabbed it and headed to the bed.

Since it was too early to go to bed, I decided that music which had always calmed my nerves in the past might work for me tonight. I hit the button on the side and switched the player on. The minute it was on and I had put the ear-phones in, I realized it was playing the last song I had listened to, which was Bon Jovi's *Living On A Prayer*. It was a good song for my current predicament, but a little depressing, so I switched it to more modern music. The song that caught my attention as I looked at titles on the screen was Lady Gaga's *Bad Romance*. I turned it on and turned the volume up and let the beat drown everything around me out. I was trying to forget about Ben, school, the creepy butler, the cook, and the manor. As the music changed through more and more songs I watched the clock and the time flash by.

When six o'clock rolled around, I decided that I would just skip dinner and get ready for bed. It had been a long day today, and putting on a show just wasn't in me tonight. They could live without me for one night. Besides, I already had a small snack that would hold me over for the night. I shut off the mp3 player and set it on the dresser and headed slowly to the bathroom to get ready for bed.

After I had had my shower and brushed my teeth, I shut off the light and headed to the big bed. I had hardly gotten any sleep since we moved here; hopefully tonight would be different. I climbed into the warm comfortable bed and pulled the comforter up to my neck and closed my eyes.

It was just like the night before.

I walked though the massive forest, stumbling on the rocks below my feet, the feeling that I was being watched sending a cold chill down my body. I could hear braches and twigs snapping in the deep dark forest. There didn't seem to be any light. The moon was set high behind the trees. I could see the cold breath coming out of my mouth. Another chill ran through my body. There was a thin fog that seemed to linger on the forest floor. But instead of light ice blue eyes, I saw him, coming in from the dark forest. It was Ethan, with the beautiful face and the ice blue eyes. I couldn't speak. I had so many questions, but no words would come out of my mouth.

Just then, he smiled. "I've been waiting for you," he said in his angelic voice. Just then I woke up. I had sweat matted in my hair and goosebumps covering every inch of my body.

This place seems to be messing with my thoughts. It's bad enough that the sun doesn't shine here, that it is almost always raining, a bunch of juvenile adolescents seem to want to torture me at school, and now, now I can't even get a night sleep without having nightmares, I ranted to myself.

I turned to look at the clock. It was only 2:30 am, too early to get up. I fell back into the pillow and closed my eyes. Then, a noise. I could hear it clearly even though it seemed to be so far away. It was a howling, but it didn't seem to be a dog. It was too loud and too strong. Then I remembered what the creepy butler had said about the woods and not going out at night. *They must have a wolf problem here.* I shrugged it off, rolled over, and pulled the covers over my head. I must have fallen back asleep. The next thing I knew, the alarm was going off and I was rushing to get ready for school. I knew why I was in a hurry, but I didn't know why it was so important.

4 Secrets

I HURRIED DOWN FOR BREAKFAST just like yesterday, and just like yesterday my mom and Ben had already had their breakfast and were off and running. I was a little too excited to eat, but I forced down the pancakes and eggs and guzzled down the juice carefully laid out on dining room table. As soon as I finished, I grabbed my bag and ran out the door, not attempting to pick up the dishes. So far I was having a good morning and I didn't want to ruin by having another confrontation with the butler. I jumped in the Jeep, which I was getting pretty good at doing by now, and as I turned the key the engine came to life.

I noticed as I put my hands on the wheel that the bruises on my wrists were almost gone, although the bump on my head was still prominent. At least I didn't have to wear that stupid bandage and my bangs hid most of the bump. I pulled out of the long drive. It wasn't raining although it was still very cloudy, almost like it could rain at any time. There weren't very many cars on the road, and I made it in plenty of time thanks to my lead foot. I pulled into the small town, and as I drove through Main Street I noticed it was almost like a ghost town. I made it to school in plenty of time. Plenty of time to think of Ethan, and the others that were his so-called friends. I started to compare him with his friends. Ethan was just as big as they were, but they all had pitch-black eyes and his were ice blue, and the way he acted was quite a bit different than the ones that confronted me in the hallway. There is just something about him, a pull. It was inevitable. Like gravity, I had no choice. I set my head down on the steering wheel.

Just then there was a knock on the window. It was Sarah. I hit the switch for the automatic windows. Before the window was all the way down she was talking. "You're here awfully early, Abby."

"Yeah," I said, "Couldn't sleep."

"Yeah, I know what you mean," she said with a sigh. "Is the town getting to you yet?"

I didn't want to be rude and tell her the truth. The truth was this town got to me the minute my mother said we were moving here. "No, I am fine," I lied.

"You know we don't have school tomorrow," Sarah stated.

"No," I said with a confused look on my face. "Why we don't have school?"

"Teachers' in-service day," she said with a smile.

"Oh that's too bad," I said with a smile on my face.

"So, what are you going to do tomorrow?" Sarah asked.

"I don't know; what do you do for fun in this town?"

"Well, nothing we are supposed to," she said with a laugh. I was shocked hearing the words come out of Sarah's mouth. She was supposed to be the quiet one. "Well, there is a place that all the kids hang out when the weather is warm; we call it the Cliffs," Sarah said.

"What are the Cliffs?" I asked.

"Just places that have massive waterfalls and small beaches. Usually we just have a bonfire and hang out."

"Sounds cool," I said with definite delight in my eyes. "But I don't think the weathers going to cooperate," I laughed.

"The weather is supposed to be warmer tomorrow," she said calmly. Besides, there are caves down there that we hang out in if the weather is bad."

"Okay, what time?" I asked.

"I will pick you up at 6:00. Make sure that you wear warm clothes and good shoes," she warned.

"Do you know where I live?"

"Abby, you're the biggest thing to hit this city in a century. Of course I know where you live," she laughed. "You're out at Ben Moore's Place, right?"

"Yeah," I confirmed it for her. *Unfortunately,* I thought. I didn't want to say it out loud, being as this was a small town and I was faking enthusiasm so my mom wouldn't get her feelings hurt. I noticed people were starting to fill into the parking lot.

I guess Sarah noticed too because she turned to me and said "I better get going to class

"Okay, see you later," I replied. She gave me a parting smile. I rolled back up the window. *The Cliffs,* I thought to myself, *well the town was called Klamath Falls. I guess it had to be named that for a reason.* I turned off the keys to the jeep. I had left it running due to the fact that it was cold and I was used to the sun. This place was my personal hell: no sun, mostly rain, strange and unusual people that seemed to stay in my thoughts and keep me up at night. Sarah had managed to distract me enough that I had stopped thinking about Ethan. Just then I heard the rumble of motorcycles. I grabbed my bag, in a hurry to get out of the jeep and get into school before I ran into the delinquents. I should have known it wouldn't be that easy. As I jumped down from the jeep with my bag, I realized I had forgotten to zip the bag and all of my books and homework was all over the ground. I closed my eyes and whispered, "Oh, crap."

I opened my eyes and was going to bend down to pick up the mess, but they were all stacked neatly in the hands of Ethan Wilkins. My mouth flew opened. I made an effort to shut it.

"Thank you," I managed to whisper.

"You're welcome," he said in that angelic voice. I tried to speak, but it seemed like my brain wasn't connected to my mouth...

"You should watch your step," he laughed. "Next time you might fall and break something," he said, still laughing.

"I'll try to remember that," I said with annoyed tone to my voice. I knew I wasn't a coordinated person but it hurt to have someone point it out to me. "Not with your friends today," I snipped. He looked over my head, which wasn't that terribly difficult seeing that I was 5 ft 3 inches and he was closer to 7 ft. He was huge. I turned to look to see what he was staring at. Then I noticed the other motorcycles, and standing next to them were the five huge boys. *It was like a gang*, I thought.

"You should be careful who you talked to..." he said with a grim look on his face.

"I'll try to remember that," I snapped back.

"You've got a little temper, don't you?" He smiled, the grim look on his face almost completely erased.

"Some people bring it out in me," I said with a sarcastic look on my face.

He was still grinning. "Don't let those guys frighten you," he said with a smile still on his face.

"Don't worry, I won't," I snapped back. I wasn't trying to be rude but something about the way Ethan was acting was starting to annoy me. "Did you need something?" I asked, trying to keep the hostility out of my voice.

He took his finger and pulled it thought his hair. "No, I was just walking by and saw you drop your books. Thought you could use my help."

"I'm a big girl. I can tie my shoes, pick up my book and even drive myself to school."

"Clearly," he said, "you don't need my help."

I shut the door to the jeep, grabbed my book bag, and started walking into the school. Just then I felt a strong grip on my upper arm.

I turned to defend myself and swung without even thinking about it, but he caught my fist. He laughed. It was like the laughter was shaking his whole body and me in turn. It seemed to awaken something deep inside me.

"Yep, you have a got a temper." He released my fist, and said once again, "Abigail, be careful who you talk to." He turned and walked away.

I stood there with my mouth wide open, watching after him. *I can't believe the nerve of that guy. What is his problem?* As he reached his friends, they were all laughing. *Like someone told a joke I wasn't privy to.* As I grumbled and walked to my first class, all I could think was, *thank god tomorrow we don't have school.* Hopefully I could find something fun to do, but I wasn't holding my breath.

The day seemed to move as slow as yesterday. I listened to all the teachers drone on in a monotone voice, except in Home Ec. where I managed to set off the smoke alarm while burning the cake I was trying to make. I guess it could have been worse; I could have set the classroom on fire. The teacher was ill-informed of my last school experience, and I was sure if she had known, she probably wouldn't let me near the stove let alone in the class room.

As soon as I got done with gym I grabbed my bag in a hurry to get out of school and get home. I wasn't sure why that was, since Ben's house wasn't my home. But anything had to be better than school. As I headed out to my jeep, I noticed Ethan standing in front of my driver side door. I groaned quietly.

After I restarted my heart and got to my truck, I said, "Can I help you?"

He had a smile on his face almost like he was amused over my irritation. "I don't think we're getting off to a very good start," he said with a smile still on his face.

"Just taking your advice and watching who I'm friends with," I sassed back.

"Am I bothering you?" He said with a smirk.

"No, not really. You don't even exist in my book," I lied, not wanting him to know how much he had been on my mind. I think he could see right through me though. Something about his eyes seemed to see right to my soul.

"Do you have plans this weekend?" He asked.

I fumed. *He has got to be kidding, is he asking me out or is he just wondering if I am so pathetic that I have nothing to do on the weekends?* "I'm busy," I snapped.

"Oh, that's too bad," he said, with the grin still on his face.

"Anything else?" I asked. He reached up to smooth one of the loose pieces of my hair behind my ear. A shiver ran through my body all the ways to my toes. I had never felt anything like it.

"It really is too bad," he said again. "Maybe some other time," he said as he turned to leave. I watched him walk toward his bike. As soon as he reached it, he kick-started it with one kick. I started to feel a little dizzy. I must have been holding my breath. As soon as I realized that I hurried to take a quick breath before I passed out. *What is with that guy, all his strange warnings, and the weird vibe that I get when I am around him?* And if he was a nice guy why was he hanging out with those jerks? Normally I am really good about reading people, but there's something about Ethan. He has secrets. *I am going to find them out.* I was a very determined person; whatever is with him I was going to figure it out.

As soon as I could compose myself, I took another deep breath and jumped into my jeep, shut the door, and turned over the keys. The jeep rumbled to life. I looked over my shoulder as I put the jeep in reverse. As I backed out of the parking lot I noticed that the parking lot was next to empty. *How long were we standing there,* I thought to myself. I put the jeep into drive and headed out of the parking lot.

As I headed out of the city, I noticed the gloomy clouds, *I can't believe the weather is going to be nice enough for a bonfire all it seems to do is rain here.* Oh well. She said there were caves in case it rained. At least I would stay dry if it started to rain. As I pulled into the drive I noticed there were quite a few people out in the fields. I assumed they were checking the harvest. I pulled my jeep into the normal parking spot and let out a sigh which seemed normal every time I was going to head to face my fate at Ben's castle.

I opened the door, and as I stepped in I could hear my mother and Ben laughing again. Don't get me wrong, I am glad my mother is over the moon about Ben. It's nice to see her happy. I just wished we didn't have to move across country in order to keep her happy.

"Mom," I said as I headed into the living room.

"In here," she said, still laughing.

As I walked through, I saw Ben kiss my mom. He said, "I have some last minutes things to do, so I will give you two some alone time." As he greeted me and said bye at the same time, I was somewhat relieved that I would get some alone time with my mom without having to see them exchange goo-goo eyes at each other. It usually nauseated me.

"How was school," she asked as I walked through the doors.

"Fine," I said automatically.

"Anything good happened?"

I think she was getting tired of my one word answers. So I began by telling her about Sarah, and her invite for a night out. Then I told her about Home Ec. and before I got though the explanations she interrupted me and asked if the classroom was still standing.

"Ha," I replied back.

"So where are you off to tomorrow??

"I'm really not sure," I lied. For some reason I didn't wasn't to divulge where we were going. "I think just to her house," I lied again. My mom was always up for anything I said, although at my other school, I never really went out, never really fit in enough to be noticed. "What did you do today?" I asked, almost like I really cared.

"Well, Ben took me to more around the property, and showed me the parts we didn't get to the other day."

If I could have rolled my eyes I would have, but instead I just said, "that sounds like fun," and I acted like I was listening intently.

"What about you, Abby? What's your school like? What're your friends like?" It was like her questions had no end. Before she could ask another one, I started to speak.

"Well, school is school, Mom, same as it was at home. Another correctional institute built on keeping kids in captivity until three. Then they let them loose on the unsuspecting townsfolk," I said with a laugh. She laughed too. I sighed; it was always nice to hear my mom laugh.

"So, where are you going tomorrow?" She asked, not realizing that she had already asked the question. She almost seemed concerned.

"Well, Sarah asked me if I wanted to hang out. I am assuming we're going to her house," I lied. I don't know why but the feeling I should not divulge too much information seemed to override my honesty button. "What are you up to tomorrow, mom?"

"Well, Ben wants to head out of town for the weekend, but I am not keen on leaving you home by yourself."

"Oh, go ahead, mom, I'll be fine." I tried to be convincing without showing her my relief that the parental figure was going to be out of town and I could do anything I wanted. Not that there was anything to do in the great town of Klamath Falls, but at least I wouldn't have to put on a brave face and convince her that I was truly happy over this move. "Mom," I started, "I will be fine. And it's not like you're really leaving me alone. The creepy butler and the crazy cook will be here," I let out a laugh.

"Abigail!" She said with a frown on her face. "That's not nice."

"Sorry, Mom," I mumbled.

"They are a little odd," she said, as she let out a small short giggle. "I don't know, Abby. If we leave tomorrow will be gone till Sunday night. He wants to take me to the great wonderful city of Las Vegas," she said with a grimace. I knew my mom wasn't keen on Las Vegas. She really never liked to gamble and she said there was a reason they called it Sin City.

" Ben has been trying to convince me that Las Vegas has a lot more to it than all the bad parts," she said with the grimace on her face. I knew she was looking for a reason to get out of it, and I was bound and determined not to give her that reason.

"Mom," I said, with a no expression at all on my face, "go and have a good time with Ben. I know you don't like the city choice but just remember you're with Ben. Forget the rest."

She looked at me almost resigned. She opened her mouth to speak, and then closed it. A smile slowly spread on her face. "You're right, Abby, it might be fun and I will only be a phone call away. Are you sure you don't mind?"

"No, go ahead. I have plenty of homework to keep me busy."

With the last statement, my mom smiled at me again gave me a hug. "All right Abby, I will go and tell Ben yes."

As she turned to head for the door, she turned back to face me. "Oh, I almost forgot," she said with a gasp. "Ben was under the impression that you would need some new clothes, because the weather is quite a bit different from Florida." She handed me a silver credit card. "Ben said get whatever you want, Abby." She said it with a smile. I was not sure if that was supposed to be for her benefit or the fact that she knew I hated to shop. As she headed out the door, my mom turned and smiled. "I love you Abby."

"Love you, too, Mom," I said as an automatic response. *That was easy,* I thought to myself. I looked at the time, not realizing that it was going so fast. It was almost dinner-time. I went upstairs to start my homework. Hopefully I could get it done before dinner. God forbid I am late for dinner; the cook might pop a blood vessel. As I sat down at my desk, I turned on my computer. I wanted to check my email, even though I figured it would be empty.

I was wrong. There was tons of stuff in there, all junk mail. I started to delete it one by one. After I got done with that, I was a little bored so I shut down the computer which took forever. I headed over to my closest to see what I should wear tonight. As I looked over the clothes in the closet, I sighed, not really finding anything that I really wanted to wear. I finally settled on a flannel shirt to put over my t-shirt and jeans. I set the clothes I had picked out for tomorrow on the dresser. As I stood there, my thoughts turned back to Ethan, wondering if he or his dysfunctional friends would be at the bonfire. I was hoping he would be there, but as for his abnormally huge and misbehaving friends, I couldn't really say I relished the idea of seeing them again.

After I got dressed I headed downstairs and into the dining room where there was a feast sprawled across the table. Ben and my mom were already sitting at the massive huge table.

"Have a seat, Abby," Ben said.

"Wow," I said under my breath, "this is a lot of food."

Ben and my mom let out a laugh. "Well," he said, "the cook doesn't really know what you both like, so she kind of made a little of everything."

"That was so nice of her," my mom said. I just sat with the shocked look on my face. "Well, dig in," my mom said. I didn't think twice. All the food looked appetizing. After I finished pasta and rolls, I accepted a chicken breast. I hadn't realized how hungry I was.

"What time is Sarah going to pick you up tomorrow?" My mom asked.

"Six," I said.

"Well, make sure to dress warm if you plan on being outside for any length of time," Ben said. It gets quite cold in Klamath Falls at night."

"I think I've got it covered," I answered back. I wasn't trying to be rude, and I hoped it didn't sound that way. With Ben I could never tell. He was a hard person to read. After I got done eating, I was so stuffed that I could barely move. I gave my mom a kiss on the cheek, told Ben good-bye, and started to head up to bed.

My mom called out, "Have fun tomorrow, Abby."

"You, too, Mom," I said with a smile. I knew that she was trying to hide her distaste for the trip tomorrow, but I could see the internal grimace on her face although Ben truly looked excited.

I didn't want to actually sleep for fear that the nightmare would come back so I took my time getting ready for bed. I stood in the shower slowly washing my hair; I even took time to shave my legs. The shower was so relaxing that I didn't want to get out. But I finally took a deep breath, turned off the water, grabbed my towel, and wrapped it around me. Like always, the mirror was fogged over. I grabbed a small towel and cleared it off like I normally did. As I stared in the mirror I noticed that the lump on my head was almost all the way gone, and the marks on my arm were completely faded. I was starting to look like myself again. I brushed my teeth slowly, still not in a hurry to go to bed. After I finished brushing my teeth I grabbed the t-shirt and shorts which I normally slept in. I got dressed and I shut off the light, and headed towards the very large bed in the middle of the room. As I closed my eyes, I prayed that the dreams would stay away for one night so I could sleep.

5 BONFIRE

I WOKE UP WITH A jolt. The dream was the same: the same forest, the same blackened covered sky, and those ice blue eyes set into the face on Ethan Wilkins. *What is wrong with me,* I thought to myself. *Why was I always dreaming of Ethan?* Since I got to Klamath Falls, I hadn't had one night of dreams that didn't include Ethan. I looked at the clock and realized that it was 9:30 am. *I can't believe I slept that long.* I staggered out of my bed and headed to the bathroom to get ready for my day. I knew that my mom and Ben were heading out to this morning for their weekend trip to Las Vegas. My mom had given me a credit card to shop for some clothes, which I did need, since all my clothes were only suitable for warmer climates.

On the other hand, I hated to shop. To be more accurate, I hated to be around women who stood in your way as you tried to shop, and listening to them ponder which undersized garment would make their butts look smaller. No, shopping was definitely not my thing. But I did need new clothes, and I could do it by myself. I did love my mom, but shopping trips always seemed longer when she was with me. I came to the conclusion that after I had had my shower, gotten dressed, brushed my teeth and got my socks and shoes on that it would probably be in my best interest to buy some new clothes. As I headed outside I noticed that the weather seemed somewhat nicer than normal, almost like the sun might make an appearance today. I climbed into the jeep, not in the mood to jump for it. I headed into town, not in any real hurry today, driving much slower than I normally drive.

I finally found the mall. I could have probably found a store as easy as Wal-Mart or Target, but I knew if I actually made the attempt to go to the mall, to one of those really fancy stores, my mom would be over the moon with joy. I walked into the first fancy clothing store, not even bothering to see which store it was. I must have looked somewhat out of place because a very nicely dressed girl came over, although my first impression of the girl was dashed by her attitude and the first words that came out of her mouth.

"Can I help you?" She said in a snobby voice.

"Just looking," I mumbled back.

"Well, I am sure we don't have anything for you in this store." It was like a slap in the face. Normally I hold my temper in fairly well. But her statement, well, it sort of pissed me off.

"That's fine," I snapped back. I set the shirt that I had in my hands back on the rack. "You work on commission, don't you?"

She looked abashed that I had come to that conclusion. "Yes," she said but I don't see why that's any of your business."

"Well, the fact that I have this here credit card," I said, holding out Ben's credit card, "and I have no limit." I said with a smile on my face. "I guess that would make it your mistake and maybe your business." Her jaw dropped to the floor as I headed out the door laughing. *Stupid stuck-up snob,* I chuckled as I headed out the door. I could now remember the other reason I hated to shop, stupid little snobs like that one.

I did however find another clothing store in the mall that seemed to have clothes that I could actually see myself wearing. I rummaged through the racks. I seemed to have picked a good time to come shopping. There were only a couple of people in the store and only two salespeople.

One of the salespeople seemed to be helping the other group, while the other one sat at the counter reading a magazine. She had short black hair that seemed to stand up in the back. Her face was albino white and she had a diamond nose ring. She looked very out of place in this store. She seemed like she would fit better in a Goth clothing store.

I must have given both of the salespeople one of those "better to leave me alone, I could be schizoid" looks, because the whole time I was looking over the clothes, they didn't bother me once. This was the kind of store I liked and could get used to. After all was said and done, I managed to get about 10 long-sleeved shirts and 10 pairs of jeans, some socks, a pair of gloves, a hat and a new coat, a warmer coat than I had. I had the impression that it got quite cold in Klamath Falls. I took my days' spoils up to the counter. As the Goth girl added them up I didn't even pay attention, and after she rang it through I merely handed her the credit card and then she bagged up my stuff. It took four big bags to get everything. I said thanks and headed out the door.

As I walked, I thought about tonight's activities, not really knowing what to expect. It shouldn't be that bad since I would be with Sarah, and Sarah seemed to have a handle on everything. She seemed to know the comings and goings regarding Klamath Falls and the High School. I walked past the first store that I had gone to, with the nasty salesperson. As I walked by, she noticed all the bags that I had in my hands. I just smirked at her, stuck my chin in the air, and breezed by her. Her jaw dropped, and as I headed out of the mall I couldn't help but laugh.

I jumped in the jeep and started it. While it thundered to life I automatically turned on the heat. While I was in shopping, the sun had hidden behind the massive cloud cover and it had gotten quite cold outside. I was relieved that I had gotten a new winter jacket for tonight's outing. I pulled out of the parking lot and headed back to Ben's place. I stopped at one of the drive-through before heading out of town to get a cheeseburger and a pop, not wanting to piss off the crazy cook at Ben's. By the time I had gotten back to Ben's house it was four and I had a couple of hours to get ready and prepare myself for the long night ahead of me. I parked the jeep in my normal parking spot at Ben's and headed into the house. Just like before, the door automatically opened -- Albert the crazy butler.

"Welcomes back, Miss."

"Thanks," I managed to mumble out. "You know you've really got to quick doing that. I can open the door myself," I informed him,

He faced showed no emotion as he shut the door, said, "Good day, Miss," and left me standing in the doorway.

Annoyed, I stomped my way up to my room, each step sounding like thunder as they bounced of the high ceilings, and then slammed my door. I am not sure why I let that guy get to me. There's just something about him. He pushes all the wrong buttons and he's just so darn creepy. I threw my bags on the bed, started to get ready to hop in the shower to get cleaned up. I had plenty of time to get ready, as long as Sarah didn't show up early. I decided to keep the original clothes that I had picked out and had left on the dresser all but the one exception; I would wear my new coat and hat.

After I had gotten as clean as possible, I got dressed. I decided to pull my hair back into a ponytail. That way it was easier to tuck under my hat. It took me a lot longer to get ready than usual. I was taking my time and my thoughts were pre-occupied by the thoughts of who would be at the bonfire tonight, or maybe who wouldn't. I noticed the clock said it was 5:30. I hurried, now trying to finish getting ready. Just then a knock sounded on the door. I opened the huge doors. It was Albert, of course.

"You have a guest, Miss; she is waiting for you in the entry."

"Thanks," I muttered. He turned and walked away. I grabbed the new coat, hat and mittens off the bed, and hurried down trying not to trip. A concussion would not be a good way to start off the night. As I came down the stairs I saw Sarah standing in the entry looking very out of place, probably the same way I look every time I come in this house.

"Hey, Sarah," I said as I headed down the stairs.

"Hey, Abby," she said, sounding very relieved that she didn't have to wait. Sarah looked like she had dressed for the weather, having a blue heavy coat, blue mittens, and a blue knitted hat. So I was relieved, to say the least, at the fact that I seemed to have worn the right clothes.

"Are you ready to go?" She asked.

"Yep."

"Don't you have to tell your parents bye?"

"Nope," I said, popping the p at the end. "My mom and Ben took a trip to Las Vegas this weekend so I can do whatever I want," I said with a laugh.

"That is so awesome," she said with a gasp. "I wish my parents were that cool." We headed out the door. As I turned to shut the door, I noticed the creepy butler was glaring at me behind the scenes. I shrugged it off and shut the door with a loud thud. We climbed into her Blazer. My first impression was that it looked like many of the other cars that were in the parking lot at the school. It looked like the typical car that someone would get for their 1st car. Most parents are smart enough to get a used car for a sixteen year old, knowing that they would use it like a bumper car.

I knew that my jeep was a lot newer than most at school, but most kids didn't have to get a bribe to like their stepparent. Although the bribe was total unnecessary, since no matter what Ben bought I wasn't going to like him or the fact that I had to move across the country to Dracula's castle. As I hopped inside and shut the door I noticed that the interior gave me a different perspective on Sarah's Blazer. The interior was actually pretty nice, neat and very clean.

"Nice car," I said as I fastened my seat belt.

"Thanks," she said. "My mom got it for my birthday. I plan on getting a different one, as soon as I turn 18, but this will do for now."

"So, where are we going again?" I asked. I hadn't actually forgotten, but striking up conversation wasn't really my thing. It worked; she really didn't need that big of a push. She started talking like it was effortless.

"Well, the kids around here call it the Cliffs. It's where all the kids hang out and have fun. During the summer when it warms up a little more all the kids hang out and go swimming."

"It warms up?" I asked, trying to picture it. For some reason I couldn't.

"So," she said, "Where are you from again?"

"We just moved from Florida," I grumbled. From the tone of my voice she could probably tell it was a sore subject.

"This must be quite a bit different," she added, trying to keep the conversation going.

"Yeah, just a bit. Does the sun ever shine here?" I asked Sarah while looking out the window.

"Yes," she giggled, "Mostly during the summer. You'll get used to it soon enough," she added.

"How far is this place out of town?" I asked, trying not to let the impatience show.

"It's about 10 miles outside of town. Most of the kids from our grade, but a few junior and some seniors will be there," she said with a smile. I groaned. She laughed again. "It will be fine, Abby. I'll introduce you the rest of the kids. I have the feeling that you are going to fit in fine," she added, trying to reassure me. "Didn't you ever go out in your old town," she asked. I knew that she had tons of questions for me.

"No, not really. I mostly kept to myself. I like it that way, but going to a small school like this, I had a feeling it wasn't going to be that way ever again."

"Well, there really isn't a whole lot to do here so it probably won't bother you that much."

But this place does bother me, I thought, not saying it out loud. We pulled off the highway on to a gravel drive. It had giant trees down the length of both sides. It seemed like the windy, curvy road would go on forever, but just then the trees opened on a large clearing with quite a few cars parked.

"Are you going to the dance next week?" She asked.

"What dance?" I asked, looking confused. I know I had only been in school a week but I thought that I would have heard something.

"It's the winter formal," she said with a smile on her face.

"I'm not sure. I really didn't know anything about it."

"Well, if you need some help getting a dress, I can go with you and show you all the coolest shops," she offered.

More shopping, I groaned silently. "That would be really nice," I conceded, "but I don't have anyone to go with."

"Oh," she said, "We're just going as a small group; me, Julie, and you."

"Okay," I agreed. The thought of dancing wasn't my favorite, but hanging out with the girls didn't seem too bad.

As she put the car into park she said, "We will have to go on foot from here." I must have had a shocked expression on my face because she added, "don't worry Abby; I won't let you get lost."

I was very reluctant, but it was very nice of Sarah to invite me and I didn't want to look like a coward, so I just nodded and reluctantly got out of her car. We started to walk through the trees; there was a small man-made path that was easy to follow. It looked like this path had been traveled many times before. As we came thought the trees I noticed a shimmering of flames, almost like the trees were on fire. As we walked around the last set of pines I noticed the bonfire and a group of twenty or so people standing around the fire. They all seemed to be laughing and joking. Someone had brought a small portable radio that seemed to playing country music. I let out a groan in my head but with some effort I was able to keep a smile on my face.

As people noticed us a couple of them called out, "hey, Sarah!"

"Hey!" She managed to yell back. As we got closer I recognized a few people from school but I couldn't remember any of their names. Chances are, she was going to introduce me to everyone anyways so I didn't need to get too worked up. I took in a few relaxed breaths, trying to keep my nerves in check. As soon as we made it to the crowd I saw Julie, who I knew from my first period class.

"Everyone, this is Abby," Sarah said, trying to get everyone's attention. I raised my hand in front of my chest and waived a short little waives,

"Hi," I said. Then she began saying names like she was going down a list: Conner, Joe, Sarah, Natalie, Melissa, John, Emma, Grace, Matt, Michael.... I couldn't keep up with all the names. I am sure if I actually stayed in this school and didn't commit suicide before my 2-year purgatory was over here, I would eventually get all their names. After she had finished her version of the roll-call, everyone headed over to sit on the logs by the bonfire. It was quite a nice atmosphere, even with the loud chatter of all the voices and the whining of country music in the background. I could see the fire reflected on the huge lake it was by, and I could hear noise like there was water rushing although I couldn't see anything since everything had gotten so dark now.

As they chatted about teachers and school and all the newest gossip in town, I looked around trying to be discreet. I didn't see Ethan or any of his juvenile friends anywhere. I really didn't care if I saw Caleb or any of his followers, but it would have been nice to see Ethan.

As the night dragged on I didn't seem to find any release. A couple of people actually started to talk to me and asked how I liked Klamath Falls. I just lied and said, "its fine." That seemed to be my response for most things these days.

Then Conner, I think that was his name, came up with a new question. "I hear you're living out at the Moore's."

"Yes, that's right," I confirmed for him.

"What's it like?" He let a grunt, like someone had just knock the breath out of him. It must have been the blonde sitting beside him on the log.

"It's fine," I said back, wondering why he had said it like that, like there was something wrong with the place. Just then everyone one looked really uncomfortable.

After he got his breath, back he started to speak. "You know, the Manor has quite a history," he said, making his voice very low and gruff.

I had a feeling that the house had a history; I knew there was more to it than it seemed and tonight maybe I would be able to find out why my hair stands on end every time I walk through the front door. "Would you like to hear the story?" Conner asked.

"Sure." I shrugged. "Why not?"

"Do you know any of our local history?" Conner asked.

I am sure that he knew that answer to that question before he asked it out loud, seeing as how I had never left Florida before my mother had dragged me across country, and it seemed that they knew more about me from all the gossip floating around than I did about them. "No, not really," I replied.

"You'll like this, then," he chuckled.

"Conner, cut it out," Sarah said with frown on her face.

"They're just stories, Sarah," he said with a smirk. "She looks like a tough girl. I am sure she can handle it."

"Yeah, if you like horror stories," she mumbled back.

"It's fine, Sarah," I said coolly. "Let Conner tell the story." It got very quiet. All around us, the only thing I could hear was the crackling of the fire and the water running in the darkness.

"Well, a long time ago," he began, "the Moores owned all the land that you see. They were a rich family like they are now. They were very prominent in the community along with six other families: Proctors, Calloways, Goodrichs, Pritchards, Landers, and Wilkins." As soon as he said the last name, Wilkins, the attention that had been so inattentive before changed and I was deeply entrenched in the story he began to tell.

"Before the Moores came to this area, these six families lived in peace with the Indians who had settled in this area. They never took more than they needed and never intruded on the land that wasn't theirs. That all changed after the Moores came. Ezekiel Moore and his family moved to the area in the year 1508. Ezekiel didn't want to share the land. He consumed every piece of land he regarded as untouched. He thought the Indians were a menace and must be dealt with. He gathered as many men as he could who would stand against the Indians. There were many. Most people agreed with Ezekiel. They thought the Indians were worthless, no better than the dirt under their feet, and that they had no right to the land even if they were there first. But the six families who had lived in peace with the Indians were against Ezekiel, and the lust he had for the land and power.

"The families knew that there would be war and casualties. They knew that there would be blood over the land. Jedidiah Wilkins, I guess you would call him the leader, went to talk to Ezekiel," Conner said. "He tried to convince him that there was enough land for everyone to share, but Ezekiel was a hard man, and he only knew of one way, his way. Jedidiah tried to reason with Ezekiel, but Ezekiel couldn't be reasoned with. His lust for land and power ran too deep. Before the fighting started, the Indians told Jedidiah to keep out of the fight, to keep his family safe, but Jedidiah was an honorable man and he could not sit by and watch mass murder being committed. Jedidiah's son had begged his father not to get involved. Jedidiah had no idea that his son had fallen in love with Ezekiel's daughter Elizabeth. For some reason I can't remember Jedidiah's son's name," Connor paused, "and I think the some of this story has been lost over the years."

"Go on," I hedged to Conner.

"Well, Jedidiah's son was frantic, not wanting to Elizabeth to get caught in the fighting. He went to her one night, climbed up her to her second story window. He told her of her father's plans for war and he begged her to run away with him. Elizabeth was a very loving, beautiful, person, the stories say," Conner smiled. "She tried to comfort him, saying it would be fine, that her father would see reason, and there was no reason to run. Elizabeth was blinded by the love that she had for her father. She told Jedidiah's son to wait for her in the forest at their spot. She would meet him so they could talk as soon as she could sneak out safely. He protested but eventually agreed. She kissed him and said, wait for me. He left and went to their spot to wait.

"She never came, and he began to get restless. After awhile he went back to her house looking for her. He noticed a large group of men standing in a circle, hovering. He moved closer to see what they were all converged around. As soon as he rounded the crowd he saw Elizabeth lying cold and lifeless on the frozen ground and blood all around. He fell to his knees screaming in horror. She had gotten caught in the crossfire of bullets meant for Ezekiel. Ezekiel was on the ground with his daughter in his arms and her blood all over his hands. You see, even though Ezekiel was a hard man set on consuming everything in his path, he loved his children. His last words were a curse on those who were responsible. He cursed them, that the firstborn daughter of each generation would be taken from them like his had been taken from him, and then a wicked smiled spread across his face.

"Then shots rang out and Ezekiel fell to the ground, blood running from the gunshot wound to his head. No one claimed the bullet that had shot Elizabeth or the one that had shot Ezekiel. The six families who had headed up the expedition to kill Ezekiel were afraid. They went to see the Indians. The Indians were known to have a power, and this was the only hope that they felt they had. Since Jedidiah had helped the Indians, the Indians were very grateful. The chief on the tribe agreed, and he granted them immortality. The firstborn males of all six families would live forever, to keep their bloodlines alive. They would be able to shape-shift into giant wolves. I guess you would call them werewolves," Conner smirked. "To protect their families and all the innocent people who would get caught in the crossfire until the day that the curse was broken and they were no longer needed." Just then he rolled his eyes, trying to show how little he believed in the legend.

"Well, what happened to Ezekiel?" I asked.

"Well, you paid attention; I'm shocked," he said with a chuckle. "Legend said that he still walks these very lands, looking to avenge his daughter. Which is a moot point," he added.

"Why?" I asked.

"Because the six families are said not to have had any girls in their families for over 500 years."

"Oh," I said. "What about Jedidah's son," I said with a confused look on his face.

"Oh, I almost forgot about him. It's said he still lives, since he was the firstborn son, still waiting...."

"Waiting for what," I gasped.

"Waiting for Elizabeth to return in one form or another," Connor whispered. I was staring at the fire so entranced that I didn't see when a couple of boys sitting on the other log got up. Just then they jumped up behind me and screamed. It's made me jump a mile. They all started laughing, and I was too busy blushing as the blood ran to my face in embarrassment.

"Gotcha," Conner said.

"Yeah, you tell great horror stories," I agreed. I didn't realize it, but Sarah must have jumped too, because the can in her hand was crushed and she had pop all over her coat.

"Stupid jerks," she mumbled.

"You all right, Sarah?" I asked, trying to be attentive.

"Yeah, just got to get cleaned up a little," she said. "I'll probably have to wash my coat tonight."

Conner still seemed to be very amused over my reaction. "Is it really creepy staying at the Manor?" he asked.

"No, not really." I replied. Or at least it hadn't been up until this point. I wasn't sure how it going to be after this night. I thought, *Ben is really nice. And my mom really loves him,* I added. "But to be honest," I said, "I could do without the creepy butler and the crazy cook."

The whole group started to laugh.

Sarah agreed with me. "Yeah, the butler is really something; he gave me the creeps as soon as he opened the door."

"So what happened to the six families," I hedged.

"Oh," Conner said, "Their descendents are still around. We even go to school with them."

"Oh really? Who?"

"Caleb Calloway, Isaac Proctor, Jeremiah Goodrich, Cain Landers, Samuel Prichard and Ethan Wilkins," he ran down the list.

"Oh," I said.

He laughed. "Know them, do you?"

"Yeah, I guess you could say I have had my run-ins with them. Have they always lived here?" I asked,

"Well, their families are from here, but they only moved back here about a year ago. Their families travel a lot. If you are a smart girl," he said, being serious, "You'll stay clear. They are known for getting into quite a bit of trouble."

"I wasn't planning on being friends with them."

"That's good," Conner said. "They get into a lot of trouble around here. Well, he laughed, "I am just glad I don't live in that creepy castle." The rest of the kids who I had forgotten were there all started laughing.

"Leave her alone," Sarah said.

"Just having a little fun, Sarah. You should try it," Conner said with a huge smile on his face. Just then I heard some twigs snap and I heard the sound of muted voices getting louder as they approached.

"Oh, crap," said Conner.

"What?" I asked Sarah.

"Seems like we have guests," Sarah said.

For some reason the way Sarah said that made my stomach jump into my throat. As they came into view one by one, I realized why Conner and Sarah had that reaction. The first through the trees was visibly the biggest. It was Caleb. He had a huge wicked smile, and his hair was gelled to stick straight up. He wore a black leather jacket with a white t-shirt. They were all dressed almost the same, except the last one. He wore no jacket, just white t-shirt and jeans, with that light brown hair and those ice blue eyes. It was Ethan. He looked up, meeting my eyes. His were so gentle, and his mouth twitched. It looked like he was trying to force back a smile that was trying to break through on his face.

"Mind if we crash the party?" Caleb said with a sneer. He still had the wicked smile on his face. No one said anything right away. It was like they were all trying to catch their breath.

"They're speechless," Caleb laughed.

Conner must have found his voice because he was the only one to speak. "We were just wrapping up."

"Don't leave on our account," said Caleb.

Only a small part of my mind paid any attention the conversation. My eyes and the rest of my attention were focused on the beautiful boy in the back. I wasn't really sure how late it was but I knew we had been out here for a while and I knew Conner's assessment of the time was right. It was time to go. To my relief, Sarah must have had the same idea that I had because she started to get off the log. Then she paused, looking to see what I was going to do. If I could have, I would have sprinted to the truck, but some reason I wasn't able to move my feet.

"Oh, and you brought the new girl." Caleb tuned his head slightly to the left and out of the blue he winked at me. A chill ran though me all the way to my toes, not a good chill but a chill that you would have if you were facing something, let's say, dangerous. I decided the tension was a little much for me and it seemed like the night was winding down so I grabbed Sarah's hand.

"Come on, Sarah, I think it's time to go," I said low to keep the trembling out of my voice. She didn't even hesitate. I could see the tension underlining her face and could tell she didn't like Caleb or his friends any more than I did. She was off the log in one fluid movement. I went out of my way to give the newcomers a wide berth, but somehow Caleb still managed to reach out and grab my left arm. His hands were so large and firm they could have wrapped around my arm twice. Also, I noticed that his hands were so warm that I could feel them burn through my coat.

"Don't leave on our account," he said, seeming to like my reaction of wanting to leave. I tried to jerk my arm away but he refused to let it go, and I glared at him but it seemed to amuse him more. Just then I heard a growl and Caleb let my arm drop. Not knowing where the grown had come from made me a little nervous. I was only hoping that none of the large predators that Ben had mentioned were in this immediate area. It only made me want to get to Sarah's Blazer quicker.

"Let's go," I said, and Sarah, who was mute during this whole interaction with Caleb, nodded and we headed back to where the cars were parked. I was very careful, watching where I walked trying not to trip and embarrass myself but moving very quickly for me. We made it back to the Blazer in half the time it took us to get to the bonfire. As soon as we made it to the truck we didn't hesitate. We jumped in and she hit the locks on the doors at the same time as she started the truck.

"Jesus," she managed to choke out,

"What was that all about, Sarah," I asked.

"They don't ever come out here," she said, still breathless.

"What is the deal with Caleb?" I asked with a little acid in my tone.

"I don't know. They don't ever talk to any of us; this is a first," she replied. I looked at the clock on the dash. It was almost 1:00 am.

"I can't believe we were out there that late."

"Yeah," she said, "Time passes fast when we're out at the Cliffs. So what did you think of the story," she asked.

"I thought it was interesting, but it's just a story," I replied.

"Yeah, but there's something to be said about stories."

"What do you mean?" I asked.

"Well, Caleb, Isaac, Jeremiah, Cain, Samuel, and Ethan, they're just like brothers. They do everything together, they pretty much keep to themselves, they all live with their families outside of town, but I don't think anyone's ever been out to their homes. They don't ever talk to anyone but each other and they don't ever notice anyone, until now.

Ever since you moved to town, well it seems like they just keep popping up. It's weird."

"Weird," I quickly agreed. "What's the deal with Ethan?"

The worried look came off her face and the corners of her mouth turned up to a smile. "You like him." It wasn't a question.

"No," I said too quickly.

She let out a laugh. "I can see it. It's all over you face."

I groaned in defeat. "Well, he is hot."

She quickly replied, "but I haven't ever seen him date anyone. Actually, I haven't seen any of them date," she added.

"He seems different from the rest of them," I hedged.

"Yeah, he doesn't get in as much trouble as the rest of them. But I still wouldn't waste my time; if you get him then you get his friends," she laughed. I shuddered.

It didn't take us very long to get back to Ben's. As we pulled up to the Manor Sarah began to speak. "Thanks for coming."

"No problem," I said back, "it actually was a lot of fun."

"Yeah, all but the last part," she laughed.

"Oh, it wasn't that bad, Sarah."

"Well I'm sure it could have been worse, knowing that pack. Hope we can hang out again," she offered.

"Anytime, although maybe at your house. This place is too much of a prison for me." I was laughing, but in her face I could see her 'deep in sympathy' look. "Thanks again, Sarah. See you in school on Monday," I said as I shut the door and waved. She pulled away and I watched as her taillights faded away. I turned, looked up at the huge mansion, and sighed. *Back to Purgatory*, I thought as I headed into the house.

6 The Drive

JUST LIKE ALWAYS, THE CREEPY butler managed to open the door before I had even reached for the door handle. "How do you do that," I said under my breath, annoyed.

He met me with a disapproving look on his face. I knew that he had been annoyed even with my mother's permission that I had broken one of his rules, about going out at night. I really didn't care as long as my mom said I could. That's all that mattered. He wasn't my boss, and the more he pushed his rules the more I was going to be like any other teenager and enjoy breaking them. I staggered back a step from the hostility rolling off his face and hurried around him, trying not to look at him. He didn't say anything as I headed up the huge staircase to my room. I glanced at him as I reached the top of the stairs, and I realized that he was still staring at me with that disapproving look on his face. I was still annoyed with all the tension in the air, or possibly I was just really tired with all the excitement from today's experiences, but I slammed the two massive doors. They made a loud thud as they shut.

I took off my coat and hat and threw them on the floor, not watching where they landed while I stepped out of my shoes. I was too tired to get out of my clothes. I just sat on the bed, collapsed back onto my pillow; I kicked my feet from over the edge onto the bed, closed my eyes, and tried to sleep.

I'm not sure how long I lay there, trying to fall asleep, before actually accomplishing my goal. When I did it was like every night before: The dream began. I walked though the massive forest, stumbling on the rocks beneath my feet, the feeling that I was being watched sending a cold chill down my body. I could hear branches and twigs snapping in the deep dark forest. There was a small amount of light from the moon that was set high behind the trees. I could see the cold breath coming out of my mouth, and another chill ran through my body. There was a thin fog that seemed to linger on the forest floor. Instead of the light ice blue eyes, I saw *him*, coming from the dark forest. It was Ethan, with the beautiful face and the ice blue eyes. I couldn't speak.

Just like before, he spoke. "I've be waiting for you," he said in his angelic voice. I waited for the jolt that would wake me from the nightmare, hoping that the time would never come. Just then his face expression changed, from that glow on his face and his beautiful smile to a hard grimace. His mouth opened, showing his teeth. A growl rumbled, ripped from his chest. My first impression was shock. *What happened? Why is Ethan acting this way?*

Another figure stepped out from the trees; he had a wicked smiled on his face. It was Caleb. Another growl ripped from Ethan's chest. Caleb was staring at me with those deep black eyes, which seemed to smolder in the darkness,

"Abby," he said in his gruff voice, and stepped towards me. Just then, the moon came from behind the trees.

Ethan yelled, "Run, Abby!"

I didn't hesitate, didn't even think, I just obeyed. As my head turned, I noticed a shift in the scene. I couldn't really tell what had changed. All I saw was Ethan lunging for Caleb. As I ran deeper into the dark forest, stumbling, I could hear growls coming from where I had just left.

I jolted awake.

I sat up, trying to remember what I had been dreaming of. As I played back the confrontation, I shuddered. I couldn't understand the confrontation in the dream. *Caleb and Ethan are friends. Why would I dream that they were fighting? It must have been the story at the bonfire*, I reasoned with myself. I got out of bed and headed to the bathroom to get ready for the uneventful day. I looked in the mirror. It looked like I hadn't slept in days; there were dark circles under my eyes and my hair that was still in the ponytail from last night. I seemed to have little pieces of hair sticking out everywhere. I was a mess. I quickly removed the rubber band that was in my hair, and then ran my fingers through it to get rid of any snarls. I turned on the shower and turned it up as hot as it would go without burning my skin off.

After I got undressed and put my clothes in the hamper, I jumped in the shower. The hot water hit my back. It was almost like adrenaline, and it woke me up while loosening my muscles. It seemed all the tension that I had was washing down the drain, just like the water. The only part of showers I hated was the time where you had to get out and face the world.

After about 20 minutes in the shower, I decided it was time to get out. I shut the water off and grabbed a towel. I wasn't sure what I was going to do today. It was Saturday, my mom and Ben were still on their trip, and the thought of hanging around the castle with the creepy butler and the crazy cook didn't do wonders for me. I hurried to get dressed. I quickly blow-dried my hair, but I was in a little bit of a hurry and some of my hair was still wet when I finished. I grabbed my sock and shoes and quickly put them on. *I think I'll take a drive and get out of here for the day*, I thought. Already my prospects were improving. I headed down the stairs and into the dining room, where I knew breakfast would be waiting for me.

I was right. Spread over the huge oak table was a feast of eggs, bacon, French toast, juice, and fruit. The cook always made too much for me. I silently wondered what they did with the extra food. I sat down and

started to eat. Everything was so good that I ate way too much. After I
fit as much in my 115 pound body as possible, I got up from the table,
tiding it up as I went. I didn't want to leave a mess and look like a pig. It
was strange I hadn't see Albert at all today. I put on my coat, grabbed my
keys from the small table by the front door, and headed out. It seemed
like the mornings around here were going to start being a tradition: get
up in the morning, get ready, come down for breakfast and get going.
At least it was easier than my first two days here.

I jumped in my jeep and started it, and without thinking about it I
turned the heat on and the music up. It actually was quite cold today. I
was really missing Florida: the warm weather, the beach, the ocean....
Thinking about home was starting to depress me, so I tried to refocus.
As I drove away from the house down the long drive, thoughts about
Ethan started to surface. I wasn't sure why he was always on my mind.
I was never one of those infatuated teenagers; boys were always on the
back burner at home. I wonder why it's so different here. I figured it
was going to take me till college to find a guy who was mature enough
to date, seeing as how guys were usually 10 years behind us girls in the
maturity department. So the fact that Ethan was on my mind 90% of
time was a little unsettling.

I started to ponder whether or not I could find the way out to the
cliffs where Sarah had taken me last night. It would be nice to see it in
the light, see the trees and the water. The thought of going to the cliffs
by myself didn't seem to bother me. I had always had an adventurous
side, although the first full day I was here had almost turned out to be
deadly. I seemed to remember the road signs as I drove, so I must have
been on the right track. I didn't realize how far Sarah had actually taken
me out. I had finally managed to find the gravel drive by remembering
the giant trees lining both sides of the road. I didn't remember the road
being this curvy, although it was dark by the time we got out here last
night.

I finally reached the little clearing that had been full of cars last
night and was empty today. An eerie feeling washed though me, but I

shrugged it away, not wanting to be distracted from my goal. I followed the small, man-made path. The trees were all around, like a huge canopy threatening to swallow me whole. The rocks clattered underneath my feet as I walked, trying not to trip. I kept a close eye on my feet. So it surprised me when I came to the opening in the trees, and there were the logs that had been full of people and the bonfire that was reduced to ashes, now still smoking from last night's bonfire.

I looked around at my surroundings and gasped. All around me were steep cliffs, and in the midst of these cliffs were giant waterfalls that cascaded down the cliffs into the water below. I walked toward the water. It was so beautiful. Last night it had been so loud. With all the kids from school out here, I really couldn't enjoy myself, but today as I closed my eyes I could hear the water rush and small birds in the background and feel the cool breeze wash over my face. It was so peaceful; I had never been to a place like this. I was so entranced that I didn't even notice that I wasn't alone. I opened my eyes and stared at the waterfall. It was amazing. And I was also a little glad that I had managed to not fall into the water last night.

Two strong hands took a firm grip grasp on my shoulder; they were flaming hot and it reminded me of last night's confrontation with Caleb. I started to scream. One massive hand covered my mouth. Then came a voice in my ears, an angelic voice. "Careful. You don't want to fall in."

I immediately relaxed and turned to confirm my suspicions. My heart sped as I turned. It was Ethan. Just like before, I was speechless.

"Klamath Falls isn't so bad that you want to drown yourself," he said with a chuckle. I finally seemed to find my voice, although my thoughts were a little jumbled.

"What?" I asked him, obviously so preoccupied that I didn't hear the first question.

"You're not going to drown yourself, are you?"

"No," I said in annoyed voice.

"Well, that's a relief. I didn't want to have to jump in to save you. The water doesn't look that appealing," he said with a laugh, "And well, frankly, my CPR is a little rusty, but I am sure it would be a fun refresher course," he said with another laugh.

"What are you doing out here?" I asked, trying to keep my voice from breaking.

"I could say the same thing to you, Abby. I come here all the time," he said. "What's your excuse?"

"Well, Sarah brought me out here last night as you well know, but I didn't get a chance to look around. It was so dark and I wanted to see where all the noises were coming from. Plus, I was bored, and being stuck in Dracula's castle wasn't an option for me."

He laughed. "Did you have fun last night," he asked.

"Actually, I did. Conner was telling some local legends," I informed him. I watched his face to see if any emotion changed his looked. But he was unreadable.

"Anything good?" He asked, not seeming to care.

"Well, he told me about the manor I live in, and my stepfather's family back in the old days way before I was born."

His face seemed to freeze. "That's right," he said. "You're living out at the Moores."

"Unfortunately," I said with a grimace on my face.

"You don't like it out there," he asked, looking into my eyes.

"No, not really," I answered.

"Why?" He pushed.

"Well, my mom and Ben barely knew each other before they got married. They sort of jumped into things a little quick and I got stuck with the end results, being dragged cross-country to a place where the sun never shines to live in Dracula's castle with a creepy butler and a crazy cook." Something in my response must have been funny, because he started to laugh. "I am glad my life amuses you so much," I said with a little acid in my voice.

"It's not that, Abby. Most girls would jump at the fact that they get to live in a mansion and get waited on twenty-four seven."

"I was just fine with the way things were, and if you'll notice, I am not like any other girl," I snapped back.

"I am getting that impression," he said. It was a relief to see him like this, away from his friends, letting his guard down. "You don't like your new stepfather," he said, with an edge in his voice.

"It's not that," I tried to explain "I just think my mom didn't think things though when it came marrying Ben." He still seemed a little amused. Then something from his earlier comment flickered. "You come here a lot?" I asked.

"Sure, all the time," he said. I was taken aback by that comment because Conner had said they didn't come out here. "Why?" He asked.

I wasn't sure if I was supposed to tell him about the stories and the comments that were made last night, so I tried to change the subject. "Where are your friends today?" I asked, not really caring.

"I don't know," he said. "I am not their keeper."

"Oh," I said. "I just thought you did everything together."

"No, not really, I have my life and they have theirs," he said. "You don't like it here in Klamath Falls?"

"Not really," I answered honestly. "Do you like it here?" I asked, trying not to show my intense curiosity.

"I don't mind it. My family is from here."

"What was the deal with Caleb last night?" I asked.

He slowly ran his fingers through his hair, and I thought this must be the question he'd hoped I wouldn't ask. "Well, Caleb is very territorial. He doesn't like changes."

"He must not like me very much," I guessed.

"It's not that exactly," Ethan started. "He doesn't particularly like the situation you're in."

"What situation is that?" I asked, a little confused.

"Your mom is married to a man who Caleb doesn't like and you're living in a house where Caleb hates the owner."

Thinking back to last night's adventure and the story that was told, I shrugged it off. *It can't be that, it was just a story.* "Oh," I said. "Why does Caleb hate Ben?"

"It's not Ben in particular," Ethan said. "It's more that he hates the whole family. Around these parts, people hold grudges for a long time."

"So..." I began. "If Caleb doesn't like me, then why are you talking to me?"

"I'm not Caleb, and I see things a little different from him," he snapped back. I could tell that this was a touchy subject and I didn't want to push him. I had a tendency when I got nervous to chatter, so, trying to avoid that, I looked back at the water and didn't speak. It was so peaceful here without all the conversations and stories of last night.

"Do you have a habit of going off on your own?" He asked. I turned back and looked at his face.

"Sometimes," I said.

"You should be careful in these parts where you choose to explore," he said, with a stern look on his face.

"What is it with you," I snapped back. "Be careful who I talk to, be careful where I explore...any more demands I should know?"

He seemed amused by my rant as he started to speak. "They're not demands, Abby. They're just warnings." My heart started to speed up as he said my name. My hands began to get sweaty and started to quiver. I wasn't used to this type of reaction in my body, and I was hoping that he didn't see how nervous I was. "Abby," he said in a calm voice, "I am just trying to keep you safe."

"Safe from what," I asked, a little annoyed. "The only dangerous things around here seem to be your friends."

He surprised me by laughing again. "They are a concern, but they're not your biggest problem, Abby."

"Then enlighten me," I said, with that annoyed tension still in my voice.

"It might be safer for you if you stay somewhat in the dark, but I hope you will heed my warnings."

"So," I started, and then paused, trying to figure how to phrase what I was trying to say. I began again, "So, would you put yourself in the same category as your friends?"

His face went somber. "Most definitely."

"Then why are you here? Just leave me be," I snapped. I could tell that my words had affected him. The grimace on his face looked like it was sketched there, never to be removed. I felt horrible at once, but I was tired of all his warnings.

"I wish I could," he said, and then he turned his head looking into the trees. It was quiet for so long that our breathing was the only sound.

"What do you want, Ethan?" I said in a more somber tone.

"The truth?" he asked.

"Of course," I replied.

"You remind me of someone I used to know a long time ago." He paused and turned his head back from the forest to look at me. "I want to get know you. Ever since I saw you in school, I've wanted to talk to and get to know you, but I want to keep you safe more."

"You don't want to be seen with me in public?" I asked.

"It's not that," he answered. "I don't want you to be seen with me. It's not safe."

The thought of not being able to talk to him, to be with him, wasn't an option, so I came up with a new plan.

"Don't tell anyone. We can be friends and nobody will have to know," I blurted out. The grimace was removed from his face, and in its place was the start of a smile.

"Abby," he started.

"Don't say anything now," I said, interrupting him. "Just think about it."

He took one step towards me, raised his hand to brush a piece of hair that had fallen in my face to behind my ear. His hand was so warm it heated my skin with one touch, almost like a flash burn. I smiled.

"Your hands are so warm," I said, and he quickly lowered his hand.

"Sorry," he mumbled.

"No, it's fine. It doesn't bother me. Will you be out here tomorrow?" I asked hopefully.

"I'm here almost every day," he said.

"Why?" I asked.

"It's peaceful," he replied, "almost like time stands still, and I don't have to worry about the world outside."

"That's sounds nice," I whispered. "I don't see why you think it wouldn't be safe for me to be around you. There's nothing about you that seems dangerous."

He let out a chuckle and then his deep eyes appraised me. "Abby, looks can be deceiving." Just then a cold breeze blew through the trees, and I shivered. "It's getting cold, Abby. You should get home." I wasn't ready to leave; I just wanted him to keep talking to me.

"You're not cold?" I asked, confused.

"No, I never get cold," he quickly answered.

"Think about what I said, Ethan. It's nobody's business who we talk to."

"And you try to remember I what I said and be very careful. Things aren't what they seem around here, Abby. Let me walk you to your truck; wouldn't want you to get lost," he said with a laugh.

"Ha ha, Ethan, I think I can find my way. There's a path."

"Even so, I wouldn't mind doing the honors," he said with a smile that seemed to fill his whole face.

I didn't put up a fight; secretly, I wanted as much time with him as I could get. I wanted to ask him about the stories from last night, but I was afraid that asking the questions would make our time together that much shorter. As he walked me to the truck, he walked beside me, making no noise, walking gracefully over the rocks. My footsteps, however, were very loud and my stumbling didn't help. When I would go to fall he would grab my arm and keep me steady, and every time he touched me, my heart beat so fast I thought it was going to leap out of my chest. Every touch felt like a shock that reached to my toes. Even my knees rattled. I had never felt this way about anyone before.

It didn't take us to long to reach me jeep.

"Will I get to see you again?" I asked, hoping he would say yes.

"Abby, give me some time to think. I don't want you to get caught in the crossfire."

"You know I have no idea what you're talking about," I said, with a confused look on my face.

"I know, Abby, but please trust me. It really is safer for you that you have no idea of what's going on here in Klamath Falls."

I didn't press; I got in the jeep, shut the door, and turned the key, starting the jeep with a roar. He stepped back from the truck. I watched him in my rearview mirror as I drove out of the forest. As I drove back to Ben's, a new thought arose. *Where was his motorcycle? I didn't see it in the little clearing. How did he get out here?* I just shook my head. It probably was one of those mysteries that I was never going to find out about. I knew that Ethan thought it was in my best interest to let things go, but it just wasn't in my genetic makeup to let things go. The thought of not being around him, not seeing him, was too much to bear. I wasn't ready for it to be over before it barely started. My mom had always called me her stubborn child, and I was. I was never a person who could roll over and take things for face value, in most cases there was something seething beneath the surface. And with Ethan, there were so many unanswered questions. One thing I was sure of, Ethan and I had a connection, a strong deep connection that was inexplicable, and even if he resisted I had to learn the truth.

As I drove back to Ben's castle, the sun was beginning to set behind the trees. I drove there in a daze, almost like I was stuck in fog. Nothing seemed clear. I pulled up to the house and noticed that only the light outside and in one room were on; it almost looked like one of those abandoned houses you see in a horror movie. I shuddered. I know my mom loves it here, but I can't help but feel creeped out every time I look at this place. I put the jeep in park, turned off the radio, and slowly pulled the keys out of the ignition. I was in no hurry to reach the front doors, knowing that the creepy butler would have the door opened before I even touched the knob. So you can imagine my surprise when I got to the door, and the door remained closed.

"Hmmm," I whispered. "No creeping butler." I turned the door handle and the door squeaked as I opened it. I notice that no one seemed to be around. I went to place my keys on the table by the door, where I often left my keys. I noticed a note left on the table. The hand writing was extremely neat. The note at the top said, "Mrs. Moore called while you were out and wanted to leave a message: Abby, we're having a great time, hope you are, too. Ben and I will be back late tomorrow. I love you. See you tomorrow. Love, mom."

It was nice to hear from her, although I could hear the stress in the note. I couldn't imagine that she was having a good time in Las Vegas. I was sure Ben's presence was helping her, but I was certain that tomorrow she would high-tail it for home as fast as she could do so without hurting his feelings.

I sighed, and then hurried up to my room, trying to avoid the creepy butler. I thought I was home free until I got to the second floor, Right before I got to my door, I noticed him in the dark shadows across the hall. The glare he was giving me was not friendly, and as I hurried to get to my room, I noticed that his nose was turned up like he had smelled something that stank. I hurried to shut the door and then froze. I heard steps pause and then walk past my door. As soon as the steps sounded farther away I exhaled as if I had been holding my breath awhile. *What the hell was that all about*, I thought? It irritated me that this guy always seemed to be lurking around, but what could I do? If I said anything to my mom, she would tell me that I was making too much out of it and was being ridiculous, or that I was overreacting.

I couldn't help but feel that something was really wrong here. Hopefully it wasn't the story that Conner had told me that was putting me on edge. I hurried to get ready for bed, though I was sure that I could have spent more time in the shower. I still wasn't relaxed when I got out, and I was sure that the thought of my little trip tomorrow to the cliffs wasn't going to help me relax. I almost felt some relief, though, at the thought that Ethan could be back at the cliffs tomorrow. I know that he wanted time to think, and of course he should take the time, but I had always been very pushy and I usually got what I wanted. I think Ethan was the only thing to keep my spirits up since we moved here. After I got done brushing my teeth and combing through my wet hair, I headed back to the bed. I paused to look out the huge windows that overlooked the drive. The sun had finally set and the only light was coming from the moon, almost covered by clouds in the darkened sky. It was so beautiful,

From out in the trees I heard a noise. It sounded like a howl, and I remembered that we had wolves here. Ben had explained that the day after I had almost fallen off the cliff, but I never thought that they were so close. I shuddered and then shut the long, heavy drapes. I climbed into the huge bed and got ready for tonight's nightmare to begin.

I was surprised that I awoke having slept more peacefully than I had since the day I moved here. I turned to look at the clock. It was 8:00 am. For some reason, I was excited to have this day begin; actually, I knew the reason. I was going to see Ethan. *Hopefully,* I thought. I got ready in a rush. Since I had a shower last night, there really was no reason to take another one, so I just wetted my hair under the faucet. Try as I might not to get water all over the place, I managed to soak the shirt I had worn to bed.

"Darn," I said. I wrapped my hair in a towel and went to the closet. I grabbed one of my new shirts and some jeans. *This should do nicely,* I thought. I settled them on the long counter and then unwrapped the towel from my head. I grabbed a brush and started to pull it through all the tangles. I figured I might as well blow it dry since I was going to be outside for a while. After I had gotten my hair dry and gotten dressed, I grabbed my socks out of the dresser. Most of my stuff from the old house still hadn't arrived, although my mom had promised that it would take no more than a few weeks. I had brought most of the stuff that I needed on the plane. I got my socks and shoes on quickly, and grabbed my coat, which was still on the floor. I opened the huge doors. They made a loud creak, but I really didn't care now, I was on a mission. I headed down for breakfast. I noticed Albert at the bottom of the stairs.

"Morning, miss," he said.

"Morning," I said, and quickly retreated into the dining room. The cook really overdid it today. I grabbed some pancakes and quickly wolfed them down; I chased them down with juice. As soon as I finished my juice, I grabbed an apple that was on the table and headed out the door. I grabbed my keys off the small table. Nothing was going to stop me from getting out the door to see Ethan. I didn't even glance back to see what Albert expression was. I'm sure he was keeping track of my coming and goings, no doubt to report back to my mom and Ben. I really didn't care about that. After all, she apparently didn't care that she'd shipped me clear across the country without asking me what I thought.

I noticed as I walked out the door that it was almost sunny and a little warmer today. The normally cloudy sky looked like it would open and let through the sun, which it normally enveloped. It almost made me smile. I jumped in the jeep and started the engine even before my door was closed. I put it into drive while trying to fasten my seat belt. I gunned the jeep down the long drive; I was trying to take slow breaths but my heart was still racing ahead, almost like it was going to pound right out of my chest. In my old school I never really noticed boys; or, should I say, they never really noticed me. *Why is so different here? Why do I feel so connected to Ethan?* I can't explain it. There is something about him. It's like my will crumbles, like I turn to jell-o when I am around him.

I made it out to the cliffs in no time at all, not even noticing the houses passing or how fast I was driving. I pulled off the road onto the twisty lane, finally making it to the parking spot. I rushed to shut off the engine and left the keys in the ignition. I was sure that no one would steal it out here. I jumped out of the jeep, realizing too late that I was going to land in the mud. I should have known it would be muddy out here. It doesn't stop raining it this place long enough for the ground to dry out. I tried to slow down as I walked down the trail so I didn't accidentally trip and go sprawling.

As I reached the logs where we had sat the night of the bonfire, I felt a little bit of terror. *What if he had thought about it and decided that he didn't really want to be friends?* My stomach dropped at the thought of it. *No, that can't be it*, I reasoned.

"He will be here," I said to myself. I took a seat on the logs. They were still a little damp from last night's rainstorm, and the trees dripped water from the canopy above. I could hear the sounds of birds singing above me. I don't know how long I sat on that log but I knew it had been awhile. The sun was finally visible and right over my head now. It felt so warm, even with me slightly hidden under the canopy of trees. I closed my eyes and let the sun hit my face, and I imagined the warm feel of Florida and palm trees and the waves rolling into the sand on the beach.

I didn't notice that I had an audience until I felt warm hands wrap around the top part of my arms. My heart sped as I opened my eyes. As I turned, a small breath came out of my mouth. It was like I was holding my breath, just waiting for the time that I would see him again. Relief flowed through my whole body as I met his beautiful eyes.

It was quiet for one long moment. "I didn't think you were going to show," I barely whispered, trying to keep my breathing under control.

"I wasn't sure if I was going to," he said in his angelic voice as he raised his hand and with his fingers gently swept back the hair that had fallen into my face.

"I'm glad you came," I said. I was hoping he wasn't hearing the excitement in my voice, but it was very hard to contain. For a moment, he just looked at me with those ice blue penetrating eyes, like he could see all the way into my soul.

"I am not sure this was the brightest move or the safest move for you, Abby," he said, "but I am very glad you came, too. Would you like to take a drive with me?" He asked.

"A drive?" I asked. "A drive where?"

"Nowhere in particular," he said with a smirk. "Unless you are afraid."

"Afraid of what?" I snapped back.

"Afraid of motorcycles," he said with another smirk. I let out a laugh.

"I will take that as a no," he laughed back. We turned to head back up the trail. He kept pace with me, and although one of his strides matched two of mine, he didn't complain at all. I was shocked. When we reached the clearing where my jeep was parked, I saw it his monstrous bike. *You would have thought I would'-ve heard the monstrous roar of the bike pull up*, I thought to myself. As he climbed on the bike and kicked up the kickstand, I paused. It was all very intimidating. He saw me pause and take a deep breath. A smile stretched across his godlike face, and my heart started to race again.

"It's quite safe Abby. I won't let anything happen to you," he said as he held out his hand to me. That promise was all that it took; I grasped onto his warm hand and kicked my right leg over the bike. I gripped onto the back of his jacket. I could hear him let out a small chuckle. It took him one kick to get the bike started. It snarled to life. In the back of my head, I knew my mom would be very disappointed with the choice that I was making now. She had never been a big fan of motorcycles, but at this point I really didn't care. I was with Ethan, and that's all that mattered.

As he pulled onto the highway and really accelerated, I let out a sound that was like, "Humph!" Then I grasped my arms all the way around his waist, and I could feel the convulsion of laughter that shook his whole frame. I wasn't sure how fast we were going, but as the wind hit my face I felt free, and I wasn't afraid, not with my arms tightly wound around Ethan. When I was with Ethan I felt completely safe, like nothing or no one could ever hurt me. I kept my eyes shut most of the trip, just concentrating on Ethan. He had a deep, musky scent coming from his jacket. It smelled so good, the warmth that was originating from him kept me warm, and he was so big and muscular that he kept most of the wind from hitting me. This was the first time that I had ever been on a motorcycle, due to all of my mother's protests that I never ride one, but as safe as I felt with Ethan on his, I couldn't understand what all her protests were about.

I was not sure how long we were out for the ride but I knew it had been awhile. We pulled into the drive and he followed the winding road to park just a few feet from my jeep. He chuckled as he carefully loosened my grip from around his waist; I hadn't realized I had been holding on to him that tightly until he loosened my grip. I realized what he was doing and let go. He turned around to look at me as he set the bike on the kickstand. I would have gotten off the bike but I wasn't sure if my balance had been affected.

"Did you have a good time," he said in his deep angelic voice.

"Yes," I said, a little breathless. "Thank you."

"I am glad you like it, Abby," he said, with that huge smile stretched across his face. "You are the first person I have ever taken for a ride," he said with the deep honesty transparent.

I laughed a little. "That's the first time I have ever been on a motorcycle and it was actually a lot of fun," I replied, trying to downplay the excitement that was coursing through my veins. As he got off the bike, he held out his hand to help me down. I tried to keep my hand from shaking, but I think he managed to see through me. He smiled just a little. As I got off the bike, being a klutz, I managed to trip over my own feet, but he caught me and held me close to his chest. It was like the warmth that was emanating from him surrounded me and it was hard to think about anything else. I looked up and he was staring down at me.

"Abby," he said as his breath grew rougher. "I think it's time for you to go."

"Why?" I asked him, a little confused.

"Well, for one thing, it's getting late," he said, "and for the other, I am sure there are people looking for you."

At this point I couldn't really care less, I thought to myself, but he was right. The sun was no longer overhead and it was starting to set. I knew Ben and my mother would be home soon, and most likely my mom would want to gush over her trip.

"Have you thought about our last conversation?" I asked. I couldn't help the hopeful smile that started to stretch across my face.

"Yes, I have," he said, his expression staying the same. My hopeful smile started to turn into a grimace, but before it could turn into a full-blown grimace, the corners of his face twitched into a smile. I relaxed.

"Abby, I think if we are going to try to be friends, it would be better to keep it our secret."

"Better for whom," I asked.

"Better for you," he said with a small laugh.

I guess it's better than nothing, I thought to myself. "What about your friends?" I asked.

"It will be better to leave them in the dark as well," he said, the grimace returning to his face.

"Alright," I agreed. Slightly relieved that he did want to be my friend, and hopefully something more soon, my heart fluttered at the thought.

"I will see you in school tomorrow," I said as I headed back to my jeep.

"See you tomorrow," he said in that deep, angelic voice. I got in my jeep and started it, watching him as I pulled out. As I drove the curving road back up the highway, I watched his face fade into the background. This was the most exciting day I have ever had. In the 16 years that I have been alive, I had never been interested in boys, and they just never appealed to me back home. That is probably because I thought boys were immature, but Ethan is different; the way he acts and talks makes it hard for me to believe that he is 16. *One thing's for sure,* I thought to myself, *I am truly and deeply falling in love with Ethan.* As I turned onto the highway and hit the accelerator I cranked up the radio as loud as it would go and sped away, hoping that I would beat my mom and Ben home.

7 Anticipation

I WAS HALFWAY UP THE long driveway when I let out a low groan, because that's when I noticed Ben's big black SUV parked under the overhang to the entry. I hadn't beaten them home, not even close, and from the way it looked, they had been home for quite some time. I groaned again. My mom was going to want to know where I had been all day, and Ethan wanted us to keep our friendship a secret. What was I going to tell my mom? *What's the story,* I thought to myself.

I parked in my usual spot, hesitating, and then I slowly turned off the jeep, also hesitating as I opened my door and got out. I was in no hurry to face the reception that was no doubt waiting for me. As I reached the door, thinking that the butler was going to keep to his routine of not answering the door, like he hadn't most of the weekend, I was wrong. The minute I raised my hand to reach for the door handle, it was already open. I let out a small groan, so low I was sure that he couldn't hear me since he was ancient and his hearing was probably gone, but from the look on his face I must have been heard.

What, is he back on the clock now, I thought sourly to myself. Before I had even stepped through the door I heard my mom's voice.

"Abigail" That was a bad sign; she was using my full first name. "Can you come in here?" I heard her call from the direction of the living room. I dropped my keys on the wood table by the door. They made a small thud as I dropped them. I took a deep breath and walked into the living room. I noticed that Ben and my mom were sitting on the couch. Their facial expressions told me they were none too happy. My guess was that the butler had spilled the beans, told them about my recent activities and the fact I had been out all night and most of the weekend. I groaned internally, and very quietly cursed the butler before they began.

"Abby," my mother started and then paused, taking in a deep breath. I am sure it was an attempt to keep her voice calm. "Where have you been?" She sounded angry.

I really didn't want to fight with my mom, not with the incredible day that I had. "I just went for a drive," I lied, hoping she wouldn't see through my lie. "You weren't supposed to be home until later tonight".

"Sorry I wrecked your plans," she said with a sarcastic tone. It was obvious that she did not have a good time on her trip. I was sure this was the reason for her hostility.

"Sorry, mom," I said, trying to make peace before she really got upset and decided to ground me. The thought of being grounded, stuck in this house with no escape, sent tremors through my body. But my apology seemed to work. Her face relaxed ever so slightly. I could still see the line creasing her forehead. She almost looked her age now.

"Well, did you have a nice trip?" I said, trying to change the subject. Knowing my mom, and the fact that Ben was sitting right next to her, I knew she was going to lie through her teeth, even though she was almost as bad at lying as I was. After all, I had gotten my bad lying skills from her.

I was shocked when Ben actually answered for her. "We had a very good time." I couldn't see sarcasm in his face or in the tone of his voice, so obviously my mother had been convincing and very good at keeping her emotions under control; though knowing her so much better than Ben, I could tell by her face that she was glad to be home. Because of the fact that she was happy about being home, I knew my mom would forgive me. Holding grudges was not my mother's thing, it was mine.

"Oh," my mother said, and turned to Ben. "Ben, where's the gift that we got for Abby?"

"It's right here," he said, and held out a box to her. It was a small, dark box with funky writing on it. I assumed it was something foreign; after all, everything in the USA is imported nowadays.

"Here, Abby, this is from Ben and me," she said, a small smile replacing the unhappy look on her face. I was glad the frown was off her face. It seemed to make me relax a little more.

I looked at the box and then opened it. "It's a cell phone," I whispered.

"Well, we thought you should have one, just in case you ran into trouble with your Jeep."

Trouble with a new truck, I thought, and then closed my mouth, trying to keep in the laughter. Translation: *we couldn't get hold of you this weekend and we want to make it easy to track you down, and keep a leash on you,* I thought and tried to smile.

"Thanks, mom," I tried to fake gratitude. I am sure she saw right through it. I was not one of those kids who were into technology. I never felt the need to have a cell phone. I guess I am being too modest; I never needed a cell phone because until we moved here, I never felt the need to escape from home.

"We thought it also would be good if Ben and I went out of town. We thought it would be easier to get a hold of you since for some reason it seemed to be so hard this weekend." I could hear the hostility return to her voice.

"Sorry, mom" I said with a sincere look on my face. "Friday night I went out with friends and yesterday and today I went for a drive. I am just exploring our new home." She seemed to buy it, but Ben, who had been mostly quiet through the whole conversation, gave me a speculative look. I was sure that he knew there was more to my story, but he didn't ask for details and I didn't offer any.

"Well," Ben said, "you must be hungry, staying out all day."

"I am famished," I said with a smile. I looked at the time and it was nearly time for dinner.

"Abby," my mother said, "Why don't you wash up? Um," she paused, "you look like you could use it."

I was taken aback by the way she said that but, I just nodded and headed to the first floor bathroom off the dining room. I didn't usually use this bathroom, preferring to stay to my bathroom. As I looked in the mirror, my jaw dropped. I could see why my mother was acting like that. My hair looked like I had stuck it out the window of my jeep as I drove. I had snarls and rats' nests all over my head; I ran my fingers through my hair, trying to get most of the snarls out. After I had gotten most of the snarls out I grabbed one of the washcloths in one of the drawer under the sink, and began washing off all the dirt that I had on my face. I hadn't realized that you could get so dirty riding on the back of a motorcycle.

Thoughts about today came flooding back and I could feel the blood rush to my cheeks, although I felt a little better after most of today's adventure was off my face. It seemed a little strange to worry about what I looked like after the day I had with Ethan. I signed and then opened the door and headed to eat dinner with Ben and my mom. The table was filled with every type of food that you could think about, it had turkey, mashed potatoes, green beans, rolls, and for desert there were 3 types of pies and cherry cheesecake. The cherry cheesecake looked very good, but seriously, who was going to eat all this, I thought to myself. Part of the problem with the cook is she always made too much food.

Dinner was a quiet affair, with only a few comments about the food that the cook had made, and some few comments about the trip that Ben and my mom had been on. I also managed to tell Mom about the dance that Sarah and Julie asked me to go to. Although my mom was curious about the fact that I was going with friends and not with a guy,

I just said everyone had decided to go in the group. That seem to pacify her and she didn't press. To be honest, there was only one person that I wanted to see at the dance, and I was sure that it wasn't his type of scene. That thought started to depress me and I was grateful that my mom seems to let the subject close. After I gotten about as much food as I could in my body, I asked if I could be excused.

"Abby, is all your homework done?"

"We really didn't have much," I answered back;

"Oh, okay Abby. 'Night, honey," she said

Ben looked at me, then said, "'Night Abby."

I hurried to get up stairs to avoid Albert. After I hurried through my bedroom door and shut it quickly and carefully, not wanting the doors to make a loud thud. I rushed to get ready for bed. After I had my shower, got into my sweats, and brushed my teeth I hurried to climb in the nice huge warm bed. I have to admit this bed is a lot more comfortable than the other one back home; you with think I would sleep better. I fell back into the pillow and relief swept through me. The thought of going to school -- not at the thought of actually going back to school; I was never excited about that-- to see Ethan made my heart flutter. I am not sure how long it took me to get to sleep. One minute I was thinking about tomorrow and the next minute I was out.

The dream tonight was different. We weren't in the forest behind the manor; no, I was at the cliffs and it wasn't raining which was different. I had barely seen the sun since the day we moved here. I just laid there soaking up as much sun as I could. I was lying on a blanket looking up at the sky. I could see the sun for once. The canopy of trees was all around. I could hear birds chirping. I closed my eyes and just listened; it was so peaceful here. Then I heard a twig snap. I opened my eyes and quickly sat up. I looked around seeing nothing. Another twig snapped

I managed to stutter out, "Hello! Is anyone there?" Although I was hoping no one would answer. Something caught my eye and I turned my head. Standing not ten feet away was a giant black wolf. A shudder ran through me. I could not move; it was like I was cemented to the ground. Before I could start to panic I noticed something strange about the giant black wolf: his eyes. They were Ice blue and didn't look angry or aggressive. Instead they were soft and full of concern.

Just then I heard another snap of a twig in the forest and the rustling of the bushes from the other direction. I turned my head slightly trying to keep an eye on the wolf in front of me. Then another giant wolf step out from the trees. His eyes were black and their expression was murderous. He let out a growl showing his dagger like teeth. It I noticed the other wolf, the black one, was looking directly at the first wolf. He let out a growl, and with him showing his teeth he lunged for the other wolf.

I jerked up so that I was sitting upright in my bed. The covers were all messed up like I had been tossing and turning all night. I glanced at the time and it was almost time for my alarm to go off. I sighed and slowly climbed out of bed, straightening the cover as I did. As I walked through the bathroom I stumbled over my shoes that I had just left in the middle of the floor. I managed to catch myself on the desk. I sighed again.

I wish I wasn't so accident prone, I thought quietly to myself. I turned on the shower and adjusted it to where it was hot but not enough to burn me. I got in and let it hit my back. I put my head under like I normally did to drown away the nightmares, or any thoughts that I didn't want to think about. After I had spent enough time in the shower without being late for school, I turned off the shower and grabbed my towel. I wrapped it around myself. I grabbed the small towel that was on the huge counter top and wiped of the mirror; this was routine. The mirror always fogged over when I took a shower. I cracked the door a little so the mirror wouldn't continue to fog over.

I stared at myself in the mirror; there were dark puffy circles under my eyes like I hadn't slept in a week. I took my finger and poked at the puffiness under my eyes thinking that by doing this it would magically disappear. I gave up, grabbed the brush, and ran it through my hear trying to get the snarls out. After I had gotten them all out I grabbed the blow dryer and blew dry my hair until it was almost dry. I never blew it completely dry because I usually got impatient. Besides, it seem to dry quicker if I just left it alone.

I went to the closet to look for clothes why trying to keep my towel around me. I finally found a nice blue t-shirt and some blue jeans. Not very fancy but after all I was going to school not a party. I grabbed my sock out of the wood dresser by the bed and got my shoes on. I grabbed my coat, and then rushed to get down stairs not even bothering to close my bedroom doors. I was hoping to beat my mom and Ben to breakfast. My hopes were soon dashed as I hit the main floor and heard laughing coming from the dining room. I slowed as I headed into the dining room hoping they would not bring up this weekend. I walked in and my mom and Ben were still laughing.

"Good morning Abby," my mom said.

"Good morning Abby," Ben said and then quickly added "Did you sleep well?"

What was this, a joke? Could he not see the dark circle under my eyes? I reined my sarcastic attitude before it could give me away on my face. "Yes" I said in reply then I sat down in the chair. I wasn't really in the mood to eat; probably still hyped up from the dream I had last night. These dreams were nothing like I had ever had before. They are so real, it's like I am actually there. It doesn't seem like they are even dreams, given the fact that I can actually remember them. When I lived in Florida I could never remember what I dreamt about. I hadn't really realized that I had zoned off until I heard my mom.

"Abby," she said. I didn't answer so she reverted to using my full name. "ABIGAIL ELIZABETH WATSON," she said in her stern motherly voice, which I never really heard that often because she didn't act like any other mother.

"I'm sorry mom; what did you say?" It looked like she actually rolled her eyes before she started to speak.

"Abby, did you say that you were invited to the dance this next weekend?" I knew that this prospect of me getting dresses up and going to the dance truly excited her.

"Yes," I replied. "Sarah and Julie asked if I wanted to go with them."

"Aren't there any guys that you want to go with?"

I groaned internally; this was never a topic I ever wanted to have with my mom or anybody for that matter. "No, mom I really don't know anyone that well here. I think it would be better just to go with friends." She looked disappointed but then she let it drop.

I was surprised that Ben didn't. "Abigail," he started, "be careful of some of the boys in school…" He paused and I had a feeling I knew where this conversation was going. "There are some boys that are labeled as trouble makers in the school; I want you to stay away from them." I knew who he was talking about, but I was sure that he had no Idea that I was already in too deep with Ethan and I wasn't going to give him up.

I shrugged. "I don't really know who you are talking about. I haven't really noticed any guys in school," I lied.

"Just the same, Abby, be careful of who you talk to in school. Not all the guys are really nice and some of them cause a lot of problems." I didn't respond. It was my mom that broke the silence. She was laughing,

"Ben," she started, "Abigail doesn't really notice guys. She has never been on date. She normally has a very good head on her shoulders; she is very responsible." She acted a little smug when she said that almost like she was very proud of her teenage daughter and the choices, up until the move, that I had made. He just nodded and then began to eat. After I was full as I was going to get. I said bye to mom and Ben.

"Drive careful" She said as I grabbed my keys and headed out. I hurried to get out to my truck, although I was watching my feet so that I didn't trip and go sprawling. I got in and turned on the truck. I turned the radio down that was blaring and then turned the heat on. It was quite cold today, like it could start snowing any time. As I looked out the window, before I put the jeep into drive, I noticed the clouds. It was almost like there was a storm coming. I put my jeep into drive and headed down the long drive.

As I arrived at school I noticed the parking lot was quite full, which surprised me. Normally the parking lot was quite empty until ten minutes before school started. It was about twenty minutes until eight and there were a lot of students outside talking and laughing. I saw Sarah and Julie outside. They had noticed me pull in and started out in my direction. A small part of me wonder why they weren't freezing since it was so cold today, and then I realized that they were probably use to this type of weather. As they reached the truck I rolled down the window not wanting to leave the sanctuary of my nice warm vehicle.

"Hey, Abby," Sarah said.

"Hi, Abby!" Julie Echoed.

"Did you have a nice weekend?" Sarah asked.

"Yeah, but it was pretty uneventful," I said keeping to my agreement, not telling anything thing about Ethan and me. "What did you guys do?" I asked quickly to keep the subject off of me.

"Nothing really," Sarah said. "Mom took me out shopping." She then rolled her eyes. I knew that if she would have been with her friends then shopping would have been a big deal, but when it was with your mom, it was just plain embarrassing.

I tried to hold back a laugh. "What about you, Julie?"

"Oh, we had a family function that I had to attend." She looked so overly thrilled. So far it looked like I had the best weekend; unfortunately I was not able to talk about it.

"Aren't you guys cold," I said trying to hold back the shivers from the cold air that came through my open window.

They both laughed. "Not really," they said.

"But we're used to this type of weather," Sarah added.

"You'll get use to it soon enough Abby," Julie said. I knew that she was probably right, but secretly I hoped that my mother would come to her senses, divorce Ben, and ship us both back to Florida. Realistically I knew that wasn't going to happen.

"Yeah you're probably right," I said faking enthusiasm.

"Did you get your dress for the dance?" Julie asked.

"No but I have a couple in my closet that still have the tags on them. I think my mom thinks of me as an oversized Barbie doll," I laughed. They both joined in.

"What does your mom do," Sarah asked.

"Well she would have liked to be a beautician, before she married Ben. I am not sure what's she is going to do now."

"Oh that's right," Sarah said. "She probably doesn't have to work if she doesn't want to; Ben is loaded isn't he?"

I rolled my eyes. "Yes he has money, but my mom will get bored soon and she is going to want something to do."

"What's it like living it that huge house?" Julie asked. Julie hadn't been one to be very nosey so she must have had to work up a lot of courage to ask me.

I laughed and then began to speak, "I wouldn't call it a house - it's more like a castle that should be a museum." I laughed again and then she joined in. But I was shocked to see Sarah not laughing but had a grimace on her face.

"What's wrong Sarah?" I asked. But I already knew before she answered. She was remembering back to the day of the bonfire, the day that she had picked me up, and the creepy butler.

"Abby," she said and then paused. "Is it always like that there?" I knew what she was talking about, but Julie looked confused.

"Yes," I answered. "I think I am getting used to it." I tried to smile.

She didn't. "What's with the butler? He almost looks hostile," she said. I laughed again.

"No he's just so old that he only has the one expression." I laughed again and this time she laughed and started to relax. I looked at the time and it was almost time to head in. It was then when I heard the noise of the motorcycles in the distant and my heart began to race.

"Oh great," Sarah said. "The juveniles are here." I could tell by the way Sarah had said that she really didn't like them, but Julie giggled. One by one the motor cycles pulled in almost running over some of the kids that were in the middle of the parking lot. I could tell it was Caleb in the front. He would usually lead his pack of friends. I could see Ethan coming up in the back. He glanced one time in my directions and then quickly looked away.

"Why don't you like them?" I asked Sarah.

"Well these guys' families showed back up about a year or so ago -- I guess that their families are originally from here like Conner said -- but they are always causing problems and getting into trouble. They pretty much run the school and no one ever messes with them."

My thought flashed back to my first couple of days here with Caleb and his friends surrounding my locker; a shiver ran through my body. "Yes, they all look very intimidating," I agreed quickly.

"I think the worse thing about it," Sarah continued, "is that even the teachers are scared of them to." I would have probably laughed but Sarah had a serious look on her face. "This gang does whatever it wants and nobody challenges them."

"Actually," Julie said, "they normally don't notice anyone, until now." Julie must have been thinking about the second day, after our first class when they were all staring at us.

"Weirder than that, they never crash a party at the cliffs, until the day you came," Sarah offered.

I just shook it off. "Maybe they just heard about the party and wanted to check it out."

"Maybe," Sarah offered.

"Well," I said, "maybe we should get to class. It looks like the parking lot is starting to clear out." They agreed and we headed off to our first class. Julie and I were the last ones to class and we hurried to take our seat that was in the back of the class while Mr. Murphy gave us the eye. I knew he hated it when students cut it a little close to the bell. The bell rang just as Julie and I took our seats and class started. I very carefully looked over to the six huge boys and saw that Ethan was looking at me from the corner of his eye, trying not to draw attention to the fact that he was looking. I quickly looked away, trying to listen to what Mr. Murphy was saying; it looked like we were going to have to write a paper on a book that had some sort of relevance to our life. Crap, I thought. Is there anything that depressing, I thought. Class seemed to pass in daze. As Julie walked off to our next class I stopped off at my locker to get my books for my next class. I heard someone clear his throat behind me and I saw Julie go rigid.

"Excuse me," a sweet rough voice behind me started. I turned to see who it was, and then my jaw dropped. I closed it quickly, realizing that I had seen this boy before: it was Adam Mills. He was the star jock of the school.

"Hello," I said after I found my voice.

"You must be Abby."

"Yes, that's right," I answered back.

"I am Adam," he said, "but I am sure that you knew that. I was wondering if you had a date to the winter formal."

"Oh," I said a little in shock. I had never actually spoken to this boy before and it took me off guard that he knew who I was, let alone wanted to go to the dance with me. I didn't want to hurt his feelings, and he was very cute, but not really my type. I was glad that I had plans already.

"Actually," I started, "I was asked to go the dance with a group of friends."

"Oh," he said, disappointed. It took only a minute and then his expression changed. "Well," he said, "I hope you will save me a dance."

"Sure," I said not wanting to hurt his feeling again.

"Great," he said. "Well, I guess I will see you later."

"Later then," I agreed. He turned and walked away. The next thing I know, I felt a fist on my shoulder.

"Abby," Julie said with irritation in her voice.

"What?" I said rubbing my arm.

"Do you know who that was?"

"Yes," I said with a shocked look on my face.

"Then why did you do that?" she said looking confused.

"Do what?" I asked.

"Why did you say no?" She almost looked furious.

"Well, for one, I have plans with you and Sarah and for two, he is really not my type."

Her jaw dropped. "Abby, Adam is every girl's dream in this school," she said looking abashed. I tried not to laugh but a small giggle escaped my lips. "Abby, if you had said yes we would have understood," she hedged.

"To tell you the truth I would probably have a better time with you guys," I said and then let out another laugh. She didn't look convinced. I don't think Julie was buying my transparent honesty, but she just shook her head and we headed off to class. I was glad when school was almost over. After burning the muffins and making the room smell in home eck I was ready to go home. And then to suffer through gym…let's just say I am glad that I didn't break any bones, although that would have been a good excuse not to have to go the dance. The whole school was buzzing about the dance. There wasn't a part of the hall walls that didn't have a reminder on it. Bright posters with every kind of color lined the walls; it looked like one huge rainbow that, of course, I was trying to forget about. I wished I could get excited, but the only way I was going to get excited was if Ethan was going with me, but I knew that wasn't going to happen. Ethan and his friends weren't the type of people that would be caught at a silly thing like a high school dance. You would most likely see these people at some Smokey bar on the wrong side of the tracks. All I wanted to do was escape, to hide from all the attention the dance would no doubt bring.

The day was coming to a close. I could feel it in the air; it was almost tangible. After I had gotten done with gym without actually hurting myself or anyone else, I made it to my locker. As I lifted up on the locker and started to open it, it made a screech like the medal door was protesting, like it wanted to keep my bag and coat locked up forever. Which I truly wouldn't of minded if It wasn't for the fact is was raining cats and dogs, and my rain jacket was in there as well as my keys. I pulled on the door with as much force as possible, cursing under my breath and grinding my teeth, secretly hoping that I was the only one around. I must have pulled it a little hard. It jerked open and almost knocked me to the floor, but swift hands caught me before I dropped.

I was horrified and a little embarrassed as my miraculous savior set me on my feet; I regained my balance, took a deep breath, and turned. He was tall dark and handsome, if you like that in a guy. It was Adam Mills. What, is he stalking me, I thought quietly to myself, trying not to show irradiation on my face.

"Thanks," I said, a little breathless. Don't get me wrong I was grateful that he had kept me from falling on my head and not embarrassing myself any further.

"No problem," he said as he raised his hand and ran is fingers through his silky black hair. "I don't suppose you have changed your mind about the dance?" he said with a hopeful glance.

"No, sorry," I said. Although I really didn't t feel sorry; I just didn't want to go with him. I knew that most girls would find him more than attractive - he was drop dead gorgeous, with those beautiful brown eyes and that dark wavy hair, looking quite stylish in his letterman jacket. He was every cheerleader's dream, but I wasn't a cheerleader and never was into school spirit. It was better to let him down easy I thought. I didn't really want to make enemies my first month here.

"No, sorry," I replied. "It would be rude to cancel on my friends, but thanks for asking," I said.

"That's alright," he said with a grin on his face. "You're still going to save me a dance right?" he said with a hopeful gleam in his eyes.

Gosh, I can't believe how persistent he is, I thought. "Sure," I said and then turned my head, biting my lip. I really didn't want to give him the wrong impression and I was still hoping that we can be friends.

"See you around," he said and smiled as he walked away. After he had turned the corner, my somewhat rigid pose relaxed. I exhaled once he was out of sight. Then I grabbed my rain jacket bag in somewhat of a hurry not to run into anyone else as I attempted to escape the school. It seemed like everyone else had the same idea I did. The once loud hall with the babbling voices and gone completely silent; I could swear you could have heard a pin drop if it weren't for my foot steps that clopped along the floor. It was starting to make me feel uneasy, like I could feel someone watching me. I took a quick peek over my shoulder, but seeing nothing I hurried to put on my jacket. I really didn't want to run into any of Caleb or his friends.

As I made my way down the rest of the hallways, almost to the doors I stopped. Standing in front in front of me and guarding my retreat was Caleb. I was frozen; I couldn't get my feet to move. A million different thoughts were running through my head, my heart started to accelerate, and it felt like my shoes were full of concrete. I didn't say anything; I couldn't. No sound escaped my throat.

Caleb was the first to speak. "Abby," he said in a menacing tone, and then smirked. Again I said nothing. "It's so nice to see you again," he said but from the tone in his voice he didn't seem to think it was nice at all. He took a step forward, my muscles locked down. "I think it's time that we talked," he said as his smirked disappeared.

"What do you want?" I said with an acid tone. My hands were starting to quiver. I closed them, quickly balling them into tight fists hoping he didn't see it. Showing fear would not be helpful in this situation. Showing fear was not an option. I didn't want him to have that type of power over me. He seemed amused at my hostility in my voice and his smirk reappeared.

"Well," he started, "you seem to be adding some complications to my life Abby." He spoke with that smirk still on his face, but now he was glaring at me too. It made the cold chill that was running through my body even colder.

"I don't know what you are talking about Caleb - I don't even know you," I answered.

"Abby, one thing I have learned in my life is history always repeats itself, and if you were smart you would pack your bags and move back to the where ever it is that you came from."

I stared at him not comprehending were all the hostility was coming from. I didn't even know him. Why did he hate me so much? Without thinking about it the words just busted out of me: "What is your problem; you don't even know me!" I couldn't help it. I was tired of be bullied by him and his followers.

He laughed; it was a deep roar that seemed to originate out of his chest. "You have a little bit of fire in you," he said with a laugh. I am not sure what emotion played on my face, but I was ready to leave.

"Are you done?" I hissed.

"Just one more thing," he said as the smirk faded. "Stay out of things that don't pertain to you," he said.

"I have no idea what you are talking about, but if you are done I am ready to leave now." He stepped out of my way allowing me access to the doors in front of me.

"Remember what I said Abby. Stay out of things, or you might end up getting hurt."

"Is that a threat?" I asked still having the acid tone to my voice.

"No." He paused. "Just a fact. People that get in my way have a tendency to get hurt."

I ignored that last bit as I hurried past him to the safety of my truck. I didn't even turn to see if he was following me. I jumped into my truck and shut the door; I hit the doors locks as I turned the key. As I backed out of the parking lot a million different thoughts were racing through my head. One thing I was sure of was Caleb truly hated me. Another: he truly hated bens family. And all those stories that Conner told us at the bonfire were they actually true. I had a lot of questions and no answers, but I was sure the next time I was with Ethan I was going to find out. If Ethan didn't tell me I was going to ask Ben. I was concentrating so hard on my thoughts that I didn't see the trees blowing past me. "Oh shoot," I said out loud as I took my foot off the accelerator and applied it gently to the break. I finally slowed to 55 mph and then felt a little relieved; getting speeding ticket would not have been helpful in my efforts to show my mom that her sixteen-year-old daughter could be responsible.

I made it home a lot earlier than expected even with the interrogation with Caleb. I sighed as I turned off the keys to my truck and open my door. From one prison to another, I thought, and then headed for the door. I was prepared for it this time, so it didn't shock me when Albert opened the door. I walked in like any other day and plopped my keys on the table, although instead of looking for my mom I headed up stairs to start on my homework. I didn't have much homework to do so I finished it fairly quickly to my dismay. Then I turned on my computer and checked my email. It was mostly junk mail in my email. I quickly deleted the junk mail and then noticed that there were a few from my friends in Florida. I opened the one that started "missing you;" it was from McKenna, one of my best friends. Her mom and my mom were friends even before I was born. So you could say that we were friend even before we were in diapers. Her opening line was the same:

Missing you Abby. How are things going? What is your new house like? Did you make any new friends? Are there in any cute boys there?

I had to giggle at that response. She knew that I wasn't into guys like she was. In her parting line she said: I miss you everyday. It's not the same without; you please write back soon.

I sighed and began to type. *McKenna, I started. Yeah I miss you to. Klamath Falls was just like I thought it would be, cold and wet. Boy do I miss the sun. School is about the same just 3,000 times smaller than our high school and it feels like I moved in to a rerun of "Leave It To Beaver." Not much happens here,* I was intentionally leaving out anything that I thought McKenna didn't need to know. Odds were that she would tell her mom everything I said and her mom and my mom still talked so it was just safer to keep her in the dark. I continued, *I have made a few friends her and I was invited to a dance this Saturday. Yeah I know, I don't dance, but I didn't want to hurt anyone's feeling so I accepted. Chances are I will be in the back trying to avoid anyone's attention. That way I don't kill anyone on the dance floor. I chuckled; I knew McKenna was going to be laughing at this point. I will right again soon... Missing you too, Abby.* I hit the send key and then turned off my computer. Not wanting to wait for it to shut down I decided to just turn off the power strip. I turned my head to look at the clock on my bed side table. Time for dinner, I thought. I headed down the stairs and headed into the dining room; of course Ben and my mom were already seated.

"Hi, Abby," my mother greeted me.

"Hi, mom," I replied.

"How was your day at school?" she asked.

"It was fine," I said, then noticed my mom's expression, her eyebrows were raise and her mouth was turned down in a grimace. Then I realized that seemed to be my response for anything these days. Not wanting to upset her I decide to go into more details. "It was pretty uneventful," I said. "Mostly people were talking about the dance this Saturday." That seemed to appease her.

"Oh," she said, "and are you still planning to go the dance with your friends?"

"Yes, mom," I said. I knew my mom was a little disappointed that I hadn't been asked, and I wasn't going to tell her that I had been because that would probably give her a stroke if she knew I had and I had turned him down.

"Did you get all your homework done?" she asked, changing the subject.

"Yes," I said. "It was a light load tonight." She just nodded. Ben was being so quiet that I had almost forgotten that he was here. "Ben," I started.

"Yes, Abby," he said as he lifted has head to look at me.

"Do you know of the Calloway Family?" I asked. I wasn't ready for his response though. Suddenly his faced changed colors, from red to blue to purple; it looked as if his heart had stop and that he wasn't breathing. He took a glance at my mom and then seemed to relax. "Are you talking about Caleb Calloway?"

"Yes," I said, weary about the next response.

"Yes, I know of the family. Why?"

"Well, he and his friends seemed to get in a lot of trouble at school and I was just wondering…"

"Have they been giving you some trouble?" he asked.

"No, not really," I lied.

"Well, Abby, it's best that you stay away from those kids. They always get into trouble and the cops have been involved more than once."

"Oh," I said. But that didn't really surprise me, I thought.

"Juvenile delinquents," Ben added under his breath, and then the food came and the subject was dropped. I ate so much food that I didn't think I was going to be able to move. Me living in this house was going to make me fat, I thought to myself. My mom looked as if she was thinking the same thing.

As I got up to leave the table, Ben looked at me and said, "Abby, please remember I what I said about Caleb and his friends; there are other people that would be better for you to hang out with. "

"No problem, Ben," I said. "I'll keep away from Caleb." I didn't add in the friend's part because nothing was going to keep me from Ethan. I headed off to get ready for bed knowing that my night sleep would be interrupted by the enviable nightmare. I slowly got ready for bed. After I got done brushing out my hair, removing any snarls, I set down the brush on the counter and then headed to the bed. I noticed a cool breeze moving through my room, as it filled the air and I shuttered. I noticed the window was cracked open. I hurried to shut it, to keep the heat in and the cold out. It made a squeak as I shut it. That's funny, I thought, I don't remember opening the window. I shrugged then shut the heavy curtains. The bed looked too irresistible to waste time staying awake and I was awfully tired. I climbed in and fell into the soft feather pillow; the pillow melted all around my head. I pulled the comforter up to my neck and tucked the blankets all around so that I was in one big cocoon. I was tired enough to sleep, and was very comfortable, but would I be able to sleep? That was the question.

I was pleasantly surprised when I woke up to the morning and realized that I had a full night sleep and no nightmare. Another positive note was the light coming from the crack in the curtain that shone directly on my bed. I almost stumbled out of bed as I tried to break free from the blanket I was swaddled in. As I grasped bother curtains and pulled them open as wide as my arms would allow I realized the sun was actually shinning. I was too happy. I didn't even want to move for fear that this was only a dream. I closed my eyes and let the sun warm my face. I felt the sun warm me from all around and I could feel my soul start to melt. I wasn't sure if this place was actually growing on me or if it was the fact that I met Ethan.

It was Ethan, I thought and then giggled. I hurried to get ready for the day, not wanting to wait for the sun to start fading away. After I had gotten ready and my teeth were as clean as they were going to get, I headed down stairs. I wasn't really that hungry so when I walked in and saw Ben and my mom at the table, I nodded at them and wished them a nice day. My mom could see that I was excited by the sunny day and she did seem to feel the need to ask any questions. I grabbed an apple out of the crystal bowl that was in the middle of the table that sparkled underneath the chandelier.

"In a hurry?" my mom said. I could see laughter behind that smile as her eyebrows raised and her grin became more pronounced. It looked like even Ben was trying to fight back the laughter.

J.L. Miller

"No not really," I said and then my face became flushed as all the blood ran to my cheeks giving me away. After I had the apple in my hands I headed out the entry, grabbed my coat and keys, and headed out for school. The sun hit my face as I jumped in my jeep. It felt wonderful. If I closed my eyes I could actually picture myself in Florida on the beach, with the sun overhead the warm breeze blowing, the sound of the ocean… And then as I opened my eyes and came back to reality. I started the jeep and off to school I went.

8 Chance Meeting

THE WEEK PAST IN A blur; before I knew it, it was Friday and the dance was just around the corner. All day long people were talking about the dance: what to wear, who they were going with, and how long they were going to stay out. It was so irritating; I tried to drown most of it out, with very little success. Hard as I tried, I just could not show the right amount of enthusiasm for the dance. I thought about calling Julie and Sarah to cancel about a dozen times, and trying to come up with some ligament excuse. The thought about cancelling was almost over whelming, but I didn't think that it would be good to cancel this short of notice especially since I was new here and I wanted to make friends and not alienate people. I kept to my word, and while I was in school I ignored Ethan. But from the corner of my eyes and the glances that I was unable to control, I had to feeling that he was glancing at me to. Anticipation curled in my stomach as the thought of Saturday rolled around. Saturday I was planning on going to the cliffs, and hopefully he would be there.

Today was one of the hardest days that I had since the day that I started in this school. My concentration was all over the place and that did little to help me. I managed to burn the cookies in Home Ec. and set the smoke alarms off. Poor Mrs. Macready had to grab the broom that was in one of the small closets that lined the room. She frantically waved the broom trying to get enough air to stop the smoke alarm while another student opened the window, letting the breeze flow through the room. She was trying to keep from laughing. And to be honest, if it was me watching this happen to someone else, I would be laughing too. As I pulled the cookies out of the oven, I groaned; they were charcoal black and hard as a rock. Now it wasn't just one student laughing; now the whole class that burst into a roar of laughter. I could feel the blood rush to my face as the embarrassment set in.

Conner, whose was the loudest of all the laughter, paused long enough to say, "Think of it this way, Abby: you can't cook, but maybe you can use them as a weapon. You can throw them at someone and it would probably kill them." And then he started laughing again.

Mrs. Macready looked very disappointed but then she began to speak. "Well," she said in her small frail voice, "it seems that I will have to make you my special project. Cooking must not be your strong suit." I wanted to say "you think," but I clenched my teeth and said nothing, not wanting to be rude. I turned my head so she couldn't see me and then I rolled my eyes. She just patted my shoulder as I dumped the burned cookies that looked like charcoal in the trash. They each made a loud thud as they hit the bottom of the aluminum trash can.

Even worse was when I had gym. We had started a section of square dancing. The boys and girl gym classes were now combined for the particular section. I groaned internally as they showed us each move and then expected us all to be able to copy it. It didn't go well at all. I managed to hit my partner in the head with one of my turns and stepped on his foot on another one. I almost felt a sense of relief as class came to a close.

As I hurried to get dressed and get out of school, I could hear some girls whispering on the other side of the lockers. I listened harder as I heard my name. It was muffled hearing it through the lockers although I could hear what they were saying.

"No, really, she turned down Adam," I heard one girl say.

"I can't believe the nerve," another one whispered.

"Who does she think she is?" I heard the one who seemed to be the leader of the group who had started the conversation say. I finished getting ready and as I rounded the corner to head for the door I saw the three girls staring at me with contempt. I just smiled, raised my head and walked out of the door. *If they want Adam, he is all theirs,* I thought to myself. Strange, the hostility that was radiating off of the three girls. I didn't even know them; I wondered why they disliked me so. *But who cares,* I thought, *it is only high school. I will just ignore them and hope they will get over there problems.*

As I headed out to my jeep I realized the parking lot was almost empty, and I was actually glad that there was no chance to run into Caleb and his followers, grateful that I didn't have to worry about hearing about the dance before I left. I would have run to escape just in case someone else happened to spot me, but I really didn't want to trip. As got into the Jeep I realized that it had gotten very cloudy and the warmth of the sun was being held prisoner by the clouds. My nice sunny day was turning into a cloudy nightmare. It was almost like an invasion, like the rain could start at any minute. I put the keys in the ignition and turned the engine over. As it roared to life, it almost made me jump. I guess my thoughts were all over the place today. I barely noticed the road as I started to head out of the city.

I did happen to notice before I made it to the highway that the city was very crowded. I noticed the line of teenage girls in the one beauty shop. *All probably getting their nails done for tomorrow,* I guessed. That was a ritual that I was not accustomed to; although I am sure my mother would have like it better if I was more into the girly fashion. As I got onto the highway, the thought of heading back to Ben's twisted my stomach. I was torn. I was always happy to escape the institution of the school; on the other hand, I was not in a hurry to get back to Ben's. And the desire to see Ethan was almost overwhelming.

As the thought of waiting to see Ethan sunk in, I slammed on my brakes, almost hitting my chest on the steering wheel before jerking back to my seat. I was only a mile from Ben's. I put the jeep in reverse, and headed out the cliffs. I wasn't sure what I was going to find, hopefully him, but I didn't want to hope all the way and then be disappointed later. The same familiar road stretched in front of me and as I grew closer to reaching my destination my breath sped and my heart thumped erratically. I started to slow, knowing the turn was coming up; as I pulled on the gravel drive, a sense of relief washed over me. I parked in the spot that I had before. A frown started to show on my face as I realized my hope of seeing Ethan was quickly dashed, when I realized his motorcycle was nowhere in sight.

Oh well, since I was already here I might as well go for a walk, I thought, not in any hurry to get back. What little light there was peeking through the clouds was starting to set behind the trees and I knew that I wasn't going to be able to put off going back to Ben's any longer. I had finally reached the logs that we had all sat on the first night around the bonfire, and to my surprise there was still smoke coming from the fire ring. *Someone must have been here last night*, I thought to myself. I took a quick look around, noticing that there were empty beer cans scattered all around and cigarette butts. *It must've been quite a party last night*, I thought, and then let out a small chuckle. It was so peaceful; I am sure that the atmosphere now was nothing like it was last night. I could just close my eyes and picture myself back home in Florida, and all the problems over the last few months with Ben and my mom seem to be a distant nightmare.

I knew I should head to Ben's but I just couldn't get my feet to move. As I stood there with my eyes closed I could heard the water. I could hear the trees rustle and feel the cool wind on my face. As I stood there, I got the feeling that I was no longer alone. My pulse quickened and my breath came rougher and it took everything in me not to turn and run. But I kept my composure as I slowly turned to confirm my suspicion. He was tall, dark, and handsome with the beautiful ice blue eyes. And then all the tension washed out of my body and my rigid pose relaxed.

"Ethan," I whispered.

"Abby," he whispered. And the fact that it was getting dark, didn't matter. The fact that my mother and Ben would be looking for me didn't matter. All that mattered was that Ethan and I were together.

"I didn't think you would be here."

He chuckled. "I sort of followed you," he said with a wicked grin. I guess most people would care that some guy was following them but I only felt relieved.

I couldn't help but ask, even knowing the answer before I did, "Are you going to the dance tomorrow?"

He just smiled and shook his head and the small hope that I was holding onto was completely crushed. "Oh," I said, trying not to show how disappointed I was. But I must not been doing a very convincing job because he smiled and let out a laugh. I could feel the blood rush up to my face.

"What's wrong?" he asked as his expression changed from a smile to a grimace.

"Nothing," I replied.

He wasn't buying it. "Abby," he said in deeper voice. And then he took a step so that he was right in front of me; he reached his hand up to brush the hair out of my face. His hand was so warm it sent vibrations all through me. I closed my eyes. I don't know why I reacted that way every time he touched me but I never wanted the feeling to stop.

"I was just hoping that you had changed your mind about things," I confessed. He kept his smile in place and slowly moved a little closer.

"You don't know how much I would love to go to the dance with you-"

"But," I said, interrupting.

"No buts, Abby," he said. "Just trying to keep you safe." I could see the sincerity when I looked into his eyes and I knew he truly believed that. But I was annoyed and when I was annoyed I tended to lash out.

"You mean keep me in the dark, don't you?"

He just smiled, an apology on his face. "I am sorry about that," he said.

"Well," I said, "why you don't tell me about the stories that I have heard about?" I hissed, not wanting to be polite because he wouldn't tell me what was really going on.

"Stories?" he said, and then lifted one eyebrow.

"Yeah, the stories," I hissed again.

"Abby, I have no Idea what you are talking about," he said, but from the look on his face, he knew that I knew that he was keeping things from me.

"Do you remember the night at the bonfire?" I said.

"Sure I do," he said.

"Well, Conner was telling me some of the local stories about Ben's family and you and your friends."

"Oh, was anything interesting?" he said, detached.

"Well, I have already guessed that you don't like Ben or his family."

"No, we don't," he said, his tone grave. "But, Abby, that doesn't have anything to do with you."

"Well," I said, "I have a feeling that Caleb and your other friends don't see it the same way as you do."

"Abigail," he said, almost sounding mad, "if you haven't realized, I am not Caleb or the other guys, and I make up my own mind about things."

"So will you tell me why?" I asked.

"Why what?" he asked looking confused.

"Well, why don't you like Ben," I hedged.

"Abby, around these parts people don't forget things, and if things happen and it hurts someone they are not forgotten."

"But you are not going to elaborate on it, are you?" I said, trying to keep composure in my voice. He lifted his hand to run his fingers through his hair, seeming a little uncomfortable in the way our conversation was going. "Ethan, you are going to find out I am just as stubborn as you are."

"Abby, I wish you would leave it alone," he said, and his eyes burned with sincerity. "It's getting dark; I think you should be heading home."

I knew he was just trying to change the subject but I wasn't ready; I had waited all week to talk to Ethan and he wasn't going to evade my questions any longer. "Well if you not going to answer my questions," I said in a rush, "Then I will go and ask Ben."

His expression went from concern to anger in less than a second. "Abby," he started, "It's better if you don't tell Moore that you are talking to me."

"Why?" I asked.

"Well, you know that thing about our families holding grudges," he said.

"Yes," I said. "I remember."

"Well, there are things between the Moores and the rest of the people here," he added.

"And you aren't going to elaborate, Ethan, are you?"

"No," he said in a grim voice.

"So, the stories are true."

"Well, since I don't exactly know what Conner told you, I can't say yes or no."

"Honestly, Ethan, I am sick of the games."

"Abby, I not playing any games," he said and I knew the secrets were only out of concern, but I wasn't going to give up that easy. I thought, *it's not like I am going anywhere; I have two years before I can leave this godforsaken place. That should be enough time for me to learn everything I need to know about Ethan.*

"What are you thinking about so closely?" He asked.

"Alright, Ethan I will leave it," and then quickly added "for now." I think I heard him sigh but I don't know for sure because I wasn't looking at him; I was staring into the forest. There was only a faint light from overhead and most of the forest was dark now.

Ethan lifted his hands to make me look at him. "Abby, promise me that you will let it go."

"I am sorry, Ethan, I can't promise you that, but I will let it go for now." His hands were so warm and I hadn't realized that I was cold until that moment. A shiver ran down through my body. He pulled his hands away,

"Abby, I will walk you to your car," he said. He seemed somewhat hesitant when he said that which made me smile in returned. Again I saw no bike as we strolled up the path and made it to my jeep. I fumbled in my pocket to get my keys.

"Ethan…" I paused.

"Yes, Abby?"

"Um…where is your bike?"

"Don't worry about that."

"Well, do you need a ride somewhere?" I couldn't even fathom how he got out here, and the thought of him having to walk somewhere in the dark with the threat of rain sent butterflies to my stomach.

He surprised me when he laughed. "Abby," he said, then chuckled again, "I am a big boy. I got out here; I can get home just fine."

"Is that another one of those things you aren't going to tell me about?"

He just smiled his wicked grin and my heart stopped. It took me a moment to catch my breath and for my heart to start again.

"I will see you later," he said in his deep, angelic voice.

"Later," I replied. He smiled again. I got into my jeep and was about to shut the door when Ethan caught the door with his hand. I was a little shocked; I hadn't been expecting that.

"Sleep tight," he said with his eyes smoldering. I couldn't say anything, I was too dazed, and before I knew it he was shutting the door. I put my keys in the ignition and turned. It hesitated, and then the jeep started with thunderous roar and I put it into drive while staring into my rear view mirror. The last thing I saw was Ethan's angelic face smiling at me as I drove away. As I turned out to the highway and hit the accelerator, millions upon millions of thought were running through my head.

Ethan had not budged one inch and now I had more questions than I had before. Asking Ben was clearly out of the question, and trying to ask Ethan wasn't helping. *For a small city this place sure has a lot of secrets*, I thought. I knew when I got to Ben's my mom would want an account of where I had been so I tried to come up with something that my mom would actually believe. Lying wasn't one of my many talents so I would have to rehearse it. As I pulled through the iron gates I realized that there were actually lots of people working in the fields and I notice barrels that were smoking. I had never seen anything like it. I slowly drove up the lane in fear that one of them would walk in front of the jeep. I parked in my usual spot and got out. I walked up the door, and already irritation was hitting me. I knew the minute I reached for the handle the crazy butler would open the door so when I reached the door, I paused, not even reaching for the handle.

Sure enough, I didn't have time to take a breath and the door was already open.

"Welcome home, miss," he said, and then all of a sudden his face changed like he smelled something bad. I didn't even take stock in it; nothing that butler ever did surprised me.

I heard a noise coming from one of the rooms down the long hall from the dining rooms, one of the rooms that I hadn't yet explored. Then I heard my mom laughing and Ben coughing. I quickly hurried down the hall to see what was going on, only to find my mom standing in the doorway with her pretty hot pick nails and hands covering her mouth. Again she laughed.

"I can't believe that we let this room get this bad," Ben said, and then he was laughing.

"Mom," I said, a little bit hesitant.

"Hi, Abby, welcome home," she said with huge grin on her face. I was starting to worry that she was having a stroke, the way her face was frozen like that. "I told Ben how much you like to read," she started to say, "and Ben told me that we had a library here in the manor and he thought you would like it."

"Oh," I said, a little stunned.

I could see now what Ben was doing. Most of the furniture was covered with white blankets. And the few that Ben had already taken off had the whole room almost filled with dust. His hands were also covering his mouth; no doubt he was trying to breathe. I let a small giggle out and my mom eyed me. That look from her conveyed her disapproval at me for laughing at Ben, especially since he was trying to do something nice for me.

"Sorry," I whispered, not loud enough for Ben to hear but my mother seemed to hear it.

"Here's the deal, Abby," Ben began to speak. "If you clean this room and take care of it, then the whole library is yours." My jaw dropped; I couldn't believe it. My mom raised her hand and lifted my jaw. Ben and she laughed in harmony.

"You are giving me a library?" I asked, stunned.

"Not giving it to you," Ben answered. "I am letting you borrow it as long as you live here." And then he reached into his pocket and pulled out an old skeleton key, and he said, "Here is the key for the room, Abby. But remember what I said; you have to clean it and organize it and I don't want any of this mess trickling into the rest of the house."

"No problem," I said. I held my hand out for the key and he dropped it into my palm.

"Well, we will let you get started then. Good luck, Abby," Ben said, and my mom laughed.

"I think she is going to need it." But I ignored that last jab; my concentration was solely on the huge room full of books. "See you in about a half an hour, Abby, for dinner," my mom reminded me.

"No problem," I said. And as soon as they were out the door and down the hall I shut the door and locked it. I leaned against the door with my eyes closed just for a minute. Just enough time to get over the shock. When I opened my eyes, I had never seen anything more glorious; besides Ethan, of course. There were thousands and thousands of books. As I walked by the book cases and my fingers tips moved gently against the biding, I sighed. I had never been more content than I was right now. Since even before we moved to this house.

It wasn't just one floor of books that amazed me. The room was tall with two floors and a metal spiral staircase that went up the second floor. In the middle of the room's back wall was a beautiful stone fire place that looked as if it hadn't been used in years. As soon as the 'Ah' factor was over, I really looked. It was really quite dirty. It looked like this room hadn't been touched in hundreds of years. It was going to take a long time to get this place presentable, which was good. This would keep my mind busy and off of Ethan and the mystery surrounding him, his friends, and Ben's family. I went to open the huge drapes that hung over the massive windows.

As I grabbed both ends of the black heavy curtains and yanked them open, all the centuries of dust covered me. I felt like I was in the ocean underwater with no breath left. I hurried to open the frail-looking antique windows. They made a creak of protested from being opened. I worried for a moment that they were going to break and was pleasantly relieved when they were opened and the cool fresh air was blowing through the room. I turned around to take stock. This room was going to take a long time to get cleaned up, I thought. But I like a challenge, I thought.

The first thing I did, leaving the windows open of coarse so I didn't suffocate, was to remove the rest of white sheets there were blanketing the room. After they were all removed and all the sheets were in a pile, I had to stick my head out the window for some fresh air. Who knew that when I said that I would clean this room it would be so much work and I had only just started, I thought and the let out a sigh. I felt comforted though, the fact that this room was all mine and I can lock myself in this room for hours and shut out the whole world.

After a while though I realized it was getting quite late, and my mom had asked me not be late for dinner. So I headed out the huge antique doors, stopping to lock them, and then headed to the bathroom on the first floor. I walked into the bathroom pausing to lock the door so no one would walk in on me, and then I turned to survey the damage. My eyes widened and my jaw dropped as I took in my reflection. I was covered in dirt from my hair to my feet. I quickly raised my hand to my hair to shake out what I could of the dust and dirt, then I opened one of the drawers to the cabinet under the sink and pulled out a dark blue washcloth. I turned on the sink and completely soaked it as I stared at my reflection and groaned. I took the washrag and slowly began to wipe all the day's dirt off of my face, rinsing out the rag a few times because my face was so dirty. After I was as clean as I was going to get I shut off the water. I opened the door and of course the door squeaked. I was getting used to that though and it wasn't making me jump as much as it did before.

When I walked into the dining room my mom and Ben where already seated, with the table completely full of food.

"Nice of you to join us," my mom said in an irritated voice.

"Sorry, mom," I said. "I lost track of the time."

"So you like your gift?" Ben said with a smile.

I wasn't used to telling Ben thanks. After all, this was the man who single-handedly wrecked my life, but this gift was over the top and I was truly thankful. "Yes," I said. "Thanks Ben; I really love it," I said with as much gratitude I was capable of.

"Well, I am glad you like it, Abby," he said with a smile. I could tell that it made him feel pretty good to do something for me that I actually liked. The move here hadn't really warmed me up to him and I got the impression that he thought things were changing, even know I knew he was dead wrong. But if he wanted to look at it that way, who was I to tell him different?

"So how far did you get?" my mother said, eyeing me with speculation. I am sure that I didn't t look too pretty, and she looked as if she was holding back a laugh.

"I didn't get too much done but I have the whole weekend to work at it," I said and then reached for the bowl of spaghetti in the middle of the table. As I scooped a heaping spoonful onto my plate, my mother started to talk again.

"Abby, aren't you supposed to go to the dance tomorrow?"

"Oh shoot," I said picking up my fork to take the first bite. I slowly chewed thinking of a response to that. "I forgot."

"You forgot?" my mom asked. "Abby, do you even know what you are going to wear to the dance?"

I paused for a minute, staring down at my food, not wanting to meet my mother's eyes. If I told her the truth, that I didn't have anything to wear, she would insist on going shopping tonight, right this minute, and I hate to shop. I hate it with a passion, a bunch of rich pricks, stopping in front of you right in the middle of the aisle. Most people have road rage... I have shopping rage. If she hadn't been looking at me so intensely, I probably would have laughed.

"Mom, don't worry. I have a dress that I can wear," I said in my most convincing tone, and I looked up to meet her glance. She didn't look like she was buying it, but it didn't look like she was going to press it, which I was truly grateful for. I finished the last bite of spaghetti and then chugged down my glass of milk.

"Wow, Abby," my mom noticed, "why you are in such a hurry tonight?"

"I want to get some sleep," I said, being honest. "I haven't been sleeping too well." As if she couldn't already tell from the dark circles under my eyes.

"Oh I am sorry; I know that this move has been somewhat of an adjustment. It will get better." Again she sounded like she was giving herself more of a pep talk than me.

"It's fine, Mom; I will get some sleep tonight and be right as rain tomorrow." She nodded in an agreement. "'Night Mom; 'night Ben," I said as I got up from the table.

"'Night, Abby," my mom said and Ben said, "Sleep well."

"Thanks again for the library, Ben; I really do love it."

"You're welcome," was his reply.

As I headed up the massive staircase, I found myself slowly dragging myself up it. I really was quite tired, holding onto the railing for support, so that I wouldn't plummet down them; although the thought of getting a concussion was appealing, to get out of the dance. I sighed as I finally reached the second floor landing and shuffled down the hall to my room. The first thing I did was head to the shower; I had centuries of dust and dirt all over me and I was relieved to get them all washed off. The water was so relaxing, loosening up my too tight muscles. I didn't even want to get out, but it was inevitable; the hot water couldn't last forever. I shut the water off and wrapped the towel around me, until it was nice and secure. Then I bent over to pick up the clothes that were on the floor. Remembering that the key to the library was still in the pocket of my jeans, I reached in to retrieve it and then tossed my dirty clothes in the hamper by the closet. I set the key on the counter and then grabbed my night clothes.

After I was dressed I took my time brushing my teeth and then brushing out all the snarls out of my hair. When I was done, I grabbed the key off the granite counter top and headed to the dresser. I was glad that the movers had finally managed to get the rest of our stuff here. I looked on my dresser; my wooden jewelry box was sitting on there. My mom must've known that I would want that. It seemed like that was the only thing of mine unpacked. I noticed in the corner of the room the desk with the rest of my boxes. I must have been so preoccupied when I walked through the door that I didn't notice. I walked over to the dresser and opened my jewelry box. It wasn't anything special. Just a oak little box, with some writing on it that my mother had told me it was French and I had no Idea what it said. It was one of the few things that my dad had left me with. As I lifted the lid the same sweet melody that I had heard many times before started to play. And as silly as it sounds, it made me feel somewhat better, having some familiar things of mine in this huge museum.

I placed the key inside the box for safe-keeping, and then shut the lid, silencing the sweet music. I set the box back on my dresser and then pulled back the covers and jumped into bed. I was too tired to even fight sleep. As I fell back into the pillow praying to have a dreamless sleep, my thoughts once again turned to Ethan.

9 The Gift

MY EYES FLEW OPEN AND a shiver ran down my body. I quickly sat up, trying to get my heart to return to its normal rate. It was the same eerie nightmare. *What is wrong with me*, I thought. Before we moved here I had never had nightmares. *There must be something psychologically wrong with me*, I thought. As I looked at the bed I noticed that the sheets were all over the place and some of the pillows that were always on the bed were on the floor. *I must have tossed all night*, I thought, and was grateful for not falling out of bed and onto the floor. I turned to the alarm clock; it was nearly ten o'clock. *You have got to be kidding*, I thought. *I can't believe I slept that long, and of course, missed breakfast. Great*, I thought, missing the old days where I could just go in to the kitchen and make a bowl of cereal. I was surprised that my mom had let me sleep that late. *She's probably out*, I thought.

I got out of bed, picked up the pillows, and straightened my sheets. I never had to make my bed in the old house, but this wasn't really my house and I felt al little bit rude just leaving it like that. After it was done I went to the closet and grabbed a pair of old jeans and old t-shirt. If I was going to get dirty today it wasn't going to be in my good clothes. After I was semi-presentable I grabbed the key out of my jewelry box and head down stairs, almost running over the creepy butler as I rounded the corner for the steps.

"Oh, sorry," I said, a little embarrassed; he just eyed me as I headed down the steps.

I spent most of the day cleaning the dust off the bookshelves. Ben must've figured that I would need cleaning stuff because a little while after I started, Albert brought in a bucket of water, wash rags, Lysol, and some dusting spray. I said, "Thanks," as he set it down and eyed me. For some reason the frozen face that had never really change looked angry, like he didn't want me in here. As he turned and walked away I could have sworn he said something under his breath a little too low for me to hear. After he was out of sight, I just shrugged it off, chalking it up to the fact he was old and grumpy and unhappy with how his life turned out. Although once he was out the door I decided to shut it and lock it. Being watched over as I cleaned was not an option.

The air in here was not as heavy as it had been; leaving the window open had been a good idea. I did notice however the light was starting to dim from the window, and wondered what time it was. It was then a knock came from the door.

"Abby," my mom said. "You had better get ready! You don't want to be late for the dance."

"Coming," I said and then dropped the wash rag in the bucket. As it hit the water and made a splash some water droplets managed to splash from the bucket unto the floor. I ignored it and headed for the door to unlock it. My mom was standing there with a smile on her face. I knew that she was happy about me going to the dance. She was forever trying to get me to do girly things.

God bless my mom; she had a sandwich in her hands. "Abby, I know you didn't get breakfast, and that you have been working all day in here. I thought you could use something to eat."

"Thanks, mom," I said with gratitude as she handed me the sandwich. "How did you get the cook to make me a sandwich? Did you have to give her your liver?" I said with a laugh.

"Abby..." she said with a frown. "Catherine is really not that bad."

"Oh come on, mom! She could be the host of Hell's Kitchen." And then I let out another laugh. My mom tried to keep the frown on her face but a small giggle managed to get out.

"Abby," she said, changing the subject. "You better get ready; you don't want to be later. What time are the girls picking you up?"

"At seven, the dance starts at eight," I said.

"Well you better get cleaned up; it's five thirty."

As I headed back up to my room, I managed to finish the sandwich right before I hit the bedroom door. I got in the shower and managed to get all the dirt off, washing in a hurry. I knew that I had no time to dawdle and I had no idea what I was going to wear, what I was going to do with my hair, or how I was going to wear my makeup. I stood there in the middle of my bathroom with the towel securely around me, frozen. The urge to call Julie and Sarah and cancel flared again. *Deep breaths*, I thought. A knock at the bathroom door almost sent me into convulsions.

"Abby," my mother said, "can I come in?"

"Just a minute," I said as I hurried to put a shirt and shorts on. When I was done I said, "Okay mom, I am decent."

She slowly opened the door and then my jaw dropped. My mom was standing in the doorway wearing a dress that flowed to the floor. It had a v-neck and two straps that fastened in back of her neck. It was black, and it looked like it had millions of diamonds woven into the dress. Her hair was beautifully piled on top of her head.

"Wow!" I said with enthusiasm. "You look wonderful," I said after I caught my breath.

"You like it?" she said. "I got it on our trip to Las Vegas; Ben bought it for me." She was glowing. Why did my mom have to look so much better? I couldn't see where I got my looks from because it obviously wasn't from my mother.

"Ben's taking me to out tonight," she said and grinned again. "I wanted to see if you wanted help getting ready."

I knew it would make my mom happy, and truthfully, since I wasn't into fashion, I probably could use the help. Okay, no probably about it - I needed the help. "Sure mom," I said. "That would be great." And that was all it took.

She grabbed the comb and the clips and curling iron; in no time it was done, my hair, that is. Then she moved to my face. I couldn't see what she was doing because she had my back to the mirror. She had said that I would ruin the effect if I looked before she was done. I just sighed and let her work.

I don't know how long she spent fixing my face, as she would call it. But all of a sudden the deep concentration lines on her forehead faded and she said, "Done; you are perfect."

"Yeah, right," I said back and then I turned to face the mirror. "Wow, mom," I said in admiration.

"I know," she said. "You turned out quite well."

My hair was pulled up to a crown on the top of my head with browns curls that trickled down my back like a waterfall. And the makeup was very subtle, nice earth tones with a hint of pink. It took me a minute to get a hold of myself.

"Where's the dress you are going to be wearing?"

"In the closet," I said. She reached into the closet and pulled one of my only dresses out; she gasped in horror.

"Abigail," she said using my whole first name. "No daughter of mine is going out wearing that," she said hissing the words. She almost looked mad. But then after a minute of frowning she turned to me with huge grin.

"What?" I asked and then she stepped out of the bathroom and was back in the same second, holding a garment bag.

"I know you hate to shop, honey," she said, still smiling, "so I took the liberty of doing it for you." She unzipped the white garment bag and pulled out a baby pick gown that was long and beautiful. It had spaghetti straps, and the bodice glittered like millions of diamonds. I had never seen anything like it. I am not a huge touchy-feely type of person, but my mom deserved a hug for this one.

"Mom," I said as I gave her a hug, "it's perfect."

"I am glad you like it," she said, the grin still spread across her face. "I thought you would be angry at me," she said with relief in her voice.

"Why?" I asked, puzzled.

"Well, frankly," she said, "every time I buy something it usually ends up in the closet collecting dust. I knew she was thinking about all the thousands of clothes that she had bought be that were in my closet in the old house. Thankfully those clothes were still packed away in the boxes; some of the price tags were even still on them.

"No, Mom. It's great, really." And I was grateful. Now I didn't have to be in the frumpy old dress that I had.

"Well, I will let you get dressed. The shoes that match this dress are on your bed."

"Thanks again, Mom."

"No problem," she said, the smile still on her face. "You better hurry," she said. "Julie and Sarah should be here anytime."

I sighed and said, "I know."

"Abby, I know that you hate dances, but try to have a good time. You might find that you will actually enjoy yourself."

From your lips to God's ears, I thought, and laughed. She raised one eyebrow.

"What's so funny?" she asked.

"Nothing, Mom. I am sure you are right."

"See you down stairs," she said and then shut the door.

After I was sure that I heard the thud of the bedroom door shut, I carefully slipped into my dress. After all the time that my mom had spent on my hair, I didn't want to mess it up. After I had successfully slipped into the dress I took a deep breath and then slowly pivoted around to look in the mirror. My first reaction was shock. I didn't recognize the girl in the mirror. I wasn't used to being dressed up. My mom had done an excellent job, but I wasn't going to tell her that.

After I finished gawking in the mirror I composed myself and headed out to the bed to grab the shoes. "Thank God," I said in whisper, "flats." I sighed; my mom had been thankfully thinking of me. They were the exact shade and color as the dress; secretly I wondered how my mom had pulled that off and then I decided that I probably didn't want to know. I noticed that my mom had gotten me a pair of sheer panty hose. I wanted to grumble about this one. I was sure that a man must have come up with panty hose, because no smart women would have come up with something so uncomfortable. Almost like thongs and stilettos, a man must have created those also to torture us.

After I had gotten the panty hose on that my mom had gotten for me, I placed the shoes on my feet. I was sure that by the end of the night my feet would be killing me and I would have plenty of blisters to count in the morning. But how many stories have I heard where the characters say, "beauty is pain." Just then I heard the door bell ring and I hurried out of my bedroom, knocking my elbow on the door as I went.

"Ouch," I said out loud, "that one is going to leave mark." As I hit the step, still rubbing my arm, I noticed Julie and Sarah at the bottom of the stairs. Julie's hair was left down; she wore a blue strapless dress that went to the floor. Sarah wore a short black number with a low 'v' neck and short sleeves.

"Wow!" I exclaimed as I made to the bottom of the steps. "You guys look great!"

"Abby, you look great," Julie said and from the look of Sarah nodding, she must have agreed. Relief flowed through me, and I didn't feel as nervous as I had earlier. I was grateful that Sarah and Julie both thought I looked good, that way I could walk onto the dance without feeling like a complete moron.

"Wait you guys," I heard my mom call down the hall. As she rounded the corner I noticed she had an expensive-looking camera in her hands. I raised one eyebrow at my mom.

"Ben?" I said. My mom just smiled at me and nodded.

"Abby, it's your first dance!" she exclaimed. "We need to document the occasion."

I just sighed. *If this makes my mom happy, then so be it*, I thought grudgingly to myself.

"Stand together, girls," she said impatiently. We all hurried to assume the position, not wanting to anger the lady with the camera. I got the impression that Julie and Sarah had been through this plenty of times because they didn't even grumble like I did.

"Say cheese," my mother said an octave higher. I guess her voiced change because of all the excitement of the night.

"Rebecca," I heard Ben say as he came down the hall, "we should get going. We don't want to be late for our reservations."

"You're right," she said. "I'm ready whenever you are," she added and then turned to me. As Ben came into view, I realized that Julie and Sarah's mouths were open. I tried to step out of the box and look at him from their point of view. Truly Ben was nice looking and the fact that he was dressed up in a suit also helped that fact.

"Well, Abby," he said as he helped my mom put on her coat, "you look very nice tonight."

"Thanks," I mumbled and then flushed with embarrassment.

"Have fun tonight," again Mom said and then kissed me on the cheek, and then quickly added, "Don't stay out too late."

"Don't worry, Mom, the dance should only be a couple hours," I said trying to comfort her. She nodded and she and Ben were out the door.

"Well," I said, "are you guys ready?"

"Um, sure," Sarah said, picking her jaw up off the floor. "Let's go," she added. As we piled into the car Julie offered to sit in back so that I could have the front seat with Sarah.

"Oh, my God," Sarah said as she reached to put her seat belt on and start the car at the same time. "Was that your step-dad?" she asked in shock.

"Yeah," I said a little confused.

"He is so hot," she added. Julie, who had been pretty quiet since they got to Ben's house, added, "You are so lucky."

I really didn't get it, although I couldn't look at it objectively, since this was the guy who dragged my mom and me across the country, to a place where you never saw the sun.

As we headed to town, Julie and Sarah kept up a consistent conversation about all the boys who would be at the dance. A couple times they had asked me if there was anyone that I wanted to dance with. I just said 'no' and told them that none of the boys that will be at the dance tonight are my type. They looked appeased by that answer and they didn't press it. When we pulled up to the school the parking lot was quite full.

"Wow!" I exclaimed.

Julie and Sarah giggled. "There really isn't a whole lot to do around here, so when a dance comes up everyone comes."

"I believe that," I said back.

10 The Dance

As Sarah, Julie and I walked into the gymnasium I almost laughed. *Unbelievable*, I thought. The whole gym was covered in streamers and balloons and crêpe paper. I don't even think there was one wall that didn't have something on it. It was very crowded. I think everyone who was in the high school was here. The teachers, who I guessed were the chaperones, were surrounding the outside of the gym floor. Strobe lights were bouncing off the large windows surrounding the gym. There was a DJ who was centered in the front of the gym on a small platform and the music was blaring from there, vibrating the soles of our feet. Everyone was dressed as if this dance was prom and not just another regular dance.

"Well, what you think?" Sarah asked.

"Wow," I said, "it sure is something, isn't it?"

"Yeah, Julie said. "We tend to get a little carried away.

"I'll say," was the only thing I could say. Just then a group of boys sauntered over in our direction, Conner leading the pack. I almost laughed at the fact that boys never seemed to able to approach a girl on their own, that they need moral support from their friends.

"Hey," Conner said to Sarah, "do you want to dance?"

"Sure," she said and flushed bright red. Sarah turned to us with a huge smile. "See you guys later; have fun," she quickly added and then winked.

Another guy named Gage – I believe that was what his name was, although having never really talked to him before, I wasn't sure – asked Julie if she wanted to dance. She looked eager, but then she looked at me.

"Go ahead, have fun. We'll talk later..."

Julie smiled and headed out to the dance floor. As for me, I said no to the first couple of boys who had asked me, and then quickly hid in a dark corner of the gym praying that I wouldn't be noticed. My plan was quickly cancelled when I noticed Adam, to my dismay, heading in my direction. I groaned.

"Hey, Abby," he said when he reached me.

"Hey, Adam," I replied trying to keep the uncomfortable tone out of my voice. I wanted to run away screaming but I managed to keep my composure. I did however notice a group a girls eyeing me, and then I realized that it was the same girls from the locker room.

"Abby, do you want to dance?" he asked sounding hopeful.

"I think I am good, but thank for asking," was my genius response. He laughed.

"Abby, I don't bite. It's just one dance; I promise that I won't step on your toes."

That wasn't even close to what I was worrying about, I thought. "I am more afraid I might step on yours," I said back and then laughed.

"Well you never know if you don't try," he said grabbing my hand, leading me out to the dance floor, and when I protested he just grip my hand tighter. As we reached the middle of the dance floor, to my horror, we assumed the normal slow dance position. I felt a little uncomfortable as he very carefully put his hands on my waist. I set my hands on his shoulders. I knew that most girls would put their arms around his neck, but I wanted a semi-safe position so I could keep an eye on my feet.

"Abby," Adam started, "you look great tonight."

"Thanks," I said and then looked down. Not in embarrassment, like he probably thought, but just to keep tabs on my feet.

"How do you like Klamath Falls," he asked.

"It's fine," I lied. To my surprise he laughed.

"Abby," he said, "you aren't that hard to read. You don't like it much here, do you?"

Honesty seemed to be the best answer in this instance. "No, not really," I said back.

"Yeah," he agreed, "it must be quite an adjustment."

"You have no idea," I mumbled under my breath.

"Ouch," Adam suddenly said as I missed a beat and crushed his foot.

"Oh my God, are you okay?" I said in horror. "I told you that I wasn't a good dancer."

He just laughed, determined to shake it off. I was grateful when a new song started, and I excused myself. He told me to save him another dance; I just laughed and said that I was going to wait until he had insurance on his feet. Adam was still laughing as I walked away. I took the moment, where no one was looking for me or at me, to sneak out the back door of the gym for some fresh air. I escaped outside and really took in the fresh air; I was pleasantly relieved to have snuck out without anyone following. As I stared out to the trees behind the school, I was in shock when I felt as if I wasn't alone. I turned to see who was there.

"Abby," Ethan said. He was like a ghost; I hadn't even heard him walk up.

"Ethan," I said, a smiled stretching across my face. I noticed that he wasn't wearing his normal white t-shirt and jeans. He was dressed in black buttoned down short sleeved shirt. His hair was smoothed back.

"Wow!" Ethan exclaimed. "You look amazing!" And then he walked up to put his warm hand against my face.

"Thanks," I said. "You don't look too bad yourself," I said, blushing. "I didn't think I would see you here, Ethan."

"Well, Abby, I was hoping I would see you tonight and that you would have saved me a dance."

"Ethan, it may be safer for your toes if we don't dance," I said with a nervous laugh.

"It's alright Abby, I like danger. I think I will take my chances," he said then pulled me a little closer. My heart stopped; it took minute for it to start again and for me to find my lungs and start breathing again. A new song began to play; the music was so loud that we could hear it perfectly outside. He pulled me closer so our chests were pressed together. Heat radiated from his body and completely engulfed me. I tried to put my arms around his neck but he was just too tall, so instead I laid them against his chest, and then I laid my head against his chest. I heard him sigh and then he laid he face against my hair. We swayed carefully from side to side, and of course I was silently praying that I wouldn't step on his feet.

"Thank you," I said in gratitude.

"For what?" he said and I could feel his hot breath in my hair. It sent electricity all through my body.

"For coming tonight, for making this night better by being here," I mumbled into his chest. I could feel his chest rattle with laughter.

"Do you really think that I would miss a night with you?"

I kept my head against his chest, totally content. It wasn't long before I noticed that the song had ended and a new song that was more of a fast type of song played. We weren't dancing anymore. I looked up at him, and he was staring down at me, with the beautiful penetrating ice blue eyes. He held me closer, and then leaned down to press his lips against mine. They were soft and warm and I could taste the sweetness of his breath as his mouth moved with mine.

Out of nowhere I heard a howl coming from the trees. All too soon, Ethan ended the kiss.

"Abby," he said in his breathless voice, "you need to go inside."

"What?" I asked in daze, not comprehending.

"Go inside," he said more urgently, and then added, "Please, trust me."

I believed the truth in his eyes. "Ethan, when will I see you again?"

"Soon," he answered. "Now go."

"When?" I asked more impatiently.

"Tomorrow, at the cliffs at ten a.m.," he said and then added, "Now get inside and join your friends."

I started to walk towards the door, taking one last look; he hadn't moved. It was like he was frozen, his eyes intent on me.

"Tomorrow," I whispered and walked through the gym door. When I walked back into the gym, and of course back to reality, it was like I hadn't even been missing. I saw Sarah dancing with Conner still, and Julie still dancing with Gage. I felt so robbed; Ethan had come to the dance and I only had gotten one really good dance. Although, for a first kiss, that was unbelievable.

I had never dated In Florida. Most of the guys seemed somewhat immature, like their brains hadn't caught up with the rest of their bodies' development. From what I have seen it doesn't get better until way later in life. But Ethan, well, he was different. Grown-up, somehow.

I turned to head to the back of the gym and hide in the shadows until the night was over, but my hopes where soon dashed when the music stopped abruptly and a new song with beat starting playing. Julie and Sarah pulled me onto the dance floor even with my protests. I didn't have time to feel annoyed; the music was playing and people from all around where stomping to the beat. It sounded almost like a stampede of a herd of elephants. I was very surprised when I caught myself actually laughing and having a good time pretending to know what I was doing. Although Sarah and Julie's expressions told me that I must not have been doing a very good job. For the rest of the evening I danced with Julie and Sarah. My guess is that most of the boys had caught the drift that I couldn't dance, and they decided to keep a safe distant to protect their feet, which I was truly grateful for. Although I did catch Adam quite a few times looking in my direction, and then the three nasty girls from my gym class would eye Adam and then look back at me with an evil eye. I wasn't that shocked that girls were capable of this hostility; I was shocked that they directed it at me, not really knowing me that well.

When the dance was finally done, Sarah, Julie and I headed out. As we got into the car the girls just went on and on about the boys they had danced with. I didn't say anything; the most fun that I had at the dance was when I was with Ethan, and I wasn't able to talk about that.

Sarah had dropped off Julie first. Julie lived in town only a few blocks away from the school. As Julie started to get out of the car she turned around. "Thanks for coming with us, Abby. I had a really good time."

"No problem," I said with huge smile on my face. "I guess dancing isn't really that bad, is it?"

"No, not bad," she said smiling and then got out and shut the car door. We pulled away once she was safely at her door. With one final wave she headed into her house. I waved back hoping she saw it.

"So..." Sarah said.

"So..." I repeated back not sure where she was leading our conversation to.

"So...where did you sneak off to during the dance?" she said with the sound of implications in her voice. I groaned internally; so she had seen me.

"What do you mean?" I asked, already knowing what she was talking about but playing dumb.

"Abby," she giggled, "I saw you sneak out after you crushed poor Adam's toes." She laughed again.

I winced. "You saw me step on Adam's feet?"

She laughed louder this time. "Abby I don't think anyone could have missed that one. His protest was quite loud, even over the music."

I winced again. I knew that was going to be the downfall of my nonexistent social life.

"Don't worry about Adam; he is a jock. They're not good at remembering things. I think it comes from all the blows to the head in football practice." She was still laughing. I slumped down lower in my seat staring out the window. We were almost out to Ben's. When she noticed that I wasn't laughing she said, "Sorry, Abby; I couldn't help it. It was funny."

"It's fine," I replied. "If it was someone else I am sure that I would have been laughing too."

"So you never answered my question."

"Which one was that?" I said faking ignorance.

"Where did you take off to?"

"I just went out to get some fresh air."

"Abby, it's freezing out tonight. You didn't have your jacket and you were gone quite a while, and you're telling me that you just went out for fresh air?" She didn't seem like she was buying it, but I promised Ethan that I wouldn't tell about him and me.

"That's right, and really it's not that cold," I lied. Although I was truthfully not cold, when I was wrapped tightly in Ethan's arms, I thought.

"Well," she said and then paused. She seemed to know that I she wasn't going to give out anymore information tonight. "Did you have fun tonight?" She finally finished her sentence.

"It was a blast." I tried to fake enthusiasm. *I did have fun, even if the dancing was a pain*, I thought. I quickly changed the subject to her so she would quit asking questions that I wasn't at liberty to answer. "So did you have fun with Conner, I asked.

"Oh my God," she started and I realized that I had just opened the flood-gates. So I sat more comfortable in my seat and let her start.

"It was so amazing Abby, Conner is such a good dancer, and I was hoping that he was going to ask me out or something," and then her face fell ever so slightly, "but he didn't."

"Sarah, I am sure he will," I said to comfort her and then added, "Guys get nervous; I bet he had a good time."

"I hope so," she said in a whisper.

"I am sure of it." It was then I realized that we had pulled into the drive. As Sarah drove up the long drive she must have noticed the tension.

"Abby"

"Yes, Sarah?"

"Can I ask you a question?"

"Sure, Sarah. Go ahead."

"You don't like living here, do you?"

"In Klamath Falls, or at the manor?" I asked.

She pulled up under the overhang to the house so that I was just a few feet from the door. "The manor," she replied.

"The truth?" I asked.

"Of course, Abby."

"Sarah, from the day that I moved into this place, I have had an odd feeling, like something's not right."

"Why do you think that?" She asked

"Lots of reasons. For one, they have a lot of strange rules about not going out a night, and no messes; and for another, it's like this house is frozen in time. It's like a museum. I have to watch myself every minute so I don't accidently knock over one of their priceless vases or something."

She laughed and said, "Yeah, Abby I could see how that might be a problem for you. Don't forget about the butler; he is pretty strange," she said, grinning.

"Oh, you noticed that, did you?" I said and let out a laugh.

"Abby, he opens the door even before you've barely rung the doorbell. I would consider that a little weird."

"Just wait till you meet the crazy cook; she is really weird," I said and then chuckled, and then she laughed too. "I'd better get inside and I am sure that you parents are wondering where you are."

"Nah, they knew I was going to be late tonight; this is actually early for me." She chuckled. "We should get together and hang out again. This was fun, Abby."

"Yeah, I had a good time, except for the fact that I crushed Adam's feet."

"Yeah," she laughed, "but it was pretty funny. Did you actually get a look at his face?"

"No, I was too embarrassed. I kept looking at the floor."

"Ha, I did. You should have seen the horror."

I groaned. "Night, Sarah," I said as I stumbled out of her car. She was still laughing when I shut the door. I'd imagine that she was probably still laughing as she drove down the lane. I headed up the steps to the door and went to reach for the door handle, and of course the door was open even before I touched the handle. The butler opened the door up wide and said, "Welcome home, miss," like every time before. A small part of my brain wondered if that was all he could say. I had to fight the urge to stick out my tongue at him, almost like I was a brooding 5 year old. As I walked by him, I noticed that his frozen face changed. Just like before, his nose was scrunched up like he smelled something bad. I couldn't help it; my teenage self was annoyed

"What," I snapped at him.

His face relaxed, he turned to shut the door and then he walked away like I hadn't said anything at all. Annoyed, I threw my keys on the table and stomped up the stairs. When I got to my room, I slammed my door as hard as I could. The sound echoed off the ceiling and I was positive that it echoed down the hall. Hopefully the butler got my annoyance. I was surprised that mom and Ben weren't home yet; it was close to midnight now. I hurried to get ready for bed. As soon as my teeth were brushed and my old t-shirt and shorts were on, I headed to the big bed. I was so tired and my feet were killing me. I was sure by morning that I was going to have a foot full of blisters. I fell back into the pillows and fell into a peaceful sleep.

When I woke up in the morning, I felt well rested. It was the best night sleep that I'd had in a long time. Then I turned to look at the clock. "Oh, crap," I said and then stumbled out of the bed. Ethan had told me to meet him at 10:00. I had only an hour to get ready, eat and get out to the cliffs. I was in such a hurry that I was more clumsy than normal, bumping into my dresser and then the desk. I hit the desk so hard trying to hurry to get ready that I said quite a few four letter words, followed by "Ouch! That's going to leave a bruise."

Afterwards I managed to get the rats out of my hair, washed my face and got dressed in less than 10 minutes. I thought to myself, quite proud of my achievement, I headed downstairs, grabbed my coat and keys and ran for the door.

"Abby, can you come in here please" I heard my mom call from the dining room.

Shoot, I thought, my quick plans for an escape was ruined.

"Coming," I said as I headed in the dining room. As I walked through the doors, I noticed that Ben wasn't at the table. "Hey mom," I said as I took a seat. I was so nervous about being late I was nearly bouncing off my seat.

"Well," she said.

"Well, what, Mom?"

"How did it go?" she asked.

"Oh, you mean the dance?"

"Of course," she said.

"It was fine; I had a good time with Sarah and Julie."

"Did any guys ask you to dance?"

I grimaced. "Yes," I said, not meeting her glance.

"What happened, Abby," she asked. She could always read my face so well that I couldn't ever keep anything from her.

"Well, I did have fun until I was asked to dance."

She interrupted, "What happened?"

"Um, well, you see, I sort of crushed the captain of the football's team's feet." I was looking down at hands on my lap when she surprised me by busting up laughing; I almost fell out of my chair. "Mom, it's really not funny," I said, a little annoyed.

"You're right," she said, between giggles. I was glad she was getting a kick out of my most embarrassing moment since I got here. Okay, well, the cliff thing was the worst, but this was right up there with it.

She finally composed herself. "Well, I hope the rest of the night wasn't that bad."

I thought back to the night, and my thoughts went to Ethan. "No, it was actually a good night." I glanced up at the clock again. It said it was after 10 but I knew this clock always ran fast. My mom happened to notice.

"Abby, are you in a hurry to go somewhere?"

"Well, I am supposed to be meeting some kids to hang out, and I don't want to be late."

"Alright, I'll let you go; but I was really hoping to spend some girl time together," she said, and her face fell a little.

"I won't be out late," I said. "I still have a lot of cleaning to do in the library. By the way, Mom, how did your night go?" I wasn't really curious; I was dying to escape. But it would hurt her feelings if I didn't ask, and I know she was dying to tell me. It was like I had opened the floodgates. She started talking; without a breath in-between, she described in great detail the restaurant and the food they had eaten and where they went dancing. It felt like it took her forever to finish, although it was nice to see her so happy, and the truth was that Klamath Falls was starting to grow on me, thanks to Ethan.

"I am really glad that you had a good night," I said after she had finished telling me about her night.

"Well, I am glad you had fun with your friends Abby. It seem like things are starting to go better for you."

"Maybe a little," I mumbled, not wanting to show my real feelings.

"Well," she said, "That's a relief."

"What is?" I asked.

"I didn't t think you were ever going to come around. Whatever has changed your outlook, I am thankful for it."

"Mom," I laughed, "I am a teenager, remember? I am so supposed to have mood swings, and get into trouble." A new thought occurred to me. "Mom, where is Ben today?"

"Oh, he is out in the vines this morning."

"Why he is out there," I asked, a little puzzled.

"Well, with the cold weather and the frost they are trying to keep the vines warm so they don't freeze."

"Oh," I said, because I had not realized that was why they had burn barrels lining the vines.

"He'll probably be out there all day," she sighed. "That's why I was hoping that you would have time for your mother today."

"Oh," I said and then glanced at the clock again. This time she noticed.

"All right, Abby. Maybe we can do something later today when you get back."

"Okay, Mom, that sounds great."

"I'm sure that you could use some help cleaning out that library," she hinted.

"That's okay, Mom. That project will keep me busy awhile, and of course that way I can't be bored."

She laughed. "Where did you say you're going?" She asked again.

"Just out with some friends." Truthfully, it wasn't a lie; I was going to be with a friend. It just wasn't going to be with the girls.

"Abby, aren't you hungry?" she asked.

"I'll just take an apple with me," I said as I reached for the fruit bowl that was in the middle of the table. My stomach was so nervous that eating was not an option.

"All right, I will see you later, Abby, but not too late," she quickly added.

"I won't be." I gave her a quick hug, followed by, "I will see you later."

As I hurried out of the dining room, I grabbed my coat and keys and hurried out the door. I almost forgot to close the door in my hurry. I turned around to get the door and right before I got up the steps I saw Albert's disapproving look and the door shut with a loud thud. I shrugged.

Oh, well. What did I really care what that creepy old butler thought anyways? I jumped in my jeep putting the keys in the ignition and starting the engine even before my door was shut. I backed out of my parking space and headed down the long drive, not noticing the people that I was sure were in the vines staring at me as I left. I had one purpose at the moment and no other distractions were going to get in my way. I was semi-lucky that the highway was pretty empty. The thought of getting a speeding ticket would not have been good since I was going 70 mph in a 55 mph zone, but I was in a hurry and the recent conversation with my mom had me running somewhat late.

I pulled off the drive into the grave road, kicking up a little gravel as I pulled into the spot where I had parked before. I let out a sigh of relief when I saw Ethan's motorcycle, standing perfect in space before me. I left the keys in the ignition after I shut off the jeep. I jumped out, catching myself on the door, not wanting fall in the huge puddle of mud right outside of my door. I took one quick breath to try to settle my stomach and then shut the door. It made a loud thud, making me jump a little. *Get a grip on yourself,* I thought to myself and started walking down the small pebbled path.

I noticed as I walked that it was very peaceful, it was as if the forest had gone dormant. There was no wind that I noticed. I could see any forest life anywhere around, nothing scared away from the sound of my approach.

How odd, I thought. As I walked up to the opening of the trees, I noticed the flames dancing through the trees, just like the night at the bonfire. As I walked through the opening, I saw him. He was standing by the logs that we had sat on, the night of the bonfire, staring down at the flames; it seemed he was in deep concentration. His head only popped up when I snapped a small twig under my feet.

"Abby," he said in acknowledgement.

"Ethan," I breathed, and then he took three long strides and I was in his arms. As he held me close I rested my face on his massive chest. I could feel the muscle on his chest through his white t-shirt. Again I noticed that he didn't wear a coat.

"Ethan, you're going to freeze," I said.

"Abby, I am not cold," he said and then laughed. I did believe him though, because with his arms wrapped around me I felt like I was on a hot beach in, let's say, Hawaii. The warmth was all around me. It felt nice. He let me go, although he took my hand to lead me by the fire. We sat down on the log and he put his arm around me. It felt so nice.

"So," he began, "Did you have a good time at the dance?" I am sure that he knew the answer to this, but I answered anyways.

"Actually," I paused, "I did have a good time, but the best part was when I got to dance with you."

"I am glad you had a good time, Abby. I love to see it when you're happy," he offered.

"But why did you have to leave so quickly?" I asked.

"Oh," he paused. "I am sorry about that." He seemed sincere when he said he was sorry. "I was starting to think that you had changed your mind, Abby."

"Changed my mind about what, Ethan?"

"About meeting me here," he said.

"Sorry, I got cornered by my mom wanting details about the dance."

"What did you tell her?" He asked in his monotone voice.

"Of course nothing about you," I offered. "You said it would be better if no one knew," I hedged.

"How it is going about the manor?" He asked, with a little too much interest.

"Same as always: the creepy butler, the crazy cook, and, of course, Ben, who my mom could not live without."

He surprised me when he laughed at my observation. I turned my head away from him to look at the fire.

"What's wrong, Abby?" he asked.

"Nothing," I lied.

"Abby, do you want to talk about what is bothering you?" I knew Ethan was only worried about me, when I talked to him and was around him, it was like he could read my mind and my emotions.

"Ethan, what would you say if I wanted to tell my mother about you?"

"Hmm," he said, and then offered, "I would think that it would be in your best interests that you kept our interactions a secret."

"But why?" I asked. "Is it your friends or your family or Ben's family?"

"It's a little of everything," he started. "I know that you have heard stories about the families around here. But like I have told you, people hold grudges for a long time, some that don't end."

"But Ethan, my mother and I aren't from around here," I told him. "We have nothing to do with the people's past around here."

"I know that, Abby, but sometimes people get stuck in the middle who aren't directly involved," he said as he reached his hand up to sweep aside the hair that fell into my face. His hand slowly put the hair behind my ear and then gradually came down on my shoulder. My heart began to beat faster and my palms began to sweat. He leaned in to kiss me and it was like my heart was going to beat right out of my chest. Before he kissed me, he giggled.

"What," I asked a little breathless.

"I can hear your heart; it sounds like a horse galloping." And without another second his mouth was on mine. It was soft and I could feel the taste of his breath in my mouth. His hand reached behind my head and his fingers wove into my hair to hold me to him. It was like Ethan and I were the only two people in the world. When he broke the kiss he did not lean away, he just set his forehead against mine, breathing just as hard as I was.

"Abby," he said, "I have been waiting a long time for you."

I didn't get a change to ask him what he meant by that because his mouth met mine and I forgot all of my worries. I had never felt like this before in my whole entire life. It was like I was it was destined for Ethan and I to meet. Like something in my life was missing until the day I met him.

All of a sudden, Ethan straightened up, like he had heard something that I couldn't hear. He sat frozen for what seemed like forever. It wasn't even two minutes later that I heard it, too. I heard a growl and then coming through the bushes was giant animal. I had never seen anything like it. It was dark black, with dark set eyes, its mouth was curled up over its fangs, and it was snarling, its eyes locked on me. Ethan shifted his body so that he was in-between me and the giant animal. I sat frozen, too afraid to move, the happiness that I had been feeling just a moment ago was gone. Fear took it's place.

Ethan's voice came out in a rush. "Abby, slowly get up and start to walk away."

"What?" I asked, confused.

Again he said, "Abby, trust me, get up slowly and head back to your jeep."

"I am not going to leave you," I said in a shaky whisper.

"I will be fine," he said, no emotion to his tone. "As soon as you get to the trees and you can't see me anymore, run. Now go!" He said.

I could tell that he would say no more on this subject. I did what he said, all the while keeping my eyes on the monstrous creature. Ethan was now on his feet in-between me and the creatures, his eyes like mine on the massive beast. As I took the first step the monster took a step forward.

"Go, Abby" Ethan said again. I didn't want to leave; I didn't want to leave Ethan with this massive beast defenseless. But I did what he said, and a growl ripped from the giant beast as my withdrawal became more evident. As soon as I hit the trees, I was running. I wasn't keeping a close eye of my feet so of course I tripped a few times. As soon as I reached the truck and jumped in the jeep I pushed down the electric locks. I turned the keys and tried to start the engine but I cranked it hard, and it started and faltered there times before I actually got it running.

Once I got it running, I didn't hesitate. I put the jeep into drive without worrying about my seatbelt. As soon as I hit the highway, I really hit the accelerator. I was sobbing almost too much to drive, wrestling with the fact that I had just left Ethan there. What I am going to do? If I told the police about the giant creature they would have me committed to a psychiatric hospital, but If I did nothing Ethan was going to get killed. But what was Ethan? He seemed very sure that he could take care of himself and he didn't really act afraid. He was more annoyed that our afternoon had been ruined.

I wrestled the whole way back to Ben's with just calling the police and reporting what had happened, but something stopped me. Something in the way that Ethan's face looked told me that he would be fine. As I pulled up the lane, I noticed that the field where so many people were working earlier was now empty. I parked in my normal spot, and then glanced at the clock, it was nearly noon, almost two hours had passed since I had left, and it didn't seem like it. It was like I could never get enough time with Ethan.

I put down my visor so I could fix my face before I headed into the house, the whole time only thinking about the fact that I had left Ethan. I put the visor up and shut off the jeep and headed to the front door. While hurrying inside, I looked over my shoulder the whole time. What if I never saw him again? What if that monstrous creature killed him? How would I live with myself? I kept running those words over my head. When I reached the door, it was already open. I shuffled in but not even the butler was around. A small note was on the table where I usually dropped my keys. *"Abby, Ben and I had to go out for a while to a meeting, we will be back later. Catherine will cook you dinner tonight. Don't forget to finish your homework before you go to bed. Love, mom"*

I was grateful that my mom was not home to see me this way. If she had, she probably would never let me hang out with my friends. I am sure that I looked as if I had been crying for days. I decided to head to my room and grab the key that I had left in my jewelry box and then head down to clean the rest of my library. Anything could be used as a distraction. I headed down the hallway to the library, I had the sense that I was being watched, but I looked around and there was no one there, not even the butler. I wasn't surprised about the butler; he was one that I expected to be always lurking in the shadows, just popping up out of nowhere.

As I came up to the library door, I realized that It wasn't locked, and I was sure that I had locked it. I went inside and quickly locked the door and then I turned around and leaned my back against the door. I was wrestling with the decision I had made to leave Ethan there, and arguing with myself about going back to check on him. Part of my mind said to trust him and the other part was worried that I would never see him again. *What was that thing*, I wondered to myself. It was almost the size of a horse, but it looked like a dog, and those teeth, the razor sharp teeth, and those eyes that looked to aware to be a simple animal.

I started looking through the books and not finding anything that would explain what I had just seen; these books were all so old like they were written over hundreds of hundreds of years ago. I did find one book, It had the title <u>Myths and Legends</u> I flipped through it was a bunch of legends about Greek gods, the Abominable Snowman, Bigfoot and vampires, I was about to shut it and give up when a black letters caught my eye on the last chapter, "Werewolves." My heart stopped, the picture on the page was exactly the creature that I had seen at the cliffs. I started to read.

The first sentence on the page was, "*Werewolf, half human and half wolf, forever dammed to walk the earth in-between two worlds, half human and half beast.*" As I continued to read, my heart sank. "*Human during the day and completely normal. You would not know that one was among you. But when the full moon is in the sky, the man becomes beast and his darker nature takes over and consumes him. There are lots of stories as to where werewolves came from, but most believers, far and wide, believe that the original one and how the story began is when a farmer's son came across a creature in the 16th century that had been hurt. He tried to help the creature, but was bitten by it. He suffered for many days before his family believed he was dead and buried him.*

"*The next day the mother had come to place flowers on his grave and his grave had been dug up and the body was gone. It was almost 10 years later that the mother saw something in the woods outside of her house that resembled her son, but when she went to get her husband he was gone. It is said that if one is bitten by the wolf, that that person on the first night of the full moon would be cursed to walk the earth for all eternity. Werewolves are nearly impossible to kill. The only things that work are silver bullets. Anything else will merely wound the animal, and as werewolf recovery is almost immediate, whoever had tangled with the werewolf would be begging for death. Anyone who has ever seen or come face-to-face with one has never survived to tell the tale.*"

I read the last sentence again "Anyone that has ever seen and come face-to-face with one has never survived to tell the tale" My mouth open as to let out a cry, but nothing would come out. The book fell to the floor with a thud. I dropped to my knees, and wrapped my arms around my chest. I was so disgusted with myself, now more than ever, that I had let Ethan find his fate on his own. I closed my eyes trying to make the image of the massive wolf out of my head. I whispered one word, "werewolf."

A second later, I heard a tap on the window and I jumped but somehow stopped myself from screaming. I quickly saw who it was as the sun was setting behind him. "Ethan," I mouthed. And then quickly ran to the window. I helped him into the first story window. I was confused. His clothes were intact, not even a tear. His hair wasn't even messed up. I opened my mouth to speak, but he quickly put his huge hand over my mouth. I looked up at him confused.

"Abby, I can't stay long, but I had to see you and let you know that I was okay."

I started to sob and he pulled me to his chest and wrapped his arms around me

"Abby, it's okay, don't worry."

What happened, Ethan?" I managed to mumble into his chest. "I saw that wolf; he was going to kill us."

"Abby," he started, "You must forget what you saw tonight, and you must not speak of this to anyone."

"But why," I asked. "Shouldn't we warn someone about that wolf? What if someone else is out at the cliffs and the wolf attacks them?" I said in a shaky voice. He pulled me away from his chest, put one hand under my chin, and lifted it so that I had to look at him.

"I promise you that everyone else is safe," and then he added, "the wolf wasn't after anyone else."

"What," I said, not comprehending.

"Abby, I can't tell you. But I can ask you to please stay out of the woods, and don't go to the cliffs."

"But why," I asked.

"Something is coming, and that is all I can tell you. I have to go now."

"But why?" I asked.

"The truth?" he asked.

"Yes, of course," I replied.

"I am not supposed to be here."

"Here at the manor?" I asked

He nodded, "And I am not supposed to be with you. It's forbidden."

"But why," I asked, still not comprehending.

"I wish I could explain to you, but it would be safer for you to be in the dark. But I promise that I will not let anything happen to you."

I could see nothing but concern in his beautiful blue eyes. "Ethan, you aren't making any sense."

"I know, Abby; all I ask is that you trust me."

I very much wanted to trust him but I couldn't get the image out of my head of the giant wolf. "Will you tell me one thing, Ethan?"

"That depends what your question is," he said with a smirk.

"How did you get away from the giant wolf?"

"Abby, wolves are normally harmless to people. We must have startled it. Once you were gone and I sat perfectly still, there was no reason for it to attack."

I didn't like his weak explanation. I opened my mouth to speak. "But," I started and he put on finger over my mouth.

"Enough, Abby, you are fine and I am fine. That is all that matters. I have to go, Abby," he said as he kissed my forehead.

"When I will see you again," I said in a whisper so my voice wouldn't shake.

"I will find a way," he said, his voice was still sure of itself. And with that he squeezed me one last time and then he was out the window. A small part of me was relieved, but the other part of me ached, for I did not know when I would see him again.

Knock, Knock, Knock, three raps on the door made me jump; I quickly went to the window and pulled the two glass windows shut. *Knock, Knock, Knock* three more raps.

"Abby" I heard my mom call. "Coming," I said, a little breathless. I took the key out of my pocket and ran to the door to quickly unlock it. I pulled the door open. "Hi, Mom, I thought you were out for a while"

"Abigail," she started, using my full first name, "Is it really necessary to lock the door every time you are in here?"

"Sorry, Mom, it's just my own private sanctuary. I didn't mean anything by it."

"Who where you just talking to?" She asked.

"What do you mean," I said, trying to play dumb.

"Oh," she said, "I could have sworn that I heard you talking to yourself."

"You probably just heard me muttering to myself about the mess in here and I what I got myself into," I said with a laugh.

"Oh, well, she shrugged, "how is it going in here," she asked.

"Slowly," I said, grabbing a book off of one of the huge shelves that went from floor to ceiling. I put my lip an inch from it and blew as all the dust flew into the air. "It's going to take me forever to get all the dust off of all these books."

Now she was laughing. "Do you want some help, Abby?" She asked, looking a little hopeful.

"Thanks, Mom, but I think I want to do this myself. It will keep me busy."

"All right, Abby, just don't forget about your schoolwork."

"No problem, Mom." She patted my head and then turned for the door. When she reached the door, she spun half way. "Abby, you might want to open a window and let some fresh air in here, it's going to be pretty hard to breathe when you start cleaning off the books."

"I actually was just about to do that when you knocked on the door."

"See you at dinner," she said, and before I could answer she shut the door. As soon as I was sure she was away, I hurried to lock the door and then ran to the window. It was just like I thought, Ethan was long gone. I was looking forward for school tomorrow, not because of classes or my friends, because that was the only place now that I would get to see Ethan. Ethan had said the cliffs were off limits, and that was the only place that we met, so what now? My heart sank as I realized my only sanity in this place was starting to teeter, and that the only peace I had here was the cliffs and I was no longer able to go there.

I spent a few more hours cleaning, and looking through the massive amounts of books. There were many different 16th century authors: Bacon, Richard, Thomas, Christopher, John Webster and my favorite, William Shakespeare. The library also held may American authors like Poe and Mark Twain. This library was my own little piece of heaven, I could spend years or centuries in here just reading through the literature in this room. It was like this room was locked up for centuries just waiting for me. It was nice of Ben to give me one piece of happiness in this nightmare.

11 The Locket

As I ran my fingers over the books, lightly touching each binding, I reveled over all the classics. *What a shame,* I thought, that *such a collection was locked up and hidden for what looked like centuries.* I ran my fingers down the long line of books, and then I got to the last one on the shelf. It was black and there was no writing on the binding. At first I thought it might be a Bible or something since it wasn't really a fancy book; it looked quite old.

How strange, I thought; curious, I carefully picked the book off of the shelf. The book looked very fragile. The edges were tattered and I didn't want it to crumble to dust. Honestly, the book looked hundreds upon hundreds of years old, with the dust to prove it. I lowered my face down to the book and blew lightly, and the dust flew into the air. I had to fight back the urge to sneeze, and I hurried to raise my hand and plug my nose, and closed my eyes. It worked - I didn't sneeze. As I opened my eyes, I looked down at the cover of the book. Still nothing: no title, no author's name.

I started to open the book, and all of a sudden something fell to the floor. I reached down to pick it up. I twirled it around in my fingers, being very careful so I didn't break the chain, and that's when I realized that it was a necklace, a book-shaped locket with crystals on it. It looked very old, like the book it was contained in, old and brittle. As I looked at it, I noticed that it has some writing the back. It was smudged, and it was very hard to read what the words said. I rubbed my thumb against the smudge, hoping to try to decipher some of the words.

As I looked at the words, I noticed what they really said was, "my only love." *Wow*, I thought, and then I noticed that it wasn't just was a necklace; it was a locket. I carefully opened the locket, and inside the locket was a painting of a face. It was black and white, and very faded. But I froze in shock as I really looked at it. Set into the locket, staring back at me, was a spitting image of me. The only difference I could tell was the way the hair was styled.

"How can this be?" I asked myself. This miniature painting has to be centuries upon centuries old. But it was me, or at least my face. And on the inside of the locket was one word. Etched in the most beautiful way it read, "Elizabeth". I stood there with a shocked look on my face.

"Conner was right," I said in a whisper. But, was he right about the other parts too? The part where the families were cursed and the first born of all the families were werewolves? I went to sit down on one of the high back chairs in front of the stone fireplace. I thought I should sit down before I collapse.

How can this be, I thought to myself, and then my thoughts went to back to this afternoon, at the cliffs and the picture of the massive wolf kept coming up in my thoughts, and the fact that Ethan wasn't afraid. I glanced down at my hand, which still held the beat-up book. I slowly open it, in the inside of the cover was a name written in black scroll: "Elizabeth Moore, 1508" I couldn't believe it, as I looked over the pages. It looked to be a diary. I knew that I shouldn't read it. I knew that this was personal and should be kept safe. But if I was being honest with myself, I wanted to confirm what I had pieced together, and this booked looked to be the key to everything. I turned to flip on the antique light that was on the rickety table, and settle myself into the must chair, and started to read.

> *1508: DAY ONE --- TODAY is the day that my dad sent for my mother, brother, and me. Mom gave me this book so I could write all my thoughts, hopes, and dreams, and about the journey that we are taking. My dad said we all have to move to Klamath Falls, that it would be in our family best interest. I wanted to laugh at him; nowhere my dad moves is in our best interest, and he conquers and consumes everything in his path. We have been on a wagon trail for weeks; I can't wait until I can clean up. I don't understand why we are moving, why we are leaving everything we know. My dad said that the manor that is being built is nothing like we have ever seen. If my dad says it, it's so. That's one thing: my dad always does what he sets out to do. I suppose you can say that my dad is a very difficult man; he sees people's worth as what they can do for him, although he seems to love Mother and my brother and me.*

As I read through the rest of the passage, about the wagon trails and the hardships, I was grateful to live in a century with cars and plumbing. So far Elizabeth seemed to be a normal girl, with normal opinions of her parents. I got to the next passage in her diary that seemed to be the day they reached the manor

> *DAY 30- I CAN'T BELIEVE how far we have traveled, but mother says that we should reach the manor today. I can't wait - not to see the house, but to be off this bumpy wagon. It is autumn here and the leaves are changing from green to brown to red. It is so beautiful. We have seen very few people from*

> *being on the wagon train. I have the highest hopes*
> *that there will be many people my age. My birthday*
> *is in a few days. My 16th birthday, and my dad has*
> *set it so my coming-of-age party will be my birthday,*
> *Sept 7th.*

My hands started to shake as I read that last line: "My birthday, Sept 7th. How can this be?" I whispered. "She has my face, my birthday."

Knock, knock, knock.

Three loud knocks pulled me out of my thoughts, and the book fell to the floor, followed by my mom's, "Abigail Watson, are you hiding in there?"

I picked up the book quickly and ascertained that it had survived the fall. "Yeah, mom," I said as clearly as I could, trying not to let her know how shaky my voice was.

"It's time for dinner, Abby."

I knew she was curious about what I was doing. I quickly put the locket back in the book and placed it back on the shelf where I had found it, and then ran to the door to unlock it and let her in. My fingers fumbled with the key in the lock. It took two tries to get the key in the lock and to turn it my hands were shaking so badly. I took one deep breath before I turned the door handle. I slowly opened the door. I saw the look on my mom's face. It had a mixture of emotions: irritation, anger, and of course her worried look. I hurried to apologize, before she could get mad about the door being locked.

"Sorry, mom; I just wanted some peace and quiet." It worked; the deep etched crinkles in her face and forehead started to smooth out.

"It's fine, Abby, but you're not hiding any boys in here are you?"

I giggled. It was a nervous giggle and I hoped she didn't hear the hysteria in it. "Mom," I said, "you know that I don't date, that I never have dated."

She was the next one to start laughing. "I know, Abby, but you are such a beautiful girl... I am sure there are plenty of guys your age that would love to take you out."

This was not a conversation that I wanted to have with my mom, and if she wouldn't have been staring at me I would have rolled my eyes. I didn't want to tell her, Yeah, but the one I want is the one Ben would want be to forget all about if he knew. "No mom; there are no guys who want to date me," I lied. If I told my mom that the star athlete of my high school was interested in me and I pretty much turned him, down she would go into shock. No, worse than that - she would have a stroke.

"Let's go eat," she said. "Ben is waiting for us."

I took one last look at the book on the shelf just to make sure it was really still there, like it was going to be gone if I closed my eyes. It was still there. I let out one breath and then said, "Okay mom; let's go." Then I shut the door and locked it as we headed to the dining room for dinner. I practically inhaled everything that was on my plate, not even tasting it to make sure of what I was eating.

"Whoa Abby," mom said. "Slow down; you are going to get a tummy ache."

"Or worse yet," Ben started. "You are going to choke and I am a little rusty on my Heimlich maneuver," he said and then laughed.

"Sorry," I said with my mouth full as I reached for the glass of milk to chug it down.

"Abby, what's the hurry?" my mother asked.

"Sorry mom," I said and then set down the glass after I had chugged every drop. "Just have a lot of homework," I lied. The truth be told, I was dying to get back to the library back to the diary. I was pretty sure I knew how Elizabeth's story ended, if all of Connors stories were right, but I wanted to hear it from her own words.

"Alright," she said, "see you tomorrow. Don't stay up too late, Abby."

"Thanks, mom," I said and hurried out the door. I felt some relief as I unlocked the door to the library, and I hurried inside and shut the door as quietly as I could. I told my mom that I was heading up to do homework, which of course was a lie. I am surprised she didn't catch that one. I was never very good at the lying thing. Normally she stopped me before I got out the door. She must be preoccupied with Ben, I thought.

As I hurried through the door, I ran over to the book case where I had placed the diary. "That's strange," I whispered noticing the book was not longer where I placed it. "I know I put it back right here," I said as I fumbled through the rest of the books on the shelf. I don't think I even noticed as the books fell to the floor and landed on my feet.

"Where is it, damn it?" I whispered under my breath. I knocked almost all of the books out of the way and still no diary. I placed my hands in my hair like I was going to tear it out. "Aaaahhh," I groaned. "The door was locked, I know it was," I whispered and then I ran over to check the window. "Locked," I said, discouraged. I walked back over to one of the overstuffed chairs and plopped down. I had forgotten how dusty everything was and found myself choking over the huge cloud of dust that had surrounded me. "Oh God," I said choking and waving my hands in the air to dispel all of the dust in the air, as if a wave of my hand was actually going to matter.

I know I put the diary back on the shelf, I know that I had shut and locked the door, and the window I had closed after Ethan had left. So how could it have vanished? I shook my head. I don't understand. *Am I going crazy*, I asked myself? "Maybe," I whispered.

I looked down at my shirt and jeans and realized I was covered from head to toe in dirt and dust. I really needed a shower. I slowly got up and walked to the door, not even bothering to pick up the mess of books that was still lying in a pile on the floor. I headed out the door. I turned to look at empty bookshelf and then sighed. I shut the door and if with my best attempts to shut the doors quietly then still made a loud thud as they shut. *Ahh*, I thought, why does this place have to echo?

I hurried to lock the door with my skeleton key, and then shoved it in my pocket so I wouldn't lose it. I hurried as fast as I could up to my room nearly knocking over a vase and then tripping on the steps. But I actually made it to my room undetected. Relief swept over me when I was in my room and the doors were shut. I hurried to get a shower and get ready for bed. I felt so much better after my teeth were brushed and my hair was combed. It had been a long day in so many ways. I couldn't get the images of the day out of my head: the giant wolf, the passage in the book, the locket, and the diary. I was so tired that I couldn't help but climb into bed right away.

I knew the minute I closed my eyes I was going to have a nightmare. I have had way too much going on for me not to have the nightmare. It's got to be this place, but truth be told I wouldn't change it if I could. For one, if I would have never come here and my mom would have never met Ben than she would be miserable, and I am really glad she is happy. For another reason, I would have never met Ethan and I couldn't even imagine that possibility.

As soon as my head hit the pillow, I could feel myself drifting off. The next thing I knew, I as in the forest again, and was dark with the only light coming from the full moon. The fog was back.

I had almost figured that that Ethan would be there, almost like all the other nights, but Ethan didn't show and I could feel the isolation from all around me. I could hear the branches and rocks crunch underneath my feet. I could feel the breeze blowing through the trees; I heard a twig snap from within the forest and I began to walk a little faster, until I had gotten into a full blown sprint.

As I came up to the cliff, the one that I had almost fallen off, I slowed to a stop. I had a feeling that I wasn't alone and I turned to see who was there. My mouth dropped and my eyes widened as I stared at the girl in front of me. I worked to compose my face. She looked at me; it was my face, but she had a dress that looked like it was from the 16th century. It was high-necked and covered almost all the way to her face and she had her hair up, piled on the top of her head. I tried to find my voice, but I had the feeling I was in shock.

The girl looked at me, her eyes soft with compassion. She raised one hand to me, fingers straight and palm up. Her lips parted and she spoke one word to me as she took a step in my direction, "Remember."

The next thing I knew I was sitting up in my bed, sweating and panting, trying to make sense of the newest nightmare. I turned to look at the clock: two minutes to six. My alarm clock is going to go off any minute. I groaned, "I don't want to go to school today." Then I fell back into the comfort of the pillow, while I put the other one over my face. I laid there, not quite asleep when my alarm clock came on. I pulled the pillow off my face and then hit the alarm clock, with a little too much force, but it managed not to fall on the floor. I sat up and hung my feet over the bed and then I hopped down from the bed and headed to the bathroom. I did feel somewhat better and more awake after the water hit my head and then flowed to my feet. I stayed in the shower even longer than I normally would to fight of the stupor. After I shut off the water and wrapped round the pink fluffy towel around me, I defogged the mirror.

"Err," I groaned, noticing the deep purplish blue circles under my eyes. I looked as I hadn't slept in months. The truth was that I haven't slept well since the day I got here. I was tired and irritable and not really in the mood to have to put on my happy fake facade. I quickly ran the brush through my hair in my irritation and lack of sleep. I think I caught more snarls than I had hair. I quickly got dressed, and then blow-dried my hair, just leaving it down today and hopefully hiding most of my face. I brushed my teeth and did feel better after that. I always felt better after my teeth were cleaned.

I went out of the bathroom to the big oak dresser by my bed and grabbed my socks and as soon as my socks and shoes where on I turned to straighten the comforter on my bed. My room was never really messy, just my books that I had scattered on the desk and the boxes that were still in the corner collecting dust and that I never managed to unpack. Yet, I didn't want to give the staff something to talk about so keeping my room clean was just a fact of life here. I grabbed my books and placed them in my back pack, grabbed my coat, and then started to head out.

As I went to shut my doors, I had a feeling that I wasn't alone. I could feel someone watching me, but when I turned to look down the long hallway there was nothing there. *Just another day in the haunted crypt*, I thought, and shrugged and then walked down the steps. I walked in the dining room thinking I was going to find Ben and my mom in there; it was a surprise that they weren't there.

"Go figure," I whispered, and then jumped as Albert came up behind me.

"They have gone out early today, miss," he said in that creepy voice. Every time he talked, it sent cold vibes that echoed even in my bones.

"Oh," I gasped.

"Your breakfast is ready," he said, not noticing that fact he made me jump a mile. Or at least he didn't show me that he noticed. His face never seemed to change from that blank look. He set the tray down on the table and then breezed out of the room, not making a sound.

"Man, that guy creeps me out," I said as I lifted the long-sleeved shirt on my arm and saw the goose bumps. "I don't think I am ever going to get used to that guy."

I sat down and hurried to eat my breakfast. It was really good today. The cook had again really outdone herself: pancakes topped with fresh strawberries, toast, and then fresh-squeezed orange juice. I have to admit the food around here is the bomb, although, if I didn't cut it out, I was going to be one of the stories in gossips magazines of the "teenagers who weigh 500 pounds." I chuckled to myself. When I finally had devoured everything on the plate I stood up and grabbed my bag, coat, and keys and headed out the door for school.

12 Explosion

As soon as I was in the Jeep and racing away from the house, I let out a sigh and felt some relief. I don't know why it always felt so weird at the manor, but somehow I felt as if there were secrets that were built into the walls, secrets that were meant to stay buried but somehow are trying to come to the surface. I drove more slowly than normal; I was sure it's due to the fact that yet another night had passed and I hadn't got much sleep. The irritation was trying to show through from the lack of sleep or from the fact that the diary had disappeared after I had only gotten a glimpse of Elizabeth's world.

"I can't believe that. I left the book in there; I should have taken it with me," I whispered to myself in irritation. I was almost to school and my heart rate hadn't returned to normal yet. If I didn't get myself in check, I was sure I was going to have a panic attack. So many secrets in this town, and no one to talk to, I couldn't even email Paige, my old friend from Florida, to tell her. No doubt she would call my mom and let her in on the plot. My mom had always been nice to all of my friends but for some reason Paige happened to be her favorite.

I pulled into the parking lot at school; no one lingered outside of their cars because of course it was raining. It was like this town was under a constant waterfall. I noticed the parking lot was almost full. I hadn't thought I was late, but between my irritation and the lack of sleep I must have lost track of the time. I hurried out of the jeep with my hood over my head so I didn't get completely drenched. I hated having to wear a rain jacket and hood.

I wasn't really into fashion, but I am sure that I looked like gossip material for looking like such a dork. Or like I had gone swimming and forgot to bring a brush. When I walked into the school I heard the final bell ring and I took off at a dead sprint down the hall, wet shoes squeaking as I ran. I made it to first hour with a quick halt at the door.

I tried to be quiet as I walked in the door, but the teacher gave me that really angry look; my face and eyes dropped. I stared at me feet as I made it back to the open desk in the very back of the room. I could feel everyone staring at me, and I tried to slow my breath and pulse rate so I didn't hyperventilate and pass out. As soon as I had sat down as quietly as I could, I reached down to open my bag and got my books out. I was very surprised that my books, even with all that rain, had stayed dry in my backpack.

Before I lifted my head and my books to the desk I took a deep breath and prayed that everyone was now paying attention to the teacher. I slowly looked around as I sat up. To my relief I found that everyone was listening, or at least they looked like they were paying attention, to the teacher. I took a chance and looked at Ethan. He was there sitting in his chair, motionless except for the pencil that he twirled around with his fingers. I couldn't help feel that he was staring at me from the corner of his eyes. My heart started to beat faster.

Class seemed to trip pretty quickly in my first hour, and then the rest of the day it dragged. It was like fate was punishing me, telling me to stay away from Ethan, too. Things got even worse when it was time for Home Ec. and my cake exploded, coating every inch of the oven. The whole class room was filled with the smell of burnt cake.

The once-patient Home Ec. teacher gave me a look through her coke-bottle glasses, her mouth turned down in a grimace. She definitely was pissed. There was no other way to explain the look on her face. And of course "oops" was my brilliant response. Then there was a small silence, followed by everyone bursting into laughter. I could feel my face getting redder and redder.

"Alright; that's enough," the teacher said in a clipped tone.

It wasn't like I did this on purpose. These things just happen when I get in the kitchen, I thought to myself. She should be glad that I didn't get it all over the room and not just in the oven.

"Abigail," she said using my whole name. She worked very hard to keep her voice level, but I could hear it waver. "Abby," she began, "once school is over you can stay and clean up the mess."

I looked at her and the less-than-noble side of me wanted to tell where to go, but knowing myself, I knew that I would never have the guts to say anything. I just nodded, keeping my eyes on the mess and my face going even redder. Just then the bell rang. Everyone gathered the books and shuffled out the door. I tried to ignore the giggles in the background and the thought that I would be the joke for the rest of the day, maybe even the rest for the week. The rest of the day couldn't even pass fast enough. Even with the thought of having to sit through the rest of the day knowing that everyone was talking about me, what was worse was the thought of having to go home and put on my happy face and play the adoring daughter.

As soon as the final bell rang, ending yet another joyful day, I hurried to my locker to put my book away and then rushed off to the Home Ec. room so I could clean up my beautiful mess. I was expecting the teacher to be there, but all I saw was a can of stove cleaner with a note underneath: *I am sure you will know how to use this; my guess is you have plenty of experience. I expect it to be as clean as before you had your accident. I will inspect your cleaning job in the morning.*

"Yep, she's still mad," I whispered under my breath. I crumpled the note and tossed into the tin trash can. *I beat my record*, I thought; with my last Home Ec. teacher, it took me six months to get her irritated at me, this one, I was able to get really pissed off within a month.

I opened the oven door and it let out a squeak; cake was all over every inch of the inside. "Crap," I whispered. "This is going to take all night," I whispered. What I wouldn't give for a self cleaning oven, I thought. And the teacher actually was wrong about one thing: my mother was obviously smarter than her. She never allowed me to be in her kitchen; I was actually banned from cooking.

I groaned, rolled up my sleeves, and grabbed the sponge and stove cleaner. As I started to scrub the stove - or should I say tried to scrub the dried-on cake - I realized something. "This is going to take forever," I groaned.

I used far more stove cleaner than I should have. I think it was starting to give me a high. After I was scrubbing for about an hour I finally had to come up for air. I wandered over to the window and opened it; hopefully, the cold air would clear out some of the fumes. As I looked down at my hands and saw how dirty they were, I was glad that I wasn't one of those "foo foo" girls that always cared about their nails. I let out a laugh at that.

I hurried back over to the stove and started to scrub it out. It took me another hour to get the rest of the stove clean, but when I was done, it was as clean as it was going to get. I threw the can and sponge in the oven and shut the door; hopefully the coke-bottle, senile teacher would not check the oven before she turned it on, but I had to laugh, not really caring if she did.

I glanced out the windows in the small class room; it had already started getting dark. I must have been scrubbing the stove for a lot longer than I thought. I knew I should hurry to get home, knowing that my mom would be wondering what I was doing, but she was probably with Ben and she wouldn't probably even noticed for awhile. My mom was used to trusting me, but after her and Ben's last trip and my almost overnighter my mom's trust was starting to falter. *Better not test her willingness to give me free reign*, I thought as I hurried back to my locker.

As I approached my locker, I realized that someone had jimmied it open; there were small scratch marks on the side and the door was bent a little like the person had had some difficulty opening the locked locker. I would have laughed if I thought it would have made me feel better. I reached for the door and opened it very slowly, afraid of what I would find in it. It let out a creek when I opened it.

Who would do such a thing? I thought to myself. Who would spend the time to jimmy my locker open? I didn't have any money on me; what could they possibly want? I finally managed to open the locker door. Inside it looked like nothing had been touched, which surprised me a little. Whoever it was had gone to great lengths to get into my locker and yet nothing was messed with; my coat was still hung up and my bag looked like it was still secure, like it hadn't been open. But down at the bottom of my locker was a note.

"Leave now, you're not welcome here. Be careful that history doesn't repeat itself" it read.

I heard the underlying threat in the note. It was quite obvious that someone didn't want me here. And what was that about, be careful that history doesn't repeat itself? The more time I spent in Klamath Falls the weirder things got. The mystery though was starting to trigger my interest. I am sure whoever left I the note wasn't thinking that it would have that effect on me. They must not know me very well.

I let out a laugh, grabbed the note, and crumbled it in my hands. I grabbed my bag and coat, slammed my locker, and threw the note in one of the many convenient trash cans that lined the halls. It was going to take more than a note and a bent-up locker to shake me up.

As I opened the door a cold whoosh of air hit me. It had gotten a lot colder than it was earlier, and I could see goose bumps all over my arms. I rushed to the jeep. The stuff with the locker being ajar was making me somewhat nervous; I had been lying to myself by telling myself that I wasn't afraid but I didn't want to be too paranoid.

I bet it was Caleb, I thought to myself. He was definitely the type of person who would do such a thing, and from the start, the feeling of me being unwelcome was written all over his face. Ethan had said that he hated the people that I lived with. But it couldn't be true, the story at the bonfire; Ethan and Caleb were my age. If that story was true, then it would make them well over 500 years old. And what about Ben? Other than marrying my mom and dragging me across country, there was nothing wrong with Ben.

It took me a second to unlock the doors; my hands were shaking so badly. *It would have been nice,* I thought, *if Ben would have opted for one of those Jeeps that had push button remote locks.* Although, it was a gift and I didn't have to buy my first car.

As soon as I was in the Jeep and my locks were safely down, I let out the breath that I had been holding since I walked outside. I put the keys in the ignition and started the jeep. I was surprised that my nerves were still a little buzzed. My hands were still shaking. All the way home I played back today's events. Nothing stood out. I hadn't seen anyone watching me, except from the occasional dark glares that Caleb and his followers were throwing at me. That was no different than any other time.

I guess I hadn't really paid attention to the road because before I knew it, I was to Ben's and getting out of the jeep and heading to the door. When I reached the door, of course the door opened the minute I reached for the handle. I was really starting to hate the damn butler. I swear he only had the one expression. He was like one a Greek statue; he face was cold and hard like the stone and the expression never changed.

I was going to say something, but before I could get the words out, my mother called from the living room. I put the nasty comment on hold and headed to the living room to face my fate. I was guessing my mom was wondering why I was home so late.

As I entered the room I saw that it was not just my mother sitting on the couch, it was Ben also. This I wasn't expecting. *What are they going to do, tag team me,* I thought with a little venom. Have you seen what happens when a tiger is cornered? Now, imagine that with a teenager hopped up on hormones. I almost laughed to myself.

My mom opened her mouth to say something but she stopped as she got a better look at me. It was Ben that asked, looking somewhat concerned, "Abby, are you all right?"

"Yeah, I'm fine," I said a little frostily.

Then my mom began, "Abby, it's almost eight o'clock - where have you been?"

"Sorry, mom," I said honestly. "I had a little trouble in Home Ec. today." That seemed to close the questioning for her, but Ben...well, Ben doesn't know my history with cooking, so I guess he was dumb enough to ask.

"Why? What happened?" he asked with a dumbfounded look, running his hand through his thick dark hair.

"Cake exploded," I said starring him down.

All of a sudden he started laughing, and it wasn't a quiet laugh. Oh no, it was roll on the floor, deep down to the soul of your shoes laugh that seem to vibrate all through the mansion.

"Well, that explains what's in your hair," my mom said with a smirk. I knew that my mom would have been laughing just as hard as Ben if she didn't know how touchy the subject was.

"Why?" I said. "What's wrong with my hair?" Automatically raising my hand to my hair to see what he was talking about. I could feel part of the cake crumbs in my hair. It was so disgusting. "Mom, if it's all right with you, I would like to take a shower now."

My mom was trying hard not to laugh; she had her hand over her mouth clenched in a fist trying to keep the giggles in. "That's fine," she said through her hands, "but next time you're late, please call."

"No problem," I said, turning to head out the door.

"Abby, I will send Albert up with a tray of food, since you missed dinner."

"That's okay, Ben; I'm not really hungry. I've been literally swimming in food."

Ben coughed to hide another laugh. I knew he was trying to be polite, but the agitation of the day was starting to wear on me. "'Night mom; 'night Ben," I said and hurried to leave the room.

I could hear Ben whisper to my mom, "Rebecca, is she really that bad of a cook?"

"Worse," she said and giggled.

"I better get the staff to put a few fire extinguishers out and a couple more smoke detectors," he said and then let out a laugh.

"Ben," my mom started, "I don't think that will be a problem. From the look of your cook I don't think she will let Abby near her kitchen. I think we're safe."

Now that they were sure that they thought I had left, they were laughing quite freely. To make matters worse, the laughter bounced off the walls and marble floor, making the sound twice as bad. I gritted my teeth and then stomped up the stairs. Hopefully this will be the last time that someone was going to laugh at me for awhile. One could only dream, right?

13 The Carnival

I DON'T KNOW IF IT is the weather here that turns my mood sour, but every single day, the thought of jumping off one of the massive cliffs here crosses my mind.

Okay, not really, but you get the point; it was like everything in this town moves in slow motion. I would always just stay in bed a few more minutes, dreading the days I was forced into the institution of school. It was worse than ever this week. All everyone talked about was the annual Klamath Falls Carnival.

I know it's tradition, but I was never one for tradition. The more I dreaded, it the closer Friday seemed to get. I told Julie and Sarah "no" about ten times but by the eleventh time my "no" turned into a "yes" just so they would stop asking. Don't get me wrong, I was grateful to have two really great friends, but I was still missing home. I wished I had someone to talk to, someone to tell my secrets to, someone to tell about all the strange things that I had happen since I moved into the mansion. Talking to Ethan, at least in public, was out of the question, but how to get him alone? There was only one place that I knew of and I was forbidden to go there.

"One thing's for sure," I whispered to myself as I drove home on the semi-darkened streets that were still wet from the rain that come earlier today, "I am going to get him alone and force him to tell me what is going on, to divulge everything I've learned since I came to Klamath Falls."

It was nearly four o'clock when I made it to the main gate; I saw a few people working in the fields and I was guessing they were getting ready for some main event having to do with harvesting, but to tell you the truth, I really didn't care. I pulled up to my normal parking place, gathered my bag, and headed into the house.

It wasn't a surprise that Albert had opened the door right when I got to the top of the steps. I didn't ever reach for the door handle. I swear this guy is has extraordinary hearing. Well, I wasn't going to worry about that now, I thought, as I gave him one quick nod and headed up the staircase.

I barely noticed when he said, "Afternoon Miss" in that cold, icy tone of his. I wasn't sure why he had such a strong dislike to me but it was apparent in every action he took. I got up the stairs in less than a minute, slammed the doors, and headed into the bathroom to get ready for tonight. I picked out some sturdy looking jeans and a heavy blue sweatshirt. No doubt it would get a little colder as the night progressed and of course it would rain, so I wanted something that would be warm. It wasn't one of those fancy tops that you would see, say, the captain of the cheerleading squad wearing, but it would do for me.

I hoped in the shower and washed up from head to toe to get the latest food fiasco out of my hair. At least I didn't smell like brownies anymore. I had to laugh at myself; if a guy used that line on me, "You look smell good enough to eat," I couldn't really slap him. After all, I always smelled like the food that had exploded all over me. I got out of the shower and wrapped the towel around me. I had cracked the bathroom door so it would semi-defog the mirror. I wasn't too afraid anymore that, other than my mom, anyone in this house would bug me.

I was guessing that Ben had had a meeting with the staff and told them to give me my space. If he had done that, I was truly grateful.

After I finished drying off I quickly got dressed I glanced at the desk clock that I had put on the bathroom counter. After being late a number of times I thought it best to leave a clock in the bathroom so I could stay on schedule. It said 4:45. "Wow," I said in a whisper and then thought. I didn't realize that I had been in the shower that long. I had only fifteen more minutes before Julie and Sarah were coming to get me. I used the blow dryer for a few minutes but my hair was way too long to dry fast, so I decided to put it in a pony tail - a quick and easy fix for a girl on the run. I put on a little concealer under my eyes just to dispel some of the black that was permanently etched under my eyes, a little blush to make my skin stand out just a bit, and then just a hint of lip gloss to make my lips shine just a bit.

I started to put my brush and make-up away when a small knock followed by "Abby, can I come in?" nearly gave me a heart attack. My mom opened the door and saw the expression on my face and one hand across my chest, and then she followed it up by saying, "Oh, I am sorry, Abby! I didn't mean to startle you."

When I could catch my breath I answered, "That's all right, Mom, I just didn't hear you come in."

"So," she began, "what are you and the girls doing tonight?"

"Well, Julie and Sarah want to go to the carnival," I said with a grimace on my face.

"Oh," she said and her face perked up in a smile. "That should be fun," she said. I knew that she was just secretly pleased that I was going out with friends and I wasn't moping around the mansion complaining about the move anymore. "You will have to tell me all about it," she gushed.

"No problem mom. Are you going to be home later?"

"Well, since you're going out tonight, Ben figured you wouldn't mind if we sneak off for a few hours of alone time."

"Well, have a good time," I said trying to look happy about it. "I want to hear all about it at breakfast, Mom," I said.

"Yes, Abby," she replied.

"Does the cook really have to make so much food? Really, I would be happy with cereal or even toast."

"I know what you mean," she said. "I am starting to gain weight," she said and then laughed. "No problem, Abby. I was meaning to have a talk with Ben about it anyway."

"Thanks, Mom," I said and the let out a sigh. "Have fun tonight, Mom."

"You too, Abby. Try not to stay out too late."

"I won't," I said. "There really isn't much to do here."

She laughed and then she added, "Stay out of trouble."

And then I was laughing. "Mom, this is Klamath Falls; what kind of trouble can I get in here?"

Sarah and Julie were there at the bottom of the massive stair case at five o'clock sharp. They seemed nervous with Albert standing watch over them. I had guessed that was why they both had come inside, rather than just one. Albert must make them just as uncomfortable as he makes me.

"Hey, Sarah and Julie," I said as I nearly ran down the steps.

"Are you ready?" Julie had asked.

"Yep, I just got to get my wallet out of my bag." I hurried over to the table by the door and grabbed my keys and my wallet and then nearly pushed them both out the door with Albert's penetrating gaze upon me. I slammed the door with a little more force than necessary so maybe he would get a clue to stop hovering.

As I got in the truck, I realized that both girls seemed to have been holding their breaths; as they sank back in their seats and relaxed they took a deep breath like they had been starved for air. I let out an involuntary laugh. I really couldn't help it - they looked like I had the first time I came here. Both girls turned to stare at me. They were looking at me with bright eyes, like, 'maybe this girl has lost her mind.' I hurried to explain.

"Sorry guys," I said. "It's just you look like the way I did when I first met Albert." I let out another giggle and then placed my hand over my mouth to try to hide it.

Julie was the first one to speak. "I don't know how you stand it," she said. "That guy is creepy. I mean, he is like one of those zombies from Day of the Dead."

I let out another laugh. "I just try to ignore him as best I can," I said, shrugging.

"And that house," Julie added, "how do you stand living in a museum?"

"It's not so bad," I answered back. "Ben essentially gave me the library and it actually has a key." They laughed; I got the feeling that reading books wasn't something they were into. "Sorry guys," I said. "I have a thing for books. I know you think they're not very interesting, but they let me escaped into another reality. There is nothing like reading a good book and dealing with their drama rather than my own."

They laughed again.

"Glad I am amusing," I said, a little stiff.

"No," Julie began, "it's fine, Abby. If I lived in this creepy house with the living dead butler," she laughed and then continued, "I would have to find different ways to escape, too."

"What about your mom?" Sarah asked. "What does she think about the staff?"

"I am not sure she ever notices them, to be honest," I said with a grimace. "She's still in that honeymoon phase. It's really sick how they look at each other; it makes me want to puke." They both looked at me and stuck their fingers in their mouths, pretending to vomit. "Yeah," I said, "exactly," and then we were all laughing.

It didn't take long till we pulled into the fairgrounds. The fairgrounds were like the hip place to go in town. Every Saturday and Sunday, people would come here for the races, like it was their religion. From the first glance I noticed it didn't look anything like the movies. It wasn't neat and tidy with fancy pretty lights. The fence that outlined the place was white and the paint was peeling. The barns alongside the fence, I'm guessing where they kept the animals, were just as run down with peeling paint and rusting metal roofs.

"Wow," I mumbled.

"I know it looks run-down," Julie began, "but really, all the kids have fun at this event."

"You aren't going to make me do anything stupid," I asked, "like ride a sheep or something?" I laughed.

"No," Julie laughed, "We usually wait until you have been here a year."

I rolled my eyes at her and then we all three started laughing. Julie finally made it to the gate. The traffic up until there was moving very slowly. They didn't have a regular parking place, so instead people were parking on the grass alongside the fences. Julie managed to fit her car between an old rusty Ford pick-up truck and a green minivan. I was surprised that she was able to squeeze between them; I wasn't sure there was enough room. I actually held my breath when she squeezed in. She swung her car in there with no trouble and I got the impression that she had done this plenty of times. The minute we stepped out of the car the atmosphere changed. I could hear the laughter coming from the direction of the rides, all of them squeals of delight.

"Welcome to the carnival," Sarah said with a laugh. The smell in the air was cotton candy with the hint of pig smell. It almost made me throw up. But with a slight tug on my arms, Julie on one side and Sarah on the other side, they led me out. "Come on, Abby," they said in unison.

They almost were running and I had to tell them to slow down a couple of times because I didn't want to break anything or to embarrass myself. It was even worse than I thought it would be. It was like everyone from the whole city was here and they were all jammed packed into the small area of the carnival; everywhere you would turn you were bumping elbows. I know I said 'excuse me' at least a thousand times. And the Carnies, as Julie and Sarah called them, they were even worse then I remembered. They were all really dirty, like they hadn't had a shower in years. I was surprised the flies weren't circling. One guy, who was running the run-down, rusted-out Ferris wheel, smiled at us and where his two front teeth should be there where gaps. I shivered at that one.

"Come on, Abby; let's go on the Ferris wheel," Sarah begged.

"That's okay. You two go ahead. I'm just going to look around," I hedged.

"Don't be a scaredy-cat," Julie taunted.

I let a short laugh. "Not scared, Julie, just very aware of my mortality." Julie and Sarah laughed but didn't push it further; they headed off to the rusted, rickety Ferris Wheel.

As they walked away, the feeling that I shouldn't have came tonight came crashing down on me. I watched them load themselves on the Ferris wheel and then took a quick breath as it started and they slowly began to lift in the air. It took me a second and then I decided that I wouldn't stay watching them have fun; I figured since I was already here, I might as well take a look to see what else was here.

As I walked through the carnival and bumped elbows with quite a few people, I realized that this was one experience I could have missed. I watched the dirty carnival people swindle the good folk of Klamath Falls. I walked through the carnival daydreaming about hot sunny beaches and the salty taste of the ocean. It was then that I felt as if I had been being watched; from the corner of my eyes I could see five massive forms. It took me less than a second for me to realize that it was Caleb and his little followers. They watched my with their deep, penetrating eyes; it made shivers run down my spine. I wrapped my arms around my chest and continued to move forward, away from Caleb and his gang. I came up to an attraction that was dark, with dark lights, and it had slightly lit steps that led up to a platform covered in what looked like Halloween decorations, and it wasn't even October.

14 Hall of Mirrors

"Come on, pretty lady," came a scruffy voice from the man on the platform. The Carney speaking to me had pale white skin and long, thin hair, and the stubble on his face looked as if he hadn't shaved in a few days.

"I'm sorry, what did you say?" was my brilliant response.

"I said, 'Come on pretty lady, come take a look.'"

As I looked up, I saw the sign: "Hall of Mirrors." I took one look behind me to notice that I was being followed by Caleb and only Caleb. I was shocked; where had the others gone? It was unlike Caleb not to have his followers with him. It only took me a second to think about it, and to reckon that the Hall of Mirrors didn't look as bad as staying out here with Caleb.

I hurried up the steps, watching my feet as I went so I wouldn't trip and embarrass myself. "How much?" I asked, trying not to let my voice shake. As I looked over the Carney a little closer I noticed he was in need of haircut too.

"One dollar," the man said in his deep, gravelly voice. Then I revised my second opinion: he could use a haircut, shave, and a breath mint.

He had so much liquor reeking off him you would have thought he had taken a bath in beer. I hurried to reach into my billfold and pull out a crumpled dollar and handed it quickly to the dirty man. I headed thorough the broad opening of the "Hall of Mirrors." As soon as I was inside, I let a relaxed sigh. I noticed the mirrors were all around, and the path seemed too narrow. Okay, maybe this wasn't one of the best ideas I had ever had. I was feeling very enclosed, and totally stupid over my latest predicament, when I got the sick feeling in my stomach that I wasn't alone.

I managed to stumble into an opening with larger mirrors all around and no hint of where the exit was. I could hear the slow, steady breathing, coming closer and closer. "Hello; is there anyone there?" I managed to get out in a choked voice, but there was no reply. My heart started to thunder. Pulse racing, my only thought was, *How do I get out of this?* I turned my face to the middle while sliding my back along the mirrors to find the hidden passage way that would lead me out of the Hall of Mirrors.

Just then, halfway around, I felt the glass disappear and relief swept through me, but that only lasted a second. I could feel warm hands wrap around me on one side and then one warm hand covered my face to keep me from screaming. Panic overtook me and I tried to struggle and scream but my thrashing was no good.

It was then I heard an angelic voice in my ear. "Shh, Abby," the voice said. "I am here to help; please don't struggle."

Without me even turning around, the terror in my stomach went away, I knew the voice behind me. He slowly moved his hand down from my mouth. "Ethan," I whispered, so softly I wasn't sure he heard me.

"Yes, Abby," he said. "It's me. We have to hurry," he said in a whisper. Then he took my cold hand in his warm one and led me out of the maze in less time then I would have thought.

"Thanks, Ethan," I said in relief once we were completely free from the Hall of Mirrors.

"It's not safe for you here, Abby; please, come with me."

"No," I said in my most stern voice. I think he was shocked, as if he hadn't expected me to protest or tell him no.

"What?" Ethan asked, abashed.

"No," I paused and then continued, "I'm not going with you until you tell me what's going on; I am tired of all the mystery."

"Abby, you know I can't tell you."

"What? Be honest with me."

"Abby," he started with a small smile on his face, "I am always truthful with you; I just don't tell you everything." The small smile on his face was just making me more irritated.

"Well, I'm afraid that I can't go with you Ethan."

"Please, Abby," Ethan said in his persuading voice.

"Ethan, I believe that you are concerned for me but I am done with the secrets. If you are going to answer my questions, then I will go with you."

Ethan stared at me with those ice blue eyes while running his hand through his hair, he looked like he was deep in thought, trying to figure out the best way to handle the situation. "Okay, Abby; come with me and we will talk."

I felt better after I heard that, although he hadn't said that he would tell me the truth, just that we would talk. I had noticed the difference.

"Just a second; I have to tell my friends I am leaving."

"We don't have time," Ethan said. I gave him one quick look, and he groaned and said "Abby, do you ever do what you are told to do?"

"No," I answered quickly. "Never have, so why start now?" I laughed but he groaned again. "Just let me tell someone that I am leaving so they can tell Julie and Sarah."

He was hesitant, but then just nodded. I was in luck. I recognized a girl named Kelly who had dark hair that was always braided as if she was in the show Little House on the Prairie, playing the part of Laura Ingalls Wilder. She wasn't very popular; actually no one really noticed that she was there most of the time. I knew that she could get my message to Julie and Sarah though.

"Kelly," I hollered, and despite the noise of the crowd she heard me.

"Oh, hi, Abby." She seemed surprised that I was actually talking to her.

"I need your help."

"Sure, Abby; what do you need?"

"Can you tell Julie and Sarah that I got a ride and left early?"

"Sure, Abby; is everything alright?" she asked.

"Oh, it's fine," I said. She didn't seem to be buying my lie, but with one raised eybrow and a stiff nod, she turned around and headed in the direction I pointed. *One thing down,* I thought, and *now onto Ethan and hopefully an explanation.*

I hurried back to where I had left Ethan and noticed he wasn't where I had left him. "Ethan," I said in a whisper as I turned around and scanned the crowd to see if I could see him. It took me a minute but I spotted something at the dark corner of the carnival grounds where there were no lights. Ethan stepped out of the shadows.

"Are you ready, Abby?" Ethan asked with a hint of worry in his voice. Whatever was worrying Ethan was starting to seep through his calm. I didn't press any questions any further at this time. He was obviously in a hurry, and I didn't want to make the situation any worse. We headed for the exit and out the front gates, away from the noise and the people. When we were in the darkest part of the make-shift parking lot I saw in the darkness the outline of Ethan's bike. My mouth dropped. Ethan felt my hesitation as I began to slow and then came to a stop, planting my feet.

"What's wrong, Abby?" he asked. I closed my jacket and then wrapped my arms around me.

"Ethan, it's freezing out here tonight; you don't expect me to ride on that tonight?" I said, staring deeply at the motorcycle. I had thought he would deliberate just a little bit, but he didn't falter; instead he let out a laugh.

"Abby," he started and then began moving to the bike. It took him one try to kick-start it, and the bike came alive roaring so loud I didn't think I could hear the rest of what he was saying. "Abby," he said again and then held out his hand in an offer to join him, "I promise you will be warm. Just wrap your arms around me."

I paused again.

"You aren't scared, are you? You have already been on the bike once; and look. you are still in one piece."

"Ha, ha," I said in reply, and without another thought I kicked one foot over the seat and wrapped my arms around Ethan, feeling his heat. I held on for dear life. The road was dark and the rain from earlier in the day made it shine under the moonlight. Despite the chill, Ethan's body heat kept me warm. I closed my eyes and laid my head against Ethan's back, taking in his sweet smell and listening to his heart. It would stay at a steady speed, until the moment I would tighten my grip. Then it would start to race, and I would let out a laugh. I was content for the first time since I had come to this place; I was relaxed, not caring about the problems that seemed to surround every aspect of my life.

It seemed the road went on forever, and then he pulled off onto a side road. It was more like a path than a road. It was not paved and it was so bumpy that I bounced up and down on the seat and my teeth chattered. I think Ethan could feel my discomfort because the bike began to slow. "Where are we going," I yelled over the roar of the engine.

"You'll see," he said and it sounded like he had a smile on his face. If we hadn't been on the motorcycle, I would have punched him in the gut. I knew it wouldn't hurt him but it would make my pride feel better. We finally pulled up to an open space. There were no lights around, so after Ethan shut off the bike, he had to guide me through the trees.

"Where are we?" I asked again. I think he could tell that I was getting impatient, so when I saw the first sign of light through the trees, Ethan finally answered, "We are at my house."

"Oh," I said and then floundered around for something to say, but he spoke first. "Abby, if we are going to have a talk, I thought my place would be the safest."

"Oh," I said again, my heart and pulse began to race again. What could I say; I had never been to a boy's house before, let alone a boy that I was attracted to. Needless to say, I knew my mother wouldn't approve; but then again, when has a sixteen-year-old girl ever done what her parents told her to do?

15 Confessions

I STOOD THERE LOOKING AT the small house; it looked very old, with rundown shutters and vines crawling over every inch of it. If you didn't look close enough, it almost looked like part of its surroundings, like the massive woods were swallowing it whole. Ethan stood beside me with a watchful eye, maybe wondering if I was going to turn around and bolt, probably forgetting my sense of direction which was as hopeless as my cooking. Millions of things were running through my head, but no words came to my mouth. Ethan was the first one to speak.

"This way," he said, and then grabbed my hand and intertwining our fingers. A jolt of electricity ran through my body the moment he touched me, and my breath caught. He looked down at me with deep ice blue eyes. "You're safe, I promise you," he said and began leading me into the house.

We entered through the front door into one large room. The first thing I noticed about the house was that everything in the house looked like it was from the 19th century, with wood table and chairs. The fireplace was already lit and looked like it was the only heat source in the house. There wasn't even a regular stove, just one of the old rusted potbelly stoves that most people nowadays use as a planter. But it was cozy and it was clean, and with Ethan's presence I felt at ease. Like I was meant to be there. Like it was home. It was the first time I had felt that since we left our little house in Florida.

The first thing he did once he was in the house was to take off his shoes. That surprised me; the teenage boys that I knew back home never did anything like that. How strange to meet a boy with manners. I followed his example and kicked off my shoes and set them neatly by his. He went into what I considered the kitchen space and sat down in the chair, which looked very small compared to his large body. He leaned forward and then pulled up another chair and tapped it so I would know he wanted me to sit there. I cocked my head to the side and smiled. I couldn't help it; being told to do something wasn't in my vocabulary, and without using any words even worse.

"Please," he said in his angelic voice.

My grin got even more pronounced as I wandered over to sit by him. I sat down, and then looked at him. He was staring at me with those deep ice blue eyes and my heart raced gain. Now I wasn't the only grinning. The grin widened across his whole face, showing that perfect smile. I couldn't help but stare at him. He was just so beautiful.

Ethan looked like he was about to speak, so I hurried to start before he even had a chance. I wasn't about to let him sidetrack me - I knew exactly what I wanted to say and what questions to ask and I wasn't going to let his beautiful face or his angelic voice waylay me.

"Ethan," I said and then paused while looking down at my hands, a nervous tone to my voice. "I know," I said still looking down not meeting his eyes.

"Abby, what are you talking?" about he said, his voice steady.

I knew if I was going to get answers from him then I would have to shake his ever-present calm demeanor. "Ethan…" I paused again. I wanted to tell him everything that I had found out and everything that I had learned since I moved to Klamath Falls, but I was hesitant. I didn't really know if I was just going crazy or if everything I had seen and found out was the truth.

"Abby," Ethan started to speak, "you aren't one who holds her tongue. You'll feel better if you get it off your chest."

I laughed and then looked up at him. He was staring at me; and my world, which was so crazy, didn't seem to matter. It was then that the words just spilled out. "I know about Elizabeth…"

He was quiet looking at me with no emotion on his face.

"You see, Ben saw that I was unhappy, and he knew that I liked books. So as a gift, he gave me the use of his library." Ethan just sat there; I couldn't even tell if he was breathing except for the fact that I could almost hear his heart pounding as if it was going to beat out of his chest. "Do you remember the day that you and your friends came out to the Cliffs and interrupted the party?"

"Yes," he said, voice solemn.

"Well, Conner decided to tell me about the history of Klamath Falls; or, should I say, the local stories."

"You don't believe everything you're told, do you?" he said with small laugh and a smile on his face.

"Not normally, Ethan," I said with an irritated look. My eyes started to narrow. He just seemed more amused at my irritation. "It wasn't until we were at the cliffs by ourselves and we were attacked by that, that wolf." A small shutter rippled through me as I remembered. "It didn't attack you - you didn't even look scared! Then when I went back to the manor, me being myself, I had to look it up in books and try to find answers as to what I had just seen."

"What did you find, Abby?" he said, and I noticed that his voice was starting to waiver.

"I found a book on werewolves, and with Conner's stories the pieces started to fit together, although it wasn't until I found the diary that everything I found made sense."

"Diary," he said his voice going flat.

"Yes. Elizabeth's diary."

He was quiet so quiet that I could only hear the popping of the last of the embers in the fireplace. "Ethan, please say something," I said in a whisper, looking back down at my hands. I felt his warm fingers lift my chin so I could not hide from his eyes.

"Abby, you have no idea what you have stumbled into."

"Tell me! Tell me, Ethan," I said in a rush. "Tell me why the locket I found has my face in it; fill in the blanks for me!"

He took a breath, closed his eyes, waited for a moment, and then started to speak. "The locket you found belonged to a girl named Elizabeth Moore." He seemed to take another breath to settle himself. "I gave her the locket over 500 years ago."

I could feel my body start to shake as I looked at him but couldn't make myself move.

"It was a gift for her sixteenth birthday," he continued. "I met Elizabeth the summer I turned eighteen, and in those days, people met and married early. I was in love with her the first day I saw her. The first time I heard her voice. She was a girl who everyone liked and wanted to be like, with one exception: Elizabeth's father, Ezekiel.

" Ezekiel, Elizabeth's father, was a hard man and almost everyone was afraid of him. He came to Klamath Falls first, and then he sent for his family."

I couldn't imagine what my face was showing, but he kept himself strong and steady while he was telling me this story. I was guessing he did it that way so he didn't lose his nerve.

After he took another breath, he looked back into my eyes and began again, "Ezekiel bought the land where the manor is now. No one around here could have imagined a house like that. Most people around these parts led a simple life, but that wasn't enough. He wanted all the land, not just the land that his house was on. He was greedy, like most rich man. The one thing, and only good thing, that people said about him was that he loved his family. And the protectiveness and the loyalty never faltered when it came to his family.

"For many months after his family arrived, they never left the grounds of the mansion, only being seen from behind the massive black iron gate that surrounded the whole property. I first met Elizabeth when her father brought her to my dad's store. We were the only general store for hundreds of miles, since this area was settled by Indians and some squatters. He was in the habit of buying his wife and daughter anything he considered beautiful. He bought them every pretty dress that my father had in the shop and any jewelry that he thought that would add to their beauty.

"She secretly slipped me notes every time she came to my dad's store, I guess out of loneliness. It was always the same - they were written on pink stationary paper that smelled of just a hint of a floral perfume. In the beginning I was guessing that Elizabeth was just lonely, never really being around anyone, but as each note came I got the feeling that it was much more.

"We began meeting in secret; I would climb over one of the iron fences and Elizabeth would meet me under the tree that we carved our initials into. It was our spot and only our spot. Far enough that it wouldn't be easily discovered but close enough that she could hurry back before she was missed. This went on for months. She was my other half, and every time that I would leave her I faced despair, knowing if her father found out about us, I would never be able to see her again. We planned to run off together fast and far enough that even Ezekiel's long arms and all his money wouldn't be able to reach us."

Ethan's eyes seemed to narrow and he wasn't looking at me anymore; he stared looking at what was left of the fire. "It was the night we were going to leave when all the trouble started." Ethan's hands started to clench and I could only guess by Conner's story that I knew what was coming now. I set my hand on top of Ethan's and I looked into his eyes, trying to comfort him.

"Ethan," I whispered.

"Abby..." he started and I could see the pain in his eyes. "I heard what Ezekiel was going to do to the Indians, to their families, and I heard what my father and the other families that lived here were going to do. There was so much bloodshed that was already happening, with people disappearing or people leaving, abandoning their land. I didn't want Elizabeth to get hurt. I went to her and actually went to her room. I had climbed the balcony and into her room. I told her that we needed to leave, but she said she couldn't leave her mother and her brother. She didn't want anything to happen to them. I begged her but she was stubborn; she told me that we would meet later at our spot under our tree…" And then Ethan stopped speaking. I knew what he was remembering.

"Ethan, I am so sorry," I said almost in tears myself. "That was the last time you saw her alive," I deduced. He merely placed his head down and into his hands. "What happened to Ezekiel?" I asked. It was then that Ethan face raised his head and I could see the anger in his eyes. It was almost like he wasn't human, and his voice seemed demonic when he spoke.

"Ezekiel," he said in his demonic voice. "When I came back to the manor after Elizabeth didn't show I saw the crowd of our six families and the Indians standing in a semi-circle looking down, their faces showing signs of anger and horror all wrapped into one. Caleb saw me approach; he was the only one that I had told about Elizabeth and me. I saw his face and began running to the crowd. He kept saying 'Ethan, no!' but I couldn't stop my feet from moving."

I could feel tears starting to run down my face and I quickly wiped them away so that Ethan wouldn't see them. I could tell that Ethan was reliving the emotion as he relived his past.

"I pushed through Caleb and the crowd and what I saw brought me to my knees." Ethan started to shake. "Ezekiel was there, and he had Elizabeth in his arms. There was blood everywhere. He looked like he was singing to her and she was just sleeping. To this day I have no idea what he said to her, but his last word to us were a curse, about our families, and that was the last thing that was uttered out of his mouth before someone took a gun and shot him."

"Ethan," I said looking at him, "it wasn't your fault. This can be left at the hands of Ezekiel, not you. Elizabeth's death is on her father."

He got up off the chair almost like someone electrocuted him. He started pacing back and forth, gripping his hair with both hands like he wanted to rip it out. "You don't get it, do you, Abby?" he snapped, shouting the words. "I couldn't protect Elizabeth, and I am not going to be able to protect you."

"Protect me?" I asked. "Protect me from what?"

"Abby, nothing is what is seems around here. You are in the heart of a war between Ezekiel and our families that has been going on for 500 years."

"What?" I said. "Ethan, you said that Ezekiel is dead, right?"

"That is what the story is, Abby, but that's not actually the case."

"What? You mean he's still out there? How can that be?" There was so much information that I was not processing it; I am not as slow as I might seem, but if you were just told that the person you are with was over five hundred years old, would you be able to process it? "Ethan, I have a feeling that you are leaving out more to this story. Please sit down and tell me the rest."

He did as I asked as he slowly sat down. "Abby, I don't want you to be frightened and the rest might scare you."

I let a laugh. "You just told me that you are over five hundred years old and that some crazy man obsessed with power is still alive and I happen to be living in his house. What could be worse?"

"I guess you are right. Well," he started again, always watching me, "my dad was a very spiritual person. I am sure that it was because he was friends with the chief of the local Indian tribe, but he really was worried. Something in the way that Ezekiel spoke his last words. It scared my dad and my dad, although spiritual, was a strong man and he didn't scare easily. He had a meeting with the chief that very night. He went into the tent and was there a long time. They whispered for a long time - my father had the other heads of the families in there as well - and when they came out they had blank faces. They were set in the course they were on. Abby, I had no idea what was settled upon, no idea what my dad had agreed to. I didn't want to live forever, I wanted to be with Elizabeth; death seemed to be a better option but it all moved so fast, and my dad said that I should have loyalty to our family and to our friends. He knew that everything that made me alive died with Elizabeth.

"It was the Chief who made my decision for me. When everyone else had left, the chief told my dad that he wanted to speak to me; my dad agreed. When I went into the chief's tent I noticed that he sat around a small fire, the smoke filling the tent. I noticed writing all over the inside of the tent but it was hard to tell whether it was words or just random pictures because smoke lingered in the small tent.

"When he began to speak I was relieved that he seemed to know English. I was never around when my dad visited when the Indians, so it was a shock that it was so easy to carry on a conversation with him."

16 Revelation

"What did he say to you," I asked, deeply entrenched in his story.

"He said that he knew about Elizabeth and he knew what happened to her. He told me things weren't what they seemed. That he knew that she had died, but she wasn't really dead, and that Elizabeth's soul would be reborn in another. He asked me if I wanted to wait and to be reunited, or to end it now and take my chances in the afterlife. He also told me that she would be the key to breaking Ezekiel's curse. So, I agreed."

"You agreed?" I asked as a question.

"Yes," he said. "I agreed to the gift - or curse, depending on which way you see it."

Things where starting to come together now: Conner's story, the hostility between the families and the Moores, the giant wolf I had encountered in the forest. "Are you saying that Conner's story is completely true? Are you a werewolf, Ethan?" I asked, my voice shaking just a bit.

"Well, I'm not sure what Conner told you, but I know the local stories and they are somewhat farfetched, more like ghosts stories or urban legends."

I noticed that he was avoiding answering me. "Ethan, is Conner right - are you and the other boys werewolves?"

He paused and it looked like he was trying to think about the best way to approach answering this question. "Yes, Abby, it's true."

I let out a big gust of air just like I had been holding my breath. It was strange though, I wasn't afraid. Why wasn't I afraid? I asked myself over and over. Ethan was starting to speak but I put one finger to his mouth. "Shhhh, Ethan, let me think." He seem to settle somewhat. "Ethan," I started, "I may look like Elizabeth but I am not."

"I know that," he said. "But to be completely honest, the first time I saw you, my heart wrenched and I felt like I took a punch in the gut. It was like I was back in the past and time stopped. I couldn't even stand to stay at school."

"So that's why you left the first day," I stated. It all made since now why Ethan had left.

"But," he stuttered, "I couldn't stay away. I was there that day at the cliffs, the day you went for a walk. I didn't mean to startle you, but when you fell-"

"Ethan, that was you," I blurted out, not even letting him finishing his sentence. Then I grasped my wrist with my other hand, remembering the bruises and then reached up to rub the place that I had bumped my head.

"I am sorry if I caused you any pain," he said sincerely. "I really didn't mean to frighten you."

"Why should you say sorry," I said, looking up at him. "You saved my life."

He was looking at me with those deep penetrating ice blue eyes and then he abruptly he stood up and pulled me up to his chest into a bear hug. "Abby, if I hadn't scared you, you would not have fallen."

I wasn't listening to his words at this point; my head was against his broad chest and the warmth of him was surrounding me. I could not have been more content if I was a kid locked in candy store all night.

"Abby," he said and I looked up to meet his eyes again. "You have no idea how deeply in love I am falling with you." And then he ducked his head down to kiss me, not just a simple kiss, but a pulse racing, heart throbbing, soul-shaking kiss. I forgot for a moment all the troubles and all the worries. When Ethan finally ended the kiss we were both out of breath. "I never thought in all the years living that I would find another reason to live," he said.

I felt so comfortable in his arms, but I knew that this couldn't last forever. "Ethan, do you have any idea where Ezekiel is?" I asked, even knowing the answer.

"No," he said. "We try to pick up his scent but he always sees us coming. There is something else you should know about him, Abby."

"What?" I asked.

"Ezekiel is a mage." He said this as if I knew what a mage was.

"Ethan, I am not trying to be dense, but what is a mage?"

He sort of laughed. "I guess you wouldn't call it a mage in this time; another word for it is sorcerer."

I knew what that word meant. "You mean, with all those spells and magic wands?"

"Spells, yes. Magic wands, no."

"Come on, Ethan, I can't believe that."

"Believe it," he said with a serious look on his face. "There is another thing, Abby; mages can shape-shift and turn into anyone or anything. Trust no one."

"Ethan, do you think that he is still in the manor?"

"Yes, Abby, I do. That is part of the reason that Caleb doesn't trust you. He thinks that you are corrupted, or soon will be."

"What do you mean by that?" I asked.

"Mages can also make people do what they want, kind of like marionettes with them pulling all the strings. You wouldn't even know that you were being controlled. And you wouldn't remember it after it was done, so you need to be aware of everything that goes on in that house."

"Ethan," I said with my voice beginning to shake. "My mom is there; she is married to Ben. She is in that house all the time and she is always with Ben."

"I know," he said and I could see the compassion and the heartbreak in his eyes.

"Is Ben a part of this?" He didn't answer; he brought his hands up and ran his fingers through his hair. I knew there was more to this story and I knew that he would try to keep me out of it, but I was sure that he knew that I wouldn't give up. "Answer me," I said, my voice getting angry.

"I know that he is part of it, I just don't know how deep Ben is in it, Abby." It was the way that he said it that made me feel helpless, like if Ben had a major role in this that I wouldn't be able to save my mom.

"Ethan, I have to go," I said getting out of the chair, almost toppling it over backwards, but I managed to catch it with my hand. To the tell truth, I wasn't trying to wreck his house, but I had to get my mom out of that house and away from Klamath Falls.

I managed to make it to the door and out before Ethan caught up with me. It took me a second to realize it was raining; Ethan grabbed my arm and I looked up at his beautiful face. My face got drenched and then the rest of me almost like I was swimming and I was underwater. I couldn't breathe; I was trying to catch my breath. Ethan put his hands on my face, brushing away the water and the hair that had fallen into my eyes. It was like time had stopped as I looked into his eyes. Nothing mattered, not the rain, not Ezekiel, not the wolves. At this moment, it was just Ethan and me. I should have been freezing with the rain being so cold, but Ethan pulled me closer to him and his aura was all around and all I could feel was heat.

"Abby, please don't leave. There is still more that we need to discuss and it's late. You can text your mom and let her know you're staying with a friend tonight."

"Ethan," I said starting to protest.

"Shh, Abby," he said. "I promise you your mom is fine; nothing will happen to her tonight. She has no idea of what is going on so she is safe enough for now." Caught in the moment, he bent his face down to mine while wrapping his hand around my hair; he pulled me into a kiss. It felt like I had died and was in the clouds; warmth started from my mouth and went to my toes. It was like everything had vanished at we were in our own little bubble.

After the kiss finally ended he set his forehead to mine; he was panting just as loud and just as rough as I was. "Come back inside; stay here tonight," he repeated.

I didn't even think; I let him lead me back in the house. I could hear my clothes dripping all over his wet floor and Ethan hurried out of the room, slipping and sliding on his wood floor in his hurry. He hadn't even bothered to put on his shoes. His socks that were once so white where now soaked and covered with mud and as he ran out of the room he left wet muddy foot prints.

When he came back his arms were full of towels; he dropped one on the floor and he headed to me dragging the towel with his feet to clean up his mess. He brought the towels to me and wrapped a fluffy dark blue towel around me. It smelled just like Ethan, and the fragrance coming off the towel was one I could just get lost in. I bent my head into the towel and took a quick smell. I heard Ethan chuckle and saw one eyebrow lift, looking at me as if I lost my mind. I let out a small laugh of embarrassment and then I could feel the blood rushing to my face. He laughed again and then took another towel and dried my soaked hair. He led me over to the fireplace so that I could finish drying off. He grabbed a couple more logs from the side of the fireplace to stoke the fire, and resurrect the flame. Then he sat next to me and grabbed the blanket that was over the makeshift couch, wrapping it around me.

"Abby, are you warm enough?" He sounded concerned, as though he thought I was going to freeze to death.

"Ethan, I really am fine," I said, trying to be convincing, but he wasn't buying it.

"Then why are you shaking?"

"I think I am just in shock over everything I have learned tonight; also, I am a little worried about my mom."

"Abby, don't worry about her; she will be fine. I promise you. But you should call her or at least text her so that she won't wonder where you are."

" I think I will text her. She has a habit when I talk to her of knowing when I am lying." *Although*, I thought mentally, *if I told her that I had no idea where I was, it wouldn't be a lie*; I had no idea where Ethan house was. And I am sure that I wouldn't be able to find it again in the day light without the assistance of Ethan.

I pulled out the cell phone that was always in my back pocket, searched the address book for Mom and then texted, "Sorry mom I am at Sarah's - the girls said it was too late to drive and with the roads and weather being bad, Sarah's mom said we could stay at her house. I will be home in the morning bright and early." After I hit send. I quickly texted Sarah just in case my mom checked. "Sarah, I texted my mom and told her I was staying with you tonight - if she calls, tell her that I am sleeping and that you will tell me when I wake up tomorrow."

It took only a few moments but Sarah was the first one to text back. "Sure Abby, but is everything okay???" she texted with three question marks at the end.

I was quick to respond: "yes, I will tell you about it on Monday." She texted back only three words: "you'd better LOL" I groaned when I read that last one. I was going to have to think of something by Monday. "Okay," I text her back.

It was just a second after I sent that to Sarah, that mom texted back. She wasn't too good with cell phones so I am sure that Ben helped. I shivered when I thought about Ben, and my skin crawled.

"Ok," she texted, "ASAP," she wrote in big letters, and I knew that I had to call as soon as I woke up. I was sure I wouldn't get grounded. I was generally a good kid and never got into trouble. I think I am making up for lost time I thought because I am knee deep in shit right now.

I turned off the phone and shut it. I had one of those flip phones, which was good because I always managed to hit numbers when I used my friends' phones back home and didn't even realize that I had called people. It was a good thing that Ben and my mom thought to get me this sturdy model as much as I toss it around. Although, what did they expect? I am a teenager after all.

I set the phone down and then focused on the crackling fire. It was just a moment when Ethan spoke: "Abby, are we all good?"

"Yep," I said somewhat cheerful now. "Now we can both relax." Although being alone with Ethan with no parents and no friends was enough to tie any girl's stomach into knots. That bubbled questions to my lips. "Ethan…."

"Yes, Abby?"

"I am not trying to pry, but where are your parents?"

Ethan was so quiet for a moment that I thought I was going to have to ask him again. Then he spoke. "Abby, when you can live forever that doesn't mean that everyone else around you will." That ended the topic; I could hear the pain in his voice and I didn't want him to continue. It was nice and cozy there in Ethan's arms and if the fire wouldn't have kept me warm, Ethan would have.

"Ethan," I asked, after he had relaxed a bit, "what about Caleb?"

He looked down at me, keeping his arms around me. What was going on here? "Um," I said biting my lower lip, "what do you think he will do?"

"Don't worry, Abby, I will keep you safe."

"Don't worry?" I gasped. "Come on, Ethan, my mother married into a devil's family and I have your whole werewolf pack-" I managed to stutter out 'wolf pack' – "that hates my guts."

"Abby, they don't even know you," he pointed out, "and if they were given the chance, I know that they would really like you. Besides, they're just like big teddy bears."

I had to laugh and then grumble, "Yeah, but with more hair and bigger teeth and claws."

He even cracked a smile at that and then growled in my ear, not an angry growl, just a low vibrating sound that ran through my body and made me shiver with pleasure.

"Ethan," I said turning my head and looking up at him. It was then he bent his head and pressed his lips to mine. I could taste his sweet breath as his mouth parted. It was the most delicious taste. I have no real way to describe it, other than I can see why people get addicted to cigarettes or to drinking or even drugs. I was so intoxicated by him that I could feel myself becoming addicted to him. He ran his hand through my hair and then pulled it up into a knot in his fist and brought it to the back of my head, locking me there so I couldn't move. But really, why would I want to move? I had never felt the feeling that I had now. It was just like one of the fairy tales, like Sleeping Beauty, and I was just now awake to emotions I had never felt before.

Finally he let go of me. We were both gasping for air. "Abby," he said in a rough voice, "I think you should go upstairs and get some sleep."

I opened my mouth and started to protest. He saw me start and he cut me off at the pass.

"Don't worry; I will stay with you until you fall asleep."

I felt a little better when he said that. "Upstairs?" I questioned.

"Yes you can sleep in my bed and I will sleep downstairs."

"Ethan," I said getting somewhat annoyed, "I can't take your bed. I can sleep on the floor."

He laughed, and after the all the silence it made me jump. "Sorry, Abby," he said after he saw that he startle me. "You're just so stubborn," he said.

"I guess I take after my mom," I said with a smile. It took him a split second to jump to his feet and the grabbed me up in his arm like he was carrying me over the threshold. "Ethan," I gasped, a little embarrassed over the gesture, "I can walk."

"But what fun would that be?" he said with a laugh. It made me feel good every time Ethan laughed. I got the impression that he had an extraordinary and heartbreaking life. I just hoped that some day that he would be comfortable enough to share it with me.

It took him only another second to carry me up the wood steps and into the only room at the top of the stairs. He opened the door with a slight push from his foot; the door wasn't latched so it opened easily with just a hint of a squeak. He held me in one warm arm and pushed back the covers with the other one. He set me down as gently as could and pulled up the covers.

"Ethan," I said and grasped his hand. "Don't go; stay with me."

"I wasn't going to leave. I was going to stay here until you fall asleep."

"Don't leave; stay with me tonight. I am sure we are both old enough that we know where the boundaries lie and the bed is big enough for both of us."

"All right," he said with a smirk. I was glad he didn't protest; the thought of him sleeping cold on the floor and me comfy in his bed was just not an option for me. Ethan laid down beside me and wrapped his arms around me; I was totally content.

I closed my eyes and the last thing I heard in my ear was Ethan whispering softly to me, "Sleep well; sweet dreams, Abby," as I drifted off to sleep.

17

WHEN I WOKE UP IN the morning, I let out a sigh and slowly opened my eyes. I turned my head to the side and looked at the one big window, light streaming through. The next thing I noticed was that Ethan wasn't by my side. I took a moment to reassess my situation and then replayed events from last night. It all came flooding back: the carnival, the motorcycle ride, the sad story of Ethan's life. I sat up and looked around the room. I noticed that it was a very simple room with wood paneled walls. There was one small dresser in the room with a large mirror over the dresser. I swung my feet over the bad and looked in the mirror.

Ahh, I silently groaned as I noticed that my hair was sticking up all over the place. I quickly ran my fingers through my hair, slightly pulling at the snarls so that it was semi-smooth. Then I headed down the steps and to the main floor; I could smell some aroma coming from the kitchen. It smelled like bacon and eggs, with a hint of orange juice, and it smelled good. When my stomach started to growl, I rounded the corner and was shocked to see Ethan standing and the old stove flipping an omelet, with bacon cooking on the other burner.

"Ethan," I said shocked, "what are you doing?"

He let out a laugh," Abby, I'm cooking you some breakfast."

"No," I said seeing that he misunderstood. "What I meant was, why are you cooking?"

He had that perfect smile on his face when he answered. "I just thought you might be hungry." He let out another laugh.

"Well, thank you," I said. I was starving but it wasn't polite to tell people that, especially a guy. I knew that breakfast and dinner at the manor was making me spoiled.

"Abby, you might not think that after you take the first bite." He started to laugh again.

"Obviously you haven't seen me cook at school," I said, and now he wasn't the only one laughing.

"Oh no, Abby, everyone knows about you and Home Ec."

I groaned and then I looked for a place to crawl under and die.

"It's fine, Abby," he said still laughing a bit. "I didn't fall for you because of your cooking abilities."

That perked me up just a little bit. "You have fallen for me?" I asked.

"Just a bit," he said and then stepped over and kissed me, just a small peck on the cheek. I could feel the tightening of my stomach and the electricity running down through my body to my toes, like every time that Ethan touched me. "Sit down and eat something, Abby. I don't want you wasting away."

"Ethan," I started, "I don't think that will happen."

"Why is that, Abby?" He actually looked curious.

"Because the staff at the mansion thinks they are cooking for a million people and there is always plenty of food."

"Oh," he said, thinking about what I had just said. "So they are treating you and your mother okay?"

"Yeah, almost too well. My mom thinks it's the greatest thing to have people waiting on us, but I just find it creepy."

"Abby, do you remember what we talk about last night?"

"Yes Ethan, I do." I looked directly into his eye so he could see my sincerity. Ethan just stared at me. After a moment I became a little uncomfortable. Someone would have to speak and it didn't look like it was going to be Ethan.

"What?" I said, looking at him.

"Abby…" he paused. "Aren't you scared?"

I was confused. What was I suppose to be scared of? "Scared of what?" I asked Ethan.

"I just told you that I was over five hundred years old and that my friends and I turn into giant wolves, and that you live in a house where a Mage is lurking around and you aren't scared?"

"No," I said looking at him. "I got passed that months ago after I heard Conner tell me the story the first time; you were just confirming what I already knew, and filling in the blanks that I didn't." I raised the fork to take my first bite of omelet and was very careful not to speak with food in my mouth, reminding myself silently that my mother had raised me with manners. I chewed slowly enjoying every savory bite. When I was done chewing, I looked up at Ethan; he was staring at me again. "Ethan you keep staring at me. Why?"

"You never cease to amaze me," he said and then smirked. I smiled right back and then continued to eat until I thought I was going to burst.

"Ethan are you going to eat?" I asked.

"I already ate a bit while you were sleeping."

"Oh," I said.

"Do you know how beautiful you are?" he said sincerely.

"I think you need to sleep more. You are obviously hallucinating," I said laughing. "Ethan," I said, "what time is it?"

"It's nearly seven," he said looking at the one and only clock that was on the kitchen wall. It looked very old like everything that was in Ethan's house.

"Ethan, I think it would be best if you took me into town and dropped me off at Sarah's so she can take me home. It might look suspicious if you drive me home on the motorcycle and my mom or Ben sees me." Although nothing happened with Ethan and me, if my mom knew that I had stayed all night with a boy she just might chain me to a wall or put me under house arrest. I really wasn't sure how she would react since I had never had a boyfriend before.

"I am guessing," he said, "that you need to get back."

I let out a sigh. As reluctant as I was to leave, and have the outside world ruin one of the best nights I had ever had, I conceded, "Yeah. I am sure if I don't leave soon, my mom will be calling Sarah to find out where I have been and when I am coming home."

"Alright Abby," he said as he rose from his chair. "I will take you back to Sarah's house. " It made me smile just a bit to see that he was just as hesitant for me to leave.

"What about out talk last night...?" I asked Ethan.

"Well, I think that you know almost everything now," he said, and then paused before speaking again. "But," he started after a deep breath - he looked directly into my eyes – "you must not let Ben or anyone in the manor know where you have been or that you know what is going on. I fear it's not safe, and I can't let anything happen to you," he said as he caressed my face, letting his warm fingers linger.

"We'd better go," I said hesitant.

"Let's go," he said, removing his hand from my face and then grasping my hand. He led me out the door after I had my coat and shoes on; I took one last look at the nice warm and cozy house before he shut the big oak door with a light thud. I headed towards the motorcycle, which was still slightly damp from the rain that had finally quit. I noticed that the woods were eerily silent. I heard no birds chirping or leaves rustling. There wasn't even a small breeze blowing through; it gave me the chills to have the forest silent.

"Ethan, do you think there is a storm brewing," I asked as he walked up behind me and set his broad warm hands on both sides of my arm.

"I fear there is a storm brewing but it has nothing doing with the weather." That was the last thing he said as got on his motorcycle; he held his hand as a silent gesture letting me know he was ready to leave. I took one last look at the forest, feeling as if we were being watched, but I let out a small shrug. After all, I always felt so safe being with Ethan, so why worry? I really had more to worry about then letting my imagination run wild and imagine a fiend watching us.

I gave Ethan my hand and he pulled me onto the motorcycle with ease. My arms were around him in the next second, letting his warmth surround me again. It took one good kick and the motorcycle was roaring and we were flying down the small path leading us away from the small house in the rocks. I closed my eyes and laid my head on Ethan's back, listening to his slow breathing and his steady heartbeat. If we weren't speeding down the muddy rock path I might have actually fallen asleep, cozy and content, only the roar of the engine reminded me of where I was.

It seemed to take only a few minutes through the darkened forest and we were back on the main road again. I could tell even with my eyes closed and head against Ethan's back when the rough gravel changed to smooth blacktop. Once we hit the blacktop he increased his speed; I couldn't even describe how free I felt being with Ethan on the bike. I never wanted it end. It wasn't long before we saw the first signs of life signaling that we were close to town. My heart started to pound, knowing we were close to Sarah's house.

"Ethan," I said as we were only a couple blocks away from Sarah's house, "Please pull over at the next block." He didn't say anything, but just nodded his head. I am guessing he knew that I didn't want to make a scene and I am sure he realized if I showed up on his bike looking dirty and disheveled Sarah would start grilling me about everything. As it was, since I had ditched her and Julie last night, she would be wondering where I had gone and who I was with.

Ethan pulled over to the curve and put his hand out to help me off the bike. "Remember what we talked about, Abby; it's better for no one to know that you were with me."

"Don't worry, Ethan. I will come up with some excuse." Lying wasn't my specialty but I seemed to be getting better at it, I thought. Ethan bent to give me a kiss on the cheek but I turned my head and wrapped my arms around him, holding him as long as I could in that lip lock before he gently pulled away.

"Please be careful," he said and I could see the despair in his eyes - he didn't want to leave me.

"Don't worry, I'll be fine. See you at school on Monday."

He cocked his head to the side. "You are so beautiful Abby."

I could feel myself blushing. "Ethan," I whispered.

"You'd better go - if you mom hasn't called yet I am sure she will soon," he said.

I sighed, letting my shoulders relax. "I will talk to you later," I said and then he revved the engine and he was off. I watched him ride off until I couldn't see him anymore and then I turned and headed toward Sarah's house. When I reached the small brown one story house with green shutters and old fashioned wrap-around porch I knocked only once and the door flung open. Sarah was standing there in flowery button-down pjs with pants. Her hair didn't even look like it had been brushed and she had a look of irritation; that's when I knew she was going to start.

"Abby, do you know how worried I have been? You left without telling us goodbye, and where have you been? And who have you been with? And then I got a text telling me to lie to your mother if she calls- what is going on?!" She said that in one whole breath, her face even was turning a little red. I put one finger up to signal that I need to break into her speech.

"Sarah, thank you for doing that for me. I do appreciate it." I hurried to think of some sort of explanation. I decided that less is more in this situation. "I ran into a friend that was just passing through town;

she happened to get a layover here. And for something to do she heard about the carnival and decided to come and check it out for herself. We went out for dinner and spent the whole night catching up." She looked at me in disapproval and she didn't seem to be buying my lie, but I continued. "I wouldn't have brought you into this but my mom doesn't really like my friends from back home and I knew she wouldn't have approved of me staying out all night."

"Your mom didn't like your friends?" She asked in disbelief.

"Not really; small town remember". She seemed to buy that part. "I am sorry," I said, trying to get her to forgive me. "Am I forgiven?" I asked.

She took one last look at me and said, "Alright Abby, just don't do that again." She seemed to thaw. "Let me take a quick shower," she said, "and then you can take one; you looked like as if you could use it," she said, a small smile forming on her face.

"Gee thanks," I said, wondering how bad I looked.

"No problem," she said and then laughed.

I have to hand it to her; she was in and out of the shower and ready in only twenty minutes. It usually took me a lot longer, almost forty-five minutes to get ready. She was in a white cotton v neck shirt and faded blue jeans; she left her hair down, which was somewhat unusually for her since she usually had it tide back into a pony tail. She noticed that I was looking at her hair. She merely said, "I feel like being lazy," and then laughed. "Shower's all yours."

"Thanks Sarah; I really appreciate it." I was surprised that Sarah had her own bathroom but being an only child in her house was probably the cause. I headed for the bathroom noticing my surroundings; it definitely was an old house and it had all the original woodwork. In most houses that were this old, all the original wood had been painted over many times, but this house was clean. I had never seen a house this clean before; not even Ben's house was this clean. When I made it to the bathroom I couldn't believe it. I thought Ben's house was nice but this bathroom was breathtaking.

Yeah I know it's a bathroom, but it had a granite counter-top with dual sinks, and the floor was slate tile that was all different shades of green that matched the light green walls. On the end of the room was the toilet and then the big garden tub with a shower. Around the tub the tile ran right up to the top. Even the towels that were hanging opposite of the toilet were another shade of green that matched the slate tiles. I had only seen bathrooms like this in magazines, or on MTV Cribs. I hurried to take my shower and towel off. I wrapped the towel around me and then there was a knock on the door.

"Abby," Sarah said, "I noticed that your clothes were a little muddy around the cuffs. We're almost the same size, so if you don't mind I will let you borrow some of mine."

"Thanks," I said and opened the door a crack and she handed the clothes through to me. "Thanks," I said again as I took the clothes and then shut the door gently. I groaned just a bit but I did it quietly, knowing that Sarah was just on the other side of the door. The shirt she passed through was baby pink with a v-neck, with pearls that buttoned down the middle, and white pants - not at all my style at all, but the clothes were clean and mine were dirty, as Sarah pointed out. I quickly got into the clothes, promising that I was taking them off as soon as I got home, and I would have them cleaned and returned by Monday when school starts. I gathered up my old clothes, trying not to get them near my new clothes, grabbed the towel that Sarah had placed out on the rack for me, and headed out of the bathroom. The clothes were just a little bit big but they would do for the ride home.

"Sarah, want do you want me to do with the towel I used?" I said, holding it out to her.

"Oh, just put it in the hamper," she said pointing at the white wicker hamper by the built-in book case. I opened the lid with a small creak, dropped the towel in, and shut it with a little thud. "Are you hungry?" Sarah asked.

"No, not really," I said thinking back to the breakfast that Ethan had made for me. "Sarah thanks for the help. I don't suppose that you can run me home? I don't want to screw up your plans."

"You're fine, Abby," she said. "By the way, those clothes look great on you," she added.

"Thanks again; it's nice to be in something clean. I will get them washed and back to you on Monday."

"Oh," she said, "it's not hurry, I have tons of clothes." She wasn't joking; she opened her walk in closet and there were hundreds of shirts, pants and shoes. Sarah was a shopper.

"Wow," I said.

Sarah started laughing. "Yeah," she said, "I know there are a lot of clothes."

"Don't forget the shoes," I added.

She laughed again. "I get somewhat obsessed when we're in a mall."

"I couldn't tell," I laughed.

"Well, let me grab my purse and keys and I can get you back out to Ben's house."

I like the way she didn't say home, and added Ben's house. "Thanks." I was saying thank you so much today I should have just grabbed one of those mini recorders and just recorded it so I could push play.

When we both had our shoes and coats on we headed outside and got into Sarah's car, which was just as clean as her house. Sarah was a good driver, looking in all of her mirrors as we pulled slowly out of the drive and onto the street. She seemed to be one who followed all the rules while driving, so it took longer to get out to Ben's than if I'd been driving. But once we went past the iron gates and up the long path to the house I felt some relief. Although I like Sarah, I didn't want to have to answer any more of her questions.

She stopped under the under hang to the house to let me out. "See you at school on Monday," she said.

"Yeah, thanks again! Hey, maybe you and Julie can tell me about the rest of the carnival on Monday."

"Sure," she said, and I thought she was going to start gushing about it now, but she looked at the clock on the dash and then said, "Got to go."

"Alright, see you," I said and shut the door. I waved as she slowly drove down the drive. I walked up to the door and on cue the butler opened the door just when I went to reach for the door handle.

18 Bliss

"MORNING, MISS," SAID THE WRINKLED old butler said as he slowly opened the heavy wooden door. I always wondered how he was able to even open the door; he looked so frail that you would think he would crumble once the door was opened. "Your mother is in the living room and she wants to speak with you," he added which was quite a surprise, since the most I have ever heard from him was a few short words, except when he went over the rules when I first got here. I just let out a short nod and headed to the living room.

To my relief, my mom was sitting in there by herself, which was different since she usually was with Ben. She was sitting on the sofa with one arm on the end of the couch and her feet on the wooden coffee table. She still had that glow to her, that glow that said 'I am extremely happy and still in the honey moon' phase. She looked deep in thought, until she saw me. "Oh, my," she said starring at me with wide eyes.

"Sarah let me borrow some clothes since I stayed at her house last night," I said, cutting her off at the pass. She pressed her lips together, smiling to keep from laughing. My mom was the fashion nut - I could care less and just wearing a t-shirt and blue jeans was fine by me - but I could see that she was overjoyed to see me actually taking pride in my appearance.

"You look great," she said letting some of her happiness shine through.

"Where is Ben?" I asked. "Usually you two are joined at the hip," I said with a little chuckle.

"Oh, he is out at the warehouse; they are getting ready for harvesting."

"Oh," I said. Translation: mom is bored. I should have known by the vacant look on her face that the wheels were up to something. Usually when my mom is bored she goes extreme on things. "What's up?" I asked.

"Well, I wanted to know how last night went. I wanted to hear about the carnival."

"Oh," I said. Relief, I thought she was going to grill me about why I didn't come home last night; either she wasn't thinking in that direction or she hadn't gotten to that point. "It was fine," I said continuing.

"Just fine?" she asked, one brown eyebrow lifted and a small smirk on her face.

"Yes," I said. "Just fine. Why you are looking at me like that?" I said.

"Well," she said, "we have been here a couple of months and we really haven't spent time together, with you in school and me learning the business."

Translation: spending time with Ben, I thought without voicing it out loud.

"And," she said continuing, "I want to hear about school and about your friends."

"Well, you have met the two friends that I hang out with, and school is the same no matter where ever you go," I said with a laugh.

"Okay, I will give you that," she said. "But...." she said and then paused.

"But what, Mom?" I asked.

"What about the boys in your school?"

I know that she was trying to be subtle, to drive this conversation in the way that she wanted, but I wasn't going to fuel her fire. "Mom, boys too are the same; they're just a bunch of hormone-riddled teenagers trying figure out their place, and boys don't get brains until they are older," I said with a laugh.

She laughed too and it was refreshing to hear that; she had been with Ben so long that I really missed her. "I'm glad that you had a good time at the carnival and I know things are a little different around here."

"You have no idea," I mumbled, low enough that I knew that she wouldn't have heard me.

"I know that you had fun staying with your friend last night," she said and I nodded to show her that I was agreeing with her. After all, it was a great night; she just didn't know that I didn't stay with Sarah, and that I actually stayed with Ethan. But parents don't need to know everything do they? I mentally asked myself, and then grinned. No they don't, I would have laughed but my mom would have insisted that I let her in on the joke.

"But," she said continuing, "next time, advance notice might be good."

"Sorry, Mom," I said. "Sarah had a long day and a long night and she was tired. I didn't want her to bring me all the way home and then turn around and drive home alone. She might have fallen asleep at the wheel or run into a deer; you know there's a lot of wildlife around here." I was fibbing when I said that, the only thing I had seen here was a wolf and he was half human so does that really count? Would you consider that wildlife?

"No Abby, you did well. If ever you are tired or your friend is tired just make sure to let me know, just like you did. That way I get the option to come get you if I want to."

"That sounds fair enough." I tried to look for a change of subject so that I wouldn't have to lie to her about last night's activities. "So, what are you and Ben going to do for the rest of the weekend?"

"Oh, Ben has meeting with some of the buyers for the wine that is getting shipped out in a few weeks, so I told him that I would help," she answered with a grimace on her face.

"You don't look too happy, Mom," I noticed.

"No, I am happy," she started to dispute my comment but she paused and then continued, "I just miss the joy of working in my shop and meeting new people or conversing with the regulars. It's great being with Ben, don't get me wrong, but I think I need the interaction with other people. I miss all the girl chat." This surprised me about my mom. Yes, I know she likes to gab, but I thought she and Ben would be wrapped in their bubble for a while and really not notice anything else. Why did she have to start coming out of the bubble, just when things were getting interesting?

"Well did you talk to Ben about it?" I asked. "Mom, the direct approach with Ben might be the correct way to handle this. I am sure that he would be up for whatever you wanted; you have got him wrapped around your fingers," I said with a laugh and a smile.

It was then that her whole face lit up and the smile spread across her face. "I do, don't I?" she said with a laugh.

"Well, I need to go get into some more manageable clothes," and I almost dashed up the stairs thinking about the possibility.

My mom face turned down in a grimace and I couldn't see the dimple that was usually so prominent since my mom smiled all the time. "Abby, you look so stylish, so beautiful in those clothes; why would you want to change them?"

"Well, mom," I said being careful; I know how disappointed she was that my clothing selection was not up to her style but I didn't want to hurt her feelings. "These really aren't my clothes, they are Sarah's. She let me borrow them so I would have clean clothes to go home in but they are so light I would hate to get them stained up."

My mom just nodded. "You know, Abby, we really haven't seen each other for a while. Maybe a shopping trip is what we need."

I tried not to grimace, I hated to shop. "Mom, I already got new clothes; I really don't need any more."

"Oh that's right, Ben let you have his credit card. Well a girl can never have too many clothes," she said with a smile, trying to get me to consider the idea. But somehow she knew I wasn't going to budge so she let it drop and moved on to another topic. "Well, I guess we can go shopping for a dress for the dance." In Klamath Falls they really didn't have a prom for just seniors; it was for the whole high school. My guess is since the school classes were so small it was supposed to put more bodies in the gym so it didn't look empty, or it could be that they were on a limited budget and this way they could wrap all the dances together, saving time and expense.

"Oh that's right that's coming up isn't it?"

"Yep," she said, beaming, and then the dimple was more pronounced. "I am sure we can take Ben's private jet anywhere you want and go shopping."

"Oh yeah," I said, faking enthusiasm; it didn't work. She could see right through me. She laughed.

"Just think about it. It might be fun, and maybe your friends would want to join us so they can get their dresses."

"I will ask them," I said as I got up preparing to exit out of the room. Mom got up at the same time as she noticed me begin to rise.

"Do you know how much I love you?" she said and gave me a hug that almost cracked my ribs.

"Ouch," I said and she released me.

"Oh sorry," she said.

I laughed. "I love you too, Mom." Her eyes actually shifted; one moment she looked happy and the next she looked like she was going to cry. Oh no, I thought; she was going sentimental on me.

"I feel like I am going to lose you soon," she said. "I feel like you are growing up so fast."

Not fast enough, I thought, smiling at the prospect of moving into my own place, far from the rain and the manor. "Mom," I said, trying to soothe her, "I am only 16 and you have me for two more years before I go to college, so don't panic yet."

She hugged me one more time, a little softer, and then released. "I probably should go and see if Ben is done with his meeting. He said the cook is preparing something special for dinner today."

That wasn't good. I thought it would be something I couldn't say or spell and I made it a rule that I never ate anything that I could say or spell. "Um Mom, I actually wanted to hide out in my library today. Can you just ask the cook to make me a sandwich and some milk?" How I long for the days that I could go into my own kitchen and get whatever I wanted and not have to answer to anyone. I thought this in my head so my mom wouldn't be disappointed in me. As far as she knew, I had starting accepting the ways around here and was adapting, so why spoil her wishful thinking?

"Sure Abby; are you sure you don't want to eat dinner with Ben and me?"

"No, not tonight. I really should catch up on my reading; I really haven't picked up a book since I have gotten here." Which was true, so that part I wouldn't have to lie about. The only book that I had ready had been part of Elizabeth's diary and that had disappeared.

"Alright," she said. "I will let you go get changed."

"Thanks, Mom." I was relieved; I hated not telling her everything but was smart enough to know if I told her everything she would make me see a shrink. "I'll talk to you later." She gave me a hug and I thought she was never going to let go. "Mom," I laughed, "what has gotten into you?"

"Nothing," she said almost like she was going to start crying, "I just miss all the time we spent together when we lived in Florida."

"Afraid I'll get lost in the manor, never to be seen again?" I laughed and she laughed with me.

"You know where my room is, so come see me anytime." She hugged me one more time before I head out the door. It was nice to have conversation with my mother but even better to get upstairs and get changed. I hurried up the stairs and headed into my room, almost knocking over the vase of the table that was right next to my door, but I caught it in time and then set it back on the table, sighing. I rushed in the door, getting out of the shirt as quickly and carefully as I could without tearing the shirt, and then shimmied the pants to my ankles. Kicking them off, I picked up both pairs of clothing and set them on the bed. Then I headed to the closet to grab a t-shirt and some sweats. I felt a little more comfortable when I was in my own clothes. I headed to the dresser that was by the bed and pulled out a clean pair socks. I reached down and took off the dirty socks that I had worn yesterday and put back on after the shower just to have something to wear. They felt really grimy and I was glad when they were off and a new pair was on. I didn't put on my shoes, really why would I? I was supposed to be making myself at home and I never wore my tennis shoes.

It took me a couple seconds to decide that I wasn't heading to the library quite yet. I would head down there eventually but right now I decided there was more to my surroundings that I hadn't seen yet, and it might be in my best interest to find out more about the surroundings that I had been living in. After all, if I was smart I would have checked out the manor the first day I was here, but the butler kind of creeped me out, and it was like he was always watching me with those beady little eyes of his. Well, he was not around now that I knew of, and my mom and Ben were having dinner, so I would be free to explore the manor and not be interrupted.

I carefully opened the heavy doors to my room, knowing if I open them too fast that they would squeak and draw attention to me. I opened them just a crack and slithered between them, looking down both ends of the hall, scanning for Albert the creepy butler. And when I didn't see him - or anyone - I made my way down the stairs as quietly as I could and down the hallway, like I was heading to the library, but when I got to the doors I walked past, heading to the last door in the hallway. It was a heavy oak wood door like all the rest, except this door had and an arch with two angels very carefully crafted on the top part of the door facing each other. How interesting that a door would have something so special over it. This must be a room of some importance.

I opened the door, and like the rest it squeaked in protest as I opened the door. Although the door was a little more hesitant than the others and that made me wonder when the last time the door had been open. When I opened the door I couldn't see anything, but I could smell the room was stagnant and I knew at that point that I was correct in my assumption this room hadn't been open in a while. I stepped into the room to look for a light switch, wishing that I had brought a flashlight. I felt around the walls looking for a light switch. It was then that the light popped on and scared me to death. I slowly turned around to see who shared the room with me.

19 The Ballroom

As I turned around, I could smell the aroma of the cologne. It was then I knew who it was but I still turned to face him. "Ben," I said in conformation.

"Abby," he replied. "I was just heading in for lunch when I noticed you headed to this end of the hall."

"I'm sorry," I said, keeping somewhat of a distance. Remembering Ethan's words, 'I know that he is part of it, I just don't know how deep Ben is in it,' I wasn't comfortable being in this room that I hadn't been in before, especially with Ben, a person that I was not particular fond of. "Where is my mother?" I said, trying to keep my voice from shaking.

"Oh, she will be down for dinner in a minute. She's just freshening up." When Ben talked, you got the feeling of someone charismatic who was sure of himself.

"So," he started, "if you wanted to be shown the rest of the house, I could have taken you on a tour. No need to sneak around."

"I wasn't..." I started to stutter and he raised one had to stop me.

"Well, I see you found the ballroom." It was then I took my first look around the room; it was very dirty and dusty, as I had ascertained from the smell. When I first opened the door I'd realized the room was enormous, with mirrors surrounding the whole room that made the space appear even bigger. It had at a glance at least twelve chandeliers, which had crystals that dangled and shimmered, and wall lights that surrounded the room. My guess: the lights had been added in later years since the manor was built so long ago they wouldn't have had electricity when it was first made. The wood floor ran through the whole room. It was undeniably beautiful. It was a picture of perfection, one like I had seen painted in art galleries. All that was missing were men in old fashioned tuxes and women with hoop-skirts, corsets, and big hair and hats.

"Wow," was my brilliant response.

"Yes, it's something, isn't it?" he said and started to pace around me. "This rooms hasn't been used since the original Moores had built it and lived here," he continued. "In the old days, when the manor was first built, there were many parties and many social events. Only the richest people would come to these parties; commoners where not welcome."

"Why haven't you used it since?" I asked, intrigued by his story.

"There hasn't been any real need for its use. To be honest, before I married your mother, I wasn't here much so that's why most of these rooms have been shut up. If you would like, I can take you and your mother on a tour; there are still many rooms as well as the greenhouse and the gardens in back."

"Gardens?" I asked.

"Well," he started, "it's more like mazes back there. The hedges have been there a long time; best not go in there without someone who knows that garden or without a compass at least. Well," he said as I continued to look and admire my surroundings, "your mom will be waiting for us."

"Actually I was just going to go to the library and I noticed the door so I thought I would have a look," I lied.

"Oh," he said. "I apologize if I read more into it," he said and added, "Abby, this is your home as much as my home now and I want you to be happy." He seemed sincere; I couldn't see any false pretense in his eyes or face. But what did I know; I had never run into any of the problems that I was facing living here.

"Actually, I think I am a little tired; a nap would probably be good." I noticed as I was heading out of the door, with Ben on my heels, that Albert was bringing a tray down the hall. I managed to say 'thank you' and grab the tray. He held onto it for a split second before letting it go, as if I was going to make him look bad if he didn't carry it. "It's okay, I can carry it; I'll bring it down when I am done."

He was still grimacing with the corners of him mouth turned down.

"It's alright, Abby," Ben said, "just place it outside the door when you are done and the staff will pick it up."

"Okay, thanks, Ben," I said and I was sincere. If this guy was supposed to be so bad how come he is so nice? And why was he so nice to my mom even we he thinks no one is looking? He is the sweetest guy, always opening the car door and pulling out her seat at the dinner table, and the way he always lays his hand at the small of her back… I could see that he truly cared for her, so it was so hard to believe what Ethan was saying, but I did believe him; something about the way he told me about his past, I could hear the truth in it. So I would hold onto that and remember it when I talked to Ben.

I started to walk with the tray to my room. Thank God I managed to get the tray up the stairs without spilling anything. I set the tray down on the desk. The cook had actually made a peanut butter sandwich. It had a small bowl of apple sauce, and a glass of milk, and for desert there was a brownie on the side. So even when I was not eating the regular lunch she still made too much food. When I ate half of everything that they had made for me I switched on my computer to check my email. I finally got to my email; the internet out here was slow. It was probably because we lived so far from town. I should probably be glad that we had internet, let alone electricity, out here in the sticks. There was mostly spam in my inbox - I quickly deleted that - but then I noticed a few from Paige. In her first email she wrote:

Hey Abby, how are things with you? Not much going on here. It's so boring without you! Have you made any friends? Write back and tell me what school is like and what you are doing the past the time since you don't have the beach to go to. Have you met any cute guys? I am trying to get my parents to let me come out and visit. But you know what parents are like when you asked them to ditch school to visit friends. Yea I know parents are a real drag. TTL
Paige.

I had to laugh at that email; she sounded just as miserable that I had been. That was, until I was with Ethan. It was nice to hear from her so I quickly looked at the other one she sent.

Hey it's me, haven't heard from you, is everything okay? You must be keeping busy. What I am saying? You probably haven't emailed me yet because you hate emailing. Lol. Well can't wait to hear from you.
Paige

I'd better write her back before she thinks that Klamath Falls has swallowed me whole.

Paige, hey girl, sorry I haven't written back to you. It's been nuts here. Nothing much has changed since I wrote to you before. Still is the same, always boring. Mom and Ben are still looking and acting like newlyweds. Yeah, I know; it's gross. And the creepy butler is still creeping me out; he is always looking as cold as ice. It's days when I am stuck here, that I miss home the most. But I have made a couple of friends, Sarah and Julie; they are pretty cool. And there is a boy that I have met and he is gorgeous of course. So things are

starting to look up. Well I have got to go. I will try to write again
soon. Take care
Abby

It was nice to have some contact with the outside world, even it was for a brief second. As soon as I was done and I had hit send I shut off the computer. I noticed that I was very tired and a nap didn't seem like such a bad thing. I headed to the bed and as soon as my head hit the pillow, and the soft fluffy comforter was wrapped me like a cocoon, I was at ease. I felt myself slip away.

It didn't take me long to start to dream, but it was a different dream. I wasn't in the forest like I had been in most of the other dreams. I was in the ballroom, and there were people in old fashioned dresses, with hoop skirts and the white wigs, that they used to wear in the old days to show prestige. And everyone was dancing in a circle to the piano playing in the background. They were swirling around with smiles on their face, and obviously having a really good time, and they all were wearing white and black masks so that you couldn't see their faces. That's when I put it all together: it was a masquerade ball, and I felt very comfortable, like I had gone to it before.

Just then a tall man with light brown hair and ice blue eyes started my direction. The crowd parted as he walked by them, giving him plenty of space. I knew exactly who he was before he even reached me. "Ethan," I whispered as the air left my lungs; when he reached me and took my hands into his warm ones I felt so safe.

"Miss Moore, would you care to dance?"

Miss Moore? I thought and realized this wasn't a dream, this was a memory. Why am I having a memory of Elizabeth's?

I took his hands and he led me out to the dance floor. I wanted ask him what was going on but I put that on hold and let him twirl me around the dance floor. I felt like I was flying and I didn't even step on his feet. That alone should have told me that this wasn't me because I can't dance. I noticed as he twirled that there were candles and tapestries all over the walls; this rooms was definitely decked out for a party. That was when the music stopped and a man that was in the beginning of the room took a spoon and tapped it on one of the many wine glasses I noticed that people held.

He was a lovely older gentleman with a tux and a white bow tie, and he had a very distinguished mustache that curled up on the ends, and his hair was parted to the side. Beside him was a beautiful lady that had taken off her mask; she had bright green eyes and rosy cheeks, and half of her hair was pulled up in a bun and the other half draped down her back in ringlets. She was stunning for women back in those times. She wore beautiful necklace full of diamonds that sparkled under the light from the candles.

The man began to speak. He had a deep voice and you could tell that he had a lot of authority in this world. Like he had given millions of speeches. He carried himself like he was sure of himself. "I want to thank all of you for coming tonight. We are happy that our friends and family have gathered to celebrate my daughter Elizabeth's sixteenth birthday." And he used his hand and gestured in my direction and the crowd parted. Ethan let go of my hands and melted into the shadows.

I walked as if was being pulled to the front of the room, but I resisted, not wanting to be pulled away from Ethan's warm hands. As I reached the front of the room the tall man reached down and gave me a kiss on the cheek.

"Happy birthday, my sweet Elizabeth," he said and then gave me a big hug, and then the women reached down and followed his example.

"Happy birthday, sweetheart," she said after she had kissed me on the other cheek.

"I have an announcement," the man had proceeded. "I have decided," he began, "that Elizabeth is at the suitable age now that she will marry."

I could feel my mouth drop and I knew that surprise crossed my face. And that was the when I woke, sweat rolling down my face and my heart beating out of my chest. The room was dark now and I looked over and noticed my alarm clock; it was just after one and I was guessing it was one in the morning. I couldn't believe it; I slept the whole day away and part of the night. I was surprised that my mom had allowed that. She must have thought I could use some sleep. But now the downfall was that I was wide awake. I ran to the window and looked out; it was so dark outside with just the moon for light, but in the distance I could see something moving outside and I quickly shut the drapes. A shiver ran down my body. Over and over, everything that Ethan had said ran through my head. But it was worse than that, I had more questions now and only Ethan would be the one to answer them.

20 TEMPER TEMPER

FOR THE REST OF THE night I tossed and turned. My guess was that I had too much sleep and that trying to get more was a hopeless process. I was awake as the light crept in between the gap in the heavy drapes. I hurried to get ready for school. I had to give myself a pat on the back; that was the quickest that I had ever gotten ready. It was twenty minutes flat from the time I hit the shower to the time I got dressed and did my hair. I drew on my socks and shoes, excited by the prospect of seeing Ethan and telling him about my dream, and getting more answers for the dozen new questions that I had. I made it down the steps in thirty second flat and to the dining room in another five seconds. My mom and Ben had still beat me to the table.

"Morning," Mom said with a smile.

"Good morning," I said smiling back.

"You're in a good mood," Ben pointed out.

"Just a bit."

"I was under the impression that most kids hated Mondays," He added and then smiled.

"Oh," I said, trying to take my enthusiasm down a notch, "they do, actually."

"Then why are you in such a hurry?" my mother asked with one raised eyebrow.

"No reason," I said as I reached for the orange juice in a glass in front of me. I took a deep swallow and prayed that they would leave me alone and not ask me any more questions. My hopes were very quickly dashed when my mom started to speak again.

"Abby," she said, "this doesn't have to do with a boy, does it?"

I could feel my face going red and I heard Ben chuckle. "No," I said, giving her the evil eye. That hopefully would close this train of conversation.

She looked once at Ben, who was still smiling, and then at me and successfully closed the conversation. She had gotten the impression from the tone of my voice and my look that this was not a conversation that I was going to have in front of my new step-dad. I took one more bite of my Belgian waffle - that really did taste good slathered in all the butter and syrup - and then stood up to leave.

"Off already?" she said.

"Yep," I replied. "If I get there early then I usually get a really good parking spot," I lied. The truth was I just wanted to get out of her line of questioning and into my own line with Ethan. "See you later, Mom," I said and then nodded at Ben to show that I was somewhat including him. It was just an attempt to appease my mother. I grabbed my coat that was on the coat rack by the door, and my bag that was underneath it, and my keys that were always on the table by the door, and headed out the front door. I reached for the handle and this time I was quicker than Albert, who had just gotten in the room as if he had been called. I flashed a smirk at him and he grimaced at me. I almost laughed but I thought that might be a little childish. So I hurried to get the door, shutting it on his surprised face.

I drove to school with my lead foot intact, watching for cops, not needing another speed ticket. I almost laughed at that thought too. I had never even seen a cop on this road. When I rounded around the corner of one of the curves, trees on either side, I had to slam on the brakes. Caleb was there, in the middle of the road, wearing his leather jacket; his bike, I noticed, was no were in sight.

I got out of my Jeep and yelled, "Are you all right?" It was first thing I thought of; he laughed at that. Then the irritation set in. "Are you crazy?" I said, putting as much anger into my words as I could. He just looked at me, without answering me. "I could have killed you. What the hell is wrong with you?" I said, still screaming. He put one finger up to show me he was going to speak. I shut my mouth, still really pissed off.

"Abby," he said. I could hear the anger is his voice. What was my brilliant response? "I have given you every opportunity to leave; obviously a straightforward approach may be the best for you," he snarled, the anger still on his face. "You are not welcome here," he said in his deep throaty voice. "You have no right to come here and uproot things."

"What are you talking about, Caleb? I never asked to come here - this was all my mother's doing. You forget; I am under 18 and I have to do what the parental figure says. Do you think that I would actually move to a place where the sun only shines when it's on vacation? Give me a break."

He almost smirked at that, with the corner on one side of the mouth curving up but then he caught himself and it turned back down. "You don't belong here," he said, changing his strategy. "Ethan is not your concern," he said, staring at me.

This was not a conversation that I was going to have with him. "Look," I said, "what is going on with Ethan and me is none of your business."

"Everything that goes on with Ethan is my business," he said.

Just then I heard the trees and the bushes rustle and my heart fluttered, suddenly scared that it would be another one of Caleb's pack. I was relieved when I saw the ice blue eyes and I began to relax. "Ethan,"

I said as he walked around the vehicle and came to stand in front of me.

"Caleb," Ethan said, "what you are doing?" His voice made me shiver.

"What you should have done from the beginning," he said in an uncaring and cold voice.

"Abby is not part of this," Ethan started to raise his voice at Caleb.

"You know that she is, Ethan; you know that she is living with our enemy."

"She is not part of this," Ethan said again.

"You know that she is not Elizabeth," Caleb said with a harsh tone to his voice.

"I know exactly who Abby is," Ethan replied.

"Don't let her face fool you. She is going to be the downfall of us all."

"The only danger I see is you Caleb."

"Why do you even bother with this one," Caleb said with his hands clenched into fist and visibly shaking.

"Calm down, Caleb; you and I can talk about this later. This involves you and me, not Abby."

"No," he said shaking his head in disagreement. "This is all about her. Didn't you learn from the first time?" he asked only looking at Ethan now. "Don't you get it," he continued, "this will not end well."

"What are you talking about, Caleb?" Ethan asked. His once-steady voice was a little shaky now.

"Don't you get it, after all this time? One thing we have learned through all the years and centuries is that history always repeats itself."

"No," Ethan said to Caleb. "I won't let it."

"How are you going to stop it," Caleb asked with one lifted brow. "For Christ's sake, she lives in that house. Her mother is married to one of them! Don't you get it? Even if you want her saved, she is already dammed. If you want the best for her, don't let this go any farther."

"It's too late," Ethan said. "I can't and I won't live without." If Ethan had not been holding me up in his strong, warm arms, that statement might have knocked me to the ground; I knew I had a connection with Ethan but he had always been so secretive about his feelings for me that I didn't realize he felt the same way about me as I did about him. He looked away from Caleb and looked down at me, still speaking to Caleb. "I love her," he said to Caleb, looking into my eyes and nowhere else.

"You are choosing her over the pack? Over the people who have been your family this whole time? We have watched each other's backs all these years and you are giving it up for nothing."

"Caleb, why are you doing this?" Ethan said.

"Because," he replied, "you are not the only one stuck in limbo. This war should have ended centuries ago and we shouldn't be living half-lives. We shouldn't be watching everyone around us die; it's not supposed to be this way. We aren't supposed to live forever frozen in time and never aging. It isn't supposed to be like this!" He was nearly screaming but I could see the sadness in Caleb's eyes; it was the first time that he had ever let his guard down and I had ever seen that side of him. I knew there was more to Caleb then I had known about. Ethan was trying to put out the fire, was trying to prevent a fight.

"Caleb," Ethan said holding up his palms showing that he didn't want to fight, "can we talk about this in private? We're not exactly in a good spot."

"Ethan, there is nothing more to discuss, and I will do what is ever necessary to end this war." And with that statement Caleb headed into the forest, slamming his fist against one small tree that cracked in half.

As he left, Ethan looked at me as though I was going to crumble like a house of cards. "Abby," he said, "are you alright?" I could feel that I was shaking but I looked up at him. I laughed. It was a hysterical laugh; I could feel my body losing control. He turned me to him and wrapped both of his strong arms around me. And I calmed a little after his arms were around me. "Abby, are you okay?" he asked again.

I finally got the use of my voice back. "I am fine," I said. "Are you okay?"

He laughed. "I am fine." That seemed to be the general response of what had been happening with Caleb. "We better get you to class, before you're late and the school gets your family involved."

"What are you going to go with me?" I asked, a little hesitant.

"Yeah, if you don't mind I will drive. You still look a little bit shaken up; maybe it might be better for you."

"Aren't you worried that people will see us together?"

"Well since Caleb is aware, now I think it may be smart for me to stay around you as much as possible now." I felt my face lift into a huge smile. "Abby..." He hesitated. "Abby, Caleb knowing about us is not a good thing."

My smile began to waiver. "Why?" I asked.

"Caleb has his own demons; you have to remember that we have lived along time and we all have our past. It wouldn't be right for me to disclose another's past."

I didn't push Ethan any farther about Caleb. It was bad enough that the once-friends were disagreeing over me. "Ethan, would it be better for you if I just stayed away? I don't want you and Caleb to fight over me."

"Oh Abby, Caleb and I would have fought over anything. Don't you worry; I'll find a way to mend things." I handed out my keys and he took them in one swoop. I walked back over to the other side of the jeep and jumped in. Ethan chuckled, "Abby you just might break your neck getting in and out of this Jeep."

"More like bruise my butt." I started laughing, remembering the first few days that I had gotten in and out of the jeep and the bruises on my legs and backside. He looked at me with one wicked smile that spread across his whole face.

"Will you let me in on the joke?" he said, still grinning.

"Oh, it's just when I first got into to the Jeep I used to get bruises because I never landed just right."

"No!" he was laughing as he put my truck it drives and I buckled my seat belt. "Yeah," he said, "I think I can see that about you."

"Ha ha," I said. "It's just so funny," I said crossing my arms and sinking down in the seat.

"Oh, you know I am only joking."

"I know," I said and started to sit back up out of my pouting pose. Ethan had already started the jeep and it was rumbling. He put it into drive and we started to move very quickly. Lots of different things were running through my head and I wasn't sure where to start. Do I tell him about the room at the manor or should I tell him about the locker? I guess I would start with Caleb.

"Caleb was the one that busted up my locker," I said looking out the window at the trees flying by.

"What?" Ethan asked and turned his eyes to look at me for a split second and then back on the road. "What are you talking about, Abby?" He seemed to be clueless to what Caleb's been up to; guess Caleb doesn't share everything with the pack.

"Well, one night after staying late at school I got to my locker and noticed that it had been jimmied open and a note was left in there telling me to leave. Okay, I'm paraphrasing," I said, "but the intention was clear."

"Why do you think it was Caleb?"

"Because he just said it; he said, 'I have given you every opportunity to leave, obviously a straightforward approached may be the best', so that tells me that everything that has been going on to get me to leave town has to be all Caleb's fault."

Ethan just nodded, now understanding what I was saying. "Yeah, that does sound like Caleb." The drive to school seemed to trip along quickly and before I knew it I was at school. It was disappointing to be at school already. I let the frown spread across my face.

He pulled into the parking lot and chose one of the farthest spots from where Caleb and his crew usually parked, which was probably a good idea, since I had a few choice words I would want to say to him - or maybe scream at him. I could see the big shiny black bikes; now there were only four of them since Ethan had come to school with me. Thank God that everyone was inside; I didn't need to be stared at again just like it was the first day of school all over again, and with Ethan by my side driving my car, there would be stares and lots of gossip. It's a small town; isn't that how it always happens?

"Shall we," Ethan said as he put the jeep in park and shut the engine off.

"I think we should have played hooky," I grumbled out.

"You know, that is always an option," he said with a smile and a wicked glint in his eyes.

"I can't, I have to work on my grade in Mrs. Teasly's class; I am sure there are things that I haven't burnt or melted yet."

His laughter shook my truck. "We all have our faults," said Ethan still laughing.

"Well then, apart from shedding and maybe some drooling, what faults do you have, Ethan?" He let out another boom of laughter that shook me to my core and vibrated down through my toes.

"Only at the full moon, Abby," he said with another laugh. He was just so free-spirited today that I had to laugh, too. It was different to see Ethan so carefree for a change; it was nice. I hoped we would have more days like this.

I straightened up in my seat; Ethan reached over and, with his face up close and personal to mine, he reached down and unhooked the latch to my seat belt. He smelled so good - he had a woodsy scent - and with the heat of his body so close my breath hitched and faltered. He grinned at me, listening to my ragged breath.

"We'd better go in," he said.

"What?" I said, shaking my head and trying to clear my thoughts.

"School, Abby. You don't want to be late," he said leaning back in his seat with one hand on the door, the other hand holding out my keys. I grabbed them out of his hand and got out of the jeep. He was right by my side as we walked to our first class. I knew that if we walked in together, we were going to be the subject of gossip.

"Are you ready for this?" I said, knowing that it was going to be worse for Ethan since I knew his friends would be very unhappy with him.

"It will be fine, Abby," he said, and he sounded calm but his hand was balled into a fist, so I know that he was worried. But I wasn't sure if he was worried about how it would look with us together, or he was more worried on how they were going to react. His other hand gripped mine firmly as we walked into the school.

I walked up the steps, my shoes squeaking with every step that I took thanks to the ever-constant rainy weather. After we got to the floor we need I turned to head to my locker noticing the halls were almost empty, with a few student scurrying to get to class. I thought Ethan was going to go to his locker but he stayed by my side.

"Ethan, don't you need your books?" I asked looking at him.

"I will get them for my next class; it would be better if we went in together."

"We are in school, Ethan. What are they going to do? Go get your books."

He took one look at me, let out a noisy sigh, and said, "All right, I will you see in class." He turned to head in the direction of his locker, still a little hesitant.

"See you in a few," I said and I turned to head to my locker. After retrieving my books and dropping off my coat and bag I headed to class. I headed back to the seat I had sat in before, with Caleb's look of hatred on me. Ethan was a just a minute or so behind me and he looked as if he was out of breath when he came into class, like he had rushed, which I knew he had. It doesn't look like Caleb's face had changed for Ethan either. I didn't want Ethan to fight with his friends over me. You could feel the cool atmosphere as Ethan sat in his normal seat.

As soon as he sat down I saw Caleb lean over and whisper something to Ethan. I couldn't see Ethan's face but I could see Caleb's; it was beyond furious. Class seemed to take longer, though maybe that was because I couldn't really pay attention to the teacher. My focus was on the pack. The bell ringing surprised me and I almost fell out of my chair.

As the other kids shuffled out of the class room along with the teacher, our trio were the last ones left in the room: Caleb, Ethan, and me. In a second Ethan moved closer and Caleb got in his face. But he was yelling and jabbing his finger at me.

"This isn't the last time we're going to talk, Abby; you'd better watch your back."

Ethan had a low growl that started deep in his chest. "Caleb, you are not going to hurt her," Ethan said, and you could feel the tension and the anger.

"You can't watch her twenty-four hours a day," Caleb said with a wicked smile.

"Don't do something you won't be able to take back," Ethan warned.

"I won't have to, Ethan," he said with a wicked smile. "Where she is living and who she is living with, you won't be able to save her and it will end just like it did before." And with that Caleb swept out of the door, the atmosphere of anger still in the air.

Ethan whirled around and I was in his arms in the next second. "I won't let it happen that way."

"Ethan," I said as he squeezed me, "I can't breathe."

He released me in that split second. "Sorry, Abby."

"It's okay, I don't mind the hugs, just maybe try not to break me." I let out a laugh. "We'd better get to our next class; I will meet you after school," I said. Ethan and I only had the one class together.

"All right," he said a little more resigned. "Just make sure you are never alone, okay?"

"Ethan, I'm at school; the worst thing that would happen today is that I will burn down the school." A little smile crossed his face. He had such a beautiful smile.

21 ATTACK

I HAD TO HURRY TO my next class, and when home eck rolled around I felt so tired, and I did not want to deal with Mrs. Teasly's crabby glares. I wondered if I burned enough food and melted enough pans if she would actually pass me just to get me out of her class, or if she would just kick me out. Both possibilities lifted my spirits.

I was trying to make angel food cake. Anyone who has ever had angel food cake knows that it is fluffy and white with a sweet taste. Yeah, like that happens when I bake. I guess when I was filling the cake I put a little too much batter in the cake pan, and most of it started spilling into the bottom of the stove, making the burnt smell fill the classroom. Angel food is suppose to be flat on the top so when you turn it over it will lay right; yeah, not so much in my case.

Once the caked was out of the oven I turned it over and waited for it to drop. If you baked it right then should just fall off, right? Nope. If it happened to anyone else I would probably be laughing too, so I shouldn't have been surprised when everyone was watching and snickering at my latest 'oops.' I caught a glance at Mrs. Teasly and she just slightly shook her head. I used a knife to get out the rest of the cake, scraping the side of the cake pan, and I started to piece the cake back together like a jigsaw puzzle. The more I pieced, the louder the laughter got. Leave it to Conner to get the class fired up. I swear when he gets older he should really take up standup comedy; the kid's a natural.

After I had the caked pieced somewhat together Mrs. Teasly came over and said, "All right, Abby, I think you have done everything you can do to fix this…." It was funny that she couldn't even call it a cake; I would have laughed but I wasn't sure that the frail little teacher's nerves could take it and I might feel bad if I caused her to have a nervous breakdown or lose whatever hair she has left. "I think we are going to have to use frosting to cover it up," she said in her frail voice.

I didn't know too much about angel food cakes but I was sure most of them were covered with strawberries or some sort of dripping topping like chocolate. I guess desperate times for Mrs. Teasly call for her to use desperate measures. She gave me what was supposed to be any easy fluffy frosting recipe - the key word was easy - and it was anything but. I got the ingredients mixed, but I forgot to shut off the electric mixer. I was covered in frosting from my hair to my waist. I would say baking and cooking were definitely not a career option for me. Even Mrs. Teasly, who was always upset at the way I baked and cooked, cracked a smile at me at my latest goof.

I managed to finish frosting and covering the jigsaw angel food cake, and it actually looked like a cake. I was pretty proud of myself, until Mrs. Teasly took the first bite. The bite of cake was in and out of her mouth in one second flat, and in the next second she was almost sticking her head under the faucet trying to get the taste out of her mouth. Conner was laughing so hard that I am sure that the whole school heard him. One student even popped his head in the open door.

"Hey, what's going on?" I heard him say and it took a split second to realize that it was a boy name Alex, one of the guys who was at the bonfire at the cliffs.

"Abby is trying to kill Mrs. Teasly," Conner managed to sputter out and then he was laughing again. My face was getting redder I could feel the blood rushing to my face and I ducked my head in embarrassment.

"How?" said Alex.

Conner managed to answer with two words in between chuckles. "Food poisoning," he said loudly.

When Mrs. Teasly was able to speak again she said, "Um, Abby, did you use sugar or salt for your cake?"

"Sugar," I said grabbing the container and handing it to her.

She took one sniff and set down the container. "Abby, this is salt. What you have here now is one big salt block."

Conner, still laughing, said, "Hey Abby, it may not be edible, but can I use it for deer hunting? They love salt blocks."

Mrs. Teasly gave Conner and the rest of the class one look and that stopped the laughing. Just then the bell rang and the class filed out. I started to clean up my mess but Mrs. Teasly said, "It's fine, Abby; I will clean up. You'd better hurry to your next class."

I think she was just trying to get me out of her classroom, and since I really didn't care about this class and couldn't wait to escape, I said, "Okay," and that I was sorry about the cake. I grabbed my books and headed out the door with her grumbling something in the background that I couldn't really hear, but it was something like: I don't know if I can take another year of this. Well, if I can't cook or bake and I have to get embarrassed on a daily basis then I will take comfort in the fact that at least my least favorite teacher has to suffer right along with me.

Lunch was a boring affair; I sat with my friends at lunch and we replayed all the events of last weekend, all the stuff that was safe to share. I also told the girls about the new room in the manor, the ballroom that I had found, and also that Ben had caught me in there.

"Oh my God," Sarah said. "Did he get mad?"

"Why?" I asked. "It's my place now, too," I said and then grumbled, "or at least that's what they keep telling me."

Sarah and Julie laughed. "Abby, it can't be that bad living in the big house," Julie added. "It's just funny that you seem to be finding more and more rooms that you haven't seen and you have lived there for months."

"Julie, I might live there but it doesn't make it my house. It's creepy looking around that house, and every room I find just seems to make the manor worse. There are secrets in the house."

"How so?" Julie asked.

"Well, there is the butler. Do we all agree that he is creepy?" I looked over at them and they were both bobbing their heads in agreement.

"Way creepy," Sarah said.

"Well, that isn't even the weirdest part: the cook is just as bad as the butler and she plays with sharp objects," I said, shuddering as I pictured the cook preparing food with the sharp utensils. "And it's Ben too; he always has the answers for everything, and he acts so suave, like nothing will ever bother him."

The girls looked at me as if I was talking crazy. I knew they thought I was lucky living in the massive house, with a new car and anything I could ever want or need, but I couldn't help but feel that everything that was given to me was going to come with a price.

"He actually has a ballroom?" Sarah asked.

"Yep," I said.

"I wonder what else he has in that house," she laughed.

"I don't know, but I know there is a whole lot more," I said. "The ballroom is pretty impressive but it hasn't been used in a long time; it's really dirty and dusty. I think I am the first person in there since the last party they had. You know what?"

"What?" they both said in unison.

"We should have a slumber party some time and then we can sneak around in the middle of the night and explore."

"Aren't you worried about the creepy butler?"

"Well, he can't stay up all night. I mean, he is like, a hundred years old; he has to sleep sometime, right?"

We all laughed at that one, and then the bell rang and it was time for gym. Having gym class right after lunch - whoever thought that was a good idea was obviously dropped on their head when they were younger. Gym couldn't get over fast enough for me, although like always my thoughts were drifting, and I wasn't paying attention. So when the gym teacher blew the whistle I wasn't just shocked, I was relieved.

This week's agenda was basketball. So naturally, no one put the basketballs away. I wasn't the only one who noticed that. Mr. Arnold was watching everyone drop the balls and head to the locker room. I was the slowest to get to the door so maybe he thought that, since I wasn't good for actually playing basketball, at least I could clean up. The school was trying to keep the gym nice and tidy since it was going to be the scene for this year's prom.

What a joke, I thought. Prom is one thing I could live without, although, knowing my mom, she would never let me. I swear she is trying to relive her youth through me. These were the days I wished that she had more children.

As I walked through the gym, I noticed how quiet it had gotten, after all the racket of the guys laughing and running up and down the court and the girls trying not to get run over and squealing when they barely missed getting hit by the boys. Each dribbling of the basket ball was like someone hammering a piece of wood with a nail. And parents wonder why kids can't hear when they are told to do something; it's because we are deaf right after gym class.

As I picked up the basketballs, I could tell the difference between the ones used by the guys and the ones used by the girl. The ones used by the guys had sweat on them in the shape of hands and fingers, and the one used by the girls looked like they had never been used at all. By this time, I was by myself and no one else was around. One quick shot, I thought picking up one of the balls that hadn't been saturated by sweat. I walked over to the free-throw line holding onto the basketball with my right hand. I looked down at the floor to make sure my feet were line up with the black free-throw line. I brought up the basket ball with the right hand and guided it with my left, bent my knees and, staring at the basket, I released.

It hit the rim of the basket, went around three times, and to my shock it actually went in. The basketball swished through the net and then bounced when it hit the floor. My mouth dropped. Of course I was excited -I had never made a basket in my whole life! - and then I was a little annoyed since no one was around to see it.

Or at least I thought no one was around.

I turned to grab the ball that had rolled behind me; it was still rolling towards the door of the gym, and without warning was stopped by an extended foot. I looked up to see Ethan standing there, one foot on the ball and clapping as he looked at me. "You know, you are pretty good," he said, a smile stretching across his face.

I frowned. "Not really," I said. "That was pure luck."

"No, no," he said, smiling, "you are a natural."

I would have been madder if Ethan wasn't so cute, with that big white smile and those beautiful ice blue eyes. He winked at me and then bent his knees and angled the ball with his hands and with one toss it swished through the net of the hoop without even touching the rim.

"Wow," I whispered. He made that shot and he was further back than I was; he wasn't even close the free throw line. "You look like the natural," I said finally, smiling at him. He just let out a bellowing laugh and it echoed and bounced off of the gym wall.

"Are you about ready?" he said when he had stopped laughing.

"I have to change, but it won't take me long," I said looking down at the black shorts and the white t-shirt that were required for any gym class in this school. The last school I had attended had school gym uniforms that were the school colors, white, yellow, and blue, so I should be happy that I could wear my own clothes. But it was gym - come on, how excited should one get over gym clothes, after all?

Ethan ran his eyes down, staring at my legs, and I had to be grateful that I always had my legs shaved. "Hmm," he said and then looked into my eyes. "If you really must," he said with a wicked gleam in his eyes and in his smile.

I could feel my face going red again and I was sure that it was bright red or at least the color of an apple. "I will be right back," I said and then I headed for the locker rooms without even waiting for an answer from him. Once I was through the door and it was closed I picked up the pace and I was rushing; I ran in and out of the all-girl shower, not even bothering for the water to warm up, just in there long enough to soap up and rinse off, smelling of the generic liquid soap they always kept hanging in the shower areas. The soap really didn't smell good but anything would smell better than the 'after gym, sweaty socks' smell. I hurried to shut off the water and dry off with the too small of a towel that the school must have thought would be big enough for teen girls.

After I had gotten my underclothes on and started to get in my jeans, I heard the front door of the locker room open and close. "Hello," I said. "Is anyone there?" Totally agitated, I hurried to get my shirt on and dry off my hair. No answer, so maybe one of the girls from gym class had forgotten something and ran in and out so fast I really hadn't noticed. I looked in the mirror and groaned looking at the massive tangles. I reached in and grabbed my comb out of my locker and began to detangle my hair. I wished I had brought some conditioner; it would have been tons better.

After I had gotten my hair brushed and I had gotten my socks and shoes on and put the stinky gym cloths back in the locker, which really never got cleaned, I shut the door with a clang. The next thing I remembered was someone grabbing my hair from behind with strong hands and slamming my head into the locker. I must've blacked out; the next thing I knew, I was on the floor and I felt like my ribs had been kicked and my face felt like it'd been run over. I raised my hands to my face; I could feel something wet, warm, and thick running down it. I lifted my hand to see what it was and with a roil of my stomach I realized it was blood pooling out of my head, enough that it saturated the floor around me. And in the darkness I realized something else; it wasn't hard to breathe because my chest felt like it had been kicked in, it was because smoke was filling the air. The locker room or even the school was on fire and I was still in the school preparing to get barbequed.

I wanted to scream but when I tried to open my mouth and scream for help my lungs filled with smoke and I choked. I realized if I didn't get the scream out that I would die in this place. I let out a blood curdling, high pitched scream and I felt my body vibrate, and the next thing I knew water was pouring over me. Just then I heard something as I floated in and out of awareness.

Someone had come in; I heard the voice as if I was in a long tunnel, and someone was calling to me. "Abby? Abby are you all right? The locker room is on fire! I have to move you; I have to get you out of here." His voice sounded panicked. I would know that voice anywhere: it was Ethan.

"Ethan," I whispered.

"Shhh, don't say anything," he said and I felt myself being lifted; he walked so steadily that I felt like I was floating. Except for the sloshing from the water we walked through that was splashing up at us. But I wasn't cold; Ethan's body heat kept me warm. And I could stay content in his arms forever.

I heard the commotion as we headed out of the school, saw the hustle and bustle of the students that had stayed after school, and the teachers that were finishing their day. Then the sirens came, and as I drifted in and out I saw the fire engine pull up with the lights flashing and the fire men with there think coats. Then I heard Ethan's beautiful voice speaking to one of the ambulance personnel. The next thing I knew I was on the uncomfortable stretcher. I heard Ethan telling the EMT that he found me unconscious on the girls' locker room floor, that he could smell smoke and hurried to see what was going on. He said it with so much hostility in his voice that I wondered if there was more to the story, but it was hard to keep track. My head and ribs were aching and I just felt like closing my eyes and sleeping.

I could hear the EMT, he was so close he sounded like he was shouting, "Miss, do you know your name?"

"It's Abby," Ethan said.

"Abby, my name is Curt. I am the paramedic on duty."

I opened my eyes just to slits; I am sure I looked like a lizard. Curt seemed to be a chubby man from the way his face looked, with beard stubble on his face like he hadn't shaved in a while. He also looked tired, with deep purplish circles under his eyes, like he had worked one too many hours of overtime.

"Abby, do you understand what I am saying?"

"Yes," I said, managing to mumble.

"Do you know what happened to you?" he asked, his eyes going wide as he examined my head wound. From that expression - eyes wide and mouth open - I am sure the cut was bad. I tried to think back but it hurt my head worse when I thought about today's event. I tried to shake my head, but Curt the paramedic protested and held his hands to my head to keep my head still.

"No don't move your head," he said. And he only released my head when I said okay.

"No," I said, "I don't remember." Every word I said seemed to be mumbled out. I knew that Curt was asking me lots of questions but I was zoning in and out too much. Curt must have turned to speak to Ethan when I felt the weight shift from over me.

"People are not allowed in the ambulance," he said and since Ethan was the only one in hearing distance I had to guess he was talking to Ethan. "If you want, you can meet us at the hospital."

I didn't hear Ethan answer. I felt the heat as Ethan leaned down to whisper in my ear, "I won't be far away; I will take care of this," he said. Even in his anger, his voice was tight yet still sexy. I felt a couple drops of water fall to my face out of his hair. It didn't really bother me; I was already soaked from my head to my toes. He leaned down kissed my fore head and then he was gone. The last thing I remember was Curt pounding on the back of the door that separated the cab from the back saying, "Let's go."

22 RECOVERY

I AWOKE TO AN UNFAMILIAR light shining in my eyes. It took quite a few tries to get my eyes to open; they were so heavy and the light shinning wasn't helping. It was like I was left in a tanning bed. I felt a hand squeeze mine.

"Abby," the voice said and I opened my eyes and tried to focus. I knew even before I opened my eyes who it was, though.

"Mom," I said in a whisper.

"Yes, honey; it's me. Do you know where you are at?" she said.

I went to shake my head and realized that I had a tube taped to my face, and when I reached up to touch the plastic tube I noticed that my arm had an IVs in it. From what I could deduce, I was in the hospital. I looked at my mom and said, "What's going on?" But it hurt to talk; it hurt to even breathe. Every part of me hurt.

She saw me wince and said, while she placed her hand on my IV-free arm, "Don't move, honey; you have a lot of injuries."

"What are you talking about?" I was totally lost.

"Abby, what is the last thing you remember?" she asked.

My mom is usually a put-together lady, but her disheveled hair and her wrinkled clothes told me that she must have been staying at the hospital and sleeping on the one couch that was in the tiny room. "What?" I asked her, since I lost my train of thought when I was evaluating my mother.

"What it is the last thing you remember?" she asked again.

"I was in the locker room," I said looking at her. "I was getting ready to come home."

"You don't remember anything else?" she asked, and I couldn't read the expression that was on her face now. Was it worry or disbelief?

"No, really, mom; I don't remember. What is going on?" I asked in a weak voice.

"Well, honey, from what I was told by the firefighters on the scene, some boy smelled smoke coming from the locker room and went to check it, and that's when he saw you lying on the floor, and flames all around."

I tried to think back to remember, but it was hard with my head pounding. If I was a cartoon character my head would have literally split in two, with a jagged line down the middle.

"You know, you are lucky, Abigail," she said, looking directly at me.

"Why?" I asked not feeling so lucky, wishing that I would just pass out so I didn't have to feel the pain or carry on with the conversation. It was exhausting trying to piece everything together and trying to talk to my mother, who was always changing the subject without even taking a breath. "Why am I so lucky?" I asked my mom.

"Hmm," she said, looking down and fussing over my blankets, making sure that every inch except for my face was covered. When I didn't speak again and it was quiet for a moment, she looked up, meeting my eyes. "Oh," she said, and then hurried the' hmmm' up very quickly when I gave her my deep stare of annoyance. "Well, after I made sure that you were going to be okay, the police and the fire chief came over to talk to me. They said the way looked was that someone was smoking in the girl's bathroom and had thrown a lit cigarette butt into the used towel cart and that's when the fired happened."

"Mom," I said. trying to think back, "that explains the fire, but what explains this massive headache and the fact that I am in the hospital?"

"Well, honey," she started, "they think you panicked and ran into your open locker and it knocked you out." For anyone who knew me, they would just assume that was what happened. "Abby, just rest; the doctor says you have a concussion. He also said that it could have been worse and that you were very lucky."

"Why does my chest hurt?" I said reaching my hand up and placing it on my chest. It felt like I had a fifty pound safe dropped on my chest. Even to breathe in and out was a work-out; it was like I had been a chain smoker. It hurt to breathe and every cough was a stab to my chest. What I wanted was my own bed, in my own home in Florida, but right now I would settle for was being unhooked and set from free from the hospital. "Mom," I said in a tired voice, "when will they let me out of here?"

"Well, the doctor said you have to at least stay overnight so they can keep an eye on your vitals. Ben will pick us up in the morning."

"Pick us up?" I asked with one eyebrow raised.

"Well I thought you might like me to stay." She seemed sincere, but I knew sleeping in the hospital wasn't fun, and she had already been here one night at least and she looked kind of rough now. If she spent another night in here she would be downright scary.

"Mom, go home. You look like you could use some rest in your own bed," I said pointing to her messed up array of hair.

She raised her hand to try to push down and straightened the mess, like she just realized that her hair was a mess. "I'm sure I don't look my best," she said and then let out a small laugh, "but I wanted to make sure that you were going to be all right."

"Mom, I am fine," I said sincerely. I knew the aches and the pains would go away. Besides, as it would seem, they were giving me plenty of painkillers. "They said I would be out tomorrow, right?" I said looking at her.

"Yes," she said, a little unwillingly.

"So," I continued, "why don't you go and get some rest?" I said repeating my last plea. I knew I would only have to suggest it twice and she would waiver and finally give in.

"All right," she said, "but I will be back here in the morning bright and early to get you."

I had no doubt she meant what she said.

My mom reached down and kissed my forehead. "I love you. You know that, right?"

"I love you too, Mom. I will see you in the morning."

She stood upright and turned to gather her coat, driving mittens, and purse, and then turned back to me. "In the morning," she said.

"Okay, Mom, tomorrow morning."

And then she blew me a kiss and head out the door. Relief swept over me. Don't get me wrong, I love my mom, but when she worries she hovers like a helicopter. I didn't feel like being hovered over; I needed some space to think about what happened.

I remember Ethan and me in the gym. I remember getting ready after that; I remember thinking I heard something and I also remember the feel of someone grabbing the back of my head and shoving it into the locker. So what my mom was saying didn't make any sense. I know there was someone else in there with me. Someone started the fire on purpose. It wasn't an accident. I was so tired that to think about the incident made my head hurt worse, like I had too many drinks, when I had never had a drink my life. But it didn't take long and my eyes were so heavy I couldn't keep them open.

The next thing that I remembered is that I opened my eyes, and it was dark. I blinked my eyes a couple times and realized that night had fallen and the nurse hadn't felt the need to shut the curtains, so I was able to stare out the window. And then panic struck me when I realized that I wasn't the only one in the room. I could hear someone else breathing; I was all prepared to scream when a hand flashed over my mouth. I tried to scream but there was silence.

"Shh. Abby it's me."

I felt the warmth of the hand and the soft, soothing words, and my fear vanished. "Ethan," I said.

"Shhh; you have to be quiet. Visiting hours are over; I had to sneak in."

"Why," I asked.

"Because I don't want to get caught," he said, with his eyebrows raised.

"No, that is not what I meant," I whispered. "Why did you come?" I knew that Ethan was trying to stay off of the radar from the Moores, although I felt relief with him here. "I had to make sure you where alright," he said, seeming to be letting out his breath.

"Other than a backache from this stiff bed and a headache, I'm great," I said faking a smile. He didn't buy it.

"Abby, are you really alright?" he said, brushing the hair back that had draped over my face tenderly with his fingers. I could feel the hands, so warm, not even touching my skin. I closed my eyes for just a second and then reopened them after I had gathered my composure.

"Well," I whispered, "I'm lying in a hospital bed after the day from hell. What do you think?" I didn't mean for it to come out sarcastically, but between the soreness and the lack of a good sleep, I am afraid that it came out that way. "I'm sorry, Ethan. I'm still really tired; please forgive me."

"Abby, there is nothing to forgive. You're tired and it has been a long couple of days."

"Do you know what happened, Ethan?" I said looking into those beautiful ice blue eyes. He had the worried look on his face, and I was sure that if he told me things it would be the truth, but it would only be parts of the truth.

"No, I don't know completely what happened, but I am going to find out. This should not have happened," he started saying and it was almost like he was conversing with himself. "I can't understand; it was broad daylight in a crowded school. Whoever it was wasn't even scared of getting caught."

"Ethan, what does that mean?"

"Abby, it means the rules have changed, that you aren't just in danger during the night or when you are alone. This person is comfortable in broad daylight."

"What do you think happened, Ethan?"

"I think it's begun."

"What's begun?" I asked.

"The war," he said in a solemn tone.

"The war?" I asked. I was really confused by this point.

"The war that should have taken place five hundred years ago," Ethan replied.

"Ethan," I said, and I could hear the heart monitor accelerate, with the beeps getting faster and closer together.

"Shh, Abby. Don't worry; everything will be fine."

"Sure Ethan. I am lying here with a cracked skull, with all tubes in almost every inch of me."

"Don't exaggerate," he laughed.

"Oh," I said sarcastically, "am I exaggerating?" And then lifted the arm with the IV, and then after lowering that arm, with my unhindered hand I pointed at my bandaged head. "I look like a freakin' mummy."

"No, actually you look cute," he said with a smirk.

And I laughed and that, and then realized that it hurt to laugh; every chuckle was like a hammer to my head. "Ouch," I said.

"What, Abby?" Ethan said with worry in his voice.

"Don't make me laugh; it hurts to laugh." And then I smiled over my own stupidity.

He grinned and showed his perfect teeth in an eye-crinkling smile. He was so beautiful. Then his head turned like he heard something. "Abby, I have to go; the nurse is coming to check on you," he repeated.

"Trust me just once Abby. I will come see you soon. Just keep your eyes and ears open, be friendly with everyone and trust no one."

"Well, I trust you," I said in act of defiance.

He laughed again. "All right, don't trust anyone but me," he said, amending his statement. Then he leaned down gave me one quick kiss on the cheek and then leaned back to have a look at me and saw my pouting look; he bent over and slowly and patiently kissed my lips. The heart monitor went wild.

I haven't had too much experience in the kissing department, but it was like someone eating their favorite ice cream, or their favorite chocolate; he was delicious. When the kissed ended, we were both breathing a little harder than normal.

"I have to go, Abby. I will see you soon," he said in a soft voice.

"Do you promise?" I asked, unsure. I didn't want him to leave. He leaned down once more, with his sweet smell surrounding me, and kissed me ever so gently. I sighed.

"I will be around," he said with a smirk and a wicked glint in his eye. I smiled at him as he walked out the door and I watched him leave.

It was a short time later when the nurse, who was dressed in all white right down to her shoes, except for the stethoscope that dangled from her neck like it was a necklace, came back and checked my vitals, and asked how I was feeling.

My normal response: "Fine, I feel just fine."

She informed me that I would be released tomorrow, and then did the whole speech about how I need to take it easy for a while. I started to close my eyes and acted tired, hoping that she would take the hint and leave me be. I think it worked.

After she was done checking me over, and the equipment, she hurried out the door. From the smell of the nurse, who smelled like cigarettes with a touch of peppermint on her breath - no doubt to cover up the raunchy odor of the cigarettes - and the gleam of craving in her eyes, my guess was she was in a hurry to get her next fix from her cigarette. It was almost funny in a sick sort of way. A nurse, who is around people all the time, picking up a worthless and deadly habit; she must have been suicidal. But who am I to judge? People die all the time. And it's not for me to have an opinion.

After that observation, the thought of the nurse skittered out of my head and back major problems on my life. And let's face it, they are major. Ethan's secret was out and so was Ben's family's, but there was something missing, some part of the history of the story that didn't fit. That was the last thought I could remember as my thoughts drifted into a deep sleep.

23 REVELATION

As I AWOKE AT THE hospital, I noticed my mother was back in the room. She was packing up the clothes I had worn to the hospital and a fresh new pair of clothes was draped across the tray at the end of the bed.

"Good morning, honey," she said in her sweet voice. "How are you feeling?"

"Better," I answered honestly. Today my head wasn't throbbing and my chest and ribs didn't feel as sore. I was definitely on the mend. "Where is Ben?" I asked, knowing they were usually joined at the hip.

"Oh," she said, looking up from the bag she was packing, "he is bringing the car around."

"Why?" I said, a little confused. "I'm going to walk with you guys out to the car?"

"Oh no, honey," she started, and then walked over to me and pushed back a lock of hair that had fallen into my eyes, "you have to ride out in a wheel chair. It's hospital policy."

"What?" I yelped in horror. "No way, Mom," I almost screeched. I was mortified; I was going to look retarded. "Seriously, mom, don't they need those wheelchairs for the really sick patients?" I asked hopefully.

"Abby, just this once, no complaints, okay?" she said and from her look I could tell there would be no more discussion on this subject.

It wasn't two minutes later when the nurse came to check on me so I could be released. She was a scary looking woman who was short and stocky, with brown grey hair that came down to her shoulders. Her face almost looked like a pit bull's, with her bottom jaw protruding past her top teeth and mouth. I swear it looked as if she was chewing at her face when she went over check-out procedures with my mom. I had to catch myself; I almost asked her if she wanted a bone. I let out a little giggle as my mother and the pit bull nurse turned to look at me with inquiring eyes.

"Sorry," I said, "I had a tickle in my throat." I hurried to recover as my mom shot me a dirty look, showing her displeasure at the way I was acting. I could tell that the nurse was not happy with me either, as she was less than careful as she pulled out the IVs and tubes that connected me to the machines. I was sure she was making her point regarding her irritation and making it hurt more than it should have. But honestly, if you have ever seen the movie The Goonie's, she looks just like the mother of the criminals. Almost exactly.

It wasn't long after she was done torturing me that I was allowed to take a shower and change out of the hideous hospital gown. I swear, whoever came up with those ugly gowns should be taken outside and beaten; they weren't complimentary to anyone's features. I felt much better after I had a shower and was dressed. I was grateful that mom had packed me some clothes, they were some of my favorites. Black sweats and one of my blue favorite t-shirts with a black hood. I know, I know; it's not a great fashion statement, but at least it's better than the ugly hospital gowns. And the number one reason I was happy about the clothes she had chosen was that they were comfortable. And comfort was my main focus as I could feel the wave of soreness wash over me, and I was ready to go back to Ben's and rest. I never thought I would ever say that.

I stepped out of the bathroom and noticed the bulldog nurse was back with the wheelchair and mom had my bag packed and slung over her shoulder. I gave a look at the wheelchair and one quick glance at my mom; I could feel my shoulders slack and my face going into pout mode. One quick nod toward the chair and my mom's face told me to get in the chair and keep my mouth shut, that I could complain about this later in private. And I was sure my mom knew I would.

I let out a sigh and then sat down. I swear the nurse was getting a kick out of my embarrassment because she stopped at every nurse's station she could on the way to the elevator. I felt like dying of embarrassment. I was actually excited to see Ben and get into his SUV. I hurried in and shut the door. And I swear I could see a vicious smile coming from the nurse, and she turned around and headed back into the hospital.

" Are you guys ready?" Ben said as he turned the key and the SUV roared to life.

"Ready," my mom said.

"Ready," I grumbled.

"I should warn you Abby," Ben started.

"Why?" I asked as we pulled out of the hospital.

"Well, it is a small city, and...um...when something happens around, here it's kind of like a dam with a crack in it with the water raging to break through. And then when it does, it floods anything in its path."

"Okay, Ben; can you get to the point?" I said, and I know I sounded grumpy but I was tired, didn't feel well, and I had just suffered some embarrassment.

"Abigail Watson," my mother said, agitated.

"No it;s okay Rebecca; Abby isn't feeling well," Ben said trying to soothe my mother, which somewhat surprised me. I figured he would be the one to snap at me after that last comment. "Well," Ben began, "everyone knows about your recent incident."

Horror washed over me. "What?" I said with terror in my voice. "Everyone?" I whispered.

Ben must have heard me. "Sorry, Abby." Ben said, and he actually sounded sincere. "It was kind of hard to hush up since it happened at the school, and such a commotion with the fire trucks and the ambulance. Don't worry Abby, I am sure that it will blow over in a few days," Ben added.

Or blow up in my face, I mentally added. It would be just like the first day and all the gossip that happened. I shivered at the thought of that. "Did they find whoever did this?" I asked, not really wanting to know the answer.

Ben shook his head while my mother added, "No honey, they don't know. But for the time being I think we should set some ground rules just so you are not alone again, and this doesn't happen again. Also, I think maybe I should drive you to school and pick you up."

"Oh, come on," I said in horror. The thought of being dropped off and picked up like a five year old terrorized me. "I can drive to school and home, Mom," I said, just like a rebellious teenager.

"I don't know, Abby. This person attacked you in broad daylight at a school. It worries me Abby." Although I couldn't see her face since she was sitting in front of me, I could hear the worry in her voice. I could see Ben was agreeing with her on this statement too. God, when they got married does that mean they share the same thoughts? *Come on,* I thought as I stayed quiet as we came to the stop light in town.

"Alright, Abby," Mom started, "you can drive to school and back but, I want you in the house before it gets dark."

"Deal," I said, quick to pick up the last deal before she changed her mind.

"Also you have to keep your cell phone on at all times." I almost groaned at that; nothing like keeping a teenager under lock and key with a cell phone. But I agreed to that to so my mom wouldn't take my car keys away from me.

We made it back to the house when the sun was directly above. "Are you hungry, Abby?" Mom asked as Ben parked his SUV.

I was starving; the hospital food was so bad it was like eating cardboard. Or, I think like eating cardboard, not knowing how it tasted myself. But one thing's for sure: if people aren't sick when they go to the hospital they are while they are there. I wasn't really in the mood for company. "Mom, can I just take a tray up to my room and eat up there?"

I think she understood. "Sure, Abby; I will have Albert bring something up to you."

As soon as the butler did his creepy 'opening the door' thing I was up the stairs, into my room, and had the door shut before you could even blink. I walked over to the bed; without even taking my coat or shoes off I collapsed into bed. It couldn't even have been ten minutes later and there was a tiny rap on the door and then a tray being set down on the floor. I waited a few minutes before I decided to open the door.

After I managed to get up and open the door I noticed a silver tray left at the door entrance; it had what looked like tomato soup in a white porcelain bowel and grilled cheese sandwiches with crackers to the side and even a glass of milk. I could only thank my mom for asking the crazy cook to make the food for me. I scarfed down the food, and the soup burned my throat as I drank it down, although it really was good. One thing I could say, even though the cook was crazy and crabby as hell, she really was a great cook.

I set the empty bowl and cup on the tray and set it quietly outside the door. Then I quickly shut the door and headed back to the bed, this time sliding my coat off and kicking off my shoes on the way. As I lay down in the bed I felt the relief of peace and quiet surrounding me, and it didn't take long until I was under and fast asleep. As I lay there in a deep sleep, my dreams started.

It was dark. The only light was the light from the torches that lined the drive. I continued to search for something or someone, with the wind was blowing, throwing my hair around my face. It was a kind of wind that chilled right to the bone. It chilled me to the deepest part of my soul. And out of the darkness I heard rocks crunch as if someone had came up behind me, but before I could turn to see who was behind someone grabbed me and wrapped a firm cold hand over my mouth, letting no scream come out. Terror rocked my body.

Then came a cold voice, whispering, "Damn the Moores and damn their lies, for every one of you shall die. I curse thee to the deepest part of hell, a place that I've known all too well. A place fit for the forsaken, so you will know the depth of my despair from what you have taken."

The next moment pain ran through my body. I looked down and a knife was pressed through my back all the way through the front of my chest. Blood was pouring from the wound and down my nightgown onto the ground, where it had the making of a small pool.

I awoke with alarm, quickly patting my chest to make sure that I was fine and there was no dagger in my chest. When I was sure it was just a nightmare, I collapsed back into my pillow; my breathing starting to go back to its normal rhythm. "Oh my God, are these dreams ever going to end?" I whispered with anger in my voice. Knowing that sleeping was a lost cause, I gazed at the clock. It was almost six; well, I suppose I could just get up and get ready, knowing that it was going to take a while to get ready since I was still a little sore.

I slithered from the bed. I had slept on top of the bedding and not under it, since I pretty much just crashed and burned last night. Although, I noticed the bedding was quite disheveled from my latest nightmare. Slowly I trudged to the bathroom, watching my feet the whole time so I didn't trip over them. It was at the last minute I caught myself, not wanting to walk into the door. I quickly undressed and turned on the shower, getting it to just the right temperature, and then ducked in quickly since there was a cold draft throughout the bathroom.

As the water hit me, my senses came alive and I was more awake than I should have been. I washed up carefully, trying to keep the soap out of the cuts that were on my forehead. I had guessed those had an occurred when my head hit the locker. And the back of my head was sore to the touch; I am sure that happened when I hit the floor. I felt like one of those blow-up plastic punching bags for kids - you know the one, where when you hit them one way, they hit the ground and then get right back up for the next go -round. It scared me to think if I would survive the next thing that came for me. And what would that be? Would it be Caleb and the pack who came for me, or would the Moores find out that I knew about their history? Was something even more dangerous than werewolves and mages lurking in the shadows?

And then I remembered my dream. "Oh my," I said, shutting off the water and grabbing a towel. Elizabeth. It was Elizabeth's memory that I had seen, of the night she had died. Was she trying to warn me? Was there really something coming for me? Then another thing came to the front of my thoughts. In the story that Conner told the first night at the cliffs, the ones that they had all laughed about, thinking it was one big joke, Conner had said that Elizabeth had been shot. Why? They had aimed for her father and hit her by mistake? But it wasn't a gun, it was a dagger. And she had been alone wandering the estate, looking for something or someone. Something wasn't adding up. I would have to see Ethan; I have to tell him about my dream - or I should say nightmare?

I hurried to get dressed and then fix my hair, which I had lightly dried since I didn't want to look like a hobo, which usually happened if I just let my hair dry naturally. I had to pace myself though; it was too early to go to school, and I didn't need to seem panicked when my mother saw me. I was assuming she thought I would stay home today. And nothing was going to keep me from seeing Ethan today. I had to see him and tell him about the recent addition to my nightmares. As I rounded the corner of the stairs I could hear voices coming from the dining room. It was almost like they were trying to whisper, except for the fact that house was so big that their whispers were bouncing off the high ceilings and walls.

As I got closer to the door that led into the dining room I could hear some of what my mom and Ben were talking about. It sounded like they were having an argument about me since every other word had my name in it.

"Ben," I heard my mom say, "it's time to tell her."

"Not yet," he said, "it's not safe."

"I thought the whole purpose of keeping her safe was staying away all these years," my mom snapped back.

What were they talking about? What did they mean, staying away all these years? At first I thought they had found out something new about my attacker. *No*, I thought, *there had to be more to this story.* My mom and I had never kept secrets. I had this awful sinking feeling in the pit of my stomach, like I had gotten a sucker punch in the gut, with the realization that my mom was lying to me about something. I stood there for a moment and then took a deep breath to keep from exposing the expression on my face. The one person in my life that I had trusted above another was keeping secrets from me. Despite my rolling emotions, I didn't want to be the source of their discomfort, so I peeked my head around the corner to interrupt them.

"What's all this?" I said as I rounded the corner. "You two are up awfully early."

"Oh, Abby," my mom said looking surprised.

"Nothing," Ben said. "We were talking about school and if you should go back until they catch the creep who tried to kill you and burn down the school."

"Oh," I said knowing that he was lying. "Well, I'm fine, and I don't want to be locked up here like some prisoner. I have friends at school and I want to hang out with them."

"Abby, do you have your cell phone?" my mom asked.

"Yep," I said it's in my bag, and fully charged." I had known my mom was going to ask about that so I was ready with the answer.

"Okay," she said sounding somewhat relieved.

"Abby, make sure that you are back before the sun goes down," Ben added.

"Yes, sir," I answered a little snippy. After all he isn't my dad, and I don't have to do what he tells me to do.

"Are you hungry, Abby?" my mom said, trying to change the subject.

"Nope, I just will take an apple with me," I said, reaching for the red apples in the center of the table that were always there. You would think we had apple orchard and not grapes with all the apples that were replenished on a daily basis.

"You have to eat more than that," she said, concerned.

With the latest nightmare and all the gossip that I knew was going to follow my first day back after the attack, greasy food in my stomach was not going to be the answer. "Mom, I am fine. I will see you later tonight," and then kissed her on the cheek. I headed out to the entryway to procure my bag and keys, and out the door I went before either Ben or my mom could protest or stop me.

I hurried to my Jeep, catching my foot on a few of the bricks on the drive, but I caught myself before I fell. *Slow it down, Abby*, I thought. I opened the door and swung my bag in; it hit the bottom of the passenger floor board with a small thud. I hurried to turn the keys and start my jeep. I pealed out of the drive, accidently sqealing my tires as I got onto the highway from the drive. I reached over and opened my console that had all my CDs; it took me a moment to find the one that I was searching for, pulling out a couple first that didn't interest me. I just placed them on the passenger seat and kept looking for the one that I wanted. After I had the one I wanted, I placed the CD in and turn up the volume. Bon Jovi's "Living on a prayer" vibrated from every speaker that I had in my jeep, and I took a moment to lose myself in the music and his beautiful voice. From some reason this song hit home. I was living on a prayer if I was going to survive another day at Klamath Falls.

24 hISTORY

WITH MY LEAD FOOT, I made it to school with plenty of time to spare. I was more than relieved to see Ethan there by himself, leaning against his black bike. He was mouth-watering; I had to remember to shut my jaw and try not to drool. His face lit up when he saw me, and the smile that I was waiting for stretched across his face. I shut off the jeep and was out of the door the next second and into his arms. He squeezed me just a little too tight.

"Oops – sorry," he said, setting me back on my feet.

"No, you are fine," I said, refusing to let him go. "Ethan, we have to talk," I blurted out the next moment. "I have so much to tell you."

"Abby, not here," he said. "After school," he said, "there is some place I want to take you."

"Where, Ethan," I asked raising one eyebrow, and leaning away from him.

"It's a surprise; please trust me."

It was hard to resist him, with those deep ice blue eyes looking into mine. "Okay," I grumbled. He smirked at my expression, which just made furious; I was surprised how that was somewhat a turn on.

"Class?" he said raising one eyebrow. I nodded as we headed to our first-period class.

"I will see you there," I said, letting him know that it was okay to leave me at my locker. Ethan gave me a look that told me that he wasn't going anywhere, but I was just as stubborn as he was. "Ethan," I said as I got to my locker and started on the lock that had been replaced since the last time someone broke into it; it would probably never shut right though since the metal looked bent beyond repair. As I opened the locker I let him see the inside to show there was nothing in there that would hurt me. He seemed a little relieved and then finally agreed to go and get his books and meet me in class.

"Don't be too long," he growled in that deep sexy voice that sent tingles from my heads to my toes. After he was gone, I noticed that more students were coming into the school and putting their books away. And as the crowed thinned a little I was grateful to see Julie and Sarah heading my direction.

"Abby!" Julie and Sarah said at the same time as they both put their arms around me and squeezed.

"Ouch," I said moving uncomfortably out of their embrace.

"Oops," they both said together.

"What are you two, Siamese twins?" We all laughed at that one.

"Are you okay?" Julie asked.

"Yes, I'm fine."

"We tried calling the house but we kept getting that creepy butler, and he wouldn't tell us anything." She sounded disgusted.

"I swear he's like a freeze pop," Sarah added.

"A what?" I asked.

"A freeze pop. You know, the frozen popsicles that have the sticks."

I laughed. "Why do you say that?" I was still giggling.

"Because he is cold as hell and acts like he has a stick up his butt. I don't even think a tractor could get it out," Julie added, finishing Sarah's comment.

I started laughing. I couldn't help it, they were so funny when they were together. "Ouch."

"What?" they both asked again.

"Don't make me laugh," I said. "It hurts to laugh."

"Sorry; so will you tell us what really happened?"

"Later, guys," I said, "we are going to be late." They both nodded, looking at the clock that hung above the lockers. Just then the bell rang and sent us running to our rooms. Since Julie had class with me, I waved goodbye to Sarah. Julie and I made it to our room just in time for the second bell to ring. I saw the relived look in Ethan's eyes as I went to sit down in my seat. And then I glanced up just in time to meet the dark eyes of Caleb. It seemed that he was reacting to Ethan.

Don't get me wrong, I know that Caleb and Ethan are friends but I can't see why. Ethan was truly a good person. As for Caleb, I don't even think the devil would keep him; he probably spat him back out, and that would explain why he was here today.

As the teacher droned on, I had no Idea what he was talking about. I was trying not to fall asleep in class and not doing a good job. Julie actually nudged me a few times when my head was going to hit the desk. *What's one more bruise to my already ravaged head?* I thought. It wasn't until I heard the chime of the PA speaker in the middle of the room that I focused my attention.

The low voice of the principle came across the speaker, "We are sorry to inform everyone that due the recent fire and the sprinklers going off and the gym being flooded, we will be unable to hold prom in the gym this year."

Muffled groans went all around the room.

"Shhh," Mr. Murphy said.

The principle continued on, not realizing that whispered denials where going throughout the school. "We have checked the hotels and banquet halls around the area and they are all full, so if anyone has another venue, please come to the office and let us know." There was slight pop as the PA system shut down.

"That sucks." I heard a few people voice their opinion. I could see Julie was a little disappointed.

"Sorry, Julie," I said. "I know how much dances mean to you."

"That's alright," she said. "We always have next year right?"

"Right," I agreed. *If I can make it through this year,* I thought but didn't say it out loud.

It took a few more minutes, and then Julie almost leapt out of here seat. "Abby, what about your place?"

"What?" I asked.

"Didn't you say they have a ballroom at the manor?"

"Yes, but it hasn't been used in forever." I saw a few more people turn around.

"What?" a few more students asked.

"We all know that Abby lives at Ben Moore's, right?" They all nodded in understanding. It was just a little uncomfortable to think that all these people knew all about me, but it was a small school after all. Everyone knew about everyone here. That was what I was telling myself, to keep me from slinking down the bottom of my chair and onto the floor.

"Well, Abby told me just the other day about this ballroom where they used to have masquerade balls."

"Julie," I whispered, knowing that I told her in confidence. *Note to self: don't tell my friends anything else.* I could feel the blood rush up to my face.

"Abby, is that true?" Mr. Murphy asked as he approached my desk.

"Yes, sir."

"Well, you would be the class savior if you would ask Mr. Moore if we could use the room for this year's prom."

"I guess I can ask," I said feeling trapped. After all it was my fault, right? I was the one who'd gotten beat up and someone had tried to barbeque me; it was my fault the gym had gotten flooded, so I had to make amends right? "I can ask him tonight." I could hear cheers as the bell rang and everyone filed out.

As I rounded the corner, someone grabbed my arm. I jerked around to realize that it was Ethan.

"Hey, what do you say we ditch the rest of the day?"

"What?" I asked in shock. "We'll get caught!"

"Don't worry, I worked it out already. Just go to the office and tell them that you still aren't feeling well and you are heading home. Then you can follow me out to the cliff where we can leave your Jeep, and you can climb on the back of my bike."

"What about you?"

He laughed at that. "Don't worry about me," he said and raised one hand to touch my chin, and with that he was on his way at the door. I raised my hand up to my cheek; I could still fill the presence of his warm fingers on my skin. I sighed as I headed to the school office.

I convinced the receptionist that I wasn't quite myself – which didn't take too long since I still look like a truck ran me over – and she said, "Okay, honey. We will see you tomorrow. I hope you start feeling better soon."

"You and me both," I whispered. She seemed to hear me and nodded in understanding and sympathy. I headed back to my locker to grab my bag, coat, and keys, but I couldn't help feeling that I was being watched. It made me go cold; I could feel goose-bumps covering my arms, yet it was quite warm. They always kept the school warm. I put my coat on in a hurry, knowing that Ethan was waiting for me. I grabbed my bag and keys, and headed out the doors.

I only got a glimpse of Ethan as I walked out the door out to the jeep. I tried to keep a steady pace, not wanting to draw any attention. I jumped into the Jeep and quickly shut the door and hit the locks, feeling much safer as I did. I started heading out in the direction of the cliffs. As I reached the highway that led out to the cliffs I finally managed to catch up with Ethan. My guess was he was waiting for me; there was no other way I would have caught up with him even with my lead foot.

Kind of like in the story of *The Tortoise and the Hare*, except in this scenario, I would be the damn turtle.

As I pulled off the highway following Ethan, the familiar trees and drive was relaxing; even after my brush with the wolf I still felt comfortable being in this place with Ethan. He waited for me to put the jeep in park. I left my book bag on the passenger seat knowing that I wouldn't need it. I checked my hair in the mirror and then I felt a little disgusted with myself. I was actually checking myself in a mirror; how superficial can one person get? I hurried to open the door and hit the locks at the same time. I slammed the door a little harder than I needed to and it made a loud thud. I paced myself on the way over to his motorcycle, not wanting him to know how excited I was to be on the back of his bike again with my arms wrapped tightly around him.

"Ready?" he asked.

"Yes," I said, a foot away with my arms wrapped around me in my pout mode. "Are you going to tell me where we are going?" I asked, knowing that it was hopeless.

"Nope," he said and then added, "Abby, get on the bike." Even when he thought he had control over me he was cute, but I knew he wasn't going to tell me. I wanted to know, and up unto this point he had been nothing but honest with me.

"Alright," I said as he stretched out his hand to take mine and help me onto the back of the bike. It felt just like last time, and then, I thought, even better: his warmth; his smell. I could stay like this forever.

"Are you ready?" he asked in his deep angelic voice.

"As ready as I am going to be," I said, letting out a nervous chuckle. He hit the accelerator and as I left, all my fears and reservations were behind me. As we traveled down the road I kept my eyes closed and my arms tightly around Ethan's chest. It didn't take long until we pulled off onto a dirt road; Ethan slowed so he wouldn't kick too much dirt up at us. I am sure it was just for my benefit. I found it hard to believe that most guys would not have a good time getting dirty and grimy.

Trees surrounded us and I could only see the path a few feet ahead at a time; the deeper into the trees we went, the darker it seemed to get, the light only shone sparsely between the trees. I could see the smaller animals scurry into hiding as we went past, and the deer that would look up and then take off as we came closer. In one word, it was peaceful. Ethan's bike began to slow as we pulled up to what looked like a little hut with grey smoke coming from one single chimney in the roof, with a small porch and three steps to it. It looked like a hut you would find in the Bahamas on the beach, but just a little more modern and with real glass windows.

"Where are we?" I whispered.

"A friend's home," Ethan answered. Before we could have more of a conversation, the front door slowly opened with a squeak, and a small frail Indian man with white hair stepped out to greet us. He looked like he was a hundred years old —no, let me restate that. He looked at least a hundred and fifty years old, with wrinkles that looked like the Grand Canyon with all its crevasses. His hair was as white as snow, and his clothes looked like a throwback to Davey Crocker's era, only without the coonskin cap. I was sure, if I went in the little hut, that he probably had one in there. As he walked closer I noticed that he used a cane.

Ethan turned off the engine and then kicked down the kickstand. He reached one hand back to me to help me off the bike. And then he followed. He held my hand and I am sure he could tell that I was extremely nervous since my hand didn't seem to want to stop shaking.

"Shh, Abby," he said soothingly. "It's alright, I promise." I could tell that he was sincere as he tried to calm me. There was just something about Ethan when he talked; it seemed to calm me to my very core.

As we reached the steps of the tiny hut I noticed why the small frail man used a cane. His eyes were completely glazed over; he was blind. Before we took one step onto the tiny porch, he began to speak.

"Welcome back, Ethan," he said in his old gravelly voice.

I was shocked that he seemed to know who Ethan was, but I was sure that the noise of the bike probably tipped him off. After all, if this was a friend of Ethan's, then I'm sure that he has been out here on his bike tons of time.

But then the man turned to me. "And who do we have here?" he said and then smiled. I went to introduce myself, but before I could, he put one finger up, pausing me. "Welcome Miss Abigail Watson."

Okay, now my mouth dropped open. *How the hell does he know who I am?* That was the first thought that ran through my mind. The second was: *what does this man know about Ethan and about the Moores?*

"Abby, this is Amar Ananta. He is the last of his tribe and he is here to help us."

"Ethan." Amar began to speak; Ethan was instantly quiet. "I need to speak with Abby." He paused for a second and then continued, "Alone."

Ethan didn't even question him; he held my hand out to the withering man. "I will be right here," he said as he placed my hand in Amar's.

Amar's hand was brittle like paper; one wrong move with my hand and I felt like I was going to break him. I looked back at Ethan as Amar led me into the little hut. As I entered into the hut I noticed that it was very dark, and the only light that was coming in was from the fire place. He brought me over to two wood chairs. They weren't pleasing to the eye but they looked sturdy, so I sat down where he pointed, still shocked that he knew where everything was, as though he still had his vision.

"Abby, I need to talk to you about something," he said as he sat down in one of the chairs across from me. It was eerie, watching the fire shadows ripple across his face like the old wrinkles where dancing.

"How did you know my name?" I asked.

"Abby, I know you have many questions, and I have some answers, but you must remember that for every action in someone's life, there is a reaction. Some people call it karma, some call it fortune, but I call it fate, and when you start messing with things it can alter the future."

"Fate," I whispered.

"Yes," he said. "Fate. Do you know why Ethan brought you here," he asked as his left eyebrow rose.

"No," I whispered in a soft voice, twiddling my fingers nervously.

"Do you know who I am, Abigail?"

"No," I answered in that soft unsure voice.

"I am the one who gave Ethan and his friends their gift. Do you understand what I'm talking about?"

I nodded, and then remembered that I was talking to a blind man. "Yes," I said.

"Ethan told you secrets?"

"Yes," I answered again.

"Did Ethan tell you about the Moores and their secrets?"

"I think he told me some," I answered honestly. He laughed at that.

"Ethan, Ethan, Ethan," he said under his voice. "For five hundred years we have lived," he said, "and for five hundred years I have been trying to figure out a way to end this gift that has been given."

"Why?" I asked, not meeting his eyes, even though I knew that he couldn't see me.

"Because, Abby, people aren't suppose to live forever. When one dies, their spirit is to be released and to be born again anew."

"Like reincarnation?" I asked.

"Yes." He nodded. "Something like that. Most souls have many different lives, but for Ethan and his friends, they have lived the same life over and over. Always moving, always changing their identities to keep their secrets, but time is drawing near when that will all end."

I looked at him this time, and I could see he was honestly sincere.

"Abby, have you noticed anything strange in the manor since you moved here?"

"Tons!" I laughed, and then composed myself.

"Do you know about the history of the Moore's and how they came to Klamath Falls?"

"I know some. I found Elizabeth's diary and a locket she used to carry."

He straightened. "Abby, do you still have the diary?" He seemed to perk up when he asked that.

"No," I said. "I left it in the library when I went to dinner, along with the locket, and when I came back they were both gone." I was still irritated at the that fact, since I had even locked the doors and placed the diary back on the shelf so no one would find it, and yet they did and it was still gone.

"Abby, things aren't what they seem at the manor."

I already knew that, but I let him continue uninterrupted anyway.

"Ezekiel Moore is still in that house, he still has a lot of power which increases every century, and he will not rest until every person in from each of the six families are dead."

"I thought it was just the first-born girls," I asked.

He shook his head. "I know there are a lot of stories told around here, but what really happened is that Ezekiel Moore cursed the Indians, and the six families, so that everyone should die. And I counteracted the spell when I cast one to protect the families. As you can tell, I am the last one of my line; my family is all gone, and my fate is intertwined with the wolves' fate now. Like it or not, you are in the middle of a war, and it will only be ended in one of two ways."

"I don't suppose you can tell me the options," I asked hopefully.

He shook his head 'no'. "Abby, do you know why you look like Elizabeth?"

"No," I said. "I have often wondered, but every time I ask Ethan, he clams up."

"Abby," he said reaching over and taking my hand, "on the day Elizabeth died, her father cast a spell. We don't know the exact words that were spoken but we do know that, although Elizabeth's body died, her soul was passed on. It sat limbo for five-hundred-years until the time drew near, that the war was coming."

"What are you saying?" I started to get agitated.

"Abby, you are Elizabeth. You can't remember it because your memories have been stolen, or locked up by some higher power, but no matter how many spells they put on someone, the truth always breaks through. Do you know what I mean?"

I hesitated a moment to compose what I was going to say. "The dreams," I whispered, and then I saw the nod of his head.

"What have you been seeing in your dreams?" he asked.

"Mostly just me wandering in the forest, and Ethan, but I hear whispers in the background."

"What whispers?" he asked.

" 'Remember' is all it says."

He seemed to nod in conviction.

"What does it mean?"

"It means the hidden part of your soul is breaking through and it won't be long. Abby, you should also know that since Ezekiel is a mage, you are one as well."

"What?" I asked.

"Abby, you will have great power, when you choose to embrace your destiny."

"Are you saying that I am going to be evil?"

He actually smiled at that. "No, Abby; not all mages are evil. Who you are deep in your soul reflects how your powers are."

"What about Ethan? What was Ethan to Elizabeth?" I asked feeling a little awkward at this question.

"Ethan and Elizabeth were soul mates, Abby; not even death will keep them apart. It is destined that they belong together no matter what life they are living; it is destined that they will find each other, no matter where they are. Ethan is your soul mate, and whatever fate you have, you share with Ethan."

"But I am not Elizabeth," I said firmly.

"But your soul is," he answered. "You will remember," he said, looking grim.

"What?" I asked. "What aren't you telling me?" I asked. "Why couldn't Ethan be in here with me?"

"Abby, I will tell you that you are going to have to make a choice in the end. It will be your choice that ends the war or keeps it going."

"Wow," I said sarcastically, "no pressure there."

He seemed to understand my frustration.

"Okay, let me just go over this one time. Ezekiel is my father and he is still in the house, which means my mom would have to know all about this, right?" He nodded. "Also, Ethan and I are soul mates, but so far last time it seems to have ended like Romeo and Juliet, only Romeo didn't die. So what do I do now?" I asked uncertain.

"Well, this conversation we had is just between you and me. Keep the secret and let things unfold. Abby, Ethan truly loves you. When Elizabeth died, a part of Ethan did too. If something happens to you this time, I won't able to save him again."

"Can I ask you something?"

He nodded.

"Why did you save Ethan?"

"Because, Abby, I was in love once and, like yours, it was ended all too soon. You are one of the lucky ones; you get a second chance to live the life that was taken from you. Not many people get that chance. Take care of each other."

And with that I knew that our conversation was over. "Thank you," I said as he released my hands.

"You're welcome."

I left him in the chair, and with one final look I headed out of the hut, shutting the door ever so quietly. Outside I fell into Ethan's arms.

25 Compromise

ETHAN DIDN'T ASK ME ANY questions as we rode along the small path that led to the highway. I noticed that the sun was starting to set and realized that we stayed out a little longer than I had planned, but grateful that he had kept me from home eck and gym, my least two favorite subjects. We made it back to the Jeep in no time, which was a curse and a blessing, no pun intended. I wanted to stay with Ethan, safe with my arms wrapped around him. As we pulled next to my jeep I tried not to look and feel disappointed; I knew I would see him at school tomorrow. He held his hand out for me again and helped me off the bike, but he didn't shut it off; I was guessing he had to get going.

"What's with the frown," he said as he put his pointer finger under my chin and pushed up so I could meet his eyes.

"Nothing," I said.

"Abby, what's wrong?"

"I'm just not ready to go," I answered honestly.

"Don't worry, I will see you tomorrow." He bent his head down to mine and kissed me. The kiss started out sweet and soft and then turned to hot and rough. I raised my hands to run my fingers through his hair and pull him closer to me. He wrapped his strong arms around me and pulled me closer to him. Every part of me was on fire. It wasn't, but after a moment we had to pull away and come up for air. We were both breathing harder than normal.

" Abby," he whispered, "you'd better go; it's getting late and I am sure that you will have to explain to your stepdad why there will be teenagers dancing in his ballroom."

"Crap, that's right." That turned my attention to the matter at hand. "Ethan, don't you think it's a bad Idea? I mean with the wolves and the Moores?"

"No, Abby; it's perfect. It will be just like the old days, a masquerade ball."

"Perfect," I said with a wicked smile.

"You'd better hurry. I am sure they will be looking for you soon."

I gave him one quicker kiss and then headed in the direction of my jeep. I got in and started it, noticing that Ethan was waiting for me to pull out first. I waived as I passed him. I couldn't understand why he didn't ask me any questions.

A new dilemma: what was I going to say to mom and Ben about the dance? Me and my big mouth. Why had I told the girl about that room? This has to be punishment. One, I hate to dance; two, there is a war between the family my mother had inducted us into and the wolves that Ethan was a part of. I had lots of things rolling around my head on the way back to the manor.

When I reached the manor I was surprised. The manor looked pretty vacant. Only a few lights were on. I parked the jeep and hurried inside. It felt like I was always rushing to the manor and away from the manor, and just like always the door was open before I even reached it. It still, after all these months, gives me chills of horror when I am around that freakin' butler. At least he didn't even try to be polite and never talked to me now. There was one blessing. I could smell the food so I knew that dinner was almost ready.

"Abby, is that you?" I heard my mom call from the dining room.

"Yes, Mom."

"Come on in the dining room; dinner's ready."

I set my bag down at the table by the door and then headed in to talk to mom and Ben. They were sitting on the same side, about an inch away from each other, facing me as I came in.

"Are you hungry, Abby?" Ben asked.

"Yeah, I guess so," I said and sat down in the normal chair I always sat in. There it was again, reverse gravity; instead of gravity keeping their grip on the ground, gravity kept its grip on Mom and Ben. It was making my stomach roll and my appetite disappear.

"So how was school," mom asked.

"Fine," I said.

"Just fine?" she hedged, looking for more information.

"Well, there is something that I need to talk to you about."

"Shoot," Ben said. And it made me jump. He actually laughed. "Geez, Abby, are you jumpy tonight."

He had no Idea.

"What did you need to talk to us about?" my mom hedged to try to get the conversation back on track.

"Well," I began, "I am sure you heard that the gym is pretty messed up from the incident the other day." They both nodded at the same time. I was going to make a stupid comment about that but I thought to get what I wanted I would have to let this one slide. "Well, the gym is unusable for prom so one of the girls asked if we could use the ballroom for prom."

The moment of silence made me feel uncomfortable. Ben was the first one to speak. "Well, we haven't really used that room in quite some time, so it would have to be cleaned and fixed up first."

I tried to cut him off at the pass. "That's okay, me and the girls can do it."

"Well how many students would be it?" he asked, unsure.

282

"Well, it's the whole high school." Back home only the juniors and seniors got to go to prom but here unfortunately freshman and sophomore got to go as well. "A couple hundred or less," I said, estimating high.

"Well the room should be big enough," he said. And he wasn't even kidding; it was even bigger than the gym, almost twice the size. "All right, but there will be some rules that must be followed. No one is to be running around the manor and no one on the grounds at night. I don't want to be responsible for anyone getting hurt here."

"Okay," I said.

"Also, what kind of a dance is it?" he asked.

"Well, everyone heard about the masquerade balls that you used to have here and they thought that would be a great idea." For some reason Ben's face went to stone, and my mom's didn't look much better. "Mom, Ben, are you alright?"

It took a second but Ben finally answered. "Okay Abby, if that is what you want, then that is fine." I was a glad that the stepdad trying to win over the new stepdaughter was still winning out. As he continued to try to play the good guy I generally got what I wanted. "Don't worry, Abby. I will hire a crew to get the room shipshape and take care of the rest of it."

"Really?" I said hopefully.

"Yep, on one condition," he said with a smirk.

"What?" I said in a grumble, my face looking down at my empty plate.

He looked at my mom and then gave her a wink and a smile. "You have to let your mom play dress up."

"You've got to be kidding," I said. I could see her over in her chair, nearly bouncing out of it. "Ben, I didn't really want to be at the dance. I was going to hide in the shadows," I offered.

"Abby, that is not how hostess behaves."

"Hostess?" I said my eyes going wide. "What do you mean?"

"Well this will be the first family function in public since we became a family, so you will have to be up front and center." I could feel l myself slipping in despair. "This is not negotiable," he said staring directly into my eyes.

"Fine," I said with a last grumble. And then I asked, "What's for dinner?" And then after she told me I wished that I hadn't even asked.

"Chinese," mom said. I frowned. "Abby, just try it you might actually like it."

"Mom, no offense but I would like to eat something minus the chicken parts or whatever animal she cuts up to put in the mix." Ben actually laughed at that. "I would kill for a pizza right about now."

"Abby," Mom said in a stern voice. The only thing that was running through my mind right now was the Little Caesar's commercial for pizza - you know when the little dude says "pizza pizza" really fast. The cook came around scooping out the food into our bowls and then brought another bowl of white rice. I scarfed down the rice. No problem there, it actually looked normal, but for the rest of it I just scattered around my plate to pretend that I actually ate something. Then I stocked up on rolls to fill me up so I wasn't hungry later.

We had two weeks left till prom, and that was what I was thinking about after I cleaned up and headed off to bed. Tonight's dream started off with me in the manor in a deep red ball gown, it was almost the color of wine the red was so dark. It had a sweet heart cut with capped sleeves and it went clear to the floor. I reached my hands up to my neck and I felt a string of pearls around my neck as I walked down the hall that led to the Manor's ballroom. I glanced in the mirrors that lined the hall. But I as I walked and passed each mirror and I looked closer, I noticed that even though the person looked like me and wore the same clothes, it wasn't me.

It was at the last mirror that I stopped to stare. I walked closer to the mirror and placed my hand on the mirror and the person in the mirror copied the movement. As I looked in the eyes that were familiar but weren't mine, the person in the mirror whispered, "I have been waiting for you."

It was at the point that the alarm clock went off, the familiar beep bringing me back to reality. *How much longer is this going to go on*, I thought myself while wiping the sweat off my forehead. First the move, and then this freakin' manor that comes with a creepy butler and a crazy cook, then the nightmares, then the wolves and now Ezekiel is somewhere in this house, and I can't even trust my own mother. Yet for my safety I am told to keep quiet. It was all very frustrating.

The next two weeks seemed to go by in a blur. Everyone was really excited that Ben has said that we could use the manor for prom, but I was dreading it. It seemed that I had made a deal with the devil in agreeing to his terms. Every chance my mom got she was dressing me up in dresses and shoes - and even jewelry! - and the worse part about that was I didn't even get to see the dress she chose until that day.

Let me tell you, some of the dresses were very scary and they ranged through many different colors. One of the scarier dresses even had black feathers on it. All the dresses were floor-length. With someone who has balance problems, this was definitely not the kind of dresses that you would put that person in. Even the shoes, there were no flats in mix. Or even less than one-inch heels. As I voiced my frustration at school and over the phone to Sarah and Julie regarding my mom's Barbie dress up phase, they laughed at me.

Sarah had said, "Abby, be grateful; not everyone gets perks like that."

Julie had said, "Are you sure that you don't want to trade parents?"

Both girls had their dresses and their dates. Sarah was going with Conner, and I shook my head at that one. Julie was going with Shane, who was a shy guy that was a junior. And me, well I wanted to go with Ethan but I just told mom that I was going stag so she would stop pestering me. I was shocked that Ben actually had kept his word about having everything done for the prom. After the cleaning and construction crew had gone through and updated everything in the ballroom, he sent them outside to work on the lawn. He even lined the hedge maze in the garden with white Christmas lights. It looks absolutely stunning. He even brought designers from Paris to get the place looking ship-shape. And I had no idea what the room looked like since it was off limits to me. The only ones who had been in the room were Ben, Mom and the teachers from the school overseeing the prom.

I could hear the squeals of delight from my mom as the days progressed. I had asked my mom if she had finally decided on a dress and her response was, "Abby finding the perfect dress for your first prom takes time. Don't worry; you will look stunning. Although it would be nice if you had a date so we could color-coordinate."

I loved how she managed to dig that last dig against my dateless status; nice, I thought. My mom would probably be horrified if she knew the truth, that I had actually been asked out by Adam and I had turned him down. I couldn't even believe he even wanted to asked me after the last dance where I hand danced all over his toes, literally. I was starting to think of him as a leech that I just couldn't get rid of. He'd had a pouting look on his face and guilt had made me feel bad. But I had my eye only on one guy in this school and he wasn't it.

As for school, it progressed just like every other day. Ethan would walk me to class and Caleb would stare daggers at me along with the rest of the boys. Talk about the prom was all over the halls and my mysterious attacker hadn't made a reappearance. Life seemed to go back to normal, or at least as normal as it was going to get. It wasn't long till the day of prom was here.

It was Saturday, and today I was getting a glimpse of the dress that my mom had picked for me. Sarah and Julie were both coming over so mom could do their hair for them. They had loved what my mom had done for the other dance and they were dying to have their hair done by my mom. My mom was in heaven; she always enjoyed anything that would give her a chance to dress up. As night drew near and Julie's, Sarah's, and my hair and make-up was done, the girls got into their gowns. They both looked great.

Julie had a black dress that had a very low v-neck and spaghetti straps, and her skirt draped all the way to the floor. Very simple, but elegant in a classic way. She opted for a silver rope necklace that fit well with the dress's low cut v-neck front; the dress was quite daring for her. Sarah had a blue dress with spaghetti straps that sparkled all over. It had a high cut slit on the front left side that went up clear to the hip. For her necklace, she hand one simple black choker with a diamond-studded flower in the middle. My mom had put up both of their hair up. Julie had more of a classic French twist. Sarah's hair had a small French twist in the back with curls on the crown of her head.

"Wow," I said, "you two look great."

"You are just saying that because you're our friend," Sarah said grinning.

"That, and because your mom did our hair," Julie chimed in, and then we were all laughing. I wasn't sure if it was the excitement of the night, or the fact for the first time since I moved here this seemed like something that a normal teenager would do.

"Okay," my mom said walking back in the room, "your turn." She was holding a black garment bag. I groaned, and then crossed my fingers praying that my mom had gone with the more practical side and the not the one that would get me killed, either from me tripping on the dress or on the high heels she had brought.

"Do I get to see the dress now," I asked.

"Nope; hair and make-up first and then we will see about the dress." I let out a small groan in protest, but from the way my mom's mouth was set I knew that she wasn't going to change her mind. Yep, I had made a deal with the devil.

"Sarah," my mom said, "will you grab the desk chair."

"What, we aren't going to do this in the bathroom?" I asked.

"Nope, you don't get to see until we are done." Sarah hurried with the chair, grinning all the way. She looked just like the Cheshire cat from <u>Alice in Wonderland</u>. Julie at least covered her mouth, to try to be less conspicuous, but the small shaking of laughter and the tears in her eyes gave her away.

"Yeah, yeah," I said sarcastically. "Funny, funny," I said in a huff and sat in the chair. My mom started pulling and separating the hair while the girls watched her work. I could tell by their faces that they liked it. My mom was done quicker than I thought she would be. I guess she worked well under pressure.

"Julie, can you grab the blind fold that I set on top of the dress's garment bag?"

"Sure," Julie said and headed over to the bed and grabbed it.

"What's all this?" I asked.

"Nope, you can't see the dress until it's on; you having to get the full effect."

"You have got to be kidding."

"There are three things I never kid about," my mom said. "One, hair; two, clothes; and the third is shopping."

The girls were dying to see the dress so they helped confine me to the blindfold. All three of them had me out of my regular clothes and into the dress in no time flat. I could tell it went clear to the floor as it brushed my toes. It took a while for them to get me laced up since the top part of the dress was a corset. That wasn't hard to tell since I couldn't breathe after they got me laced up. I couldn't remember my mom making me try on a dress like this so at this point I was getting just as excited as Sarah and Julie.

Then I felt my foot being lifted and then the other one. I could feel the shoes as I put my foot down. Heels, she had got me heels.

"Mom," I managed to mumble.

"Don't panic," she said. "It's not as bad as it looks. Now just stand right there."

"What are you doing?" I asked curiously.

"I am getting the mirror I had Albert bring up for me," she answered. I could feel Sarah and Julie pushing me, I was guessing towards the mirror. When mom was happy where I was standing, she finally let Julie and Sarah take off the blindfold.

"Wow," I said. It was red like a rose, which fit since roses were all over the top of the dress on the corset. It was off the shoulder and had roses that wrapped around the arms instead of sleeves. It went clear to the floor with little poof. It was a ball gown. It was unbelievable. "Wow," I said.

"Do you like it," she said hopefully.

I nodded. And then I lifted the dress to see the shoes. They were red to match the dress, and yes, they had heels but they were tiny heels. I was pretty sure I was going to be able to walk in them. My hair looked great too. It was slicked back with curls that started at the top of my head and went to the back, not a lot of curls, but slicked back and smooth almost like a crown.

My mom stepped behind me and reached around me to place a necklace on me. The necklace was diamonds and rubies in the shape of roses that alternated between the stones. It was so beautiful.

My mom went to whisper in my ear. "The necklace and these ruby earrings," she said holding out the ruby earrings, "are from Ben."

"Ben bought me jewelry."

She nodded. "You are the only daughter he has. He was excited to do something for you."

"Stepdad," I corrected, "and that was very nice of him."

"That's good; you can tell him later tonight."

"What, you guys are going to be in the ballroom?"

"Well, they asked us to chaperone," she said sheepishly, "since it's Ben's house, he agreed."

"You are not going to embarrass me, are you?" I asked in horror.

"No different than any other day," she said grinning and gave me one good squeeze. She laughed. "I will be good, I promise. Now you girls better get downstairs, and here," she said handing us our masks.

They were all different; they all match our dresses. This was the first time I saw my mask - it was red with diamonds and had red feathers on it.

"This is going to be so great," Sarah said putting on her mask.

"I can't wait," Julie said as she placed hers on.

"Here goes nothing," I said placing on mine. "Wow," I said, "they really do hide your identity well, don't they?"

"No kidding," Sarah and Julie said at nearly the same time, and then laughed at that.

"Let's go girls," my mom said. "You don't want to miss prom, do you?" With one final glance in the mirror I took a deep sigh, and then I headed out the door, shutting it with a light thud.

26 PROM

AS WE LEFT THE ROOM and headed down the stairs, I could hear the music coming from the ballroom. It was official: prom had started. As we rounded the corner, I was surprised to see that the front entry was teeming with tons of kids who had just shown up. Since they all had their masks on I wasn't sure who everyone was, but they all looked great, and I saw they were going along with the classic theme of the prom. I was relieved to see other girls going along with the ball-gown look so I didn't feel like a freak. I noticed that the doors were shut that led to the rest of the house, and what couldn't be locked had been roped off with those kind of ropes that they used in the moved theaters to guide people where they wanted them to go. I guess it was like herding cattle.

We got in line with the other kids to head to the ballroom. It was refreshing that no one was pushing or shoving to get in. It took a little while to get through to the room and I had plenty of time to look at myself in the mirrors that lined the walls on the way. I guess I had to give my mom props; I didn't look like myself and I am guessing that was her goal, but I did look okay. And since it was a special occasion even the shoes didn't bother me that much.

When we got to the room, my mouth dropped along with Julie's and Sarah's. "Wow," they both said.

"No kidding," I gasped.

"Didn't you see the room before this?" Sarah asked.

"Are you kidding?" I said. "I have been pretty much in lock-down in the house. The only thing that I have seen is people coming and going."

"Well, he did a great job," Julie added.

I had to agree with them. "I guess when you have money, you can get anything you want," I scoffed.

"Abby, I would kill to have a stepdad like yours; I am so jealous."

"Don't be," I said in a stern voice, not meeting their eyes. "Not all things are like they seem." I could feel their eyes on me but I wasn't going to elaborate; some subjects are better left untouched. As I looked around the room, I noticed that the DJ was in the front of the room and the tables for dinner were in the back. Lining the back walls were appetizers and the buffet. There were light strung up all over the place and it looked like people were dancing under the stars. The tables in the back were black with red rose petals on the top and candles lit the tables up; it was gorgeous. Ben had actually outdone himself. He even had new chandlers installed one small one every few feet. They glistened off the lights, adding a simple strobe light look.

It was just then that Julie's and Sarah's dates found them.

"Care to dance, ladies?" Conner said with a smirk.

I was surprised to see that Conner actually cleaned up nice. Shane was a quiet guy, who stayed behind Conner, letting him take the lead. Shane and Conner held out their hands and the girls took hold as they started out to the dance floor where the rest of the kids where dancing.

"Wait," Sarah said making her date pause. "Abby, do you want us to stay behind with you?"

"No, go ahead; have some fun. I think it's better for everyone involved if I stay off the dance floor and off of people's feet." I let out a laugh and they joined me. I was happy to see them having a good time, but I was a little anxious, not knowing if Ethan would come tonight. It was then I felt a tap on the shoulder and turned around to see Adam standing there with his puppy dog eyes.

"Abby," he said in a whisper.

"Yes, Adam, it's me." He really did look nice in his tux, but he still wasn't my type. From the corner behind him I could see three girls eyeing us. One was tall and blonde; she had a short dress that was really not a ball gown at all. She looked like she would be better served on a street corner than being at prom. And the other two had simple floor-length dresses with short sleeves. They were petite. It didn't take me long at all to know who they where: the cheerleaders, and with the looks they were giving me, I was surprised that I wasn't writhing in pain on the floor. The tall blonde didn't like that fact that Adam was talking to me, which made it all the more appetizing. I wasn't interested in Adam, but she didn't need to know that.

"Abby, you look wonderful," he said, interrupting my thoughts. "Would you care to dance?"

I took one more look at the girls in the back who were still glaring at me and decided that I wasn't doing anything at the moment - it might be interesting to have a little fun at the cheerleaders' expense.

"Are you sure you're so recovered from the last dance that you are ready for round two?" I said with a laugh.

He gave me a sheepish look and then a smile. "Don't worry; I wore steel toe boots this time," he said with a grin.

I rolled my eyes at him and then gave him a smile.

"My lady," he said and the put his arm out so I could take it.

"Thank you, good sir," I said taking his arm. As he led me out to the dance floor I took a quick glance at the blonde girl in the corner. If she could have blown fire, I would have been toast, burnt toast that is, and I winked at her and smiled. It looked like she was going to take a step after me if it wasn't for the girl holding her arm back and whispering in her ear. My guess was that she was reminding her that this was the place where I lived and they didn't want her to get thrown out on her butt. I would have liked to see her try, though; it would have been entertaining. I would have made tread marks all over that pretty face of hers.

Don't get me wrong, I am not the least bit interested in Adam, but the fact that it was pissing off the head cheer leader, and a real snob, made me feel wonderful. As we reached the middle of the dance floor, the song "Love of a Lifetime" by Fire House started to play, and I grimaced. Not the type of song that I wanted to be dancing with Adam to. Relief swept through me as someone tapped Adam on the shoulder asking to cut in.

I took one look at him, and even with the mask on I knew exactly who he was. "Ethan," I whispered, staring into those beautiful ice blue eyes.

Adam hesitated for one short second, and then conceded. I was guessing he was taking in the fact that Ethan towered over him in to account. He let go of my hand and hip and graciously bowed out.

"Thank you, Adam," I said.

"Anytime, Abby." He turned to walk away and I realized that his smile had turned to a frown; I felt bad for him, that he was interested in me when really he wasn't my type. I preferred tall, dark, and handsome, with a touch of dangerous. That distraction didn't last too long, because a greater portion of me knew that Ethan was beside me. Ethan took my hand and placed one arm on my hip. He was smiling and he looked gorgeous.

"Having fun," he said with a smirk.

I knew what he was implying; I shrugged that off and said, "I am now."

"I think you just crushed his ego," Ethan said, still laughing.

I think he will live; there are plenty of girls who will want to date him," I said nodding to the girls still lurking in the corner watching me with those beady eyes.

"Yes," he said. "I see; they don't like you much, do they?"

I laughed. "Oh well," I said, "when have I ever cared what people think?"

"Wow, you look like you just fell from heaven," he said and then smiled.

Okay, it was a cheesy line but it still made me fill pretty good. He wore a plan black mask that would remind you of Zorro. "You don't look too bad yourself," I said smiling. "As for my dress and hair, all my mom's doing."

"Well then, I must meet her someday so that I can offer my thanks for making my date so hot."

"Where is this date?" I said with a smirk; obviously he wasn't talking about me. "My mom must've done more girls' hair and make-up than I thought," I said with a laugh. "I will take her out back and kick the crap out of her."

He laughed once and then pulled me closer so that our bodies were pressed together. I could feel the heat coming off him and it made everything in my body tingle.

He bent down to whisper in my ear. "The only person or date I am interested is you," he said smiling.

We danced there for awhile and I lost count of the songs they were playing; I wasn't even paying attention to if they were fast or slow. I was in Ethan's arms and I was content. After a while Ethan asked me if I wanted to take a walk.

"Do I need my coat?" I said.

"No," he said looking down at me and smiling. "I will keep you warm."

We headed out the door and I was praying that my mom and Ben weren't watching me. As the breeze hit me as we went out the back door that was off the kitchen, Ethan pulled me close and wrapped his arm around me.

"Are you having a good time?" Ethan asked.

"You have no idea," I said into his chest, giggling as we walked toward the hedge maze that was lit up with thousands upon thousands of lights. It was so beautiful with the greenery and the lights; it was perfect. As we walked he kept his word. I wasn't cold; he kept we warm with his body heat.

"You clean up nice, Ethan," I said sincerely.

"Thanks," he said, "but these suits are a little confining if you know what I mean," he said pulling at the collar and then loosening his tie.

I laughed. "Let me," I said as I reached up to help him loosen his tie.

He caught my hands in his as I reached for the tie and then just held them. Looking down at me with those ice blue eyes, he whispered only for me, "You are so beautiful." And his words made me melt as he reached down to kiss me.

When his lips reached mine it was like an explosion; heat surged through me. And I forgot everything. I forgot the manor and the prom, the stupid shoes my mom had gotten for me...it was just Ethan and me. This type of reaction seems to happen a lot around Ethan. After the kiss broke, with us both panting and trying to catch our breath, he whispered, "I have waited for you for five hundred years," he said as he leaned his forehead against mine, "and you didn't disappoint me. You were worth the wait."

"Am I?" I asked.

"Yes, I love everything about you - your eyes, your face, your lips, the way your body moves, and your heart, for the way you love me."

"What are we going to do, Ethan?"

"Yes, what are you going to do?"

I heard something come from behind a hedge. My mouth dropped and I went to step away from Ethan but he stepped with me, holding me to him.

"Ben," I whispered. And from the look on his face he was not happy; anger glinted in his eyes. It was almost deadly. His face was set down in a frown and his eyebrows were lowered. His eyes looked like they were lizard's eyes, with his eyes having the hooded look to them. " Ben, what are you doing?" I said.

But he didn't seem to see me or was ignoring me. "You don't belong here," he said staring at Ethan. Ethan didn't move and kept his arms firmly around me. "Abby, go to the manor," Ben said still looking at Ethan.

Just then Caleb and three massive wolves stepped out of the trees snarling, their fangs exposed; they were dark black.

"Oh my God," I said staring at the wolves.

"Did we miss the fight," Caleb said with a wicked smile. Ethan shot Caleb an aggravated look that froze him in place.

"Get your hand off my daughter," Ben snarled.

"What?" I said. "Stepdaughter," I said correcting Ben. I am sure that my face was showing the same outrage that Ben's did. "You can't order me around," I said in defiance. He was really pissing me off; I could tell Ben could hear that in the tone of my voice.

And with the wolves creeping closer I had a chance to re- evaluate their size. There were huge and as big as horses; they had deep black eyes and razor sharp teeth which they had no problem exposing. Ethan raised one hand at the wolves and then they stopped.

"Ethan, why are you wasting your time? She wasn't worth it before and she isn't worth it now," Caleb spit the words with venom in his tone.

"Stay out of this," Ethan said to Caleb in a deep demonic voice that didn't sound like him.

"You can't have her," Ben said. "She doesn't belong to you."

Ethan's response was quick and direct. "She doesn't belong to you either."

"Abby, your mom is worried; go inside."

My mom is worried, I thought, snapping for a mere second from my anger. Why would she be worried? How much did my mom know? "What, are you joking?" I said. "Enough with the lies; why don't you tell me what is really going on, Ben?"

He looked irritated, like he didn't want to answer.

"Yes, Ben," Ethan said. "Tell Abby what is going on, what you have been keeping from her."

Ben shot a look at Ethan, and if looks could kill Ethan would have been dead on the spot.

Ben took a breath and then began to speak. "You shall not die, but only sleep, around you the world will weep, five hundred years will pass until the time is right, your soul will be born again, you will live a new life." The words flowed fluidly out of his mouth.

"What is that?" I asked looking directly at Ben.

"Those were the words that I whispered in your ear the day you died in my arms."

My mouth dropped and eyes widened. "What?" I said.

"Abby," Ben paused, "you are not my stepdaughter. My real name is Ezekiel Moore and you are my daughter, Elizabeth."

"What?" I asked again in horror. "That can't be," I said in denial, and then remembered what the Indian had said, that I was Elizabeth and Ezekiel was still here. "That can't be true," I said. "My mom wouldn't lie to me. She would have told me if it was true."

"Your mom knows all about this," he said sincerely. "We have been frozen in time, until the day the spell played out and you were born again. Your mother took you to Florida, the furthest place in this country, to keep you safe and away from the people who killed you," he said and looked at Ethan, Caleb, and the wolves.

"Why would you bring me back here then?" I said.

"Because it was time," he said. "Your sixteenth birthday was the day that your powers started to reemerge."

"What?" I said again.

"Abby, you were born into a family that has many privileges and great power. You are a mage, Abby."

I felt like my ears were stopped up; my head was spinning like I had been run over by a train. "What powers?" I said. "I am just a normal human being." There was nothing about me that screamed powers.

He shook his head at the denial. "Abby, the day the gym was set on fire, the sprinklers came on before it had gotten hot enough; you heard your mother. I know she told you."

I nodded at that.

"Self preservation," he said. "You saved your own life - you set off the sprinklers so the fire wouldn't get you."

Nothing he had said made any since. "Why didn't you tell me this a long time ago? Why now?"

"It wasn't safe, it's still not safe. Do you see that we have done all of this to protect you?"

"What, by lying to me?" I yelled back in fury. I could feel my pulse racing and heart beating like it was going to pound right out of my chest. Still, Ethan stayed by my side, and that alone was the only thing keeping me together and sane. "Why would anyone what to hurt me," I said.

"I don't know," Ben said, "and I still have no idea of who tried to hurt you the first time. I wish I knew who shot you." I was shaking my head at him but looking at the ground.

"Elizabeth wasn't shot." I still wasn't able to process that in my former life I was Elizabeth. It was just easier to say Elizabeth than I.

"What?" both Ethan and Ben said together.

"She was stabbed," I said raising my head and looking directly at Ben.

"How you know that? You can't even remember back then."

I was still shaking my head. "I saw it in my dreams – I saw everything, I couldn't see the person, but Elizabeth was stabbed from behind," I said and started to shiver.

"That can't be," Ben said. "It's all your fault," he accused, looking at Ethan. "Why couldn't you just leave her alone; she was innocent."

"You think this is my fault, Ezekiel? Why don't you look in the mirror? You caused all of this; you came to this land and tried to take everything from the good people who lived here. Blame you own greed and ambition. Elizabeth died because of you, and I won't let you do what you did to Elizabeth, to Abby."

"Why are you even bothering?" Caleb started to snarl. "Enough with this – let's finish it. Five hundred years is long enough for pay-back."

Ethan looked back at Caleb and said, "If you touch Abby, there won't be a place you can run, a place you can hide; I will find you and I will kill you." There was no indecision in his eyes/ he meant what he said.

"You are choosing that slut over your friends."

"What?" Ethan said, giving Caleb that deadly look. Caleb started visibly shaking, and it looked like he was doing everything in his power to keep himself together.

" Abigail," Ben said, "I love you. You are my daughter, and I would never hurt you. Ethan has brainwashed you, trying to mix up what really happened. I only wanted to keep you safe; I stayed away until I knew it would be safe enough to train you in the mage way. You have to be trained; you are young and your powers are unstable. If you don't learn to use them, people around you will get hurt."

"People will get hurt," I said, and then I looked at Ethan.

"Don't listen, Abby. He is just trying to keep you locked away like he did before," he said cupping my face. The minute that Ethan touched my face, Caleb started to vibrate, like the thought of Ethan picking me over them and touching me was too much for him.

"So be it," Caleb snarled and then shifted into a big black wolf with a grey streak down his back. He was bigger than the others and looked even scarier than the others.

"No," Ethan said as he went to block Caleb's attack on me. One minute Ethan was human and the next he was a snarling beast. As he changed, his clothes were shredded to the winds that were now blowing.

Ethan was a light grey wolf with those beautiful blue eyes. Even as an animal I couldn't help but have some pride that he was beautiful. I felt a pull from behind me and realized that Ben had used some of his powers to move me closer and away from the snarling beasts that were fighting.

"Abby, please," Ben said. "There is more to tell you; we have to talk."

"Why don't you tell me where you put the locket and the diary that you took from me?"

"What?" Ben said, honestly astonished. "What diary and what locket?"

"You know exactly what I am taking about. Elizabeth's diary and the locket Ethan had given her."

"Abby, I never took anything like that. I knew that Elizabeth wrote in a diary because I was the one that gave it to her, but," he paused, "I thought it had been lost in the fire that had consumed the house the night you died. The six families set fire to everything the night that I supposedly died. I looked for what I could salvage later on after everyone had left. But everything was gone, consumed by the flames. It took me a full century to rebuild the house the way it had been."

I could hear the growling and snapping from the wolves. I looked at the fight that was still going. Rage filled every part of me of the thought that Ethan would be harmed. I could feel the fire start in my body. It started in my toes, moved up through my body to my fingertips. I raised my hands and screamed at the top of my lungs and light shot from my hands at the two giant wolves that were fighting. I meant to just stun Caleb, but hit Ethan to by mistake. They both flew ten feet and hit the ground with a loud thud. The waves from the blast were so powerful that it hit the wolves that surrounded the two that were fighting.

Horror filled me about what I had done. I looked over at the two wolves; they both laying there, limp. The others got on all fours and shook their heads as if they were dazed, and trying to clear their heads. They ran off on to the trees, whimpering.

Ben's words ran through my head: "You have to be trained; you are young and your powers are unstable. If you don't learn to use them people around you will get hurt." I had hurt Ethan. My intentions were to stop Caleb and Ethan from fighting; I had done that, but not in the way I had intended.

Finally the black wolf seemed to stir, and then get up on his feet. He looked down at Ethan's wolf form and then snorted. My guess was he thought that Ethan had gotten what he deserved; Caleb took one more look at me and bared his teeth with a growl and then turned and shot off into the forest.

"Abby," Ben said, "do see, you have to be trained? There is still someone out there who wants to hurt you and we have no idea who it is."

I ran over to Ethan, ignoring Ezekiel or Ben or whatever you want to call him; "the devil" worked for me. I knelt down in front of Ethan slowly and ran my finger through his soft fur. Shallow fast breaths came out of the giant wolf.

"What have I done?" I whispered over and over, and Amar's words ran through my head: *you are going to have to make a choice. In the end it will be your choice that ends the war or keeps it going.*

My choice.

Ben walked over to me. I looked up with tears in my eyes. "Can you save him?" I said. Anger was written on his face; I could see the thought of helping the wolf was disgusting to him. And then it smoothed.

"Yes," he said with no emotion now.

"Please save him. This is my entirely my fault; I have to make it right."

"I will save him on one condition," Ben said.

"Whatever it is, I will do it," I said promising before I even heard what he was he had to offer.

"You can't ever see him again, it's forbidden; it's a betrayal of our family for you to consort with him."

I looked down at Ethan once more and shook my head, knowing that I would not be able to live if Ethan died because of me. "But," I said with a knot in my throat, "is it in your power to wipe his memory and the wolves' memories?" I could live with the fact that I had loved Ethan, but I didn't want him to remember me and what we had shared; that pain I would save for myself.

He nodded.

"I don't want him to suffer for my mistakes; please wipe all traces of me out of his memory." I bent down and whisper in Ethan's ear. "I love you and will always love you; I am sorry."

Ben nodded once more said a few words, so low that I didn't understand, and with a flash Ethan was gone.

"Where did he go?" I said panicking.

"I assure you he is fine, and will be better by tomorrow and will have no memory of you or this night. As a mage you are bound by your word, Abby; you can't break it."

If Ethan is okay I can live through anything, I thought, no matter how much pain it will cause me to be separated from him. And then I gathered myself and got to my feet. I looked at Ben with anger in my eyes. "I would never forgive you for this," I said.

"It's for the best," he said with a stern tone.

How insulting, that he thought that he knew what was best for me.

"You are young, Abby and you have a lot to learn. You are old enough for me to teach you now, how to use your powers and how to control them. You have a lot to learn and you don't need any more distractions. Now come inside; your mother and I have lots of things to discuss with you."

As we headed to the manor, I noticed from the trees a hooded figure with a snarl on its face; clutching something to their chest. It was then that I saw it: Elizabeth's diary. I closed my eyes and then reopened them to see if it was real. The person had vanished like a ghost in the night. From the look in the person's eyes, I was yet again on another person's hit list. I groaned as I headed into the manor. I couldn't help but feel like I made a deal with the devil. I just wondered what was next.

LaVergne, TN USA
21 May 2010
183429LV00001B/182/P